DEATH IN SIBERIA

By Alex Dryden and available from Headline

Red to Black
Moscow Sting
The Blind Spy
Death in Siberia

ALEX DRYDEN

DEATH IN SIBERIA

headline

First published in 2011 by
HEADLINE PUBLISHING GROUP

1

Cataloguing in Publication Data is available from the British Library

ISBN 978 0 7553 7337 6 (Hardback)
ISBN 978 0 7553 7338 3 (Trade paperback)

Typeset in Bembo by Avon DataSet Ltd,
Bidford-on-Avon, Warwickshire

Printed and bound in Great Britain by
Clays Ltd, St Ives plc

Headline's policy is to use papers that are natural, renewable and
recyclable products and made from wood grown in sustainable forests.
The logging and manufacturing processes are expected to conform to the
environmental regulations of the country of origin.

HEADLINE PUBLISHING GROUP
An Hachette UK Company
338 Euston Road
London NW1 3BH

www.headline.co.uk
www.hachette.co.uk

To my god–daughter Daisy Bell

Russian Claimed Territory
in the Arctic Ocean

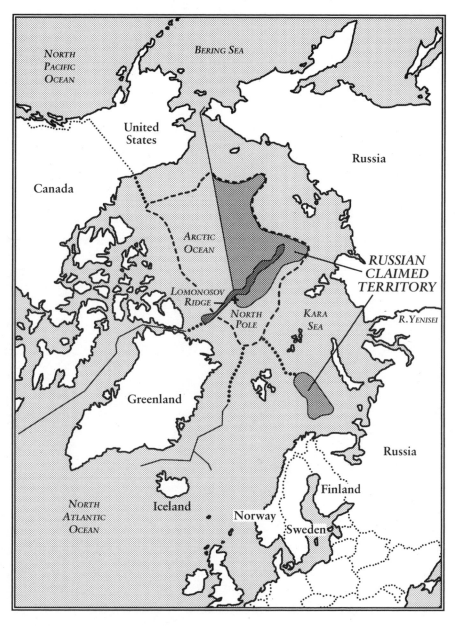

——— Agreed Borders   - - - - 200-Mile Line

•••••• Equidistant Border   ▓ Russian Claimed Territory

'We're not afraid to down nine shots of vodka,
Or eat cabbage pickled in permafrost.
For, you see, we're the men,
We're the men of the seventieth parallel'

An Arctic Siberian miner's song

'Trees completely ceased to grow. Grass withered.
There were no animals. And no children were born.'

From a tale of the Evenki tribe in Arctic Siberia

'The Arctic is Russian'

Artur Chilingarov, Vladimir Putin's Arctic exploration
leader and a Russian parliamentary deputy, July 2007

PROLOGUE

THE FOOTSTEPS BEHIND him seemed to be getting closer. To Gunther Bachman – or Herr Professor Gunther Bachman, to give him his full title – they had become a constant threat.

He heard the *slap slap slap* of the steps again now on the wet concrete of the Siberian street. Bachman's reaction was a constriction in his heart, a shortness of breath. For in Gunther Bachman's alternately declining and rising tide of panic, the steps had begun to seem like the approach of his own execution.

He'd read somewhere about false executions. In Vietnam, was it? No, it was Cambodia under the Khmer Rouge. They were a particularly Oriental variation of cruelty, as Professor Bachman had understood it.

But that was what this torture of the footsteps in this Siberian city had become, as night began to fall like the lowered hood of the executioner himself. He may not have been strung up with a rope around his neck, only to be allowed to fall half-alive to the ground, as they'd done to their victims in Cambodia. But what was following him in the driving rain through the ever more obscure maze of streets contained the same terrifying promise.

1

He turned around another corner, blindly now, and into one more anonymous street. There was the same fragmented concrete, the rain sloshing off it in rivulets on to the trash-strewn roadway.

Here he saw a row of nineteenth-century, one-storey wood houses abutting the street, some with faded paint just visible where once it had been bright – greens and blues and even pink. The houses were tilting into the ground, cock-eyed like drunks, where the Siberian earth had frozen and thawed repeatedly for more than a century and slowly sucked them into its bottomless maw.

Bachman walked on past the once pretty houses. But their strange, crooked angles seemed sinister to him now. Like something from a middle European fairy tale where the faded beauty of a woman turns out to be the harbinger of death.

And no matter how much he wanted to, he dared not look back.

The steps behind him were so close now he thought that he could hear panting. Or was it his own breath? It sounded like the panting of something inhuman that was tracking him and had been since he'd left the airport.

He patted the sides of his coat with both hands, as if he were looking for something in the pockets. His dark-blue, water-streaked raincoat from Karstadt in Munich's Kaufinger Street swished in the downpour.

He quickened his pace. A choking noise came from his throat, and the thick, dangling craw of his turkey neck tightened against the collar of his shirt.

The brief fantasy of the civilised city of Munich – his

city, his world – and the department store Karstadt where he'd bought the coat, momentarily gave him an illusion of calm; the memory of the smooth, silent elevators, the well-heeled customers, the bright lights, the friendly, caring faces of the store's assistants, the shelves of reassuring consumer goods.

But all those comforting memories might as well have been a million miles away. He was here, not in Munich, not at home. He was walking the pitiless Siberian city of Krasnoyarsk. He was in a city where life had little or no meaning. A dead dog lay upended by a car and left in the broken street. A frozen tramp with a beard like Rasputin's slumped on a corner, looking more like a drenched and shaggy animal than a human being; sets of aggressive eyes shone in the gathering gloom – the desperate, moneyless and addicts who would cut your throat for a kopeck. Out here in the industrial wasteland of Krasnoyarsk, Munich might as well have not existed.

He thought back to his last and recent encounter with a friendly human being. It had been earlier that day, up beyond the Arctic Circle, in the city of Norilsk from where he'd taken the flight this afternoon. In his miserable prefabricated hotel room in Norilsk on this very morning, Vasily's man was sitting across from him on the edge of the bed. It was Vasily's man who had told him only hours earlier how to conceal the documents he was carrying. 'Take a spare pair of shoes with you. That way you can stash your own shoes,' he had added by way of explanation. 'And so hide what's in them. Then if they stop you, you're clean.'

But he hadn't remembered – or had thought it super-fluous – to buy another pair of shoes before he'd got on the plane at Norilsk, or when he'd stepped off the plane here in Krasnoyarsk from that hellish, slave-built city up beyond the Arctic Circle. And so he couldn't stash what he was carrying in his shoes by removing them and hiding them in some anonymous locker – at the rail station, perhaps. That was what Vasily's man had suggested, he now remembered, the rail station.

He shuddered. He knew he was out of his depth.

The self-pity soon returned, washing over him once more, as if the acid rain of the industrial city contained it.

He wasn't trained for this. He wasn't trained for the management of fear, or in the art of subterfuge. He was a scientist, a professor, a respected nuclear expert on the international stage. He wasn't a spy. How had he got himself into this? How had he agreed to be the courier? How had he come to be carrying something so valuable? Why had Vasily passed on to *him* the documents via his go-between, and not to some other foreigner who could have taken them to safety – and to glory?

But as soon as these thoughts surfaced he realised it had been exactly that – personal glory – which had led him to accept the documents. It was his own over-arching ambition that had prompted him to take the documents from Vasily's man. From what he had seen of them at the hotel, before they'd been sewn into his shoes, the documents were apparently so important that they would make his whole career, right at the twilight period of it. A Nobel prize awaited him, perhaps. That was what the documents portended. Professor Gunther Bachman, Nobel laureate.

But in his denial of the risks back then, sunk in the grim, empty hotel in Norilsk where he'd been told by the go-between that Professor Vasily Kryuchkov would not be meeting him, he had suppressed the fact that the documents were also something that the Russians would kill for.

His international colleague Professor Kryuchkov's so-called 'inability' to meet him had been explained to Bachman by the go-between as the authorities' *prevention* of their meeting. That should have been warning enough. It seemed that Vasily Kryuchkov was in any practical sense of the word a prisoner of his own people above the Arctic Circle. He was too valuable to be allowed out of the closed military area up there, let alone to meet any-one from the West. Bachman had been told as much, as he drained the last drink from the hotel mini-bar for courage and studied the documents. What Vasily Kryuchkov had discovered must never leave Russia. The warning came back to haunt him and it wasn't his career he cared for any longer, Nobel laureate or not – it was his life.

Through the gloom of evening and the murk of the driving rain which the cold was now turning to sleet on this night at the start of June, he knew he was lost in this dreadful city.

He looked up and saw rail yards in the far distance, lit by high orange arc lights. Maybe he should head for the light? But the fear that had gripped him for nearly an hour as he'd tried to make it to the hotel when he couldn't get a taxi at the airport had addled his thoughts.

'When you reach Krasnoyarsk, get to the hotel immediately,' Vasily's man had told him, 'the big, American hotel. Then call your embassy in Moscow' – that was the second part of his instructions after the ones about the spare pair of shoes. To get his own embassy's protection. But where was the hotel?

He put his hand into the pocket of his coat and felt his mobile phone. But who could he phone?

Then he saw a man step out ahead of him. There were two men now, ahead and behind him. He crossed the street, slipping on some mud in the gutter. He fell and felt a sharp pain in his hand. He sobbed with the humiliation of it. Scrambling to his feet, he looked at his right hand. Something sharp, broken glass perhaps, had sliced his flesh. His clothes were drenched and coated with slime and mud. His beautiful raincoat.

He wondered again if he were hearing things; if he had been hearing things all along. But slumped in the gutter, he saw behind him, from the corner of his eye, a man, his head shaven to the skull, and hands that were holding a chain. On the end of the chain was a brute of a dog.

Professor Bachman scrambled up, gripped his case, and hurried across the street, blood pulsing from his wounded hand. Then he thought he heard the man and dog step into the road's gutter. And ahead he saw the second man who stared at him from under a broken street light. He realised he'd lost his phone. He must have dropped it when he'd fallen. He felt a sweat break out all over his body.

Before darkness had begun to fall he'd kept to the river

where Vasily's man had said it would be more open. There would be other people and cars – even police cars – which would provide some protection. And it was the riverside that led to the American hotel; lights, a cocktail bar, muzak, people with smiles on their faces, a phone line to the German embassy.

But he'd left the riverside to escape his pursuer. Maybe he should end it here, turn and face his own death. Better to look it in the face than be struck down in some fearful surprise attack.

He began to sob. Now, Bachman knew he would have turned himself in, confessed everything, betrayed his friend and erstwhile colleague Professor Vasily Kryuchkov, begged Russia for forgiveness, handed over the shoes with the incriminating evidence in them, gone to jail. If only he could have found a cop, or even one of the thugs from the MVD, the Ministry of Internal Affairs, or a fully fledged KGB officer – anyone to whom he could divest the evidence of his guilt. Bachman would have given them anything, anything to escape; his own daughter, his wife.

He stopped and turned and caught the glint of the dog's chain crossing under another flickering street lamp and the boot-shod feet of the shaven-headed man behind the beast. Bachman could hardly breathe. He shuddered, tripped and almost fell again. Then he felt an enormous explosion in his chest; he staggered on a few steps further, but fell to his knees, groping on the concrete.

He turned from his kneeling position, feeling the agony spread across his chest, and saw the eyes of evil at the level of his own. The dog was straining to get at him, its yellow teeth bared. Bachman thought he heard a man's laugh.

He felt something else, something cold and metallic pressing into the back of his neck. But he never felt the second explosion after the one in his chest. It blew his atlas bone to pieces, severed his spine from his brain stem and ended all his hopes of greater glory, along with his life. Professor Bachman fell forward and his stricken face smashed into the gutter.

CHAPTER ONE

FOUR DAYS BEFORE Professor Gunther Bachman knelt, unprompted, for his execution, three men and a woman were approaching the steeply mountainous Russian border from the Mongolian side. Five hundred miles to the south of the city of Krasnoyarsk, the border presented its usual forbidding obstacle to anyone foolish or brave enough to attempt any crossing, let alone an illegal one. The woman, Anna Resnikov, was certainly brave enough.

Now, as May broke into June, the snow had gone from the waving sea of the lower grasslands of northern Mongolia but the night air was still icy and the soaring Tuva mountains, snow capped throughout the year, were a perfect natural fortress against incursion.

But Anna Resnikov's was no ordinary illegal crossing. It was not a smuggling operation bringing cheap Chinese electrical goods into Russia, or a hunting party looking for rare wild animals whose body parts were destined for the Chinese medicinal markets, or even just the casual to-and-fro of Mongolians clandestinely visiting their ethnic relations across the border in Russia. This was a fully fledged act of espionage and for that an illegal crossing was of necessary importance. Anna Resnikov – formerly KGB Colonel Anna Resnikov until her defection to the West five years before – was on a mission into the heart of Siberia. It was an operation that was conceived, planned, financed, and concealed even from his CIA friends, by Burt Miller, the flamboyant multi-billionaire, one-time CIA agent, and now head of the world's largest private intelligence company, Cougar Intelligence Applications. It was said of Burt Miller in some intelligence circles that he'd started out working for the CIA until it ended up working for him. Those in Washington who feared or hated him said that the CIA had become just an adjunct to his own mighty, private intelligence agency and military hardware supplier, Cougar. By this particular night, Anna had worked for Miller for over three years and their partnership, professional in her case, but also personal in his, was the talk of the Washington political and spy elite. Some said Anna simply reminded Miller of the huge, if reckless, success he'd enjoyed in his own youth, a youth spent as an American spy in Central Asia. Others said that Anna was more like a favourite daughter to him, even his heir. Others still, more cynical perhaps, sneered that her unparalleled skill and knowledge had become just another gold seam that Burt was so famous for exposing. But those closest to Miller pointed out that Anna Resnikov was simply the best covert agent Burt had ever met in more than fifty years of intelligence work; and that his admiration for her was as one of the few, if any, human beings, who had managed to put the great man himself in the shade.

They were still crossing the northern Mongolian grasslands but all the time they were coming closer to the mountains. The way ahead was clear of border patrols, at least on this, the Mongolian side. The recently fitted Mercedes engine in an ancient *jifeng* Chinese army truck was having no difficulty driving its way along the military road. The dirt track on which the truck was bumping along now was passing just to the east of Lake Uvs. Apart from pools of water with a thin layer of ice that lay sluggish in the road's deep potholes and glinted silkily in the thin sliver of moonlight, the road was dry enough.

The track flowed up and over small hills and rose not far from the lake to the east. It would disappear altogether into darkness where a grassy bump rose in front of the truck. In the back of the truck were two special forces Americans hired by Cougar, while in the front cab sat Anna and Larry, her minder, general worrier and secret admirer for three years now. Larry was Burt Miller's only trusted guardian of Anna. In his late thirties, the same age roughly as she was, he'd been a Navy Seal, then an intelligence officer in the field for the CIA, until Miller had plucked him out of government service to work for Cougar, as he had done with so many others. And they were always the best ones, as Miller's admirers and critics both agreed on.

From inside the truck's cab, the two occupants could make out the darker shapes of the ancient Mongolian burial mounds – the *kurgans* – that stood out against a purple-black sky which was perfectly printed with a linocut of stars. The grasslands around them could be felt rather than seen, the flowing grass like a living thing swaying for hundreds of miles in every direction. In the daylight they had indeed resembled the movement of waves on the sea. There was a light breeze and, despite the night's chill, Anna had her window open three inches or so. Her head was turned towards it and up, as if sniffing the air for a trail to follow.

Larry turned the wheel to avoid a large rut and the quiet, brand new engine hauled the beast of the ancient truck up over another hill, then down again into a gully. The truck's lights were switched off but the eyes of the man and the woman were accustomed by now after four hours of darkness and Larry saw reddish mud banks on either side. Ahead of them, the snow-capped peaks were becoming visibly sharper. The backdrop of the approaching Tuva mountains, where Mongolia gave way to Russia, and the Russian border itself, towered higher and higher from across the empty stage of grassland.

Larry looked across at Anna, over her alpine pack which was wedged between them on the middle seat of the truck. She had her knees drawn up on the seat, arms hugging them, and her long back stretched up in a gentle curve so that she was poised over her haunches – like a greyhound, he thought, waiting to seize the certain moment to spot its prey before leaping from the cab in pursuit.

She'd cropped her hair short, an inch long, perhaps, and dyed it black, so that he could see the shape of her sinuous neck whitish against the black night. She wore a thick sheepskin waistcoat over mountaineering gear. A well-worn brown leather coat was draped over the alpine pack. Alongside the pack, on the seat between them, there were also coils of strong cordage and carabiners, an alpine harness, ice axe and ice screws and webbing. In the pack itself were the bare essentials; a sleeping bag, food and water, and the Thompson Contender handgun she always used. Its eighteen-inch barrel was perfectly sighted and she could drop a man at up to two hundred yards.

Larry turned back to the road. He knew sometimes that he watched her in ways that were not in the strictly defined limits of his job. After two years together on missions in areas of Russian influence, he would have died for her. But this time she was going into Russia itself for the first time since her defection and he was worried.

'It's over there,' he said, pointing ahead, 'between those two peaks.'

But she didn't turn towards him or the mountains.

Two greyish-white peaks that denoted the mountain border loomed ahead of them against the clerical purple of the sky, like a ghostly and unforgiving priesthood.

'The gorge is just to the right of where we're heading,' Larry persisted. 'Between the peaks. There's a narrow entrance to it, invisible until you're on it. You'll see it when you get close.'

'I know, Larry,' she said, but she addressed it to the window where her head was still angled upwards. They'd been over the route on maps back at Cougar's headquarters in the United States a hundred times already.

Cool to the point of unfriendly, Larry thought, but he guessed she was already in her own world, somewhere up ahead of them – after they'd dropped her off – and that in her mind she was making the crossing over the border.

'This was the least-guarded stretch of border when the tensions were high between Russia and China,' Larry was saying in his usual attempt to cover her still silence with reassuring facts. 'Both sides relied on the mountains. You can't get a vehicle through those. Not on this stretch. It was to the east where the stand-off was most dangerous.'

But Anna knew the borderlands well, even though she'd never been on this, the Mongolian side. When there were two million men on either side of the border, she'd been a teenager, but later, when she'd joined the SVR, the new KGB's foreign intelligence service, studying the potential of a Chinese attack against Russia had been mandatory. And when she'd become a colonel in Russian foreign intelligence – the youngest female colonel in its history – she'd visited the border east of here where it went up directly against China itself.

Larry now fell silent. If she didn't want to talk, so be it. That was her way.

But tonight, for once, it wasn't what she had to do that Anna was thinking about. She wasn't mentally following the route ahead that she would have to take later that night, nor analysing her mission that lay beyond that, a mission that was intended to bring her up ever northwards into the heart of Arctic Siberia. Her mind was occupied in a way that was neither appropriate nor usual for her just before a mission. It was distracted and the distraction was caused by news she had received five days before. She had received this news in the curious combination of both a body blow and a cause for celebration.

Her father was dead. That was what had been picked up out of Moscow. The old devil had suddenly fallen ill and was dead three days later at the age of seventy-three. It went unreported, due to the disgrace his daughter's defection had brought upon him. So the news had been filtered out of the country by her mother who had been estranged from him for nearly ten years now. But Anna had hated him for a lot longer than that.

Once, back in her childhood, her father had been the KGB Head of Station in Damascus, a hero of the Soviet Union. He'd been a tyrant to his subordinates, as well as to her mother, and a cold and finally sinister figure to her. And all the time, during the years of her childhood, he was a true, unreconstructed Stalinist who, after Stalin's death, had concealed his real leanings and consequently had made his way steadily up the ladder of promotion during the gentler years of Khrushchev's thaw and afterwards. Her father had always been a secret apologist for the Gulag camps of Siberia where millions had died in slavery.

But finally, after Putin's takeover of Russia in 2000, he'd seen those 'glory years' reviving. He saw in Putin's new Petersburg spy elite, who had taken control of the country, a last hope for national resurgence in the years of his own decline. Once more, the KGB – his KGB – was victorious. And it was more powerful, in fact, than it had ever been in its history. The Communist Party that once ruled it no longer existed in power to give it orders. The spies, the spy elite, Russia's parallel society to which her father had devoted his life, now ruled Russia completely.

Looking into the blackness of the steppe, Anna now recalled that she had spoken to her father for the last time five years before. It was just months before her defection to the West. And it was her father who'd been a window into her reasoning to defect, and her defining excuse to leave this new Russia. A foreign intelligence spy like herself, in his retirement he had been given a hero's grace and favour apartment near the Kremlin, reserved for upper echelons of the KGB. In the 1990s, he'd taken even more heavily and angrily to drink than he had done in his active service, as he saw democracy make a brief flicker of an appearance in the country. He had raged against her mother, his now estranged wife, for working for the Sakharov Foundation. And finally – to Anna's ultimate horror of him and of what he represented – he had seen his evil opportunity to help the new KGB in his twilight years. And he had seized it in the vilest way imaginable. In order to snare a Swiss banker who was making a routine visit to Moscow, the new KGB had procured small girls, some as young as ten years old. They were photographed at Anna's father's apartment, where the banker had performed on them his disgusting acts of depravity under the remote, watchful eye of Anna's father. The Russians' cameras had captured it all and turned it back to use against the banker.

To Anna, that was the kind of man her father was and had always been. But when she'd seen the photographs in a hotel room in Geneva, and recognised his apartment, the well of her hatred for him exploded.

And so his sudden death, as well as being a body blow, was also a cause for her celebration.

But it was actually the body blow that accompanied the news that was more complex. For in a subtle and inverse way, it was her father who had provided the incentive for her to be as good as she became, to be better than any other graduate of the KGB's foreign intelligence service, and to become its youngest female colonel. As the old Soviet empire collapsed in 1989, she had initially decided to take her revenge on him by being better than he was at the same game, the spy game, to be more senior and successful, a greater operative and hero than he had been. And she'd decided back then that she would do this in a country that was apparently turning to democracy for the first time in its history.

That was to be her revenge on him, simply to be better than him, in a better cause.

But Russia's democracy soon turned out to be an illusion. She'd watched her father then, gloating once more as Putin's spies seized the country. And after she'd seen the photographs, she'd done the only thing she could think of to damage him most. Her defection brought him a shame and humiliation in the dying years of his life which could not have been made greater by anything else she might have done. And it was a far greater revenge. At the end of his life, he was disgraced in the eyes of his superiors, shunned by his peers, because of the defection of his daughter. He was destined for no place in history, and an unmarked grave.

As Anna now sat in the truck that bounced them all

from side to side on the Mongolian military road, she wondered where that incentive to excel at her work would come from now that he was dead. She no longer had a personalised hatred against which to struggle. Her father was gone – and good riddance – but was she the same person she'd been when he was alive?

She turned away from the window and back to the track ahead, focused again on the present.

They'd left the last proper metalled road at the Mongolian settlement of Dzuungovi and headed north to the lake along the deserted military track. She heard the two pumped-up special forces men talking under the tarpaulin in the back, armed to the teeth in case of trouble. They were talking loudly over the noise of the truck.

Larry and a team of five other men had already been watching her route through the gorge for three weeks now, as deep inside it as they'd dared to go, where they could just about survey the border itself two miles beyond. Unlike other stretches, they'd confirmed this area was relatively clear, the way through deemed by the Russians impossible for any infantry attack and a complete barrier to any vehicle. The locals said that even a horse couldn't make its way through the gorge. Only the eagles and the agile Siberian big horn sheep could move around in these mountains – or a determined and lucky mountaineer.

Larry didn't like the prospect of her going over at all, but to cross over here seemed madness. There were fewer border guards for a very good reason.

But Anna, as always, had prevailed with Miller – initially with gaining the assignment in the first place and then with the chosen method to reach the start point. If she made it across tonight it was still two hundred miles by bus from Erzin just across the border to Kyzyl further inside Russia, then another three hundred miles to Abakan and a hundred miles or so after that to Krasnoyarsk. And Krasnoyarsk was just where her mission began.

It was a few minutes after midnight when Larry heaved the truck off the road and into some pasture. Anna saw a corral roughly made with untrimmed branches inside which were several horses. There was a man, too, in the corral, one of Larry's who had been assigned this part of the mission; he was a former cowboy from Montana, Larry had told her. Larry turned the key to Off, the engine died and the cowboy unhooked the crude gate and approached. Anna was already out of the cab, taking the leather coat and the pack and gear with her. She put on the coat and dropped the rest of her equipment in the grass. In the open air, it was icy cold after the heated cab.

She nodded to the man without a greeting, though whether he saw her nod in the darkness was doubtful. Nervous, the man thought, nevertheless. But in her relentless pursuit of perfection in her work, Anna Resnikov had never yet been afflicted by nerves.

She walked with the man over to the corral as Larry and the others stepped out of the truck.

She saw that the horses were native Mongolian; short legs, big heads, extremely hardy animals that lived through very hot summers and minus forty-degree winters with equanimity.

'I recommend him.' The cowboy indicated the horse

nearest to the front. 'Look at him. He's eager to get going. You can gallop him for twenty miles. He won't tire. Or when he does, you'll already be at the mouth of the gorge.'

Anna touched the muzzle of the horse and felt his forelegs. They were immensely strong. 'Okay,' she said.

She swung herself into a high saddle and her pack and climbing gear were strapped on to the rear of the saddle by the men.

'When you get there, release him and give him a tap,' the cowboy said. 'He'll come home by himself.'

Larry came up to her.

'Remember, Anna. Get rid of everything before you cross,' he said urgently. 'Including the gun.'

'Don't worry, Larry. I will.'

But she knew Larry would worry anyway. He'd become almost like a personal bodyguard, Burt Miller's shadow who had followed her for three years now. But here he couldn't follow. That was what always bothered him.

The horse was good. She reached the entrance to the gorge in under two hours at a gallop. Should she go through now? Or wait for another night? She got down and unstrapped the pack and gear and tapped the horse on the rump. It didn't like to leave her. She smiled up at it. 'Go on,' she said. 'It's finished.' She tapped it again and the horse turned, began to trot and then broke into a canter into the dark plains.

Before it was lost in the darkness she heard it whinny once.

Anna slung the pack over her shoulders and looped the

cordage around her neck. The rest of the equipment she hung from various belts and over the top of the pack. Then she began to walk.

There was a way along the bank of the river at first. The water was icy clear, tinkling and rushing over black and red rocks. It caught the moon until the walls of the gorge rose up high around it and shut out the thin fingernail of light. Soon she was winding around overhangs, sometimes walking into the edge of the water to clear the towering rock. The route became harder. She was climbing so far without the gear. Then there was a high, flat rectangle of pasture that she climbed towards, and she had an easy way for a while. All the time the unmarked route rose upwards, sometimes gradually, sometimes sharply, towards the gap between the snow peaks.

Once, as she was crossing up high above the river, she caught sight of the moon again and then she dipped down a scree slope and it disappeared behind the crags once more. Where the gorge was at its most forbidding, she stopped finally to rest before the final assault.

Her mission filled her mind in those moments of quiet, the noise of the river too far below now for her to hear it.

Some six hundred miles lay ahead of her before she would reach Krasnoyarsk. Then it depended on her finding a way downriver towards and beyond the Arctic Circle. That was another fifteen hundred miles as the river flowed. Intelligence suggested that the scientist, Professor Vasily Kryuchkov, was in or around Norilsk. But it was possible they'd moved him further east, to the secret nuclear development facilities in the Putorana mountains, where the grim guardians were also hidden – the missiles of Russian's northernmost ICBM, their Intercontinental Ballistic Missile site. It was from this nuclear research and development facility that reports of Kryuchkov's discovery had filtered – in hearsay, in dribbles of information sufficiently reliable only in as far as it required her mission to confirm or deny them. But if the talk were true, what Kryuchkov had finally discovered was too momentous to ignore. And there were other pointers that had indicated to Burt Miller that the talk was true. Three recent visits by nuclear scientists from the West had resulted in no meeting with Kryuchkov and the Russian scientist had been forbidden to travel to international nuclear forums in the West for over a year now.

The Russians were apparently keeping Kryuchkov to themselves, guarding him closely, afraid perhaps that what he had supposedly discovered would find a way out of Russia. For Vasily Kryuchkov, Anna thought, his genius – if the rumours were true – meant permanent exile under guard and a denial of any further contact with the West.

Once she was rested sufficiently, she unclipped the pitons from a belt around her midriff and took some cordage in her right hand. Then she looked up at the high wall of rock above her and began to climb.

It was long and slow, but she climbed crabwise up a rock face in the darkness. Sometimes there was a ledge she could cling on to, or take a brief rest on, but mostly the face was smooth and she needed the pegs and carabiners to make the agonisingly slow progress. For an hour she ascended and when she looked up there was still a great chunk of the face still to scale. She was tired, unseeing, knowing her way up only through touch. And then suddenly her hand went over the craggy edge at the top and she hauled herself over it and lay panting face down on the ice and rock, too exhausted to think.

But down the other side of the face was another rock wall she would have to descend in similar fashion. At least here she would make progress more quickly with the aid of a rope, and below that was the river again, leveller ground for a while. She would have to do this by climbing, then abseiling, downwards several times, scaling and descending the near impenetrable vertical rock walls. Clouds had appeared. Sleet began to lance down in sharp-angled darts, stinging her face. Then, as she went higher, the sleet turned to snow and the climbing became more treacherous.

Finally, some two hours before dawn, up ahead of where she crouched low on a snowy slab of granite, she saw the black outline she was looking for against the purple sky. It was the old Czarist mud fort Larry and his team had identified from two miles back down the canyon as the border with Russia.

Towards this she now made her way, scrambling over scree slopes and down sharp drops, using the axe some-times to arrest her accelerating slides, or hammering in more pitons for climbing. Within another hour – almost too late with the dawn beginning to show on the far horizon to the east – she saw that she was close to the fort. Down here in the dark gorge, she had, perhaps, another hour before the light could penetrate.

What she saw as the fort came nearer were its ancient, crumbling mud walls, the beams all rotted and gone long ago, just a roofless frontier post abandoned more than a century before. But it was the place. It was the border and she would get through before dawn came.

She climbed up towards the fort and approached it concealed in the lee of a large rock that towered ten times her height above and around her. When she was almost at the mud walls of the old fort, she rested for the last time behind the rock. She lay on her back behind it and looked up at the sky, where the stars had disappeared behind the low snow clouds which scudded below the higher peaks of the mountains. The clouds would delay the light of the dawn here, just as the high walls of the gorge would. That was good. She sighed with relief from the pain of the climb and with the thought that the first stage was almost done. She lay on her back in the snow and looked with almost total blankness at the snow clouds. One last rest.

It was then that she heard something. To her acute senses, it was an unnatural sound in this emptiest of places.

In the discreet still of the night before the dawn was fully dressed for her appearance, and with the river inaudible three hundred feet below, Anna heard the unmistakable click of an automatic weapon. It was muffled by the steadily falling snow, certainly, but it was a sound she'd heard a thousand times. She sat up, rolled over on her front, her gun drawn at once from its sheath in the back of her coat. The noise seemed to have come from behind her, from where she'd come, from where she'd just made the final ascent towards the fort. But perhaps the sound was reflected off the rocks. She would have to be careful of that. She had no way of perfectly telling where it came from. But the sound was the unmistakable snap of a heavy ammunition clip being shot home.

Instinctively, Anna rolled over to her left in order to avoid the burst of gunfire she expected swiftly to follow.

CHAPTER TWO

*M*ILITSIYA LIEUTENANT ALEXEI Petrov opened the door to his kitchen cupboard at 5.15 in the morning, about the same time he did every day of the year. On this particular morning, from the selection of tins and packets on the eye-level shelf he chose a can labelled '*ryby*' – fish – the species of which went unidentified. Probably the scrapings from the bottom of the hold in a factory ship up in the Arctic, he thought. The good stuff – the actual fish – they sold abroad.

Behind him a dented tin kettle half full of water on the gas stove was beginning to simmer and the water was destined for two spoons of loose black tea which waited in a brown china pot on the chipped, faded yellow plastic surface.

As he waited for the water to boil, he took up a stance by the window that to any observer might have had a strange, unearthly grace about it for a tough, stocky Russian police lieutenant. He looked out at the city from his cramped, one-bedroom, eleventh-floor apartment and was completely, consciously relaxed as he did so. He left his arms hanging loosely by his side, his narrow slitted eyes were focused on nothing, and he maintained a steady, almost imperceptible breathing. It was his moment of calm before the day began. Then his mind went to blank.

It was what might be called in polite Western circles his morning meditation. But Petrov had actually learned it from his native Evenk grandfather, Gannyka, a nomadic Siberian who'd lived his whole life in a reindeer-hide tent. And now, Petrov had heard just a few days earlier, the old man was dying, in a deer-hide tent just as he had lived.

It was the second day in June and the sun had already been up since 4 o'clock. With his mind in neutral, he was aware now, through the poisonous yellow smoke that belched from Krasnoyarsk's smokestacks twenty-four hours a day, that the sun was illuminating the half-dead, polluted city with a dull haze, as if through gauze. He was aware too that the city spread out to the east of where he stood, towards the sun – known as the Eastern Gate to the Evenk people. His meditative consciousness took in the grim industrial surroundings without the judgement or anger, the resentment or bitterness it might otherwise have done.

Thus, *militsiya* Lieutenant Alexei Petrov began his day and, from this detached beginning, the day's events would unfold in whatever way they did without those life-destroying mental compulsions his Slav colleagues seemed to be plagued by.

Beneath the window, this quarter – his quarter of the city from the point of view of the *ment*, or cop, that he was – consisted of decayed workers' blocks from the Brezhnev era that looked like they'd been hurled

petulantly on to the cityscape by dysfunctional gods;
a few potholed streets, some of which were more hole
than street; some broken concrete structures annexed
by drug dealers, meths drinkers and various other addicts
– they were decaying humans in a decaying landscape, in
other words. But as the lieutenant in charge of this
quarter, it was his job to know everyone as closely as he
possibly could, including each former convict and each
dealer or addict, in order to take pre-emptive action
where necessary.

It was a rough place, even by the standards of a rough
city. In his quarter, the stall-holders who elsewhere in the
city sold newspapers and cigarettes by the packet, or just
singly, dared not set up shop for fear of robbery or worse.

Unfolding in his consciousness, and away now beyond
his quarter, the rest of the Siberian city of Krasnoyarsk
smoked incessantly, like an addict itself, from its towering
industrial chimneys. And half a mile from the window,
the great river glittered as if in anger at the foul factory
substances it was forced to ingest. But Alexei Petrov had
no critique about all of this, just a blank, calm acceptance.

He was finally brought back to physical reality by the
kettle that had been whistling for some time behind him
and he turned and filled the pot.

At thirty-nine years old, Petrov was of medium height,
and an extremely strong and leanly muscled man of mainly
native blood. His few Slavic features came from his Slav
Russian father, as did his name, but these were almost
obliterated by his strong, tribal Evenk ancestry. Certainly,
apart from his mother's and father's brief union with each

other, there may have been other encounters of a sexual kind, casual and violent, between his tribal family and the invading Russians ever since the Czar's Cossacks surged across Siberia more than three hundred years before. But back then even bands of largely undiscriminating Cossacks might have baulked at a native woman who hadn't washed for six months. And up until modern times the Evenk could disappear into the vast wastes of their once unpolluted Siberia where no one could follow.

Petrov had a sculpted, nut-brown face, with high, prominent cheekbones – a feature shared with the Evenk's genetic relations in Mongolia. His eyes were set well back in his head and there was a kind of imprint in the centre of his forehead that looked like a faint, fleshy medallion. His straight nose and protected nostrils were an Evenki feature and his strong jawline had deterred many a potential antagonist who might otherwise have taken a swing at him. He had black, shiny, cropped hair, which he would have preferred long – over his shoulders – but which his *militsiya* position, he felt, prevented. His mouth was straight, with slightly prominent lips, and had not quite lost its once prodigious ability to laugh. Regular exposure to humorous situations, however, had hung by a thread for some time now.

It was his Russian father who had ruthlessly tried to Russian-ise him, ashamed perhaps that he had taken a native woman for a wife, and trying to compensate by beating the nativeness out of their son. When his father had finally sent his wife back to her own people – reindeer herders and fishermen way up beyond the Arctic Circle, north of one of the villages called Potapovo – he'd had Alexei's papers changed. He'd claimed a Kazakh mother for him instead. At least the Kazakhs had a nation of their own and a useful one – after all, the Russians used Kazakhstan to test their nuclear bombs. But to Petrov's father, the Evenk people had nothing; no country, no polity – no *possessions* – and as far as Alexei's father was concerned, they therefore could not have any meaningful identity at all.

And so Alexei Petrov the police lieutenant was a man caught between two worlds and he floated in the melange they both created. One world was ancient, deeply traditional and governed by the spirits of nature; the other was violent, atavistic and responsible for much of the charnel house of recent Russian history that had laid the land and its own people to waste.

But in the mirror in his bathroom, Petrov the Russian thought he looked pretty good in his military-style police lieutenant's uniform. He certainly looked tough and was known for being so in his quarter. Now ready for work, he wore the uniform, except for the jacket. That was hanging on a chair, impeccably cleaned and pressed, with its shining buttons and twin shoulder insignia of two yellow stars and a yellow dot on grey, all of which was bordered with neat red lines.

It was his nomadic ancestry that had made him naturally as strong as he was. But he had complemented that by rigorous training since his early youth. Now, aside from his sometimes strenuous police duties as an *operativnik* – detective – he played squash three times a week and ran half-marathons at weekends when he wasn't on duty. He had even been a member of the national *militsiya* long-distance running team in his twenties and was given a trial for the Olympics sixteen years before, back in the middle of the 1990s.

But since his wife had died of some officially 'mysterious illness' two years before, which he suspected – no, which he knew – had been caused by a radiation leak at the military facility outside the city where she'd worked as a laboratory assistant, he had taken even greater care to look and to be fit. And sometimes he was ashamed of this, as if nowadays he were looking after himself in order to find another woman. Was it possible to betray the dead? Absolutely, was his resolute, Evenk conclusion. And betraying both the living and the dead was anyway a signature feature of the people who ruled Russia, the Kremlin's spy elite.

While he waited for the tea to brew, he looked out of the window again – his mind now at rest in observance – and watched the icy river, swollen by melted snow from Mongolia to the south, that wound its way fifteen hundred miles to the north and into the Arctic seas.

In Siberia, he thought, as he often did with a certain morbid regularity, the bones of the dead millions still waited for the crimes committed against them to be acknowledged, let alone waited for a decent burial. The latter would never happen – he was sure of that, it was impossible now anyway. But, who knew, perhaps one day there would be a regime in Moscow that at least recognised the enormity of the country's crimes against its own citizens. His own people, the Evenk, were merely an afterthought in Moscow's mass murders, an almost accidental appendix, the swishing of the old Soviet monster's tail.

He doubted, however, that an actual apology would ever intrude into the thoughts of the average state official in the twenty-first-century Kremlin, even for the Siberian slaughter of its own people, the Russians themselves.

He turned back to the kitchen counter and opened the can of fish which turned out to be an indistinguishable, rust-coloured mush. He thought that the contents were most likely a bouillabaisse of fishes' heads, tails and arseholes. Whatever it was, it was all mixed up with a thick, gluey tomato-like sauce. Then he spread half the contents on to some black bread and poured the brewed tea into a chipped mug. As he was poised to take the first sip of the day, his mobile phone screamed into the silence inside his head.

'*Da?*'

Young Corporal Temov was at the other end, finishing the night shift at the station.

The thought flashed across Petrov's mind that soon his subordinate – a pale 23 year old with an ambitious urge to please his masters – would be promoted to his own level, and then, sometime in the future, above him.

At thirty-nine and with his general diligence and recognised crime-solving skills, Petrov knew that he should have been at least a *militsiya* major by now. But he also knew that it wasn't just his ethnicity that stood in the way. He was guilty of an even worse offence against the state than that. He was guilty of avoiding becoming part of the 'corruptocracy' – the venal system that stretched from the top of the Kremlin to the lowliest traffic cop ruled supreme in all of Russia's law enforcement agencies. In the myriad law and spy organs that sought to control, suppress, grow fat and, very occasionally, solve crimes in the country, there was no one who was more distrusted by the spy elite than a straight cop or a clean security officer – if you could find one. There was no one who came under more suspicion. Until he took his first bribe, Petrov knew he would remain forever a lieutenant.

Over the phone Temov reeled off the night's events in Petrov's quarter of the city; the new drunk-tank occupants, the knifings, the overdoses, the thieving, the accidental or not-so-accidental deaths. He sounded bored, or maybe just tired from the shift. But he had left the best until last. There had been a murder reported, Temov told him, unable to suppress some excitement in his voice. The report had come in just five minutes earlier at 5.47. The dead body was at a block not far from Petrov's own apartment. And according to the anonymous caller, there was 'something odd' about the murder victim. But then the anonymous caller had rung off quickly from what was found to be a public phone. A public phone in his quarter that actually worked, Petrov noted with some surprise.

Corporal Temov suggested that he could pick up the lieutenant in a squad car and they could both go together.

'I'll walk,' Petrov told him. 'Meet me there. Seal it off.'

Petrov sat in the kitchen for a moment longer. For some reason – perhaps the old man's imminent death – his mind turned back to his grandfather, Gannyka, dying in a reindeer-hide tent up above the Arctic Circle. He automatically looked across at the window-sill where he kept the deer-hide drum the old man had given him as a child and which he hadn't touched in years. A magic drum, an Evenk tambour, Gannyka had told him, made from the wood of a tree struck by lightning, and then stretched with deerskin. It was made from the same tree from which Gannyka had made his own shaman's drum, back in the 1930s. Petrov stood and walked to the window. He picked up the small drum and turned it over in his hands. Then he began to tap a rhythm that scattered the layer of dust from the drum-skin into the rays of sunlight. He decided then that he would like to see his grandfather for one last time before the old man died.

He returned to the table, finished his tea and smeared the rest of the fish mush on to another slice of black bread. He washed his hands carefully, buttoned up his jacket, put on his *militsiya* cap and took the urine-stained and stinking elevator to the foot of the building.

The walk itself was just a little over ten minutes away from the street exit from his block and he arrived before Temov had time to scream up in a cop car with its light flashing.

There was a small throng of people outside the chipped concrete entrance to the block. They were *babas* with their black shawls and shopping bags, a few very young and unwashed children, a couple of youths who stared at the ground, kicked chips of concrete, and kept their hands in their pockets.

'Where?' Petrov asked quietly and to the group in general.

One of the *babas* pointed silently behind her into the alley where the trash was kept and, mostly, left to rot.

Then Temov ran up behind him and seemed to be about to push the placid little circle of residents back as if they were fomenting a dangerous public riot. But something in his lieutenant's quiet demeanour pre-empted his carefully learned officious arrogance.

'Get some tape,' Petrov told him.

Temov walked back to the car.

The block was not far from the great river's dock area, just a street or two away from the river, in fact, in Sverdlovsk Street. It was much like Petrov's own block, badly built of poor materials, dilapidated further by the extreme temperatures which in winter could reach minus forty-five degrees centigrade or more, and littered around its edges with the detritus of its chemically unhinged inhabitants.

He walked down the damp alley next to it. It had started to drizzle and he now wished he'd brought his coat. Down here in the dark warren of the blocks, he hadn't even noticed the sun had disappeared.

When he reached the end, just before the overflowing trash cans blocked the path, he saw the body. It was the corpse of a man, lying face up.

Petrov knelt down beside the dead man. He studied him patiently and with care, as if he might suddenly pop back to life.

Despite the dirt on it, the body was well dressed, Petrov noted first of all, and therefore the man could not be from around here. That was certain. He peeled back the man's upper lip. Foreign dental work, he noted. A rich Russian, then. Then he placed his right hand behind the man's neck, between it and the concrete. There was a bullet hole, the shot fired from close up – he could feel the hole and the burn marks around it. An assassination, by the look of it. The Krasnoyarsk *mafiya* doing its night work. They'd shot him in the back of the neck, then left him face up away from the crime scene in someone else's trash alley. Sometime during the night. Forensics would know when.

Petrov turned around, still kneeling, to look behind him.

For some reason that he couldn't explain to himself, he wanted to know if he was being observed. But there was no one. All he heard was Temov's commanding arrogance from around the corner at the far end of the alley. Now, without Petrov's influence, all his official state aggression appeared to have been released.

Petrov turned back to the corpse. He slid his hand under the man's raincoat and into an expensive-looking tweed jacket and took out an air ticket; it was for a seat on board the flight from Norilsk up beyond the Arctic Circle to Krasnoyarsk. It was from the previous afternoon. He then rooted further down into the pocket and brought out a passport, which was protected in a black leather wallet. He slipped it out of the wallet and looked at the cover of the passport and saw at once that it wasn't

Russian. The man was a citizen of the European Union, apparently. Then he flicked to the end page. This made him pause again. The assassin's victim was a foreigner, that was certain. But he was also a professor. He mentally noted the name of the man, Gunther Bachman, and his country of origin, Germany. A professor? Well, in Germany everyone called themselves *Herr Doktor* or *Herr Professor*, didn't they?'

So that was what was 'odd' about the corpse, he thought. A well-off foreigner in a back alley of Krasnoyarsk's most unpleasant, filthy and poverty-stricken quarter. He put the passport back into its leather wallet and then returned it and the air ticket to the pocket of the man's tweed jacket.

If whoever had killed Bachman had left the passport, there must be a reason. They could have got good money on the black market for it. Perhaps, then, whoever killed him didn't have the wherewithal to deal with a foreign passport, had nowhere to fence it – that was the simplest explanation. So maybe it wasn't a *mafiya* murder after all. The *mafiya* would know how to make good money from a European Union passport. Perhaps instead it was some opportunistic delinquent who had killed the German professor. Perhaps Bachman had been unlucky enough to wander off the beaten track, then been mugged and casually killed. A delinquent, perhaps, who imitated the style of the *mafiya*.

Petrov remained, squatting on his haunches by the body now. If they'd left the passport, it was surely certain they would have stolen any cash the German had in his pockets. Petrov dug around in the opposite inside pocket of the jacket and came out with a well-worn money wallet. He flicked it open and, sure enough, there was nothing, not a euro, not a kopeck, not a sou. The credit cards were gone too, but there was no sign of torture on the body in order to gain the pin numbers. Perhaps fear had been enough, and the promise of life, if he'd cooperated. Evidently, someone – the killer – had been through the pockets, but it seemed he was just a petty thief – perhaps even the anonymous caller himself. At any rate, it must have been someone so low in the local order of criminality that they hadn't known what to do with a passport, and were too afraid to take it.

But Petrov still crouched by the corpse. He began to run his hand across and around the other areas of the coat and jacket, lapels first. In doing so, he noticed the jacket had been apparently expertly slit to reveal the lining. After checking the lapels, he then traced the sleeves of the jacket, then the shoulders, the front and around the lower edges. All were slit with something very sharp, a razor most likely. He turned his attention to the man's trousers and ran his hand up and down the legs until he was clutching the man's genitals through the material. The trousers, too, had been expertly slit, he noted. They were lined with something like silk. All of this was odd too.

Petrov pursed his lips and summed up what he had before him: a foreigner who had arrived the previous afternoon from Norilsk on a return ticket to Krasnoyarsk: whose passport had not been stolen, but whose money and credit cards had been; a bullet hole at point–blank range in the back of the neck, execution-style; and the mysterious slits in the man's clothing. Whoever had killed Bachman was, it seemed, looking for something expertly concealed, something far more valuable or important than a passport. Had the killer or killers found what they were looking for? Or had they missed whatever it was? Petrov's second diagnosis, of an opportunistic killing by an addict and a thief, began to fade like the first *mafiya* one had.

He paused, looked behind him again. Still no one was watching him.

He now noted the professor's shoes were unlaced. They were very expensive shoes, he guessed. He slipped them off, checking the inside of the socks first, feeling around with his hand. Finding nothing inside the socks, he looked the shoes over carefully, turning them one by one in his hands, scraping off the dirt. They were covered with the street filth, muddied almost beyond recognition as a once fine pair of shoes, in fact. But something caught his eye, nevertheless – and only when he scraped the filth away from the soles with his fingers. One shoe, the left one, had clearly been re-soled. And despite the wear and tear it had undergone on the vile night before – the night of Bachman's death – the stitching work on the left shoe looked like it was very recent and not particularly expert. A cheap Russian job, by the look of it, not one done by a professional German shoemaker.

Petrov checked down the alley behind him again and, finding the coast clear, slid a knife from the pocket of his uniform and began to cut the tight, thick thread that bound the sole to the inner leather and the shoe itself. It was a difficult task even though the re-soling stitches weren't particularly good. By the time he'd prised the sole away, from the toe down to the instep, he was sweating, but more from anxiety that he'd be caught interfering with the evidence than from the effort. For this was no longer a job for a humble *militsiya operativnik*. It was a job for the higher-ups, the spook departments of the law. The MVD. The victim was a foreigner.

Between the two pieces of leather, the sole of which he'd bent back as far as he could, and tightly wrapped in thin, transparent plastic, he found a closely folded wad of paper. Maybe it had been folded six or eight times, he guessed, into a wedge – as many times as it could have been folded, anyway. The wedge would have made it uncomfortable for the man to walk perhaps. But the packet was invisible, even when looking directly at the shoe's sole, until he had prised the sole away.

Something made Petrov still pause, now in the kneeling position again. Finally his mind cleared. He clutched the folded papers in their plastic protection into the ball of his large fist, unbuttoned his jacket with the other hand, and slipped the wedge of papers into the pocket of his immaculate *militsiya* jacket, now stained by the dirt on his hand, before buttoning it up again.

He didn't think about what he was doing. Indeed he had never done such a thing before, tamper with evidence. Perhaps it was some thought of an imminent cover-up that flickered across his mind; he didn't know, later, and he couldn't explain it to himself now.

And perhaps the cover-up that followed his wife's

death from a radiation leak had something to do with that. Never again, he thought. If there was one thing you could rely on in Russia's law enforcement bodies, it was a corrupt disregard for the truth. And if he'd failed with his wife, he wasn't going to fail Bachman. No cover-ups. Never again.

Now at last he stood, still alone in the alley. He was back to being Lieutenant Petrov again. One last thing he mentally noted; Bachman had no suitcase with him, neither an overnight bag nor a briefcase. Stolen, presumably, like the cash and credit cards. He filed away that fact for later.

Finally he looked down at the victim and thought about his early morning musings at his apartment, about the dead, whose bones littered Siberia. Against the millions – the tens of millions – of unnatural deaths meted out in this vast empty land over the previous decades, what was significant about this one? For, to Alexei Petrov, every death was significant, indeed important and individual. As well as his imperviousness to bribery, that was one other thing that distinguished him from his masters. Everyone was someone. A death in Siberia might, to them, be as insignificant as a snowflake in Siberia – lost, surplus, irrelevant. But not to Petrov.

But now he knew he had to act quickly like *militsiya* Lieutenant Petrov should do.

That the victim was a foreigner changed everything, he'd known that from the moment he'd seen the man's foreign passport. This was now a job for others, not for him, not for the ordinary *militsiya*. He would have to report it immediately to other state organs, the high-ups. The MVD people must be informed without delay or it would be his neck on the block. It was they who would deal with such a murder. And these Ministry of Interior police wouldn't conscience a wait of any time at all before they were handed the job of dealing with it.

CHAPTER THREE

Anna Resnikov stood in the shuffling line of the unemployed that snaked along the quays of Krasnoyarsk's riverside docks. It was 2 June, three days after her arrival in the city. In the cold air at six in the morning she waited – sullenly, in imitation of the others – to be at the head of the line where the hiring office was taking on workers for the lumber mills downriver in Igarka.

But in her mind she was troubled, unusually, uncharacteristically so. And it wasn't the prospect of going through the next stage of her mission – the hiring for Igarka's lumber mills – that was worrying her. It was her own conduct at the border four nights before. She went back in her mind over the previous three days – and that particular moment at the border – with a mixture of surprise, almost shock, but most of all with a fiercely analytical self-criticism.

She'd made it to the city on schedule and so the mission was on track – that much was true, certainly. But her own reactions as she'd crossed the border and had heard the arming of the automatic weapon were deeply out of character, way outside her normal, instinctive

45

ruthlessness in the face of impending danger. That was what was bothering her now as she stood in the dejected line, as it had done ever since the incident itself. It was a needling anxiety that hadn't gone away.

When she'd heard the gun and the sound of the ammunition clip ratcheting into place, she'd frozen. Exactly as she should have done, her training inch perfect. Then she'd rolled away from any risk of immediate gunfire in her direction and had ducked down further behind the rock she was using as cover. So far so good. It was then that she'd heard the voice.

'*Kto etu?*' The nervous, young male voice that rang out in the predawn darkness at the border had spoken in Russian. 'Who goes there?'

From that, she'd known that she hadn't been seen and was not in the cross hairs of the man's weapon.

She'd drawn the Thompson Contender from behind her back where the long, eighteen-inch barrel had greater freedom of movement when she was climbing. Then she'd removed her gloves and silently fitted the ice-cold, metal silencer taken from her breast pocket over the barrel, easing it tight. Now she was deadly. Again, so far so good.

She'd waited then. Let him make a move. The man with the weapon was in the dark, both literally and figuratively, and she had the advantage. Soon she would be able to pinpoint the direction of the voice, once she'd worked out the sound shadow and the echoes from the surrounding rock formations.

The unearthly quiet that followed at the top of the

gorge where the old Czarist border post was crumbling to dust stretched out for a long time and then she'd heard the arming of another, second automatic. She'd realised she would have to kill two of them. More than two, perhaps. Well, surprise was on her side, that was okay. She would have to kill them. That was how it would be. How it had always been, ever since her training at the SVR's headquarters, from the age of seventeen.

'*Te haanaas irsen be?*' This time the challenge had been in Mongolian. The same young voice, she judged.

He, or they – she knew there were at least two of them now – were close, but not behind her as she'd feared. Somewhere up ahead down the slope behind the rock. From the sound shadow, she estimated they were, in fact, just beyond the rock which she'd hidden behind. So that fact, along with the interrogatory challenge, assured her further that they hadn't actually seen her.

She'd then off-loaded the mountaineering gear she was carrying, careful not to let the metal parts clash against each other, and crept upwards away from where she guessed they were standing. She followed the line of the rock until she could look around its upper edge, nearest to the fort.

What she'd seen from her cover were two young Russian border guards of tribal ancestry, Buryats, most likely. They were standing below her. They were in their twenties, she'd thought, maybe even younger, recruits still just in their teens, and they'd been stationed out here where the danger of incursion was at a low level and where any encounter was most likely only to be with an illegal Mongolian trader. She could see they were nervous, under-trained rather than tensed for action, and they were facing down the gorge from where she'd come. Facing away from her. She was now well above them. On the declining slope from where she'd come, their heads were just lower than her feet.

The shot was easy, two shots, to be exact. She could drop them both without either of them knowing what hit them. And it would be done, thanks to the silencer, without anyone else knowing, either. Then dispose of the bodies. The snow would cover her tracks.

She took aim along the long barrel of the handgun. Her index finger closed on the trigger, a light, delicate, almost loving touch, the touch of a long familiarity with an instrument of death. She felt its resistance and steadied her aim.

But it was then that she'd hesitated. The back of the first brown-skinned boy's head was fixed in the sight, just below the cranium. A dead shot, an instant end. He wouldn't even know what happened. But still she'd hesitated and that was what was bothering her now as she stood in the line of unemployed leading to the hiring office at Krasnoyarsk.

Why had she paused? They were two quick and easy shots for a person of her high calibre and skills. One for each of them, in the backs of their heads. Down, gone. She could be on her way, relentless in the pursuit of her mission. Just as she'd always been.

The reason she'd hesitated, as she thought about it now – for the hundredth time since she'd made the border crossing – was a sudden and unfamiliar surge of doubt. Thoughts had entered her mind that had nothing to do with the mission, nothing to do with her training, or even with her own personal safety and survival. She'd suddenly seen the two guards for what they were, that was what had happened. She'd felt an eerie feeling that she was in a theatre, she onstage, the youths across the boards from her. But on top of that, she'd felt she was also watching herself, as if from the audience, levelling a deadly weapon at two defenceless kids. This vision of herself, this self-reflection, had deeply unnerved her.

What she'd seen in her mind's eye was the humanity of her intended victims, the flesh and blood, the mothers, brothers and sisters of the two nervous guards who fingered their too-heavy weapons as if they might go off in their hands. In this mental scenario, they were not border guards per se, but just two innocent local boys, forced into conscripted service against their will. In short, they were human, and that was not a thought that should intrude before a killing. She was trained to think about, to concentrate on, the action of killing, not the death itself. An immediate death would now come from the slightest increase of pressure.

Her rational mind had tried to reassert itself. It was just a double killing, two shots where necessary. That was the game she was in, wasn't it, and had always been in since she'd graduated from the KGB's training school at Balashiha outside Moscow. Kill or be killed, that was the bottom line. That was the lesson which was relentlessly drummed into the new intelligence recruit as she had once been. Or more than that, even – just kill to make life a bit easier. In this case, her crossing at the border four nights before would have been eased considerably by the simple pressure on the trigger. It was routine, a necessary act in her world, in order to be sure of avoiding detection. After all, they would have killed her if they'd had the chance, or out of fear, perhaps. It didn't matter. That was their job too.

But the unfamiliar, and potentially suicidal, doubts had proliferated, upsetting the normal, smooth mechanism of her mind. Was she really anything more than a killer? It seemed to her then that the dead bodies which had steadily mounted in her lethal career were becoming a dead end. In her sudden, unprecedented doubt, she had lain there in the steadily falling snow and listened. And as she did so, she'd wondered if she'd reached her breaking point; if she could no longer trust herself to kill – to kill anyone who was in her way – in order to make herself safe. As she lay there in mental confusion, she'd lowered the gun.

The thought of her father had crossed her mind again then. Had his death removed her killer instinct? She felt a clamminess on her hands. Then she heard a shuffle on the terrain below her and was immediately alert again.

'It must have been a rock or a stone falling,' one of the kids had said, in Russian again this time. But as she'd watched them, she noted that he'd kept the automatic trained down the gorge while the other boy slung his over his shoulder.

'Come on,' the second boy had said. 'It's nothing. Let's get some breakfast.'

Anna had watched them slowly retreat after that, one walking backwards at first, training his weapon down the gorge, as if he were in some safe-training session. She could have taken them both down at any moment. That had been the obvious thing to do, the thing she would normally have done in the circumstances. But she hadn't done it and now she felt a deep misgiving that she'd endangered herself and the whole mission in the process.

She'd waited for them to go, watching them all the time. Then she'd crept up past and behind the old fort and left a wide berth around a concrete pillbox further into the high valley which Larry's men hadn't been able to see from their line of surveillance in the previous weeks. The pillbox was the new border post, and where the boys had gone and had begun to brew some tea in the freezing morning. As the first dull beginning of the dawn began to tint the upper edges of the mountains with a grey light muffled by the snow clouds, she saw a fire they'd lit.

They could have spotted her at any time as she passed. She must have been mad not to kill them. They could have radioed to others, for reinforcements, in order to make sure there really was no one coming across the border. She'd put her life at risk. She'd betrayed a ruthlessness that had always kept her alive.

After she'd left the pillbox behind her, her head had cleared at last. Things had become more straightforward, though no less dangerous. She tried to put her doubt out of her mind. She dumped the climbing equipment into the ravine and then she looked at the gun. Larry's instructions came back to her. But she unscrewed the silencer and hid it and the gun deep inside her clothing with the three hundred rounds of ammunition. Any strip search would reveal it. It was a deeply risky thing to do.

On the day that followed the crossing, she'd walked for some thirty miles into Russia. The only people she'd seen were a few Buryat horsemen in the distance. The empty landscape. There were similar endless grasslands on this side of the border and the mountains to the grasslands of northern Mongolia which she'd crossed with Larry and the others the day before. The journey northwards across the emptiness was a relief, arduous certainly, but a respite from her tangled thoughts at that time of crisis.

She had rested up in a stone *kurgan* during the night after her crossing, then walked on in the hours before the second dawn to the hamlet of Erzin. She'd seen a few yurts and some more native Buryat horsemen, but there were no Russians in evidence. And no more border guards until she'd reached the first proper roads.

At Erzin she'd bought two large string sacks of apples from a Buryat family at the side of the road, which had been stored and preserved underground over the winter. And then she'd found some old clothes at a market stall, changing her appearance to that of a peasant farm worker, before boarding the bus to Kyzyl.

The old bus crawled slowly across the same wilderness landscape. Here, still close enough to the border to attract attention from Interior Ministry troops, the bus was stopped several times by border patrols and by the local police. Their methods were simple. Huge iron chains with spikes were dragged across the road to stop all traffic. Abrupt questions, long looks at her papers, snapped remarks, and the occasional gloating, lustful look at her body. But her papers had worked, the forgers at Cougar had done their job well. She had the two sacks of apples, in which the gun and ammunition were now concealed. She was going to the market in Abakan to sell the apples – that was her story. She must have repeated it eight times or more on the interrupted journey.

At Kyzyl, she'd taken another bus to Abakan. This was a bustling town and she could more easily lose herself now. At a marketplace in the centre near the bus station, she'd taken the gun and ammunition, then dumped the apples and hitched an overnight ride to Krasnoyarsk in a rasping truck that was taking cheap Chinese goods to the city.

When she'd arrived in the city she paid the driver of the truck on the outskirts and walked. Then she'd scouted the area where she'd needed to stay in order to be near the port and the hiring office. The plan was all worked out in a control room at Burt Miller's Cougar ranch in New Mexico. She'd first marked out several old *babas* at the marketplace nearest to where she'd wanted to be. There'd be one who would rent her a room for a few nights. She'd finally taken a room from a 76-year-old woman named Zhenya with whom she'd fallen into conversation at the street market, a conversation that was instigated on Anna's part for just that purpose. Zhenya's apartment was in the slums of the slum city, in a filthy dilapidated block on Sverdlovsk Street, not far from the docks. It was ideal.

Now, Anna looked up at the greying skies of Krasnoyarsk. The sun had crept behind the clouds after its early dawn display, a broken promise. The city was mantled in dullness and unseasonal cold. She'd been at the apartment for two nights already, looking for work downriver towards the Arctic – and her destination. And this hiring today was her final chance of obtaining the job that would get her part of the way there, as far as Igarka. Her mission was at the starting blocks. But now she must make her way north, towards the ever colder destinations where she would find, or not, Professor Kryuchkov and the answer to Burt Miller's question.

And so now she waited, for the second tired morning of the hiring process. And she tried to put her troubled thoughts from the incident at the border crossing behind her.

CHAPTER FOUR

FROM THE CRIME scene Lieutenant Petrov first went back to his apartment. It was just after seven-thirty in the morning. Normally he would have gone straight to the *militsiya* station, but he didn't wish to have the papers he had taken from the sole of Bachman's shoe on his person when he arrived at work. He'd left a telephone message for his superior, Major Sadko, about the foreigner's body and would leave it to him to gain whatever thin glory there was in informing the MVD. Sadko enjoyed keeping possession of such access to himself.

And now Petrov sat at his kitchen table for the second time that morning and unfolded the papers he'd taken from the corpse from their waterproof wrapping. He flattened each sheet one by one and placed two books at the top and bottom to keep them flat. There were just three sheets in all, each about three inches high, torn from a cheap, lined Russian notebook.

He'd made a cup of coffee and now placed the cup on the kitchen top far away from the table. Like an experienced climber who fears an uncharacteristic loss of balance when perched on a precarious ledge, he suddenly imagined that he could lose control of his normally smooth physical functions and that, at any moment, his hand might involuntarily knock the cup over and destroy whatever was written on the papers. Then he turned his attention to what was written on them.

What he'd expected to find in their carefully concealed manifestation he wasn't sure. Writing, obviously, but in truth he'd hoped for more prose than he could see, something plainly put that any man could understand, even a lowly *militsiya* lieutenant like himself. So when he saw a sea of figures, calculations and equations that covered the three pages on both sides and were interspersed by only the occasional explanatory paragraph of prose, which the figures put him off from reading, he was disheartened. And everything on the papers was also written in terribly small handwriting. He felt that his meticulous preparations for the event of reading them – the carefully placed chair, the cup of coffee, the objects to flatten the documents and his intensively calmed mind – had been misplaced. There was nothing for him to prepare for if the papers were incomprehensible to him. Only the prose, in Russian, made any sense to him and even that was written in some kind of scientific language that all but eluded his understanding. He didn't bother even to try and take it in.

He got up from the chair and went to the tiny sitting room next to the kitchen. These apartments were like chicken coops, he thought. Just enough room for a man and a woman to lay the eggs the State required of them. Well, he and his deceased wife hadn't fulfilled any State quota. They'd been childless when she'd died.

He rooted in the drawers of a desk that contained mostly his former wife's belongings – knick-knacks she'd found in the market, a small religious icon painted on cheap wood, postcards which were never sent to people who existed anyway only in her imagination, a ball of string, a pair of gloves – until he found a smudged magnifying glass she used to examine postage stamps from around the world and which she'd collected from a man with a stall on Leninskaya, in exchange for apples and honey from Petrov's small allotment out of the city near old Afasiev's place.

Without closing the drawers, he returned to the kitchen, cleaned the glass on a fresh tea towel, sat down and squinted at the jumble of figures. But even magnified – particularly magnified, he decided – they were still just as incomprehensible as they had been before.

Petrov sat, magnifying glass in hand, and wondered if there were anyone he knew well enough to whom he could show at least a line or two.

His deceased wife had worked as a laboratory assistant at the military industrial complex outside the city, known as Krasnoyarsk B. In Soviet times the mountain from which it was hollowed appeared on no maps. She had made friends with a few of the scientists there – women – one of whom had even visited the apartment on an occasion when Petrov had cooked dinner for the three of them. Petrov supposed he could call her. He could look in his wife's address book for the name which he'd forgotten.

But what if even a few lines of the mathematical jungle

on the pages in front of him contained something she recognised to be highly secret and sensitive – and surely they did, or they wouldn't have been so carefully concealed? The woman would feel obliged to ask him how he had got hold of them, at the very least, and, more than likely, would also feel obliged to report their existence to her superiors. Then he'd be a suspect, possibly laying himself open to charges of treason, let alone tampering with evidence.

He sat back in the chair and stared at the pages, laid out side by side, as if watching them would provide some clue to their decipherment. Then he stood, gathered them together in a bundle, clipped them with a paperclip, and went to the bathroom holding them in his hand. He lifted an asbestos panel above the toilet and was about to slide them inside the ceiling when he thought of the mice. He stepped down, walked back into the living room and dug around again in the drawers of his wife's desk. Finally he came up with a large tin in which his wife had kept her stamp collection. He buried the papers under the stamps, closed the tin and sealed it with tape. Then he returned to the bathroom where he placed the tin in the ceiling and slid the asbestos panel shut again. He would think about the documents at greater leisure later in the day.

On the way to the *militsiya* station Petrov listened to the new Krasnoyarsk ballet company on the car radio. They were performing Stravinsky's *Rite of Spring* that evening and the radio programme was by way of an advertisement. It was a ballet in which, as Stravinsky himself had noted, *In a circle of sage elders a young girl dances herself to death.*

Though not a patch on Moscow's or Petersburg's ballet companies, the city, nevertheless, was trying to nurture a Siberian company without the help of the State or of the billionaires who sucked the people and the place dry with their aluminium factories.

As Petrov listened to the violent magic of the music, he decided what he would do. Maybe it was the music that set his mind running, its discordant, tuneless cacophony supposedly echoing a ritualistic, pre-Russian folk practice – an Evenk practice, perhaps – at least in the Slav Stravinsky's mind, Petrov thought. It was amazing how the Slavs fantasised about his own people, and the Evenk were only one of dozens of ethnic Siberian tribes that seemed to set their imaginations racing. So, what was he to do?

It all came together for him in a flash. He would take a vacation from work, extended leave for a few weeks at least – that was the decision that came to him. His leave could be combined with his thoughts from earlier that morning. He decided to tell Major Sadko that his grandfather was ill and undoubtedly dying. That he wished to see him once more before he died.

The thought of seeing Gannyka before the old shaman left this world filled Petrov with a sudden happiness that he couldn't explain. He hadn't been north, up to where his family tribe lived, for more than five years. Somehow it had never crossed his mind. But he could take his leave any time and the urgent immediacy of his request of absence would only be granted because of family illness or death.

The music tumbled around in his head in its repetitive way that was supposed to imitate the ecstatic chants and out-of-body experiences of so-called primitive people. The shamans perhaps. Yet somehow it seemed to connect him with another way of life, theirs, his mother's and his grandfather's.

But then what? It was more than a thousand miles downriver to the village and they'd be gone from there by now with the reindeer herds. And what would he do with the papers? He decided he couldn't risk leaving them behind. He would have to take them with him.

He parked the police car on some waste ground behind the station and walked around the front and into the reception. No expense spent, he thought, as he surveyed the decayed infrastructure of the building and recalled that the toilets hadn't been working the day before. The girl behind the metal grille nodded sharply at him.

'Major Sadko wants to see you right away.'

He nodded in return but didn't reply. The door next to the grille was unlocked by the woman from the inside and he went straight to Sadko's office, down a hall of peeling paint, if you could call the colourless daub put on to the walls, God knew how long ago, paint. He knocked and entered.

Sadko was sitting, or slumping, in a wheeled, swivel office chair. He was a large Slav with a drinker's gut and russet cheeks beneath a wrinkled brow, bushy eyebrows, and grey, thinning hair that stuck to his sweating scalp.

The picture of a true, corrupt police officer, in Petrov's mind, and there was no love lost between them.

'Sit down,' Sadko said without a greeting.

Petrov took the chair on the far side of the desk.

'You were the first to look at the body of the foreigner this morning,' the major snapped before Petrov was even seated.

'Yes, Major.'

'Find anything interesting?'

Sadko sat back in his swivel chair and pressed his thumbs together as if he were conducting some kind of sign language.

'Nothing. Apart from the fact that he's a foreigner.'

'*Was* a foreigner. After I informed them, the MVD have been back on the phone.'

Petrov saw no need to reply.

'They want to talk to you, Petrov.' There was a hint of triumph in his voice.

'When?' He didn't give the major the satisfaction of asking him why.

'Now. Right away. Get down to their headquarters. A major called Robolev.'

'Good.'

Sadko raised an eyebrow. 'What's good about it, lieutenant?'

'I mean it's good that it's now,' Petrov replied. 'I've had news that my grandfather is dying. I'd come to ask you if I could take time off.'

'Well. If the MVD let you go,' Sadko sneered, 'you can take a few days off, if you must.'

'It'll take a few days just to get there. He's in the wilderness above the Arctic Circle. I'll need a couple of weeks at least. I can take my summer vacation now, if that's all right.'

'Any more than that and it's unpaid,' Sadko replied. 'But let's see what the MVD have to say first, shall we?'

When Petrov left the building, no one asked him about his grandfather. Nothing interested anyone except their own day's fulfilment. Why should they ask about his grandfather? He was just a nomad who was on nobody's mental screen.

The MVD building was a grim façade of stone with small windows, barred on the inside, that seemed to exert some sort of malevolent presence on the street. Petrov imagined that pedestrians would cross to the other side to avoid it. He waited in a huge chamber of a lobby, two storeys high, until a woman in a tight skirt and clacking high heels, like a secretary in a fifties American movie, came to summon him upstairs. In the elevator she clutched a clipboard to her chest as if she'd forgotten to put on her blouse. An elevator! Petrov thought. The State still spent its money on monitoring its population and looking for spies or subversives, yet it didn't give a damn about ordinary criminality or the daily death count.

He was shown into a large bare room with an outsize desk of the kind favoured by the bureaucrats and intelligence people. Robolev, in uniform, was sitting behind it making a credible pass at being interested in a pile of paperwork. When he looked up, like an enemy interrogator, he fixed Petrov through the lenses of round, Gestapo-like spectacles.

'Take a seat.' His tone was more jovial than his expression. 'You're . . . Petrov.'

'Lieutenant Alexei Petrov, that's right.'

'What we want to know is how far you searched the foreigner's body this morning.'

'Just to the point where I found his passport. Then I knew it was a job for someone else. For the MVD.'

'What happened to him?'

'He was shot in the back of the neck at close range,' Petrov replied, knowing the MVD would also know the information.

'A hit?'

'I doubt it.'

'Why?' Robolev asked, and leaned back in the chair, resting his elbows on the arms and swinging gently from side to side.

'They − or he − left his passport. A proper hit man would know how to get money for that.'

Robolev leaned forward, elbows now placed on the desk. 'And why were his clothes sliced open, all the linings?'

'I didn't see that,' Petrov lied. 'Maybe they were looking for something.'

'Something they expected to be well concealed.'

'Presumably, major, yes, that would be my guess.'

'A foreigner with something concealed in the lining of his clothes.'

Petrov didn't see the need to reply.

'And then there's his right shoe, isn't there?'

'It seemed to have come away from the sole, as far as I could see,' Petrov said.

'Did you examine it?'

'No, major. Maybe he caught it on something when he was running away from whoever killed him. But, as I say, as soon as I saw the passport I knew it was something for the MVD.'

'Your lack of curiosity is . . .' Robolev seemed to struggle for the right word, 'unusual,' he finally decided on.

'I do my job. I have enough to do in my quarter. I judged the shoe must have come off when the body was moved,' Petrov said, retreating into police observation. 'Maybe the sole was partially removed, broken in the probable chase, or maybe it was slit, like the clothes.'

'How do you know the body was moved?' Robolev asked suddenly and leaned in triumphantly.

Petrov shrugged. This was common police work. 'In the area around it there was no sign of a struggle, only signs of the legs being dragged. You could see that in the dust and dirt in the alley. And that's what they do.'

'Who do?'

'Killers. Assassins. They move their victims in case there's evidence of the ordnance used or if the killing took place too close to people and they didn't want a victim to be discovered too quickly.'

'So why *did* the victim's body show signs of being so comprehensively searched?' Robolev said, and focused the flashing lenses of his spectacles more closely into Petrov's eyes. 'There were slits in his coat, his hat, he'd been all but strip-searched elsewhere . . .'

'As I say, I didn't see them, major. But they were looking for something, I suppose.'

'Did they find what they were looking for? In your opinion?'

'I've no idea, major.'

Robolev looked hard at him. 'But you found nothing,' he said eventually.

'After the passport, I handed the case straight over to my boss for referral to your department.'

Then Robolev leaned further forward over the desk and placed his elbows flat on the surface, his knuckles supporting his chin. Once more his spectacles, like gun sights, zeroed in on Petrov. 'It would be a terrible mistake if a *militsiya* officer took anything from the scene of a crime,' he said.

'I quite agree,' Petrov replied and stared right back.

On the way out, he realised that Robolev hadn't asked him to keep himself available, either from oversight or because he was dismissed from his mind as well as his office. But at least it meant he could now say to Sadko that he wasn't prevented from leaving work.

Chapter Five

Anna's main efforts as she stood in the line of unemployed were devoted to being inconspicuous, transparent. Transparency was the dearest ally of the agent on foreign soil. Nothing was more important than that. Transparency was the best camouflage.

The most successful agents were the ones nobody ever noticed, the kinds of people you passed by in the street but didn't really see, or met at a party and whose faces you couldn't remember later; the people whose names somehow never stuck. The thought crossed her mind that, in an ideal world, she would simply have been invisible.

Her head, like the others' in the line, was cast down, her demeanour was submissive and her expression was blank. In the other Russian workers in the line, this blankness and submission was the kind of look that came from daring not to hope. And in their case this came from never having very much to hope for in the first place. It was the predominant look in the line and she'd seen it for two days now. The dejection could be seen in the half-hidden faces all along it and she impersonated it well.

What she knew she couldn't impersonate, however, was the poor state of their physical health. She couldn't hide what, relative to the others ahead of and behind her in the line, was a robust, good-looking freshness. For one thing, even under her baggy, dirty worker's clothes, she knew she looked too well fed. And the skin on her face was too clear and had a brightness to it.

The others, for the most part, were thin, pinched and drawn, with grey-looking skin and asthmatic breath that betrayed lives of forced ill-health under the city's smokestacks.

Her fellow job-seekers reminded her of those dismal newspaper pictures of refugees waiting, unwanted, at frontiers. In any case, they seemed to come from the same tribe of the desperate, the dispossessed, the betrayed and the hopeless. These unemployed Russians pinned any hope they might be able to summon up, from the deepest resources they possessed, on the hiring office and the hiring office alone.

They stood like slumped statues, she thought, only to break the spell of their pained stillness with a foot-dragged shuffle forwards when the line inched towards the concrete hut. It was after eight o'clock in the morning and they'd been in line for more than three hours. But they still formed a sinuous thread that stretched back for almost thirty yards along the river front. It was a weak and pitiful human trickle next to the confident power and muscular strength of the river itself.

There were both men and women in the line and most of them had spent the long Siberian winter unemployed, and in some cases hungry. Dressed in old, faded and colourless working clothes, with tattered quilted jackets slung over their shoulders for warmth, they nevertheless shivered in the cold early June morning. The women wore scarves over their heads in most cases, the men wore fur hats or Russian military winter caps from their conscription days. Except at the city's aluminium factories, work was scarce here and even in those satanic furnaces it was underpaid. The people in the line knew that if they were lucky enough to be hired for the hard summer labour at the timber mills in Igarka, downriver towards the Arctic Circle, their wages would be barely enough to live on.

As a picture of human dejection, this creeping filament of the miserable and deprived seemed to have leached somehow from the choking smokestacks located pitilessly in the centre of the once triumphantly propagandised industrial Soviet city and which, with their variously poisonous chemical effluents, clouded the air the people breathed and the skies above them.

And behind the slumped human flotsam on the quayside, the broad, tumbling green and brown Yenisei river worked its icy way through the dockyards and the shabby piers toothed with cranes and derricks. It, too, was heading north, beyond the Arctic Circle to the Kara Sea, though with a force and energy that made the humans on the quay seem half-dead.

The line shifted and Anna shuffled forward a step.

She noted that the city's tilting quays through which the river rushed had only recently been released from snow. The rusted vessels that lay alongside them had been laid up for the winter when the river was partially iced, but they looked as if they'd been discarded decades ago and left to rot beneath the aluminium smog of Krasnoyarsk.

In most cases, however, the ships' engines were kept in surprisingly good working order – she could hear them now – thanks to the necessity of eking out everything that could be summoned from machinery and man combined. Many of the ships were over a hundred years old. The river water on which they operated didn't have the corrosive effect that salt did on seagoing vessels.

And behind everything – the hiring office, the line of people and the busy quays – she was aware of the polluted city that squatted on the vast Siberian land like a sick and rasping ogre.

Anna forced her eyes down again, while occasionally flicking a glance from under her peaked cap to right or left. It was an instinctive reaction, born of a life of watchfulness, the life of a spy. The real Anna Resnikov had always been one of two things; either the hunter or the hunted. Here, on enemy territory, she was undoubtedly the latter. And she could afford no more lapses of the kind that had afflicted her at the border.

A ship tooted its horn in the background, as if impatient to be off downstream. Several ships were preparing for the first voyage of the year down the Yenisei. The various rust buckets leaned exhaustedly up against the quays, their half-loaded holds tilting them this way and that. Only the newer passenger ferry that took the few tourists part of the way to the Arctic Circle and rested on a quay of its own seemed fit for the journey.

The sound of diesel engines being test-run for the

1500-mile journey downriver towards and beyond the Arctic Circle numbed the hearing. Perhaps this, too, explained the bent heads of the unemployed. Conversation was almost impossible above the engines and the shouted instructions of the foreman or the whooping cries of stevedores.

The foreman was a rumbustious six-foot-four giant by the name of Ivan, born and bred in the Siberian taiga and descended from nineteenth-century Russian settlers – as he'd lost no time in proudly explaining to the people in the line. He was looking up and down the line now with his sneer of contempt. But when his eyes rested on Anna, as they had done several times already, his expression changed to one of intense, and greedy, study. It was just what she did not wish for – to be noticed at all, let alone studied with the foreman's fixed stare.

Nearing the front of the line, Anna had now almost reached the door of the hiring office.

She averted her eyes from his gaze. She was close enough to the hiring office to be able to see inside the small building, which was little more than a concrete box. What she saw was a dark room, furnished – if that was the word – with only a worn wooden table and two wooden chairs, one of which was to receive each applicant for the summer jobs. The lumber mills down river at Igarka were changing from their pared-down winter shift and increasing their workforce for the few months of the summer. With the ice broken, the ships were now able to take the work crews downriver at last. Up in the river's huge bays around Igarka, a thousand miles to the north, the great rafts of loose logs would soon also find the way free to the northern Arctic sea port of Dikson.

To take her attention away from the foreman Ivan, Anna looked at the decrepit building that was the hiring office. It was made of poor materials – that much was clear – which the ice winters had made worse with chips and gouges in the concrete. It was little more than a block of pale, disintegrating cement.

From the look of it, it had been erected more than half a century before by Stalin's slaves before the dictator's death. The starved and beaten political exiles whose job it had been back then to build it either didn't know how to make concrete or they lacked the proper equipment to do so.

Directing her eyes around the foot of the building, she also now observed four courses of uneven brickwork. They were so poorly made that her eyes fixed on them for a long time and it was then that the foreman seized the opportunity. He came up too close to her and spoke, breathing hotly in her ear as he did so. He'd been looking for just such a chance as this.

'That's what you get when low-life political exile scum do the work for you!' he sneered and nodded at the brickwork.

Anna turned away from him and fixed her mind ahead in time.

Fifteen hundred miles to the north of where she stood, up in the Kara Sea where the river disgorged itself into the salt waters of the Arctic, the ice was still solid – nearly ten feet thick in places. Now in spring the disparity between the melted waters of the south and the frozen ice in the north was causing its annual, cataclysmic freak of nature. Backed up against the northern ice, the melted water down here built up into a dangerous surge that carried thousands of trees torn from the river's banks and tons of boulders in a headlong rush that would now be finally smashing the ice floes at the river's mouth. The furious torrent ground the floes and broke them with ear-splitting cracks that could be heard ten miles away. Finally it reduced the ice by hurling it against the bare cliffs to the north and against itself.

This event signified the end of winter at the other end, where the river met the Kara Sea. The thousands of blocks of broken ice were then dispersed by the rage of fresh water out into the Arctic and, for a time after that, the Kara Sea was filled with a small forest of broken trees bleaching slowly in the salt and the thin northern sun.

The end of May or the first half of June – depending on the severity of the winter – was the time when vessels could at last begin to head north after the seven-month grip of the Ice King. Up in Igarka and, beyond, in Dudinka, they would have begun the annual task of reconstructing the wooden piers and wharfs and port facilities which had to be dismantled every year to avoid being smashed and washed away by the surge of melted waters.

Anna glanced around casually again without perceptibly lifting her head, and again she saw the foreman watching her. She didn't like it and he was still keeping his gaze steady. Did he suspect something? No, that was impossible. More likely, his interest in her, despite her dishevelled, dirty appearance, was that he wanted to imagine her in one of Krasnoyarsk's pole-dancing bars and brothels. She was used to men like the foreman. So be it. She had the papers.

Then she shifted her eyes calmly past his level stare to look back at the port and the river and, behind everything, the dreadful city.

She wore old plastic yellow boots, faded brown overalls a size too big for her, and a quilted blue jacket over the top, also marked with dirt and grime, and faded like the overalls. All had been bought in one of the cheap shops on the edge of the city. Her hair, cut short and dyed black, was concealed under a military green felt cap with felt ear flaps. Her face was almost too carefully touched with worker's grime, grease and engine oil. But the particles from the yellow-grey smog of the city that clung to her otherwise clear skin were real.

Once more she shuffled forward as another worker was admitted to the office.

To anyone watching her, including, she trusted, the over-curious foreman, she was just another impoverished twenty-first-century Russian citizen looking for work. But if anyone should doubt it, she had the false papers in her jacket to prove who she was. She was travelling under the name of Valentina Asayev.

She was a citizen of the Siberian city of Bratsk to the east – so the papers said, anyway. Her internal Russian passport, made dirty and scuffed with apparent use like her clothes, allowed her to move anywhere in the *Krai* of Krasnoyarsk that stretched from the Mongolian border to the Arctic seas. Only the Arctic city of Norilsk – the initial destination of her mission after Igarka – was a closed area. It was the second biggest city in the world beyond the Arctic Circle, and had been closed to anyone without a special pass since 2001. It was barred not just to foreigners but also to any Russian without the pass.

Anna's thoughts drifted almost in a dream to her mission and the next journey that now lay ahead towards it. Even she, a woman of extreme courage and belief in herself, had to admit it was a desperate throw of the dice into the unknown.

But somewhere – she knew this for sure – somewhere up there above the Arctic Circle, she would find the man she was looking for, Vasily Kryuchkov. Whether it would be in the slave-built Norilsk itself – the filthy, degraded city whose pollutants had killed every tree within a fifty-mile radius – or whether it would be in the Putorana mountain nuclear facilities to the east of there, or in Dudinka to the west of Norilsk, or even further north at Dikson, the island port out on the far edge of the Gulf of Yenisei in the Kara Sea – wherever Kryuchkov could be found up there in the bitter far north she would find him and the secrets he was said to possess.

But for now, her immediate aim – her necessity – was to get the next boat to Igarka, the lumber town two thirds of the way downriver towards Norilsk. Igarka was her next base and a journey she could make with at least the pretence of legality. But to reach there, she needed to be hired.

Aside from her false identity papers, other false papers zipped in her jacket pocket declared her to be a skilled lumber machinist and maintenance worker on the type of vast saw machines that day and night cut the Siberian forest into logs or planks for export. She had endlessly studied similar Swedish saw machines back in America until she knew them back to front. She knew she could do the work for as long as she needed to remain in Igarka.

But at some moment, after she reached the lumber town outpost, she would have to break free – alone – and head north again.

Then, through these thoughts, she again felt the sudden and unwelcome presence.

'Ivan,' the voice said next to her suddenly, and she felt the foreman's alcohol and onion breath wash down again on her face from above. He was standing over her, much too close to her body now. 'My name is Ivan,' he explained, and she saw his chipped and yellowed broken teeth and a red, pock-marked nose, with the pitted skin of childhood smallpox on his face. There was a charcoal stubble on his chin that was collecting the light particles of industrial smog.

But it was his eyes, which had a lustful, fevered and decided look about them that she liked the least.

'And you?'

'Valentina,' she replied, with just enough of a pause to demonstrate she intended no further intimacy.

Suddenly he gripped her arm in his big, greasy hand. He was a powerful man. He didn't let her go or lighten his grip and she didn't resist. No matter how much she wanted to – and could have – throw him back on the pitted cement forecourt of the hiring office, she resisted the temptation. She might need him later, certainly. But most of all she couldn't afford to cross him now and fail to be hired.

She had the training to break his neck in two, or drive his nasal bone into his brain, or any number of lesser moves to render him harmless. But it was certainly not the type of training she could afford to reveal here. Her real training was not the training of a machine operator at a sawmill, but of a highly decorated, former intelligence officer in Russia's foreign service. A service to which she had become a most hated and most wanted traitor.

So for now, Ivan the foreman might be useful to her. Later, she thought grimly, I'm going to have to deal with him, one way or another.

'Come with me,' he said loudly over the top of her head. The volume of his voice boasted his superior, official position. 'I'll clear things with the office.' But still he stood there, looking at her for too long, as before. The leer on his mouth and the glint in his eyes communicated an unmistakable and deeply unwelcome message.

'I can wait my turn,' she replied passively. She must be passive, she must be just like the others. She must show no knowledge, no fight, no resistance at all – and above all no special training.

His hand was still on her arm, gripping it too tightly. 'You're strong,' he said, now with some admiration, and feeling the muscles under the jacket. 'Where did you get to be so strong?'

'Nothing but work,' she said dully.

This time, he didn't pose his words as a question. 'Come with me,' he said, and pulled her forcibly out of the line. She followed him ahead of the three people in front of her and meekly entered the darkness of the hiring office.

'Papers!' he commanded when they were inside.

She offered him her false internal passport and the false paperwork that qualified her for the job. He took them and threw them on to the table in front of the seated hiring officer, a man with a puffed alcoholic face and running snot on his upper lip, which he wiped from time to time with the sleeve of his coat.

The hiring officer looked bored having to deal with the sickening line of feeble losers in front of him. But she was different, he could see that at once. He looked up questioningly at Ivan with bloodshot eyes.

The foreman just nodded for him to get on with it. The hiring officer exhaled a cloud of bitter smoke from a *Kosmos* cigarette gripped in the gap between his two front teeth and casually looked through her papers. Then he cast his eyes up at her, lingering too long on her face and on the outline of her breasts, an outline which, despite her baggy overalls and jacket, could still be faintly seen. Finally he took out a form from a drawer in the table, copied her details, and stamped the form with the name of the lumber company. Then he scribbed his initials over the stamp. He winked at Ivan with a lascivious smile, then turned to her.

'Where are your things?' he said.

The others in the line mostly carried their possessions with them – as if that were some kind of reinforcement of the hope that they would be on the ship to Igarka.

'I can get them in a few minutes,' she said, and she said it with the tone of barely dared hope in her voice that characterised the others.

He pushed the paperwork back across the table to her and she put the documents inside her jacket, zipping the pocket.

'The boat leaves at five,' the hiring officer said. 'It's the *Rossiya*. Quay three.'

Just under eleven hours from now, she thought.

Ivan turned to her. 'I'll see you on board then.' The foreman grinned openly now, and the suggestion was clear. But he wasn't satisfied with just the implicit suggestion. 'I'll look forward to that,' he said. 'You can be sure I'll look after you as a woman like you needs to be.'

Then he pushed her out of the door. It was still drizzling.

The foreman's promise turned her attention to this new danger. If necessary . . . if necessary she would break his neck, fell him like a tree. She felt nothing of the doubt she had felt four days before at the border.

She hurried along the quay through the drizzle and beyond the line of people who shuffled forward the space of another human being. She felt elated, she had the job, a way was free to her as far as Igarka.

Away from the quay now, she felt the heavy gaze of the foreman Ivan vanish. Behind the docks, in a side street whose surface was holed by frost-made craters that made it look like an urban battlefield, was the cheap room, which she'd hired from the old *baba* at black market rates three nights before. It was where she'd left her bag, minus the gun and ammunition. Eleven hours. She would return to Zhenya's apartment, take a coffee with the old lady, do some shopping for food for the journey and then return to pick up her bag for the voyage north. Maybe sleep a little until the ship left.

But as she turned the corner on to Sverdlovsk Street, she stopped dead. It was a barely perceptible pause to anyone watching, even someone who was studying her closely. For she at once broke into step again and walked slowly to the left of the building on the far side of the street from it, so that anyone observing her would have hardly noticed a gap in her steps.

What she had seen switched her mood of elation from moments before to a cold, dark readiness. An automatic preparation for action.

She kept her head down as she passed by on the far side of the street, staying as far away from the block where her bag was as she could. She walked on in a transparent haze of oblivion, though with her mind entirely alert to a challenge, one more shuffling human. Her reflexes were taut, her consciousness raised to the maximum.

What she'd seen outside the block was a police tape and beyond that a ring of Ministry of Interior troopers and their MVD investigators who surrounded the entrance and the alley to the side of the building. The double-eagle insignia of the MVD imprinted itself, then became magnified in her sharpened mind.

Chapter Six

An agent on foreign soil is essentially alone, and it is an aloneness all the more bleak for the presence of the mass of humanity all around in a hostile territory, any one of whom might be the one to betray, or simply to notice and report an inconsistency of behaviour. But Anna Resnikov was not running completely solo in Krasnoyarsk. That was not how Burt Miller would have done it, not how any intelligence agency, private or government, would have conceived of such a complex and high-risk operation. Burt had been meticulously preparing her mission for nearly a year.

First there had been the slivers of 'information', hearsay and mere guesswork that had filtered into Cougar's worldwide intelligence stations for many months; each tiny particle of which was isolated and protected like a precious collection of individually useless pottery shards that are sealed in bags by careful archaeologists. It was certainly only the few, Burt chief among them, who got to see and eventually connect them all. Perhaps, indeed, it was only Burt himself who knew the full picture that slowly began to emerge. The information came from Burt's own company officers scattered across the globe, as well as from other, government, agencies that sold their secrets to Cougar. But Burt's eyes and ears seemed to be everywhere and they included individuals too. There were people – sources – as diverse as a disgruntled KGB operative overlooked for promotion and farmed out to a dead-end post in Lima; a Pakistani nuclear physicist who had been extensively questioned by the CIA itself under suspicion of selling nuclear technology – but who, according to Burt, had not even himself realised the importance of some fragment of detail he possessed and so had not thought to impart it to his CIA interrogators. Then there had been a German oil pipe manufacturer with a contract in eastern Siberia who, under threats and coercion – and finally the sight of photographs of himself in a foursome in a Moscow hotel room – had divulged something of complete insignificance on its own. A Canadian Arctic geologist; a Danish timber merchant with connections and trade in the northernmost wilderness of Siberia; an operative of India's foreign intelligence service, RAW, stationed in Moscow; another KGB intelligence officer – this time in Burt's pay – who worked out of the Federal Security Service's, the FSB's, economic department; the boss of a high-end Moscow escort agency, later murdered by a bullet straight through the top of his head and fired from a bridge below which he was walking – all of these and more had provided the shattered pieces of the hoped-for priceless intelligence amphora that Burt was trying to construct. And finally there'd been another German – this time a nuclear physicist – who Burt had made a point of befriending at the annual, secret Bilderberg conference of world leaders and their guests. Burt had later wined and dined the portly, bespectacled German and offered his personal financial support for research work, as if the man were his closest friend. It was this German, by the name of Bachman, a one-off guest at the Bilderberg, who according to those closest to Burt at Cougar, had put a different light into Burt's eye. After several meetings with Bachman, they said, it was as if Burt had seen the construct he had been building so painstakingly, then lost it, and then seen it again. The ghost of an intelligence objective seemed to flit before Burt's vision. He himself said that it was like seeing a computer image of a building though with none of the hardware that made the building real. But, certainly, it was after a month of private dinners and lavish financial research grants to Bachman that Burt finally ordered his troops into action. The picture came and went, and now he wished to find the evidence that would make it real, three-dimensional, indissoluble. And the light in his eye now, those close to him said, was the prospect of an intelligence coup that would at some future date be placed at the apex of his life's achievements. The golden cupola of Burt's giant life. But for this to occur an agent had to be put into Russia itself.

And so from this point, it became an operation. The forgers at Cougar were suddenly hard at work, each one kept separated from the other so that no one should know it was Anna whose identity, whose fiction, was being created. Agents on the ground in Mongolia, Finland, and Russia itself, came up with routes, itineraries, likely problems and their solutions. An uninhabited island off the far north coast of Finland was acquired for Anna's extraction from Arctic Russia. It was a three-day journey from this island to the mouth of the Yenisei River, where it was decided she would be picked up, but it was the best they could do. Extracting her from Russia's Arctic coastline would be hard enough simply on its own. Then Larry himself was stationed with three others at the Mongolian gorge for three weeks before Anna's infiltration. And all the while, back in America at Burt's 93,000 acre New Mexican ranch, Anna herself was plumbed for information which only a former KGB colonel would know, and then tutored in how to use it once she was on the ground. She was, perhaps, the only person other than Burt who knew the whole story.

And last of all, there were three Cougar operatives who were moved undercover into Russia, and whose job it was to watch her, guard her back, die for her if necessary – at least for as long as they could before she disappeared into the northern wilderness where they could not follow. These were the watchers on the ground, here in Krasnoyarsk, and so – for a time at least – Anna would not be entirely alone.

The team of Burt Miller's who had monitored her movements in the city since her arrival, by a system of prearranged dead-drops, were also watching events unfold at the block on Sverdlovsk Street as the MVD investigators arrived. They had observed them before Anna returned from the docks and before she had seen them herself.

They'd spotted the cop first, a *militsiya* guy, then a cop

car arrived with a younger man at the wheel, and then the first cop making a mobile phone call that apparently resulted in the arrival of the MVD. Why the MVD? That was the greatest shock to Anna's watchers. MVD involvement indicated something far bigger than an ordinary crime. Did it then indicate Anna's discovery? But after that the watchers had seen the MVD troops take a dead body from an alley beside the block and their initial fears were allayed – only to be replaced by others.

The two men in the team, Clay and Sky, and the one woman, Eileen – all pre-assigned to Anna's protection in the lead-up to her mission – had been tracking her progress in the city for three days now, since her arrival. They had themselves arrived nearly a week before that. Now, as the block was ringed by MVD troops and the hatchet-faced MVD investigators first examined and then took away the body, the implications were lost on none of the three. The Interior people would be questioning the block's inhabitants next. It was surely simply a matter of time before the name 'Valentina Asayev' became known to them, the name of an itinerant woman who must come under suspicion.

As far as it was possible to achieve in the heart of enemy territory, the diligent and highly trained back-up team had lain low in the city for a week and were pretty sure Anna, let alone anyone hostile, hadn't spotted them. They reported back to Burt Miller personally, as well as to an operations centre at Miller's ranch in New Mexico, set up for the single aim of her mission. Apart from the 'dark' period when she was necessarily lost to them – from the border to the city itself – they had seen her arrive, watched as she had engaged the old lady at the market – and then as she'd rented a room in the block on Sverdlovsk Street. They had kept up their surveillance of her when, as planned, she went to the docks looking for work down-river and they watched from afar as she went on brief expeditions to buy food, or to check their prearranged dead-drops around the city.

The team's relief when she'd arrived in Krasnoyarsk had been immediately relayed to America and simul-taneously to Miller's emergency 'agent ex-filtration base', as it was known, situated on the island in the north of Finland closest to the Russian Arctic. And now this team in Krasnoyarsk was watching with growing anxiety how events would unfold at the block on Sverdlovsk Street and wondering how they could warn her.

For a group of watchers, Sverdlovsk Street and the block where Anna had found a room for rent had represented something of a nightmare. It was a hard place to watch without their own surveillance being itself surveyed. There were no cafés across the street for a team to change in rotation while sipping filthy coffee or twice-brewed tea; no shops in which a person could loiter with a reason, however thin; no market stalls where a man might buy a paper and smoke a cigarette and discuss the day's events with other idle jobless individuals. There was no street furniture of any kind, in fact – a laughable notion in itself for a place like Sverdlovsk Street. The block where Anna had lodged was a towering monument to Soviet brutalism in decay, and it stood on a wasteland of the damned. There was no cover for a watcher but to simply stand and stare until you were either arrested for vagrancy or were knifed by a passing thief.

Nor, unless you were in the sort of deep cover Anna was in, and dressed in the clothes of a Russian worker, was there the possibility for the watchers to rent another room across the street, in a block of such decayed exactness to hers that it seemed like a bad Soviet joke.

For, unlike Anna, her watchers were not Russian, but Americans who spoke the language too perfectly. Clever Americans, certainly; Americans with the highest training you could receive in covert work. But language skills were never enough and in order to run a covert operation you had to have cover in the first place. The two men and one woman who comprised the team would have aroused suspicion swiftly if they had attempted to rent a place, especially in an area as poor as this one.

Clay and Sky were deceptively boyish adults, both educated in the arts of observation, close and distant combat, and code work. Eileen was their leader, in charge of watching the watchers themselves. Her skills lay in keeping them and their true identities secret, unnoticed. Eileen was an artist of transparency but there was nowhere transparent for a watcher in Sverdlovsk Street.

They'd been travelling through Russia under the cover of postgraduate students, joyfully released from their studies. Krasnoyarsk was just another place with a history along the Trans-Siberian railroad. Lenin had stayed there once, on a boat on the river. In Soviet times, the military industrial complex had been closed to foreigners. The city's pre- and post-revolutionary status was of interest certainly, but it was the tourist ferry that went down the Yenisei River which was their principal aim. Once Anna had departed downriver, assuming she could secure the work at Igarka, the ferry was the only plausible way for her watchers to keep track of her. At least that far. After that, she'd be on her own.

For the three of them it had been a twisting and turning journey to Russia. There'd been a roundabout flight to Moscow from Athens, a few days sightseeing in the capital, then a reserved trip along the Trans-Siberian railroad on the route that ended eventually in Beijing, their stated destination. They'd bought tickets that allowed them to break the journey at places of interest across western Russia and then on through Siberia. The cover of a postgrad tourist trip was low-key, believable; a final fling before depositing their lives with wives or, in Eileen's case, a husband, as well as jobs, kids and adult responsibilities.

And so, like proper tourists, they'd visited the places they'd be expected to visit. After Moscow, they took a trip to Nizhni-Novgorod for its fine churches, then turned south and walked the estate grounds at Tolstoy's home of Yasnaya Polyana, then on to Ekaterinburg, the now booming city which, a century earlier, had been the place of assassination of the last Czar and his family, and then on further east, rejoining the Trans-Siberian railway to Novosibirsk where Siberia began.

They'd collected souvenirs from the places they'd visited, lit votive candles in old, restored or unrestored and near-derelict Orthodox churches, sent postcards home to fictive parents and friends, taken steam baths in the open air, under stars, or in the great city *banyas* – and all the time they'd watched the endless steppe unfold towards Siberia with its awesome flat vastness broken only by the Ural mountains, and its occasional picturesque onion-dome churches poised on the iced land now emerging into spring that looked like fairy-tale mirages in a cold desert. The three of them had thus slowly made their way towards central Siberia and arrived finally in the city of Krasnoyarsk.

Krasnoyarsk was one of the major junctions on the Trans-Siberian railroad. There was a rail line that went south-east to the Chinese border – and Beijing – but then there was the river, the great river that flowed north to the Arctic Circle and beyond. It was the river that interested them, the only route that went north.

And so as an excuse to stop for any length of time in Krasnoyarsk – and as a major detour – their general cover in the city was to get permits and tickets for the tourist ferry up the Yenisei. Norilsk and the areas north of Norilsk were closed areas and needed special permits, but they could go part of the way towards it. All had been granted and sold to them by bona fide travel agents in Holland before they'd left Europe, but once they'd arrived in the city a week before Anna, a further walk through Russian bureaucracy – to give it its proper name, bribery – had been necessary to secure the berths they'd already paid for. Corruption, as ever, was the saving grace for anyone operating in a clandestine way in Russia.

Corruption was the Achilles heel of a system that other-wise crushed its own citizens, let alone foreign tourists, with the gigantic weight of mass surveillance. But this delay, as they found their way with dollars through the bureaucracy, suited them well. They needed to keep pace with Anna Resnikov, day for day, or Burt Miller would have their scalps.

But Sverdlovsk Street had been a major problem from the beginning that nobody had foreseen. How to watch her, how to guard her back, how to observe other possible observers, when there was no way the watchers could even walk unnoticed through such an area.

Finally, Clay – a 27-year-old special forces officer who had operated in Afghanistan before Burt Miller plucked him out – came up with the only idea that might work. He had bought an iron brazier from an itinerant who was upping sticks and leaving the city after the winter, and going in search of work elsewhere. The three watchers then found an angle of sight from where they could observe Anna's block from nearly a quarter of a mile away. It was in a park dotted with sickly trees, otherwise bare except for a graffitied statue of Lenin, still intact, still in place on its pedestal. The iron revolutionary's left hand was either beckoning its watchers to their doom or guid-ing them to a promised land, depending on your point of view, and the old revolutionary's studious-looking book was tucked inside the wrist of his other arm.

In vagrant's clothes which the watchers had pieced together from remnants in second-hand shops or, in one case, dug out of a pile of trash for the purpose, they had agreed that at least two of them would man the brazier at any one time, lighting a small fire at night to keep warm. The third, meanwhile, was headquartered at the Business-Hotel Kupechesky, as befitted well-heeled international student travellers, and, in fact, they all had rooms there.

It was an improvisation that couldn't possibly have lasted for more than a few days – even if they were lucky. There was the ever-present danger of questioning by the *militsiya*, not to mention the dangers posed by other actual tramps and addicts in the area. But it had seen them through – just, and with a few narrow scrapes. Now, however, what Clay and Eileen, who were on duty on this early June morning at the brazier, saw from the Lenin park was first a *militsiya* cop arriving at the block on foot, then another *ment* in a cop car screaming up with its light flashing and finally, a little under twenty minutes later, four MVD cars descended on the place like arrows to a target.

The two of them watched for a while with increasing dread. Anna would be back at some time early in the morning, either hired or not for the work in Igarka. She would walk straight into a nest of MVD troops.

What the watchers did next was all pre-planned. Such eventualities had been rehearsed for months. Every danger had been anticipated – as far as possible. So when they saw the Interior Ministry forces arrive at the block they went into automatic action. First, Clay and Eileen left the park in the opposite direction from the block. Eileen was deputed to remain between the block and the docks in order to head off Anna. She and Clay had watched her walk to the docks earlier when dawn was already up around at just after 5 a.m. Anna was safe for now at least, away from the block, and that was something. But they had to prevent her from walking into a trap.

Clay was to return to the hotel, connect with Sky and then both of them would contact Cougar and Burt Miller.

By a circuitous route Clay made his way to the historical district of the city, shaving and changing clothes at a steam bath on the way, where all three of them kept rented lockers. He then hurried to the Business-Hotel Kupechesky, once more the student traveller, but at an almost suspicious speed, to any observer, for a student. The arrival of the MVD had been a very bad shock. Something had gone terribly wrong.

After Clay and Sky had conferred in a public area at the back of the hotel, they knew that Miller had to be informed at once. It was Sky – a 25-year-old MIT graduate and rising star in Burt Miller's Cougar Intelligence Applications Corporation – who went to the hotel's business centre. He brought up his Facebook page in the name of Smokey Bear and began to type.

> Hoping to get on the ferry north. But Charlie's gone down with something. Don't know what. It's an intestinal thing, he thinks. Throwing up all night. Major symptoms.

Back at Cougar's headquarters in New Mexico the Facebook page was visible on a dozen screens. It was almost instantly decoded. A Red Alert went out. MVD interest in Anna Resnikov. Her place of residence actually surrounded. Her not there – at least there was that – but otherwise everything looked black.

There was absolutely no hesitation in the response. Abort the mission. That was the sole possibility. Burt Miller, whether from the uninhabited island in Finland, which he'd colonised for the purpose of the mission, or from somewhere else on the planet, issued the order personally. A message flashed up on Sky's Facebook page at the business centre in the Kupechesky.

So sorry to hear about that. It's imperative he gets some decent medical attention at once. Just bad luck that it curtails what sounded like a fun trip. Hey! Larry's got a place at the NBA. Wow!

For Sky and Clay, Cougar's response was clear.

Eileen, on watch between the docks and Sverdlovsk Street, had finally seen Anna as she'd rounded the corner to the street. It was completely against all ground rules for her to be seen by Anna, let alone to make direct contact, and so she was relieved as she watched Anna first see the MVD herself and then take evasive action, walking on past the block without drawing attention.

Back at the Kupechesky, the mission was crumbling fast. It was, in effect, over. Months of preparation for nothing. But those were their orders and Clay and Sky greeted them with a mixture of relief as well as a sense of being cheated. It was a huge operation in terms of importance and in the work they and those behind them had put in. Burt Miller had impressed its importance on everyone, in one briefing after another, though without the detail Anna knew.

But they went on to a war footing at once. The three of them, and Anna, had a system of signals and dead-drops in the city. Anna was to check the signal twice a day, three times, if possible. The way it worked was that the initial signal told her which of the dead-drops to check. That way, the watchers could keep an eye on any drop that became unsafe. The signal itself was always at the bus station in the centre of town, a place that saw several hundred people come and go in the day, and which made it difficult for anyone trying to observe an individual. Clay walked from the hotel – a taxi might be remembered.

It took him twenty-two minutes, maybe a minute or two more, he thought nervously, as he checked his watch for the third time.

But finally he arrived on the broad concrete landscape of the bus station where ancient buses choked their butane and petrol fumes into the air and moved in and out in the constant ballet of journeys begun and ended.

Over to the side, there were stalls selling fruit and cigarettes. And everywhere milling groups of travellers, loaded with bags and boxes of electrical goods to take home from the city, while others arrived with sacks of produce to sell at the markets. It was just the sort of mayhem that did nicely.

Clay walked into the covered area under a concrete portico to where the ticket counters were. There were queues of people here, shouting and talking, sacks and bags of every kind littered the floor, and there was noise, mainly noise, and that gave the illusion of muffling an illegal action.

To the left of the far-left ticket counter was a regular bus station shop – a hole in the wall. It sold sweets, cigarettes and lighters, and newspapers. Under the narrow counter of the shop was a timetable, glued eternally to the concrete wall and the most obscure of several in the building.

Clay took a notebook and a purple-tipped felt pen from his pocket and crouched down on his heels to look at the bizarrely placed schedule which necessitated crouching or kneeling to read its information. It was faded and peeling in places but essentially immovable and well used despite its awkward position. He ran a finger down the timetable, obscuring it all the time with his body, and wrote three times of departures to different places near the city in the book in his hand.

And as he did so, he made a small mark on the timetable itself, against the name Bugachevo, a large village about twenty miles outside Krasnoyarsk. The motion of his hand marking the timetable was seamlessly disguised with his writing in the notebook and both were hidden by his crouched body.

Then he stood, looked down at what he had written in the notebook, frowned, and walked to a board which clacked destinations on a mechanical rotary system up above the heads of the travellers. He watched the board for a few moments, pocketed the notebook, and walked out of the building into the grey drizzle that now seemed as if it would last for the rest of the day.

CHAPTER SEVEN

AFTER SHE'D SEEN the MVD troops, Anna walked on, head down, along the length of Sverdlovsk Street. She turned left on a rubble-strewn corner at the end of Sverdlovsk, until she was out of sight. Then she stopped and leaned against a wall as if she were looking at some beautiful view and had come a long way to find it. Her breathing and heart rate slowed to normal, her primed reflexes eased. Muscles which moments before were tensed and hard now softened. She began to notice what else existed in the world apart from the MVD's double-eagle insignia which had temporarily shut everything else out.

She watched two small boys climbing up a pile of broken concrete in the street, then jumping off, highly delighted by the game. A bone-thin black cat scowled from a doorway a few feet away from her. The resilience of the children's laughter caught and then quietened her mind.

She'd been maybe twenty-five yards from the MVD raid on the block, twenty-five yards from the *baba* who'd rented her the room three nights before. But she hadn't been challenged. Maybe Zhenya had seen her and stayed silent . . . and maybe she wouldn't stay silent for long. The Ministry of Interior investigators were there to flay the minds of the block's occupants. There was never anything trivial about their presence.

Anna stood up away from the wall and began to consider her options. But then one of the boys came up to her before her thoughts could come together.

'Give us money, give us money!' He had a big grin on his dirty face while the other boy, more shy, hung back.

'Here,' she said. She took two chocolate bars from her jacket pocket and the boy seized them, eyes bright.

'Give us money!' he repeated without going away.

'No money,' she said.

Then she turned and continued to walk away from the depressed quarter of the city, in the direction of the railroad yards. The boy followed on her heels at first, then his pace became slower as he fell away behind her until he stopped altogether and soon she'd lost him.

Anna stopped only once, a few streets away from the block, in order to buy an apple at a stall in Orjonikidze Street from an ancient *baba* with veined and bulbous legs that sprung like disfigured fungi from beneath her black dress. The *baba* had twinkling eyes, grey hair under a scarf and she smiled toothlessly in gratitude at the few kopecks. Anna stood by the stall and chatted to her, ate the apple, looked back carefully in the direction from where she'd come, and then went on towards the rail yards.

Her walk took her away from the river at first, then across a buttressed bridge over it near the centre of the city, and on past the huge city monument to Lenin. From time to time, she stopped to look in a window or find something in her jacket, but it was done only in order to check behind her. She saw nothing that made her suspicious.

Finally she reached the Krasnoyarsk Pass, the mainline station for the Trans-Siberian railroad. But she didn't stop there. She continued along a small street next to the tracks and, following them, she watched the long, heaving freight trains that brought the bauxite from Bratsk into Krasnoyarsk's aluminium factories. Now in June, the unloading was easy. But in winter when the bauxite came in, it was frozen to the metal sides of the freight cars and had to be jack-hammered out. From the minus 45-degree centigrade exterior of the yards it was transferred into the 120-degree interior of the smelting factories. Everybody knew that workers didn't last long under those conditions. Marriages were short here, and children grew up fast if they grew at all in the stunting atmosphere.

When she'd reached as far as the street allowed her to go, before it was blocked off by a tattered, drooping barbed-wire fence eight feet high, she doubled back, first turning to the right, and stopping again to see if she was alone. No walkers behind her, a line of cars passing her in a normal fashion. A beaten-up Lada drove by more slowly. It was not an official car but you never knew.

Then she continued on her seemingly aimless way, into a set of side streets where she could observe more easily if one car stayed with her or came out ahead of her when previously it had been behind her. When she was finally satisfied she hadn't been watched or followed, she headed under the M53 trunk road and walked directly along a litter-strewn gutter at its edge, the cars and trucks throwing up noise and smoke, until finally she reached the bus station. The drizzle seemed now like a leaking tap in the sky.

At the hole-in-the-wall shop inside the bus station she bought a packet of *Astra* cigarettes from Arek, the Armenian man behind the counter, as she had done every time she'd come to check the signal in the past three days.

'Spring,' he said to her, and grinned from under a large, drooping black moustache. 'And it drizzles for us,' he laughed. 'Are you still looking for work?'

'Still looking,' she replied.

'Something will happen,' he said. And it was a common enough phrase that covered all points between the out-and-out mystical and the blindingly obvious.

'I'm expecting my mother to come in today,' she said, lighting a cigarette.

'Tell her to come and buy something from Arek.' He grinned. 'What time's she coming?'

'This afternoon. Around four.'

She crouched down in front of the counter and looked at the timetable. She immediately saw the purple mark against Bugachevo. Then she stood again, smoking and looking at the magazines behind Arek's head. 'At four twenty,' she said.

'A woman like you,' he said. 'You should find it easy to get work.' His watery, doleful eyes and drooping moustache gave him the look of a floppy-eared hound. 'Here. Have this on me,' he said. He handed her an

Alenka chocolate bar, the best in the shop, just as he did every time she'd visited in the past three days. 'You smoke too much,' he observed, 'even if it's crashing my business to tell you so.' She'd bought eight packets of cigarettes in three days.

'Thank you, Arek,' she said. 'See you later maybe.'

He thought she lived rough, somewhere around the bus station, while she looked for work.

'Make sure you bring your mother here,' he said cheerfully. Her visits had become the high point in his day and she could bring her mother along too if that was necessary and what she wanted. 'And you take care, Valentina. Come to me if you're in trouble. Come to Arek,' he said with a puffed dignity, as if he were the world's premier fixer.

Anna walked out of the bus station, grinding the cigarette under her heel when she was out of sight of the shop.

Bugachevo. The name of the village indicated the nearest dead-drop to the bus station. And that meant it was serious, as she'd known it would be. No doubt they'd seen the MVD surrounding her block just as she had. They were certainly good enough, her watchers. It had impressed her that she hadn't caught a glimpse of any of them over the three days she'd been there.

Across the plaza from the bus station were a few *kafes* and stalls out on the street, waiting for the sun to re-emerge.

The *kafe* nearest the centre was named the *Chaika*. She sat outside on the pavement under a parasol in the drizzle and ordered a glass of water and a coffee and when it came it was bitter and sweet at the same time. She left some coins on the table and sat and watched with barely seeing eyes the passers-by, flimsy umbrellas up, rubber overshoes on their feet. And as she did so she turned over in her mind what the shrinking options were for her now. The MVD at the block changed everything. But, even before she'd picked up their message, and despite what Miller ordered, she knew she would reach her own conclusion.

She looked at her situation dispassionately. In reality, it seemed extremely unlikely that the MVD knew of her presence in Russia, let alone here in Krasnoyarsk. She had entered the country illegally and that was where she would have been stopped if there was a leak. There was nothing she could see that could have compromised her – not yet, anyway – and of that she was sure, almost sure, as sure as one could be, anyway.

The *baba* who'd rented the room to her, or one of the other residents who had seen her in the block, they were the weak links. But no matter how curious they were about her, perhaps, there was nothing that could have made them call in the MVD of all people. The *militsiya* maybe, but not the MVD. So there must be something else, she concluded, something that had nothing to do with her. Maybe there was some other fugitive who was also in the building and whom they did know about, and it was all bad luck. Someone else they wanted. A coincidence, certainly, but coincidences were not as unusual as people thought.

She finished her coffee, left some more kopecks on the table for a tip, and went inside the *kafe*.

At the rear of the *kafe* there was a women's room she'd visited on one occasion. It was empty now, the door ajar. She entered and locked the door with a thin, wobbly bolt that had lost two of its screws. She stood in the small space and listened. The women's room was at the end of a dark corridor, painted a dull red. There was a fire door to the outside at the end of the corridor but it was always locked with a chain and padlock. It was just there for taking out the trash. They didn't want people drinking and then disappearing without payment. So no one would be coming down the corridor unless they were visiting the toilets. She heard nothing.

She climbed on to the toilet seat and lifted the lid away from a high cistern up on the wall behind it. She couldn't see inside the cistern, it was too high for her eye line, but she fished around with her hand until she found the plastic ballcock. She lifted it. With both hands now, and still unable to see, she unscrewed the two halves of the plastic ballcock. It was well sealed, and waterproof when it was screwed up tight. Then she felt around inside one of its hemispheres until her hand touched a packet, also waterproof for extra safety. She lifted this out, and dropped it into a dirty, chipped basin beside the toilet.

She stepped down, listened again.

The ballcock was new, it all fitted together perfectly. It had been placed there by Eileen five days before.

She stripped the plastic away from the packet lying in the basin. Inside was a folded piece of paper. It contained instructions for the assembling of the ballcock. All in Russian. But inside the text, as they'd arranged back at

Miller's in America, was the hidden coding. She held it up to the light.

Of course, it was as she'd expected. She was being recalled at once, immediately. Get out now. There would be a rendezvous on the Mongolian border, tonight, tomorrow night, the next – as soon as she could make it. They'd be on the other side, all as planned. Another custom-fitted Chinese military truck; colleagues, good food and drink. And a safe passage home. The thought made her pause. Home. But it was Russia that had always been her real home and America had never come to replace it in her mind. Russia, whose rulers would execute her if they caught her. But it was still more home than anywhere else.

She screwed up the paper and flushed it down the toilet. From her pocket she drew a two-inch sheet of paper from a notebook. She wrote in Russian, in long-hand. What she wrote were 'notes' from the plumber on how to assemble the ballcock. And inside her text, there lay the concealed message.

It was terse, as all such communications were. But it was terse for another reason too.

They need not wait tonight, tomorrow night or any other night on the other side of the border. She wasn't going to abort the mission. She told them that she was going ahead and somehow the coded words distanced her from their actual meaning. But it was a firm 'No' to their order, to the great Burt Miller's order.

She put the notepaper inside the waterproof package, sealed it with tape, then stepped up on to the toilet seat again and placed it inside one of the hemispheres of the ballcock, screwing the two shut tight together. She let the ballcock drop back, the water hissed momentarily. Then she replaced the lid of the cistern and stepped down again.

She flushed the toilet, then left the women's room after washing her hands in the filthy basin and walked back up the dark passage, lit dimly by a low-wattage bulb, out into the interior of the *kafe* and, beyond, to the street.

She kept walking, the apparent purposefulness of her step belying the conflict in her mind. The drizzle drained over her face and down her neck. It nibbled at her ankles and crept up the sleeves of her jacket. She felt that it was washing her of something. She hadn't agreed with them, that was what struck her in the first few moments of her confused thoughts. Why not? They were – in any operational sense, anyway – correct. And yet failure should not be so easy. If she were going to run at the first raised fist of the MVD, or any of Russia's myriad security agencies, why come to Russia in the first place? It was this, winning against the odds, that was her purpose – at least that's how it seemed to her as she walked the dull, wet street. In the rarest of moments for her, she examined the complex motives that lay behind her actions, in whose simplicity lay a kind of beauty. Revenge against the Russian intelligence service that had killed the only man she'd ever loved, was that it? But revenge was merely banal. And she knew she contained a hate that was far greater than a hate just for them.

No, it was this mission, like all the others, which was

what defined her. This was what she was for, why she existed, what had given her life its meaning for as long as she remembered.

She gave no thought to the fact of disobeying their order. Burt's personal authority, his corporate power and political cunning meant nothing to her. He, in ways that were hard to fathom, was as useful to her as she was to him. She and Burt were parallel lines of independent thought that flung sparks between them, but no more than that.

She paused at a corner of a street, uncertain suddenly of how far she'd walked and where she was in the city. And then suddenly she knew. Burt had put her safety before the outcome of the operation. That too was banal. The operation, the mission, was too important for the triviality of her safety or otherwise to interfere with it. And she realised then that this was Burt Miller's weakness and it wouldn't be hers. Her life meant everything and nothing, but she wouldn't allow it to stand in the way of a chance, however slim, of success. Burt himself had told her that it was the most important ten days of his entire life.

Her mind cleared then. She'd understood her motives by seeing his. Within a few seconds her mind was free of confusion and she was once more the coolest of operatives. A second and almost instantaneous thought swam into her mind. She was going to the far north, up into the Russian Arctic, unprotected, maintaining her mission intact, and with the possibility – no, probability – that the MVD would soon know the name of Valentina Asayev.

Her watchers would follow her, certainly – but only as far as they could, to Igarka. Miller would be furious that she'd disobeyed and would barely be able to conceal his fury as he ordered her watchers to follow her. But they could follow only as far as the ferry went.

Whether the MVD were specifically looking for her or not at the block, their investigations would eventually and undoubtedly reveal a Valentina Asayev who hadn't returned to pick up her bag. The manifest of the ship *Rossiya* would also, eventually, be consulted and found to contain the same name, once they'd tracked her down that far. The only question was how much time did she have? Enough time to reach Igarka? Maybe. Then, with luck, she could lose herself in the vast tundra to the north.

She began to prepare for what lay ahead.

She walked back towards the docks, avoiding Sverdlovsk Street and the market where she'd first met the *babas*. She stopped to buy a small bag and some good boots and warm clothes to replace the belongings she had left at the apartment block, as well as to buy provisions for the journey.

Finally, in a dead-end alley where even the addicts didn't venture, she retrieved the gun and the ammunition, wrapped, waterproofed and concealed inside a disused electrical box somewhere at the rear of the dock area.

CHAPTER EIGHT

LIEUTENANT ALEXEI PETROV decided to wait until it was dark before he made the risky return trip to the apartment block.

The afternoon had gone according to his improvised and swiftly developing plans. After he'd visited the MVD office, he'd returned to the *militsiya* station where, with surprisingly little ceremony, Sadko had granted him two to three weeks' leave to visit his grandfather. Three or four days downriver, Petrov had explained, and then there was still a trek into the wilderness where his people would be gathering their reindeer for the spring feeding and birthing in the Putorana. So two weeks at least was necessary. Sadko waved his hand at him in dismissal. Petrov and his efficiency were a thorn in his side, not to mention the major's feelings of disdain for the lieutenant's undesirable Evenk relatives. Petrov was free to go.

But, to himself, Petrov didn't actually have the faintest idea what he was going to do with the time apart from making the trip. Certainly, he now had an overwhelming desire to see Gannyka, to touch the old man's forehead, hear his dying words, even to listen to what the old man had been wanting to tell him since he'd been five years old – but Petrov had never given him time to do. But now he had a second overwhelming desire too – to make some kind of progress with the documents. Their importance was growing on him hourly. And that was why he wanted to revisit Sverdlovsk Street a second time, no matter what the risk.

He left his own apartment at just after eight o'clock in the evening. If the MVD were still at the grim concrete blocks where the body had been found, he wouldn't be able to conduct any further inquiries there. The last thing he wanted was to be immediately reported for returning to the scene of a crime from which the ordinary *militsiya* was now specifically excluded.

But if they'd finished their work – if they'd squeezed the memories of the block's inhabitants dry and also, no doubt, noted down a load of false stories made up by individuals to please the MVD – then perhaps he would be able to sit and take tea with one of the *babas* he'd seen that morning.

That was his one advantage over the Interior Ministry police; he knew, and had for a long time taken care to know, the lives of the block's occupants, their successes and failures, their great losses and tiny triumphs, their children and grandchildren, and all the convoluted family stories which consisted mostly of tragic happenings. He, Alexei Petrov, had bothered to listen to people and it was perhaps the most valuable lesson he could have given to anyone in any position of power or influence, whether political or domestic. To listen. But this was a gift which came naturally to him.

As he walked with a steady stride away from his apartment he noted a thin rain was now coming from the low mountains that ringed the city and, in the lights of the river bridge nearest to him, he could see steam rising off the river. Upriver from the city, the water was constantly warmed by the crumbling and ancient hydroelectric dam that powered the aluminium factories, so that the river was usually warmer than the air around the city of Krasnoyarsk.

He walked along the broken concrete pavement, tossed a few kopecks to some beggar children, and kept his hands in his pockets in case theirs tried to find a way into them. He was wearing his scuffed brown civilian leather jacket, a beret-type cap pulled over his head and thick winter boots into which were tucked warm, lined trousers. It was still cold at night, even in the early days of June. Further north where his mother lived it could still occasionally fall to twenty degrees below even in the spring months.

It didn't take him long to reach the street where the block was located, the grim urban shipwreck of Sverdlovsk Street. From the corner, he was able to take a long view down the street in order to establish that there were no MVD cars in the area. No doubt they'd have kept a presence there, however. He would have to bluff his way past whoever was left to ask visitors awkward questions, to make life difficult for anyone entering or leaving.

Suddenly, without his uniform, he realised with some astonishment that he was no longer Lieutenant Alexei Petrov. He was just a friend and sympathiser of the city's dispossessed and damned. It was a long time, he realised, since his rank and his job had taken second place to the man he was – or had once been.

As he approached the block, he saw he'd been right. There were two uniformed MVD troopers at the entrance, stopping anyone they chose. Petrov felt in his pocket for his papers. It was always better to offer than to be ordered. Quite often in a country where fear and corruption were the norm, willingness on the part of a suspect – and everyone was a suspect – was misinterpreted as innocence. If you showed your papers, the power-crazed little men who were the vital cogs in the machine controlled by the truly powerful simply waved you through.

But in the papers that he now held in his hand he was no longer Lieutenant Petrov. The papers he was preparing to offer the MVD represented his other side, his non–Russian identity. He'd quietly obtained them from his ethnic tribal family, the Evenk, in his mother's name. There'd been nothing calculated about obtaining and then prolonging the existence of the papers, they were merely a link, as Petrov saw it, to a past that was as much a part of him as his present, if not more so. Up to this moment, he had never thought of using them for anything, let alone dared to do so.

He held them just in the right way as he approached the troops who flanked the entrance to the block; not too eagerly, not too much in their faces, but modestly and in a quietly helpful way, but not too close to his own chest either. It was always important with authority to let them believe they were in control, had the power to grant or deny, or just to snatch something away. He stopped under an arc light the MVD had erected and waited while the soldier nearer to him took them from Petrov's half-stretched hand. Then he stood in the light so that he could be seen and matched with the photograph.

The men were cold, they had a brazier burning nearby and the second soldier wandered off towards it to warm his hands and turn something they were cooking — chestnuts, Petrov thought, judging from the aroma.

The remaining soldier took his papers in thick-gloved hands and cast a look of infinite weariness over them. He made a play of doubting Petrov's photo match with a series of rehearsed expressions. God knows, Petrov thought, perhaps they all stand in a room at MVD training camps and practise looking sceptical or angry.

'What are you doing here?' the guard demanded.

'Visiting my mother's cousin.'

'Who?'

'Irina Demidova. They're close, but my grandfather's been ill for some time so I come here on Thursdays instead of her.' Petrov embellished his story a little, pretending his mother lived in the city, enjoying the pretence, and he now found himself comfortable with his own grandfather's illness.

'How long are you staying?' the soldier asked nastily.

'A half-hour, maybe an hour.'

'Report to me when you leave.'

The guard made a note with a Biro whose ink seemed to come and go; first Petrov's Evenk name, *Munnukan,* then the identity number that matched it on the papers. *Mannukan* meant 'hare' in the Evenk language.

'I will,' Petrov replied.

He held out his hand for his papers and the soldier withheld them for an instant. Just trying to get a reaction, Petrov thought. They love a reaction. It gave them a chance to do something mean. But then he was through and into the filthy entrance lobby, with its broken ceiling and missing floor tiles and the ubiquitous stench of urine.

Irina Demidova's two-room chicken coop was, in its interior decoration, an almost exact replica of the home where she'd been brought up nearly eighty years before, a wooden log cabin by the river way up near the Arctic Circle.

There were dozens of little Russian icons mingled with spirit pictures and prayer feathers from the Evenk side of her family. The walls were completely covered in these and other prayer flags that might have had some Buddhist origin, from closer to the Mongolian border and the Evenk's genetic relations. In the few spaces where the walls were bare, small rugs were hung, one or two original, hand-woven Evenk rugs – probably quite valuable now, Petrov thought. But mainly the rugs were cheap Chinese imports.

Otherwise, vegetables hung in baskets from hooks in the ceiling, two dogs slept by an electric fire and there was a samovar in one corner. Petrov looked about him as he always did. A bit of straw and a pig was all it needed to be a stage set for some peasant *Yolki Palki* pageant, he thought.

A few feet away from the old woman, a television was switched on and it was showing a Brazilian soap opera with subtitles. Irina Demidova now switched down the sound to silence.

Petrov greeted the old woman warmly. He was a frequent visitor.

Irina Demidova was cracked and wizened like an old leather wine flask, mostly toothless, and looking pale under her ethnically brown skin. The whites of her eyes were, in fact, yellow but the pupils were hard and the colour of beaten copper. A heart condition was what it looked like, and then Petrov saw a bottle of pills on a small cabinet by the chair in which she clearly spent all her waking hours. Her most prized possession hung over the back of this chair. It was a shaman's coat, not unlike Petrov's grandfather's. She'd told him once, on one of his visits, that the coat had once belonged to her brother. Stalin's men had thrown him from a helicopter and told him to show them how a shaman could fly.

'Fetch me the vodka and pour us both one,' she demanded. Requests were a thing of the distant past for her.

Petrov dutifully found a half-full bottle of cheap vodka on a bookcase near the chair and a tin tray with glasses on it. He poured two measures and handed her one. She motioned to him to sit on an ottoman next to her. She had failing hearing, he knew from past visits.

She raised her glass shakily to him and he saw her grin toothlessly. 'You're here about the dead foreigner,' she said. 'But let's drink to life.'

She sipped delicately, then took a larger swig, half draining the glass. Petrov raised his glass silently but just sipped.

He wanted to ask her how she, or anyone, knew the body found that morning was that of a foreigner, but he knew better than to ask. Maybe some of the local kids had flicked through Bachman's clothing and got frightened when they'd found the passport, before they locked on to the wallet.

'Yes, *baba*, I'm here about the foreigner,' he said.

'I told them nothing,' she exclaimed. 'They've had their brains sucked out of them, those Interior people. Look at them. Morons. Why would I tell them a thing, the bastards.'

'I agree with you,' Petrov replied and sipped again. He wondered how many bottles the old woman managed to polish off in a week, or if she only drank when she had a visitor. 'Did they find anything that interested them though?' he asked.

'How can you tell what might interest those pigs?' she said, and waved her empty glass for a refill.

Petrov stood and topped up the glass and she seemed content this time to wait before she tasted it.

'No arrests, then?' Petrov enquired. 'No suspects, no leads, and nothing you didn't tell them, *baba*, that might have helped them?'

She looked at him and he saw a great cunning in her copper eyes. 'Oh yes,' she said. 'Everyone made up lots of stories, that's certain. Noises in the night, men with guns, flashes and bangs, groans and cries for help. The MVD were given very graphic descriptions of what didn't happen.'

'And you know something, don't you?' he asked gently. 'But only if you want to tell me. It won't go any further.'

'You know something yourself too,' she replied in a mock-accusatory way. 'That's why you're here, isn't it? I can see it in your eyes, Lieutenant Alexei Petrov.'

Petrov wondered whether he should tell the old woman now that he had come this evening, not as Lieutenant Petrov, but as a private citizen under his mother's name. He was *Mannukan*. Or whether he should tell her at all. There was a risk either way. The MVD might question her about her visitor.

'I'm not on the case, *baba*,' he said.

'So why are you here? To share my vodka?' She cackled with enjoyment.

'Just for your wise thoughts,' he replied. 'Anything you might like to tell me that you didn't tell them.'

She went into herself for a while and Petrov waited patiently while she decided what to say and how to say it.

'You like pretty women?' she demanded, out of the blue, and Petrov wondered whether the vodka had gone too swiftly to her brain. He looked back at her and shrugged, smiling with a slight embarrassment. 'Of course you do,' she persisted. 'Even since the sad death of your own pretty wife,' she said. 'Well, there was a very pretty one staying in the block the last few days. In the apartment of Zhenya. Upstairs, you know.'

Petrov nodded. Another old piece of faded human

parchment on the floor above, skin like rice paper, a hooked nose out of a pantomime, and a taste for the national drink that made Irina's seem abstemious.

'She paid in money' – cash she meant, Petrov knew – 'and upfront for seven nights. Tonight was the second night, or third night, wasn't it. I can't remember exactly. But she's gone, and left her things. Disappeared. Wearing only what she was wearing at five this morning. Before the body was found,' she added, with a hint of melodrama that wouldn't have been out of place in the Brazilian soap opera that still played out silently on the screen.

'Who was she?' Petrov prompted gently.

But she wasn't going to be that easy.

'Who knows?' Demidova replied flirtatiously. 'Her papers said she came from Bratsk. She said she was running away from a drunk husband and looking for work here. So she said,' Irina added.

Petrov sipped his drink thoughtfully. He knew well enough not to hurry a storyteller.

'But you didn't believe her story did you, *baba*?' he said finally. 'Did you, you clever old witch.' He laughed in an openly conspiratorial way and she looked at him with appreciation at his perspicacity.

Then Irina Demidova laughed with a sound like a child's rattle. 'You see, she was healthy,' she said. 'A very healthy young woman. No one around here, or in Bratsk, for that matter, looks like she did, not unless they're married to one of those thieving pirates who run the country and steal our money. And those people all buy their looks in the West, don't they? Or maybe in one of those fancy salons they have in Moscow and Petersburg now.'

She shook her empty glass at him peremptorily. He stood and took it and filled his own too. At this point, he withdrew the present he'd brought for her from the pocket of his leather jacket. It was another bottle, but unlike hers it was expensive vodka. She seized it in her thin claw-like hands and her eyes again showed him a deep appreciation. Then she thrust it down the side of the armchair where she was sitting. 'I'll keep this one for myself, Alexei,' she said.

'That's what it's for,' he answered, suppressing a grin. 'Just for you.'

She settled herself back into the chair and sipped delicately from the glass.

'So, then. This too-healthy woman somehow finds Zhenya down at the market,' she continued, 'as if she'd been looking for just anyone at all. But it's convenient for the job she was looking for, this block, wasn't it? Just two streets away from the docks.'

'She was looking for a job at the docks?' he asked, and she laughed scornfully at his deduction.

'You detectives!' she exclaimed. 'No, she was trying to get work at Igarka! In the lumber mills. Zhenya got it all out of her, her qualifications as a mill operator, her papers to say she knew how to service the saws up there. But take a look at her hands!' Demidova exclaimed, as if Anna Resnikov were in the room with them. 'They were strong, certainly, but they weren't *worked*, if you know what I mean. How does a woman who wants a shitty apartment to stay in for a few roubles a night afford hands like that, Zhenya thought. And why does a woman like that want to work in those saw mills?'

'I see,' Petrov said, though he wasn't sure he did.

'I see you want to know her name,' Demidova stated.

'Well . . .' Petrov demurred.

'She called herself Valentina Asayev,' Demidova said triumphantly, as if she were placing a winning poker hand on the table – but also with enough scepticism in her voice to suit the plot structure of an entire series of Brazilian soaps. 'But those bastards don't know that.'

'The MVD don't know?'

'Of course not. Only Zhenya and I know.'

Petrov sipped his vodka. She wanted to lead him on to questions, but he knew to be patient again. She would beat about the bush as long as he followed her by the nose, but if he sat and waited, her eagerness to tell everything would soon overcome her.

'But we all thought that couldn't be her real name,' Demidova said finally and in a defiant tone of voice.

'Oh?' Petrov said.

'We saw – Zhenya and I – that she wasn't who she said she was, that's all, so her name was doubtless false too.'

'Maybe she was just hiding from her husband,' Petrov ventured. 'That would be reason enough to conceal who she was. Maybe her husband is a violent man, maybe he tried to kill her.'

'She looked like she could kill ten husbands,' Demidova replied dismissively.

'And the foreigner too?' Petrov asked. 'You think she killed him?'

'No. Not the foreigner, not that Zhenya and I believe, anyway.' She paused. 'She was a Russian all right, no doubt of that. From the west around Moscow. She was educated too. But I tell you . . .' Then she grabbed Petrov's wrist with surprising force and pierced his eyes with her own copper ones. '. . . she was Russian, but she smelled of foreign countries,' she said.

CHAPTER NINE

THE *ROSSIYA* HEAVED sluggishly away from the dockside at just after ten o'clock in the evening. The old ship was only five hours late departing. Not bad timing, Anna Resnikov considered. It was something of a miracle the vessel worked at all.

A raging orange and purple Siberian sunset still coloured the sky to the west, out beyond the Ural Mountains, and the drizzle clouds had disappeared leaving a clear sky in which stars had slowly begun to appear.

She stood on her own at the guard rail, the blue quilted jacket tugged around her neck and her feet cold through the boots she'd bought. The temperature had dropped with the ship's departure and it had turned icy again, maybe down to a few degrees below zero, but something in the air told her that the brief, hot Siberian summer down here was not far away.

She stayed on deck as the light faded and, looking down vertically at the ship's side, she watched the rusted hull of the *Rossiya* wallow for a moment as if unsure if it could still float after the long winter, then slip away from the quay into the fast-moving current.

The engines were built by Vickers in the early

twentieth century at the British industrial town of Barrow-in-Furness, according to a proud bronze plate at the stern. They rattled every rivet and clattered the metal sheets of the deck, shaking chains and davits, stanchions and guard rails. Their loud throb made it seem as if the ship had some kind of shaking sickness. In the beginning there had been the steady, insistent thumping of the old 1913 engine. The crosshead, four-stroke cycle diesel wasn't up to much any more in terms of speed and probably never had been. It could propel the *Rossiya* at five knots at the most, and only more than that with the aid of the strong current. But its deafening cacophony was, if anything, worse than it had ever been in its long history. The resulting, incessant throbbing of the ship invaded Anna's every thought. It jarred every inch of the metal decks and companion ways, shuddered the guard rails and the narrow sheet-iron passages that made up the claustrophobic internal parts of the ship. The tortured movement of ancient, riveted metal made her feel as if she were being shaken herself. The ship's cargo and fittings all became the engine's dissonant orchestral accompaniment. Finally the grumpy vessel settled a little nervously, it seemed to Anna, into the centre of the river just as true night fell.

As she stood on the deck watching the last of the light, her immediate thoughts concerned the foreman Ivan. He was the imminent threat. She knew that from his remarks at the hiring office. After her encounter with him her priority on the *Rossiya* must be to keep well clear of him.

But then there were the other, for the time being more

distant, threats too that had accumulated since the MVD raid. She had to assume the Interior police would find the name Valentina Asayev, her forged alias, in connection with the block and Zhenya's apartment, and eventually they would find her name on the *Rossiya*'s manifest.

Despite the extreme, last-minute tensions of her departure, however, the upside was that she had what she wanted – the job at the saw mills and principally the journey towards them. She had no intention of remaining in Igarka for any length of time. It all depended on whether she could make it to the lumber town before the MVD caught up with her. And she also wondered what her watchers would do now that she had disobeyed Miller's orders. They were certain to follow, that was her only conclusion.

But it was Ivan she would have to deal with first. She knew he would come for what he wanted in return for getting her hired. Now it was more imperative than ever to avoid his attention, and Ivan was not just invasive and potentially dangerous to her, he was also too curious about her by far.

She hadn't seen the foreman since she'd boarded the ship and she wondered where below decks she could put her bedroll for the night without him finding and bothering her. To hide herself among the other female hands hired for Igarka's lumber mills was the obvious choice. But even going down to the women's section – simply a freight hold in the bowels of the ship – wouldn't stop a man like him, for whom power was simply an invitation to abuse it. She wondered just how aggressive he might become, and how – now she was on the ship – she could most effectively deal with him.

Finally she turned from the guard rail and faced to the north where the river led and where her mission lay. As the ship passed Ennolaevksy, Dodonovo and Komonovo in the brief few hours of darkness, she remained on deck – out of sight, she hoped. She looked almost blindly into the near-darkness towards the Arctic until the early tinge of dawn began to appear to the east.

Then she turned from the night's greying end ahead of the ship, picked up her bag and went below.

The permanent noise of the ship *Rossiya* became unnoticeable after the initial twelve hours on board. But in that early dawn it wouldn't let her rest and, in the vast silence of the Siberian wilderness around the ship, it was as if the *Rossiya* was the landscape's lone and angry presence; a minotaur in the unending cave of Siberia.

During the few hours before breakfast, the first thing she had done was to conceal the gun and the ammunition in the latrines. She needed to keep it in the women's quarters, where she was most likely to have to retrieve it quickly and then, while the other women were sleeping, she found an old disused and blocked pipe, stuffed with wire and rubble and some old rags. She emptied it, placed the wire four feet inside, then the gun and ammunition, finally filling the remaining hole with the rubble and rags. On top of it all she stuffed a few sanitary towels.

Then she had lain on a wooden bench in a large open area in the hold, a cargo space which had its hatch all but battened down at night, as if its human cargo were prisoners, not paid workers. But the other women seemed to know it was reserved for them and so she'd followed their lead. In that early morning, she'd hardly slept. Whether she expected Ivan to come for her, or whether it was the tension of the mission that was now properly emerging into its grim reality which kept her awake, she wasn't sure. But at least she hadn't seen Ivan.

As she lay on the hard surface, her bedroll beneath her, she felt the fetid warmth of the other female bodies stacked so tightly on the benches and on the floor that there was hardly room to move once everyone had fallen asleep.

When she woke after a fitful, dawn sleep early on the first morning on the ship, she slipped off the bench. The sun had been up for a while. The smell in the hold was rank. She picked her way among the still-sleeping bodies, opened the hatch, then went through a metal door and up some metal steps out on to the deck. She leaned on the guard rail, breathed the clean air, and watched the sun soaring in the sky across eastern Siberia from the Pacific two thousand miles away.

As the light illuminated the Yenisei Basin and the unimaginable vastness of Siberia, it was hard to believe she was heading somewhere more desolate than the scene in front of her.

Yazaevka, Porog, Mamatovo . . . In the expanding dawn the ship was passing a few small fishing villages which were not even on the map – just settlements of scattered wooden houses in each, dotted on the banks. A small boat with an outboard might come out and try to sell something, but the *Rossiya* wasn't stopping except at certain designated places on the route. Sometimes the river widened to half a mile across, sometimes sheer cliffs rose up on either side of it and when they did, the water rushed with greater speed through the narrows. The trees on the eastern bank – pines, spruce and fir – stretched away to the horizon while the flat, western bank was almost bare as far as the Ural Mountains, which rose between the river and Moscow. Ahead of the ship there was still a thousand miles to the Arctic Circle.

It was at around midday when she saw Ivan. The deck was busy with other hired workers eating bread and chicken, smoking cheap Russian cigarettes, or drinking beers and playing cards. But she spotted Ivan easily. He was watching her intently as before, a slight smile on one side of his mouth. When he saw her looking at him he came over at once and gave her the same leering smile he'd made at the hiring office.

He said nothing at first, stood almost limply. But then suddenly he sprang forward at her. With one hand he took a mobile phone out of his jacket pocket, with the other he swiftly snatched the cap off her head. Then he took a picture of her with the phone. As he looked at the picture, he laughed at the angry look that crossed her face.

Only a great effort of self-control, once again, prevented her from getting up off the deck with all the speed and strength she possessed and throwing him and the phone over the rails.

Instead, she quietly picked up the cap he'd dropped beside her and put it back on. Be passive, she told herself.

Be like the others. But even in her old clothes and with her dishevelled, dirty appearance, she knew she couldn't be quite like them. Something of her health and strength set her apart. She could not disguise that.

She looked away from the bulk of Ivan's body that stood between her and a thin sun. But he wasn't going to leave.

'Why are you on your own?' he said aggressively.

She didn't reply.

'Look,' he said, 'the others all know each other. Why not you?' His tone of voice was somewhere between a plaintive question and an angry accusation.

'Maybe they work up in Igarka every year,' she replied, looking at him at last. 'I've never worked up there.'

'Why not? What brings you here for work?'

She shrugged.

'Where have you worked before?' he insisted again, even more aggressively this time.

She stiffened. 'What are you,' she snapped back and looked him directly in the face, a challenge. 'OMON?'

He laughed. 'Would that bother you?' Through his chipped and yellowed teeth he chanted in a sing-song voice the motto of the Otryad Militsii Osobogo Naznacheniya, another of Russia's nastier internal security police forces. 'We show no mercy and expect none!' he sang. Then he laughed his huge and unpitying laugh.

She said nothing.

He looked at the picture of her on his phone. 'Maybe up in Igarka I'll say you're my woman,' he said insolently, and then stared at her face in the flesh. 'And maybe you will be. Look,' he said again, demanding her attention, 'a woman like you will need protection up there. It's a rough place, believe me.' When again she refused to reply, his impatient expression hardened. 'What makes you so tough? You think you can ignore me maybe. I can fire you at the next stop, if I choose. At Yeniseiysk or Vorogovo or Bakhta. Easy. You're off the ship.' He snapped his fingers. 'Just like that.'

'Then I'll have to find work somewhere else, won't I,' she replied, looking at him for the first time.

'What work? Where have you worked before, then?' he said.

'Bratsk. Where I was born.'

'In the mills there?'

'Yes, the mills. Other odd jobs. Whatever I could get. I'm not idle. My parents died when I was young. I know how to look after myself. What does it matter to you?'

He leaned over her and again she could smell the alcohol on his breath. 'You're too good to be doing this, that's why.' He paused. 'I can see it,' he hissed.

Her heart missed a beat.

He tossed the phone in his hand a few times, as if to taunt her with the picture on it, and then he walked away.

CHAPTER TEN

ALEXEI PETROV'S MOTHER was an uncomplicated, tribal and deeply traditional woman. She'd raised four children in the far north, doing the work of men as well as women, herding reindeer in summer and winter, the sacred animals that kept the tribe alive with their skins and meat, hair and bones. They were sacred beasts, deeply honoured in life as well as in death. But his father was a very different creature. Petrov Senior had been a minor Russian state official from Moscow with burning communist sympathies who was sent out to Siberia at the end of the 1940s. For some time before he'd been assigned to a place that only the most fevered Party enthusiasts would ever want to visit, let alone live. Stalin had ordered the development of huge military-industrial complexes throughout the region, including the highly secret Krasnoyarsk B complex. Though it officially didn't exist, it was hollowed out of a mountain near the city, and it was the place where Alexei's wife had died from a radiation leak in the 1990s. A laboratory assistant who was forgotten by all but Alexei Petrov.

But back in that long distant past, his father had fallen foul of Stalin's final purge in 1953 and was given ten years in the camps. He was released early, in a general amnesty after Stalin's death and thanks to Khrushchev's thaw, having served just two years. Still buried alive in the wilderness up in the northern reaches of the Yenisei River, however, and without the necessary papers to travel elsewhere in the Soviet Union, let alone the money to do so, Petrov Senior had worked in various menial industrial jobs – little more than slave labour in themselves – in the Arctic city of Norilsk, until he'd met and married Petrov's mother in 1972.

By then he was in his mid-fifties and she was twenty-three years old. He was a former *zek* – a convict – though he still retained his loyalty to the Communist Party, an institution that, in his eyes, could do no wrong. She was the daughter of reindeer herders and fishermen who went back tens of generations living in the same vast wilderness, unknown and fearful to anyone else, but to her own tribe a home where every tree and rock and river were known as if they were objects in a family living room.

After the brief marriage, Petrov's father had finally managed to make his way south to Krasnoyarsk and, due to the lack of people willing to move to Siberia to become police officers, he'd eventually found his way into the *militsiya*, his slate wiped clean by a needy recruiting officer desperate to fill quotas.

His marriage to Petrov's mother had lasted less than two years, in which time Petrov was born.

From his mother and grandfather, Petrov had learned that the Evenk people occasionally helped Russian convicts when they escaped from the gulag, as well as befriending the freed who, having nowhere else to go, were still all but slaves. Perhaps his father had simply used his mother to get out of the bitter north, Petrov had often thought in his thirty-nine years. His father was certainly far older than his mother, more than double her age. From Petrov's knowledge of both his parents, there seemed to be little in common between them and Petrov Senior was able to use all the power of the State as well as his new policeman's role, to keep his son with him and evict his mother back to the Siberian tundra and *taiga* 'where she belongs'.

As Petrov now approached the hiring office in Krasnoyarsk's dockland which recruited workers for the Igarka lumber companies downriver, he suddenly found himself thinking about the rootlessness of his now dead father compared to the deeply traditional tribal affinities of his mother's family. Despite the repeated attempts throughout the history of the Soviet Union to wipe out the Evenk and other tribal groups or, at the very least, assimilate them until there was nothing left of their heritage, there was still a thin culture among them that kept them staggering on, from one generation to another, their language in decline and their way of life slowly eroded by the metals factories and oil pollution of the reindeer feeding grounds in the Arctic, not to mention the nuclear testing on the far northern island of Novaya Zemlya. But Petrov knew that one day – soon perhaps – that thin culture, too, would be wiped out and then the Evenk would have effectively ceased to exist. Gannyka might be the last, not just of his generation, but of a group who knew the old ways by heart and instinct. Part of the landscape that was itself slowly being destroyed.

Perhaps it was the Evenk identity papers he had used the night before at the block, but he suddenly felt a wave of affinity for his tribal past that he hadn't felt for years.

He studied the concrete box of the hiring office before entering. Though prohibited now from pursuing any direct lines of inquiry into the death of the foreigner, Petrov wore his *militsiya* uniform and he commanded the authority that came with it. He wasn't asking anything about the dead foreigner, after all. He told himself that he was simply following up a missing woman who called herself Valentina Asayev.

He approached the hiring office and entered. The officer didn't bother to look up. Petrov rapped his knuckles on the table and demanded to see the list of the hired employees from the day before.

From an initially reluctant, grunting response from the drunk who was apparently in charge of the hiring process, there followed a string of expletives. But finally here was the list and on it, sure enough, Petrov found the name 'Valentina Asayev'. She had gone north to Igarka the evening before aboard the *Rossiya*, a few hours after he'd been in the apartment block with Irina Demidova. But he remembered that she hadn't returned to the block to pick up her belongings before the ship had left. Why? Who would go north without carefully prepared clothes and provisions, and he had seen and searched her bag at the old woman Zhenya's before he'd left the apartment.

Petrov ran his eyes down the list, carefully going past

her name, then turning the page until he reached the end.

Simply because she hadn't returned to Zhenya's apartment, it didn't mean there was any connection between her and the corpse of the German. But it was strange, nevertheless, the conjunction of events. She'd had the whole day to walk two streets from the docks to Sverdlovsk Street to pick up her things and she hadn't done so. 'She was Russian but she smelled of foreign countries', Petrov suddenly recalled Irina Demidova saying before he'd left. Were they simply the ramblings of an old woman who watched too many Brazilian soap operas? How do you smell of foreign countries anyway, he wondered?

But Petrov knew he had no choice but to follow the young woman, even if it were only to put his mind at rest. If she were connected to Bachman, then she must also be connected to the papers.

'Found who you want?' the hiring officer asked him.

'No,' Petrov replied. 'He's not here.'

'They used to get sent up there to the Gulag,' the officer sneered. 'Now half the low-lifes in Russia go there to escape.'

Petrov left the wooden office building and walked back towards his apartment, steering clear of Sverdlovsk Street.

When he reached home, he carefully hung up his uniform before packing a rucksack with food and water, a few items of clothing and heavy boots. He wrapped his police gun in a pair of trousers and took an old hunting rifle Gannyka had given him when he was seven years old. Called a *berdianka*, it was more than a hundred and twenty years old but, if you learned to shoot with it as he had, you could bring down a deer at a hundred yards. He strapped his fishing rod in sections to the outside of the pack and added a few traps for small animals. When he thought he was ready and had the pack on his back, he suddenly put it down again. He walked over to the window and looked at the tambour. Then he finally took the old shaman's drum from the windowsill and tied it on to the top of the pack and stuffed an old pair of reindeer-hide breeches into one of the outer pockets.

But before he left he went to the bathroom and tipped the asbestos panel upwards and retrieved the tin. He took out the documents and wrapped them tightly in a new waterproof bundle. He didn't imagine that he would need them where he was going, but he couldn't leave them here. He didn't trust Robolev and the MVD. If they didn't find what they wanted to find, it was easily possible that they would raid his apartment, particularly if they found out that he'd returned to Sverdlovsk Street or gone to the hiring office. Now that he recalled it, he hadn't entirely trusted Robolev's relatively easy manner, nor the way he'd been allowed to go without further questioning.

Finally, he locked the door of the apartment and headed for the city centre.

He walked away in the opposite direction from Sverdlovsk Street and continued walking for two miles until he reached a thoroughfare that contained a few restaurants and a couple of hotels. It was a commercial district of sorts and he was heading for an Internet café he knew. He dared not use his own computer.

Once inside the café, he saw that it was occupied only by a youth behind the counter and another sallow young man – possibly a friend of the barman – sitting at one of a dozen screens. Petrov ordered a coffee and paid a few roubles for the use of a screen at the far end.

He took the cup to the far end of the bank of screens and sipped from it as he brought up Rustler, the Russian Google. Then he put the name Professor Gunther Bachman into the system and waited an age for a link to appear.

Petrov blindly pored over the German's biography when it finally came. It was in English and German and he spoke neither language. And so he focused on some of the initials attached to the professor's name and which had links to a Russian translation. From these it seemed Bachman was a member of something called the IAEA. Petrov tapped the link and found the Russian initials of the organisation and noted that they signified the International Atomic Energy Association. Then he was back to the German professor again. He repeated the process several times, with several sets of initials for international organisations. Bachman, it turned out, was a member of the Nuclear Science Committee, among others. He was also the Alexander von Humboldt Fellow at Munich University. It seemed Bachman had written numerous papers on aspects of nuclear technology.

Petrov was able to use the server's translation to discover the list of prizes and honours the great Bachman had won in his lifetime, and the names of the universities where he'd apparently enjoyed visiting professorships abroad, particularly in America. His learned articles in specialist, academic publications from Sweden to South Africa, Israel to America – the names of these publications Petrov also noted – marked him out clearly as a leader in his field. One press article with Bachman's photograph caught Petrov's eye, but it was also only in English and German, with no translation, and he couldn't understand it. The picture emerging of the man Petrov had seen the previous morning, dead in a pile of trash, was of a highly thought-of individual in a highly sensitive field. And he had visited Norilsk two days earlier, dying within hours of returning.

Petrov sought a translation into Russian of other papers by Bachman. One finally came up. It was a limited overview – a precis – of the foreign language text and in an atrocious form of Russian that was only barely easier to understand. But Petrov was able to join the dots some more. He jotted down the main features of Bachman's research, his academic achievements and major papers on the subject of nuclear energy. '*Professor Bachman*', the atrocious translation read, '*has worked for more than a decade of ten years on a highly top-secret confidential nuclear project, but has, as things stand today, not made the breakthrough he hoped for.*'

Finally, Petrov noted that Bachman had been invited to attend a meeting of the Bilderberg Committee. Petrov looked up the link to Bilderberg and read the story of the committee. It was a secret composition of world leaders and industrialists, it seemed. Its Byzantine structure – or more accurately its lack of any formal structure – was essential to its secret meetings. The committee's invitation-only, annual get-togethers in obscure parts of the world were, according to some, where the world's affairs were hashed out. Deals made at the Bilderberg Committee affected billions of people, so it seemed.

It seemed to Petrov that Bachman had been merely a guest at this meeting of the Bilderberg, invited in order to explain his – so far failed – research project which he had been working on for so long. *Decade of ten years . . .*

Petrov folded the notes he'd made. He didn't want the record of a printed copy. Then he erased his search just for good measure. He shut down the computer and left the café.

It was a clear day, cold with a blue sky that stretched too far for the eye to properly comprehend. The kind of far-off, wide landscape only a wide camera lens can capture. He felt a great wave of freedom wash over him after the months of winter, the tiny apartment and the relentless duties of his job. He hardly cared why he was leaving the city. Even the documents – his unspoken reason for taking time off – and his brief look at Bachman's identity seemed suddenly boring compared to the vastness and the light that spread out to the north and east of Krasnoyarsk. He was elated to be leaving, to be going north towards his roots and to be saying his goodbyes to his dying grandfather Gannyka.

At the port, the tourist ferry was preparing to leave in just over an hour. Petrov flashed his *militsiya* identification and found a place on deck, the cheapest ticket. The ferry would be carrying mostly, if not entirely, Russians this early in the season.

As the ferry left the quay, something about returning towards his mother's family and the north brought out in him the complete normality of what he was doing. The journey itself, perhaps, contained a clue. In his heart, he guessed he was still a nomad, even one on a modern well-appointed ferry. It was at times like this – so rare he could hardly remember the last one – that he realised how much he had forced himself into the job and into the Slavic culture, just as he had forced himself into the uniform that went with it. His father had made it so. Certainly, he was proud of his achievements – he was a good cop, the best – but it was the pride of merely superseding his ancestry, not of adapting to a culture that he'd ever thought, for a single moment, was superior to his own. It was really the pride of cunning, he thought, of concealing himself, of being able to operate in the alien Russian world. His heart, as he was always aware on the few occasions he allowed himself to think about it, lay in the north, the so-called wilderness, and in the ancient spirit of his people.

He went below the viewing deck and found the bar open. There was a motley collection of travellers mostly bringing supplies northward to their families and friends – fruit and vegetables and alcohol, mainly – packed in boxes or sacks. He ordered a *Stary Melnik* beer and walked over to the panoramic window of the boat as it slipped away from the quay. He gazed at each tree of the thousands they passed, noted the teal and garganey, a high buzzard and some circling kestrels. He watched them describing their perfect circles until suddenly one would close its wings and dive like an arrow, skimming the grass as it rose again, successful or not. Curlews, plovers, some geese and mallards, all heading south or east. He began to think of their names in the Evenk language.

When finally he turned an hour or more after the vessel had left the city altogether, he saw three people sitting at the table. You could tell instantly they were foreign. They were youngsters, students probably, Petrov thought. They stood out as being obviously not Russian. They were Americans, he guessed, two men and a woman. They were looking at two or three brand new guidebooks and one of them had a map opened fully on the table.

CHAPTER ELEVEN

IN THE MIDDLE of the afternoon on the first full day out from Krasnoyarsk, Anna sat alone, cross-legged on the deck. The Siberian *taiga* – its dark forest – was now massed thick against the banks on either side like a green infantry army cut in two by the cavalry of the great river.

She considered her vulnerability and she knew now that this vulnerability on board the *Rossiya* was increased by her solitariness. Aside from the false papers and the mission itself, there was Ivan to think about, a constantly looming presence she could never get away from in the prison of the ship. He lurked, never far away, and now he had made it amply clear to her that her isolation was not only suspicious but also a card in his hand that he was determined to play.

She saw that the others on board all seemed to know each other. Presumably they worked the mills in Igarka every year. But by trying to make herself inconspicuous, she realised, she had cut herself off from the other workers. And so she began to look at the faces around her, deciding who she would approach in case of a crisis with the foreman. It was an automatic action, as well as a sudden desire to be part of the work gang in order to give herself better cover. Here on the ship, it was apparent that to be inconspicuous meant being part of the group.

She had learned to tell a lot from the study of a human face. The Russians had a section in foreign intelligence which had made the study of the face – and the deduction of the psychological nature of a person from this study – into what they called a science. The method, which was not recognised internationally as an actual science, had been invented in America in the 1930s, then dropped and taken up later by the French. It had a name – morpho-psychology – and a literature that had grown up around it. The Russian intelligence services, particularly the KGB's foreign service, had seized on this – some said – pseudo-science in the 1950s. Anna recalled how she had been assigned to the section for nearly three months, nearly twenty years before, in the KGB's training section at Balashiha when she was a new recruit to foreign intelligence.

Morphopsychology wasn't described as a pseudo-science by her SVR teachers, however, but simply as an 'alternative' science. In Russia, the intelligence services made use of anything, no matter what the rest of the world thought. Some of what took place in the spy laboratories were, to be sure, just cranky, pseudo-studies but, in her experience, the study of morphopsychology could be a highly reliable method of gauging a person's character at speed. It might make a difference in a situation where only a few seconds counted between life and death. Was a person capable of killing? Would they fight, even? Could they be trusted or should they be distrusted? A person's reliability or otherwise, likewise their discretion, bravery, recklessness and all manner of things, could be told from a face. Her studies at Balashiha had taught that there was a correspondence between the shape and configuration of the human face, and its component parts, and the individual personality – and most importantly, its capabilities – the person's potential. And Anna knew from experience it could be extremely accurate.

So on this bright Siberian morning on the *Rossiya* – partly as an exercise and partly to try to get to know her fellow workers and their potential usefulness to her – she began to take in their faces.

First, she looked at the three men sitting nearest her. They were playing cards ten yards along the deck from where she sat, concentrating on the game, the only sounds a low muttering which was occasionally disturbed by a curse of failure or a cry of triumph.

The man nearest to her had a round face, dilated like a baby's. He was jovial, with a tight, closed mouth when he wasn't laughing. His lower lip was large – he was a man with an appetite, then, a baby's insatiable appetite – and his upper lip came over the lower one. Anna watched him and mentally assessed him in the way she'd been taught twenty years before. He was someone who wanted all the attention – a man baby. He was, most likely, a grasping, greedy person. His face told her that he was a man with needy, childlike desires – and someone who couldn't hold his tongue. Unreliable, indiscreet. He was someone who undoubtedly needed to be supported, but who wasn't much good at supporting others.

The man next to him in the circle of card-players had a strong jawline, a big square forehead and a taut face with no excess skin. This was a very 'masculine' man, then, with a force about him and the ability to go for what he wanted and, mostly, to get it. And next to him was a third man whose face she noted when it turned towards her from his profile. This card-player had a big nose, a wide face and straight, protected nostrils. His nose rose smoothly to the head. That signified he was cerebral – in the language of morphopsychology anyway. He was a man who could feel what was going on around him but who didn't show his feelings, a reflective character, someone who took a distance and thought before he spoke or expressed his thoughts.

As an exercise it was something that had a soothing effect on Anna, like a quiet mental game. But it was also potentially useful as she looked around the deck at those closest to her – useful, if she needed to approach someone and required a quick assessment of their natural discretion, for example, or their willingness to take another's side. Sometime, she might need somebody's help on the *Rossiya*, someone she could trust.

None of the men she studied thus saw her as she studied them. They were too absorbed in the game, or others were focused on eating and drinking, laughing or just half-asleep in the sun. Her gaze travelled further around to a group of women, apparently gossiping incessantly. It didn't seem to matter about what. Every subject they seemed to be talking about held the same resonant urgency, the same tense flow of words, the same tone of voice. They would have talked in the same way, she thought, if they had been discussing anything from the price of bread to an imminent nuclear attack. Theirs was a steady flow of exchange, a calmness – or acceptance of their lot – that most of the men lacked. But she assessed them in the way she had the men.

She went from person to person across the deck near her like this, group to group, studying who was strong or weak, who was honest or dishonest, who might be a potential help to her in a time of crisis and who to avoid and expect nothing from in such an event. It could be valuable information and was nearly always correct if she was rigorous in the initial study of each face.

Finally her eyes fell on a young man. Sometimes he seemed to be on his own. She'd noticed that earlier in the day. But at other times, he appeared to consort with a group similar to him, and in a quiet, conspiratorial sort of way. They were a group apart from the rest of the work gang.

The young man was in his early twenties, she guessed. Then she stiffened for a moment and she forgot her analytical exercise. The man was looking straight back at her. There was something intense in his stare, almost intimate. It was as if he knew her. And when she caught his eyes, he didn't look away, but continued his level gaze, and the first thing she noticed about him was that his eyes were fiercely bright, almost flaming.

Anna tried to remember if she'd seen him in the line at the hiring office. But she couldn't remember having seen him as she remembered some of the others. And yet his face seemed familiar. She studied him, but with a jolt of recognition that she couldn't place. Now it was this thin recognition she felt which took up her thoughts, not the study of his face.

The young man was part of this group who looked more like students than workers. It was partly the way they dressed, and their boyish conspiracy of friendship, rather than a friendship which naturally evolved and flowed. The young man wore nothing that made any concession to the cold; a flimsy grey jacket with one of the pockets torn right down the side, which he'd worn the night before in the harsh low night-time temperatures. The jacket looked as though it had once been part of a cheap suit, she thought. There was an artfulness about his dress which was the mark of youthful disregard for appearances – while all the time being highly aware of them. Around his neck was a very long red wool scarf, like some Petersburg student, she thought. And under the jacket a thin, striped shirt. His head was up, too high, the arrogance of a youthful confidence which hadn't been defeated by life's difficulties. He had a narrow, pale face with cavernous, undernourished cheeks – but again, she noted, his physical appearance like his clothes seemed to have an artfulness about it that was an act. He seemed to be conscious of the type of figure he was performing. A thin, wispy, tangled beard worked its way around his chin like a strangled winter vine. But it was still his eyes which set him apart from the others most of all, his eyes which she had first, and startlingly, noticed about him. They contained the same fierce, burning light they'd done ever since she'd started watching him. There was a fire in them that hadn't yet been extinguished.

As she stared back at him, both of them unwavering in their looks, she found herself confused between the science of what she had been applying and the act that he seemed to have adopted. He could have been a generic poster boy for any revolution, she thought, the thin, gangly, propagandised student with the patriotic flag in his hands, standing legs apart on the barricades, burning shot flying around him, as his fierce eyes and fiercer beliefs scorched away the capitalist oppressor. He was a figure who might have walked right out of a short story by Dostoyevksy.

There was an intensity now, too, in the way that he looked at her. But it was not the intensity of Ivan, or a man like Ivan. It was not a lusting, lecherous look. It expected nothing. His gaze was a dispassionate assessment of her, just as hers was of him.

When she looked away for a while and then turned back to him again, he was still looking, studying her almost like a specimen in a jar, it seemed, just as she had been studying him. It was as if he were performing the same experiment that she was. And this time as she watched him, she knew she *had* seen him before – but she also knew it hadn't been in the line at the hiring office. And this sent a disturbing feeling of uncertainty coursing through her.

Troubled at not being able either to place him in the recent past or to dismiss him altogether from her mind, she fell into a lulled state, leaned back against some lifebelts and fell into an uneasy doze. She wanted now just to put him out of her mind.

Savino, Tunguska, Rudikovka . . . The small settlements and wooden villages drifted by. As the afternoon fell into its grey decline over the *taiga*, a hazy, puffy cloud bank descended on the landscape like a dirty pillow and the *Rossiya* pulled groaning to starboard, dropping its anchor off the bank by the town of Tomonovo. The rattling of the chain from the ship's hawses stirred her from her torpor.

The ship was expected in the town. More boats with outboards came out to sell vegetables or bread, but the main product on offer seemed to be fish. From time to time the river here still supported sturgeon, despite the unchecked pollution further north.

Anna got to her feet and watched the captain of the *Rossiya* descend metal steps that had been dropped down the side of the hull and he climbed on to one of these small boats that waited. He shouted back up the steps at nobody in particular that the ship would depart in two hours.

She descended the steps after him, along with a few of the other passengers, and they paid a few kopecks each to be taken ashore.

The 'town' was more like a small village and all the more strange for the way it had suddenly loomed out of the dense green forest like a mirage. It seemed to be made up largely of semi-wild dogs. There were mostly Samoyeds from the north, or Siberian huskies, which ran at high speed towards the boats as they beached on the shore. There were also various long-legged wolf-hunting dogs. The Samoyeds whined and growled but didn't bark, while the hunting dogs bayed furiously and had a dangerous pack mentality about them. There were other dogs – for hunting wolves – tied up on chains and there were two captured wolves and a small bear kept on chains further away. Now and again, one of the old women who had produce for sale on the few rickety tables by the beach threw them a fish head or scrap of bone.

A few unshaven men in the extreme stages of inebriation slumped against walls or sat on the rocks by the beach. They were offering mangy sable pelts for sale, in exchange for vodka. The women in these lonely impoverished places were the ones who, as ever, worked, while the men hardly cared any more as long as they had vodka.

There were just two streets in the village. They were both made of earth and the two dozen or so wooden houses that lined them were sunk into the mud at crazy angles, as if the town itself and not just most of its inhabitants were drunk. Anything built here without proper foundations sank into the earth when the frost melted in the summer. She paused on the beach and looked at what was for sale at the tables. There were some root vegetables, more mangy-looking fur pelts, a pair of live sables and two sturgeon, one of the fish over six feet in length.

Anna walked off into the main street without any plan other than to stretch her legs on dry land. A few children in filthy clothes played around a hole in the ground full of stagnant water with a thin coating of ice. A man reeled down the street unsteadily towards her, his eyes glassy, and holding out a hand for alms. But it was a gesture without any hope, let alone expectation.

When she'd reached the edge of the village, a distance of a hundred yards or so, she saw the forest pressing in close, as if intent on pushing the houses and the entire village with all its decayed humanity back into the river from where it had come.

She turned and, as she did so, immediately the hackles on her neck rose. She saw Ivan. He was skulking in the shade of a wood store on the far side of the street. And then, looking to the left of him, she saw that he wasn't alone.

He was talking closely with a tall man, fit and healthy-looking, not like the men on the ship or in the village. He wore smart polished black leather boots. Slung loosely over the second man's shoulders she saw what seemed to be an American military jacket. Her first thought was that he'd got it on the black market from one of the American military bases in Kyrgizstan, which supplied their endless war across the border in Afghanistan. But his boots seemed to be too good to come from the black market. The two men were about twenty-five or thirty yards away from her, and behind her, as she walked up the mud street of the village. She knew at once that Ivan, or more likely both of them, had been following her, watching to see where she would go.

Now, as she watched Ivan talking with the man, she saw the second man turn and look in her direction. Then he looked away, back towards Ivan, and she saw Ivan make an obscene gesture and both he and the man began to laugh in her direction, Ivan with his big, crude laugh, while other man made a pinched, mirthless bark that was as close to laughter as, most likely, he ever got.

Anna crossed the street, dipped behind a house, unhurried, affecting not to care about their presence. She walked around behind the few other houses on this side of the street until she was well out of their sight. She was walking across rough ground now, half wild ground bush, half village, but all the time keeping away from the street. She expected them to follow her, but she needed to know.

Her mind was not calm, but it was focused now on danger. She knew that Ivan was never going to leave her alone. She wondered if he had shown the second man the picture he had taken of her on the phone. Ivan, she realised, was becoming an unacceptable danger to her. The photograph – even in her current state of disguise – could jeopardise everything about her alias. They had her pictures in every security service establishment in Russia and, even disguised as she was, a sharp eye might just – might easily – make the connection. Her life was now in danger. She would have to move on to a new, aggressive footing.

She was very well known to the highly secret foreign intelligence services at their headquarters in Balashiha to the east of Moscow. She'd once been one of the SVR's best officers in Department 'S', the so-called *patriotiy*, and their youngest female colonel until her defection. And the foreign intelligence service to which she'd belonged had placed her on their most wanted list for the past five years. She'd even gleaned from Burt Miller, via one of his informants in Russia, that recruits to the SVR were being encouraged to use photographs of her for target practice at the Balashiha headquarters.

Not for the first time in the past few hours she considered the existence of her photograph on Ivan's mobile phone. Maybe – and the inevitable thought came to her without reluctance or even pause – she would now have to kill Ivan, destroy him and his mobile phone along with him.

But when she came out from behind the few houses, she saw that the two men hadn't followed her but had remained in the same place. They knew she would have to come back eventually in their direction. She was just ten yards away from them now.

The second man was staring at her as she came out in front of the house and on to the street. The house was a tilting wooden structure like the others, with a wood porch on which an old man was gutting fish.

It was as if the two men watching her had judged her movements in advance. Ivan was smoking a cigarette and he smiled unpleasantly at her. Both of them were staring directly at her.

The second man possessed a pronounced asymmetry between the two sides of his face; a man who lived in great tension, she thought; a man who was capable of great imbalances in his character. The two halves of his face were alternately concave and convex, retracted and dilated. Such an imbalance, she judged, would lead to the man's inner tensions creating in him a great propensity for violence. His skin was very taut over his forehead, and his eyes were very different from each other. The left eye curved in its socket, and the eyebrow above it was lowered over it, protecting it from external influences. His right eye, on the other hand, was piercing, and set on a horizontal line. The left side of his face was angular and tense; the right more dilated. His flaring nostrils were like a bull's, sensing everything around him. An instigator of actions – and, more than likely, violent ones. And his tight, straight lips suggested that he would never admit to whatever life it was he led.

And now she was closer to them, she saw that the American-looking military jacket the second man wore slung over his shoulder was, in fact, a Russian military jacket. It had a Russian military badge sewn at the top of the right arm.

But it was the badge that made her catch her breath. The badge was an embroidered wolf's head. The white outlines of the creature were embossed on to a black background. The wolf was snarling. Anna recognised it at once as the badge of the OMON special forces.

She paused, too close to them to walk away and pretend she hadn't seen them. The badge, like the MVD insignia she'd seen outside the apartment block, was a red warning light, but it represented something far more dangerous than the MVD. The wolf demonstrated the man was in some section of the OMON, the dreaded paramilitary force attached to Russia's security services. The men who were recruited into this force were greatly feared, trained to the highest degree in physical combat. They were reared through their training like fighting dogs. Many of them had been formed into special brigades in the brutal war in Chechnya in order to commit the numerous, inhumane atrocities there. They were killers, torturers, rapists, who cared neither for the sex nor age of their victims in pursuit of absolute control and humiliation.

Anna nodded at them curtly and walked on with an apparent calm, avoiding their stares. But inside her head her mind was racing. What was an OMON special forces officer doing here, in an insignificant village with a few houses, two hundred miles north of Krasnoyarsk?

Maybe there were twenty thousand like him in the whole of Russia, but not much more than that. So why was he here? She sensed her pulse quickening. Perhaps it was a coincidence, she told herself, and no more than that. It must be another coincidence. Her entry into the country had been seamless.

But she felt herself sweating under the work overalls and the quilt jacket. She pulled her hat down lower, from some obscure instinct for anonymity. She knew she was in danger of starting to imagine things now; alone in the presence of people. The looks in the faces of others, even the villagers here, began to insinuate themselves into her consciousness. Were they looking at her too? Were they seeing through her, into her? Into Valentina Asayev, or into someone else, the person she really was? Did they know? She shivered, though not from the cold. She had to bring herself back to the present, to focus on the real, not the imagined. She shook herself out of her thoughts and began to think of what she had to do.

By the time the captain and the few passengers who'd disembarked had all re-boarded the *Rossiya*, the darkness of the short night was approaching. She saw that the captain was lit up on the bridge, silhouetted against the window. And she could see he was lit up in other ways, too – drunk, it looked like, even from this distance. She could see that he was holding a bottle in his hand that didn't seem to have a label. The second mate was at the wheel, receiving the captain's orders. Then she heard the loud clanking of the chain coming up from the floor of the river and locking back into the hawses like the metal trap of a prison gate.

And at the last minute, coming across the silver moonlit water in an aluminium launch that glinted in the moon's mysterious light, she saw the man with the wolf badge emblazoned on his shoulder. He was standing up in the boat, alone apart from the boatman. She didn't know what had become of Ivan. He must have boarded via another boat, before the Wolf.

CHAPTER TWELVE

ANNA DECIDED TO stay on deck after the *Rossiya* left its mooring and had departed from Tomonovo. From the guard rail she watched the last of the sun's livid orange hangover fade into a dull grey-pink beyond the Urals to the West.

She stayed in the lee of some davits built to hold non-existent lifeboats. She remained there for several hours as the temperature dropped to near freezing. She was motionless, sprung for some action as yet unknown. Her training, repressed since the line at the hiring office, was bursting to be released. It was as if she were waiting to be attacked.

The first time she looked at her watch she saw it was now after one o'clock in the morning, but still she remained. It was icy up on the ship's superstructure and a cold wind was coming down the river from the north. But still she waited motionless.

Most of the women had turned in for the night, but there was a group of four or five men playing cards and drinking on the cold deck. They had a small wood burner flaring beside them. She envied its warmth. Once the sky had receded into a purple blackness and there emerged a million stars, Anna sought a place away from the guard rails, out of sight of inquisitive eyes. She sat or coiled herself in the cold darkness, her back against a bulkhead, her feet placed apart, ready to spring in the face of an attacker. From here nobody could approach her from the rear and she could see if anyone was coming towards her.

And now, after hours in the darkness, there was a figure, just as she'd expected. It was coming up the steps from below, up the staircase that led down to the women's area. From the height and bulk of the figure she knew it was Ivan, even if she hadn't expected him. She realised she'd been expecting he would come for her either here or in the hold, maybe both. Clearly he had gone to the hold first and, not finding her there, had come back up to the deck.

The broad silhouette of the foreman stopped at the top of the staircase, his big head turning around as his eyes adjusted to the darkness. Eventually he must either have seen her dark shadow by the bulkhead, or gone there because he couldn't penetrate the shadows and had deduced her presence by a process of elimination. He walked towards her with a swaying gait that could either be the macho slope of a predator or simply caused by drink.

'It's cold out here,' he said, when he'd approached and was standing over her, six feet four inches of male threat and ugly stench.

'Yes it is cold,' she replied. She got to her feet. 'I was about to go below and get some sleep.'

'Why all of a sudden?' He moved in front of her,

blocking her way past him. Close up, she smelled his sweat and the topped-up alcohol on his breath. 'Why not have a drink with me?' he said in a voice that contained no invitation, just command. 'That'll warm you up.'

He drew a bottle of vodka from the pocket of his coat like a weapon from a sheath. Then he grinned in the darkness at her and she saw his yellow teeth in the moonlight.

She looked down at the label-free bottle in his hand. 'All right,' she said. 'I'll have a drink with you. But I'll get my own bottle.' She turned to go past him. She heard his hollow laugh. But she couldn't make out his expression in the blackness. Then she felt his big hand stop her passing him as he placed it deliberately across her chest. She tensed to strike him, but he spoke.

'I've got another bottle,' he said triumphantly. 'If you drink this, you're a real hard case, Valentina,' he added. He drew out another bottle from deep inside his thick jacket, ceremonially, as before. 'Take it. Home-made vodka,' he said. 'I wouldn't say it was the best, but . . .' He uncorked his bottle and raised it to her. She took the second bottle, felt its cold, brittle glass in her hand, and looked past him.

Anna watched the silhouettes of the men further along the deck. She saw their shadow shapes hauling themselves to their feet. A shake of hands. Quietness. As she looked, she saw they were leaving. Was that Ivan's intention? No witnesses for what he planned to do? Were they under his orders? Highly likely. Whatever the case, she was going to have to deal with Ivan on her own and there would be no witnesses to what she would have to do with him, either way.

She clutched on to the bottle he had given her and slowly uncorked it, popping the cork in the darkness with a sound like a child's toy gun. 'So what are we drinking to?' she asked slowly. As far as she could see behind him, they were now completely alone on the deck.

'Why not to us?' he said, yellow teeth bared like an animal, and she felt his intent like a bad smell.

'Why not,' she replied. 'To us, then.'

They both tipped the bottles to their lips and drank. She felt the raw, home-made vodka sear her throat.

She saw now that he'd brought two blankets with him that were draped over his shoulders. They were what had made him look even bigger. 'Get under these,' he commanded, throwing them on the deck against the bulkhead. 'Stay nice and warm,' he added in the same leering tone of voice.

She did as she was told and he pushed in beside her underneath the thin warmth the blankets offered.

'We'll keep each other warm,' he said.

They both leaned against the bulkhead. There were no words between them. Ivan drank steadily and in big gulps, like a man who intended to get very drunk. The silence between them lifted the noise of the ship into her consciousness for the first time since the first twelve hours of the voyage. Theirs was a long silence. The great, dark, empty land passed by in silent witness.

'Either we can make this easy,' he said at last, 'or you'll pay the price.'

She didn't reply immediately, as if she were giving his proposal some thought. 'All right then,' she said finally. 'When we finish the vodka, you can do what you like.'

'That's better,' he snarled, and drank hugely.

They sat with the kind of silence between them that only presaged some violent act.

Finally, when he was halfway down the vodka in his bottle, he said, 'I bet you want to know who that was I was talking to. At the village.'

'No. What does it matter?'

'You're not curious enough, that's why,' he said.

'It doesn't pay to be curious,' she replied. 'I saw his badge, if that's what you want to know. If it was a real one.'

'Oh, it was real.'

'So what's he doing in this dump, then?'

He laughed again, a reckless, cruel sound. 'The SOBR unit of OMON elite commandos. He's on an assignment tracking some highly dangerous criminals.'

'Has there been another Siberian serial killer out here?' she asked facetiously. 'Gorging himself on human flesh?'

'You really are a tough bitch, aren't you,' he replied and tried to see her expression in the darkness.

Then when she didn't respond he drank and looked around the dark, empty deck. 'He didn't say exactly why he was here . . .' He paused. 'But don't worry, I didn't show him the picture of you.'

'I'm not a highly dangerous criminal, am I?' she answered. But it was good, she thought, that he hadn't shown the man with the wolf on his shoulder her picture

– if, that is, he was telling her the truth. If he was, then there was only Ivan who had seen it. And only Ivan she would have to deal with. 'So it doesn't matter if you did show him, does it?' she said.

He tilted the last dregs of the vodka into his wide, broken mouth and threw the bottle sideways over the guard rail. He didn't see where it went and, above the ship's noise, they didn't hear the cracking of the glass as it bounced on the rail or the splash it made in the river.

Then he reached over her, roughly shoving her against the bulkhead. He came up into a kneeling position over her, towering above her head, his legs either side of hers, and he began trying to pull the quilt jacket off her shoulders. With his other hand he started to loosen the belt around his trousers. 'You'd better make this easy,' he said.

Anna raised the free hand that held the bottle by its neck and smashed the glass against the bulkhead behind her. Whipping the bottle round with all her force, she drove the jagged edges into his face.

Ivan screamed and loosened his grip on her jacket. She threw him off, but he was on her again before she could get completely free, his hand at her throat. In the darkness, with his other hand, he was frantically searching for her arm which held the broken bottle. She jammed it again under his flailing arm, once, twice – maybe more, she didn't know; she was fighting for her life now. And once, certainly, she felt the broken glass dig into something softer than flesh. She'd struck him in the yielding plasma of his eye socket. As part of the jagged edges of the bottle struck one of his eyes he let out a roar of pain and fury. He lunged wildly at his face for protection. But he still kept his other hand at her throat.

She made a sudden duck and a roll of her body, an instinctive aikido move. Her training was now released in a pent-up flood of aggression. Her move left his hand suddenly loose, without its downward pressure on her throat, and she found she could pull away, half rolling, half kicking against him with her feet like a wild animal. She sprang up immediately, on her feet in a second as he was getting on to his. 'I'll kill you, you bitch,' he shouted. And she knew for sure that he would.

As he got up in the blackness of the deck, she chopped him with the edge of her hand, precisely at the side of his neck, and he dropped like a dead man. Then she kicked the side of his head hard with the heavy working boots.

There was the silence between them again, behind which the engine's throb was like a distant, reassuring landscape. She crouched back down in the shadow of the bulkhead and listened over the noise of the engines. For the first time in twenty-four hours, as she heard the engines again, and the clank and rattle of the ship, it felt as if the world itself were being shaken to death. But now she was grateful for the noise.

She crouched in the shadows of the moon for maybe a minute or more. When she was sure they were truly alone apart from the nagging, guttural sounds of the ship, she dragged the foreman's heavy, inert body to the guard rail and leaned it against the rails, supporting it with both her arms. She was up close to his face, slumped forward over it as she dragged the body, and she smelled his rank, animal sweat and felt his blood congealing on her face. Then, with a huge effort, she heaved the considerable bulk of his body on to the rail, swaying momentarily, until she used its weight to drop it over the side. If he wasn't dead now, she thought, he wouldn't last more than a minute or two in the icy water.

Anna crouched down again, hidden this time in the shadow of some davits that leaned over the guard rails like hangman's posts. She listened again, but could pick out no living sound. Only the friendly engine and the shaking ship made any noise at all. And beyond the banks of the river, the empty, unseeing green of the *taiga* grinned its all-consuming nothingness in the light of the moon.

As best she could, she gathered the glass fragments together and threw them and the broken bottle into the fast-flowing water after him. Then she wiped her face and the deck around the bulkhead where she guessed the stains of his blood would be, using the blankets to mop up whatever was there in the moon's darkness. Finally she dropped the blankets too, over the side, and they fell silently into the churning moon-white wash at the *Rossiya*'s stern.

CHAPTER THIRTEEN

S HE HAD HIS blood on her sleeve. And she had the spit that dribbled freely from his dying lips as she'd dragged him to the rail. During the night as she lay in the women's hold, she could almost feel him alive on her arm through his excretions, a crawling, vengeful facsimile of him in blood and mucus.

She hadn't been able to wash it out properly on the deck and down below in the latrines she couldn't afford to be seen washing her coat. Not with a missing, dead man around. Or no longer around.

As the dawn of the third day rose at just before three o'clock on the *Rossiya*, creeping through the cracks in the hatches and glowing through a dirty porthole on the far side of where she lay, she considered her changed circumstances. First, she wondered how long it would be before they found out that the foreman was missing. And then, she wondered if his body would be taken by the current to the side of the river, somewhere remote, where it wouldn't be discovered for a long while, or ever. Or worse, if it would land up near a village, or be discovered by a hunting or fishing party, or by trappers checking their mink traps, and be found in a matter of days or hours.

But, worst of all, she wondered if it would follow the current, a nightmare of a corpse that stayed in the centre of the stream and tracked both her and the ship as it headed north. As she lay on the hard bench, she imagined Ivan's dead body following her as he had done in life.

She finally got up off the bench and picked her way among the sleeping bodies towards the dirty light of the porthole. In the thin illumination of the early rays of sun, she saw the bloodstains still on her sleeve. They were dry and cracked and she was able to scrape some of the crust of them away with her fingernails. Then she saw some oil leaking from a pipe that led down through the deck, perhaps into the engine room, and she began to wipe the drips of oil with her fingers on to the sleeve of the arm which had held the broken bottle. When she was satisfied the oil concealed the dried blood, she looked out at the flat grey light of dawn.

What she saw through the porthole was a landscape beginning to change as the Russian *taiga* began to lose its grip and they neared the tundra. The subarctic forest was now different, thicker yet more stark than the country they'd passed so far. Up here, the air had turned colder, dryer, and the forest was even more supreme. She'd felt all that change on the deck the night before as she'd waited for Ivan, drank with him, and then killed him. Now, as she looked out at the landscape, she could see no evidence of man's existence. No history, even, of man's presence. The nights of light were now visibly lengthening and would soon become one endless day as they steamed inexorably north.

Though she wanted some clean air, she decided to stay in the sleeping hold as the dawn changed to day and the morning progressed in the semi-gloom of the hold. The other women slowly rose from sleep, in twos and threes, unhurried and apparently untroubled by anything their lives contained. They divided up loaves of bread, brewed tea, talked in low voices. They were completely uninterested in either the bleakness or anything else outside the ship.

It was safer now to be in this group of women, she decided. No more going out alone. She needed company and the slow fatalism she felt among the women around her seemed to be of a quality that attracted no attention. If it hadn't been for Ivan singling her out at the hiring office, she, too, might have passed unnoticed like the others.

She returned to the bench, shared her own few provisions with two women near her, and then she sat or lay listlessly on the bench as the other women did, hour after hour. The day crawled by with punishing slowness.

At just before midday, the metal door to the hold opened and she saw one of the crew members standing in the entrance. He stayed stock still by the door. Behind him the door clanged shut like a brutal announcement.

She watched him looking around the large space, studying the faces of the women. He wasn't more than nineteen years old and was smoking a cigarette. He wore a blue beret and a heavy wool jacket with big plastic buttons, the informal uniform of the crew. He seemed to Anna to be trying to look arrogant and self-possessed in the roomful of women. But it was a thin attempt at

169

self-confidence. He could have been a youth entering a brothel for the first time, nervously surveying the merchandise.

Like the others, Anna didn't move.

Finally she heard the youth say in an over-pumped voice, 'Valentina Asayev!' It was her name, the name in her papers.

She kept her eyes averted as she stood up. 'Yes?'

'You're to come with me.'

His ill-founded pomposity was absurd, she thought. But another feeling in the pit of her stomach wrenched her back into the situation.

'Who wants me?'

'The Captain, that's who. Come on!'

She walked across the floor among the semi-comatose women and stopped in front of him. She looked him full in the face and he blushed.

'You're the one they're looking for,' he said. 'Come with me.'

She turned around and saw the eyes of the other women stirring and turned on her, their expressions a mixture of relief and indignation.

Anna didn't move from the spot in front of him. 'Why?' she said insolently and the boy looked momentarily wrong-footed.

There was a ripple of laughter from the other women in the hold at her confidence.

'Never mind why,' he said. 'You're wanted above.' Then he stuttered, 'I don't know why. I was just sent.'

He was crumbling before her eyes. Then he stepped

back and indicated with his hand that he wished her to precede him to the metal door.

Up on the deck, it was a relief to be in the sparkling clean air after a night and a whole morning in the rancid hold. He took her arm above the elbow, not roughly but not gently either.

'My name is Yuri,' he said sympathetically.

'Well, Yuri, it's a beautiful day,' she said.

'Is it?' he said.

Then he smiled nervously at her and led her up a companionway, along the deck, and stopped outside another metal door beneath the bridge. 'You're to go in there,' he said.

There were three men inside the room. It was a small office, by the look of it. Then she heard the crackling of static and she realised it was the radio room.

All three men sat behind a table. The captain sat to the left, the man she'd seen with Ivan, the man with the embroidered special forces wolf on his shoulder, sat in the centre, and another man she hadn't seen before sat to the right.

On shelves above where they were sitting were charts of the river, updated every few months to keep up with constant changes in the silting channel, and there were a few bits and pieces of what looked like radio equipment, spares maybe. The room was small. The table was five feet long and there were only two feet at either end of it. There were two steps to the chair that she was to sit on, facing the men across the table.

'Sit down,' the captain said. 'Papers!'

She sat in the chair and reached inside the quilt jacket and took out her identity papers, the internal passport and her qualifications for the saw mill. In the bright sunlight shining through a porthole from the south of where the ship was steaming, he studied the documents closely, then passed them to the special forces officer. The Wolf. He, too, studied them for a long time and then put them down on the table between them.

'Why are you here?' the Wolf said.

For a moment she was confused. Here in the room, or here on the ship?

'For work,' she replied, her mind clearing.

'Where did you learn to be a machine operator?'

'Bratsk.'

'Your . . . birthplace.'

'Yes.'

The Wolf was silent for a long time, staring at her as if to force her to admit a mistake.

Anna thought back six years to the time before she had defected. Back then, before she had met the Englishman for whom she had left Russia and her past, and before she had faced the final disillusionment with her father, she had dated one of these men in special forces, considerably senior to the one in front of her now. He'd been a man in the Alpha Group, Russia's most highly specialised military force.

'Is there a problem with my papers?' she asked, in order to break the spell of mistrust he was trying to create.

'Apparently not,' the Wolf replied. 'Where is the man who hired you?' he said casually. 'The foreman Ivan?'

'I don't know. I haven't seen him since yesterday on the ship.'

'You saw him last night,' he stated.

'And I hope it's the last time I see him.' She decided now to sound defiant.

'Oh yes? And why is that?'

'He tried to attack me, that's why.'

'Attack?'

'Rape, then.'

She saw the captain smirk.

The Wolf leaned across the table at her. 'And what did you do?'

'I ran away.'

He snorted.

'You ran away! On a ship! You ran away from a man who's six-feet four inches and built like a tank!' The Wolf laughed, then his mouth pursed in an angry line. 'So it was as easy as that, eh?' He sat back in his seat, as if the verdict was now clear.

She shrugged. 'It was pitch-dark. He'd drunk a great deal. I personally saw him drink a bottle of vodka. Who knows what else he'd drunk before that. Yes, it was easy.'

'He's a big man. A strong man,' the Wolf said.

'But not a smart man,' she replied. 'He was dead drunk. Perhaps that's why he attacked me. Who knows? Maybe he attacks a lot of women.'

The Wolf turned to the captain. 'There's too much drinking on this ship,' he said, now wishing to find another avenue of blame.

'Yes, major,' the captain answered him. 'There's not much else.'

The Wolf looked at him angrily, as if his rank were not public property. Then he turned again to Anna.

'Some men saw you drinking with him last night. On the deck.'

'He threatened me. He said if I didn't have a drink with him, he'd rape me. I was hoping he'd be too drunk by the time he'd finished the bottle he had. That's why.'

'What happened . . . when you ran away?'

'I hid on the deck at first, to make sure he wasn't following me. Then when I was sure he'd gone or fallen asleep, I made my way to the hold where the women sleep.'

'You know where he is now?'

'No. Why should I?'

'Because he's disappeared, that's why,' the Wolf snarled.

Anna looked back into his eyes.

'Then he's probably in the river, isn't he.' she said.

CHAPTER FOURTEEN

STANDING ON TOP of the world was something Burt Miller was accustomed to, but only in a purely metaphorical sense, as the head of the world's most powerful private intelligence agency Cougar. Actually standing on top of the world, however, above the Arctic Circle and within a few hundred miles of the North Pole, was a new experience.

Wearing a knee-length, shining dark brown sable coat from Saks in New York, Miller didn't exactly cut the figure of an average leader, or even wealthy patron, of the geography field expedition that his presence on the uninhabited island purported to be connected with. And standing on a deserted and freezing pebble beach on this uninhabited island in the far north-east of Finland, the incongruity of his attire seemed especially glaring.

Some of his so-called 'students' – in reality, employees of Cougar brought on to the island – had speculated on the cost of the coat and came to the conclusion that it couldn't have left a lot of change out of a hundred thousand dollars. One of them, a 25-year-old Jewish New Yorker with a bob of black hair and an attitude by the name of Charlie, airily claimed to have seen such coats before. But her grandfather had been in the fur trade a few streets downtown from Broadway. The other so-called geography students at Burt Miller's icy mission HQ – and his agent ex-filtration point for Anna Resnikov – looked at the coat with a mixture of awe and ignorance.

And then there was Burt's fur hat, similarly beyond the financial reach of a university professor – which was Burt's current identity for the purpose of this period when he needed an uninhabited island in the north of the world. He was Professor Burt Miller (though he'd actually given himself another name, not his own); he had acquired all the fake qualifications, he had essays published in scholarly, if obscure, American journals and, to round off the fiction, he could show off the necessary plaudits of 'fellow' academics in the field to anyone who cared to ask. He had even taken the trouble for the most vital mission of his life, as he was letting it be known it was, to acquire a Chair at a small mid-western university.

As for his other accessories – the gold watch, for example – a keen eye might have spotted these, too, as excessive for the location, let alone for the academic profession.

But Burt Miller seemed unabashed by the figure he cut on the deserted beach and it was a mercy, Larry thought, that in this godforsaken spot at the top of the earth there was nobody outside Burt's religiously loyal Cougar employees who could wonder at the coat and other luxuries and consequently question his boss's false credentials.

Legs astride on the smooth, round pebbles, his fur boot-shod feet crunching the stones, and his large stomach pushing the coat out in a comfortable globe of priceless fur, Burt Miller watched through high-powered binoculars towards a line of three trawlers returning from still higher up in the Arctic. Judging by the low line of their gunwhales, he noted, they were returning with a good catch.

'Three days . . .' Burt said in contemplation, and in a repetition of the recently given answer from the man standing next to him.

Larry had arrived on the island only hours before Miller, after the urgent summons that had brought him racing to the north. Landing from Mongolia first at Ankara and from there on to Helsinki in one of Miller's private jets, he had finally reached the island by another flight north in a small prop-driven plane and then a trawler — another of Cougar's possessions — which was fitted out with high-powered satellite and other general spy equipment.

Larry was a heavy-set, tall brute of a figure with a crew cut and an ugly scar down one side of his face. He had eyes like diamond cutters and each of his hands, when they weren't thrust in the pockets of an army-issue jacket, were big enough to pick up a basketball. He was always the sharp end of Burt's operations — some might say the violent end. But this afternoon on the freezing pebble beach he looked every inch the practical and, indeed, sensible military man, down to a white goose-down polar military jacket used by Canada's Arctic regiment. But his expression told a different story. Lines of worry and anger that betrayed a loss of control over Anna's mission crossed his face. He sucked his teeth and wondered if Anna Resnikov had lost her mind.

'Three days, yes, Burt. Three days if the ice isn't too

bad,' Larry replied. 'This time of year, it's still tricky up here.'

'Yes?' Miller queried.

'Otherwise you need an ice-breaker and only the Russians have them. The Russians have twenty ice-breakers, seven of them nuclear-powered. The US has only one active,' he added with a trace of bitterness.

'I don't see any ice,' Burt replied gruffly, waving the binoculars about wildly as if some iceberg invisible to the naked eye might hove into view.

'Here, no,' Larry said patiently, though a careful listener might have detected a grinding of teeth. 'Up here in the north of Norway and Finland a combination of the tail of the Gulf Stream and a continental climate that comes in from north America keeps the sea free through-out the year. But there,' Larry pointed to the east and south, out into the sea which had now been turned a deep blue by the cloud-free sky, 'out there in the Barents Sea and, beyond that, the Kara Sea above the Yenisei river, none of that applies. Even though it's slightly south of where we're standing, the Kara's frozen solid in winter. Impassable without a breaker. This time of year the ice is breaking up, sure, but that's more dangerous, if anything, for a normal vessel. You still need a way cleared by an ice-breaker for an ordinary ship to get between the floes and growlers that come down from the north when the wind's coming from up there.'

Burt seemed momentarily at a loss that his own com-pany, Cougar Intelligence Applications, didn't possess a nuclear-powered ice-breaker of its own. After all, Cougar produced a great deal of military hardware, including satellites and unmanned drones, as well as rivalling the CIA itself in its intelligence-gathering activities. But ice-breaking hadn't been a necessity – until now, perhaps. A flash of anxiety at this lapse crossed his brow.

Burt lowered the binoculars. 'So that's three days to the mouth of the Yenisei, right?'

'Best to allow four, probably, to the Yenisei itself,' Larry answered, again patiently, even though this informa-tion had been conveyed to Burt on several occasions, in lengthy briefings, in the several months before they'd left American soil. 'There's a long run in to the mouth of the river itself. A ship comes down from the Arctic Ocean which we're looking at now, into the Kara Sea and then the mouth of the Yenisei.'

Was the old man more worried than he thought? Larry wondered. Burt certainly hadn't wanted Anna in there, inside Russia, in the first place. But she'd insisted it had to be her. And now she'd gone out on her own, against all instructions, disobeying Miller openly. And with the MVD by now undoubtedly somewhere behind her.

'Four, in case the weather's bad,' Larry explained. 'And depending on which of the pick-up points she goes for.'

'And where's the nearest pick-up point to here?' Burt queried. 'That's where she'll go.'

Larry imagined that this statement – as if one of fact – had something to do with Burt's self-proclaimed 'Line to God'. But he took out of his jacket a satellite map of Cougar's that showed the top of the world.

It demonstrated a great expanse of ice around the

North Pole and, circling half of this Arctic ice-cap, was Russian Siberian territory. The other half of the circle around the ice-cap was divided roughly between the American state of Alaska, Canada, Danish-owned Greenland, and Norway and Finland.

'There.' Larry pointed. He pinned his finger to a point at the edge of the Kara Sea, a promontory where the northern Siberian coast turned to the right for another four thousand miles, almost as far as Alaska. Near his finger, a single town by the name of Dikson was marked. 'That's the northernmost port,' Larry explained, 'but it's barely more than a jumble of warehouses and barracks.'

'Dikson?' Burt said. 'That's where the Russians have been building their new transportable nuclear reactor.'

'That's right.'

Larry now withdrew a more detailed map of the area. The pick-up point was about a hundred miles eastwards of this northernmost town of Dikson, in a small gulf.

'That's where she'll go,' Burt affirmed, without really looking at the map and certainly without inviting any possibility of demurral.

'If she can make it that far,' Larry replied, knowing better than to openly doubt Burt's pronouncements. 'And if she isn't already in some torture cell in Moscow,' he added cruelly. He drew himself up. 'Look, Burt.' He pointed at the map. 'Norilsk and the Putorana mountains are three hundred miles south of the pick-up point. Three hundred miles of nothing that she'd have to cross. Dudinka is slightly less far than that. But it would be much more dangerous to try to pick her up from there. If she's decided to go through with the mission as originally planned, then if she succeeds, and if she survives, she's still got around three hundred miles to the pick-up, north all the way, nothing by way of transport and in the middle of a highly militarised and hostile territory.'

Burt thought about this, but not for long. 'That's where she'll go,' he repeated. 'It's the closest to us here. That's where she'll go.' Then he turned sharply to Larry. 'Now you look, Larry. She's gone against orders. But don't start fretting on me. We either work up a sweat about it or we work to get her out, just as planned. So let's deal with what's happening, shall we?' After fixing Larry with a cold stare, his face broke into its habitual grin, as it always did when well-laid plans had broken down and improvisation was all that was left. He even clapped Larry on the back with a fur-gloved hand. 'So. When's the earliest possible rendezvous there?' he said, and pointed at the pick-up point.

'Tenth of June. After that, every three days, but it gets riskier each time.'

'But we have that all arranged, haven't we?' Burt objected. 'Nothing's changed in terms of our plans, as far as I know.'

Larry paused to compose his answer. 'No. Nothing's changed. We have the three ships, two based in Hamburg, one in Svarlborg. All old tubs that have been regular visitors to the Yenisei for years in the summer months when they pick up timber there. There have been no name changes on any of the vessels, the Russians have seen all the papers they carry before. But they're ours now in all but name. Each ship will make journeys to and fro from Hamburg, coal on the way to Siberia, timber on the return. With three ships going both ways, it means we can pass not too far from the pick-up every three days. And on each ship, of course, we have our own teams. Small boats that look like the kind of local fishing vessels you find up in the Kara, but which can travel at four times the speed and pick someone up off a beach.' He paused. 'So, yes, nothing's changed.' He looked up and out to sea to the east. 'The first vessel should be making its way into the Barents Sea tomorrow, escorted by a Russian ice-breaker. That's the only way they're allowed to go. The Russians say it's the necessity of having an ice-breaker accompany each ship, which is partly true. But they're also there as an escort to make sure nothing happens the Russians don't like. The route to the Yenisei will take the ship past the island of Novaya Zemlya where the Russians have tested their nuclear weapons in the past, and then into the Kara. They either pick up the timber in Dikson, or they can go on into the Yenisei as far as Igarka.'

'Then that's fine, isn't it,' Burt said, as if they were deciding on a venue for lunch.

The two men began to walk back along the beach to give the morning briefing. They remained in silence. But, to Larry, Anna's mission now seemed little more than a suicide run.

And twenty minutes later, back at field expedition headquarters higher up from the beach, Burt also seemed deep in thought, preoccupied by the same questions, perhaps, and there seemed to Larry an uncharacteristic sense of doom about him that his best operative was now committed on Russian territory with a net that was sure to be closing around her already.

There were three prefabricated huts higher up from the beach. Against his own explicitly dictated regulations on the subject, Burt nevertheless called the geography field expedition headquarters the 'Arctic Psy Ops' centre. From these three huts, day and night, the members of the so-called geography field team Burt had gathered together from the youngest employees of Cougar's Russian intelligence unit went about the normal activities of a university field trip above the Arctic Circle.

But all the time what they were actually monitoring was shipping activity across the maritime border in Russian waters, as well as Russian air presence in the area. They tapped into Russian communications signals coming from the military base near Murmansk and other places on Russian soil. They zeroed in from Cougar's satellite on to the Russian ICBM base and nuclear research facility buried in the Putorana mountains to the east of Norilsk and the Yenisei, and they picked up snippets of coded intelligence from Krasnoyarsk that had told them, most recently, about Anna's departure on the *Rossiya*. And against Burt's explicit orders.

The geography field trip was, in fact, a full-tilt intelligence operation aimed at Russia's northernmost territorial limits above the Arctic Circle. But these territorial limits were claims only and the government in the Kremlin wished to extend them all the time. Burt and the CIA believed, in fact, that the Russians wanted to extend them as far as and even beyond the North Pole itself. And if they did that, they would be treading right on America's toes.

Only two years earlier, Vladimir Putin had personally ordered the Russian tricolour flag, this one made of titanium, to be planted on the sea bed directly beneath the North Pole itself. And the planting of the flag was achieved, with the mini-submersible the Russians used somehow managing to find its way back up again to the small hole in the ice where it had begun its descent. The other countries with an interest in the Arctic polar region apart from America – Canada, Denmark and Norway – were equally nervous about Russia's latest ambitions there.

To the so-called geography students, the real purpose of Anna's mission was concealed. It was this, Russia's proposed and vast extension of its sovereign territory beneath the North Pole, that the team believed they were there to monitor. This, and gathering intelligence concerning the nuclear reactor the Russians had built far north of the Arctic Circle; a conventional nuclear reactor in every way, except that it could be moved across ice or sea to where it was needed to power the Russians' proposed Arctic oil explorations.

To the team, there was never any mention of a Professor Vasily Kryuchkov, or of his supposed earth-shattering discovery. What they believed they were there to study on the island were Russia's next moves up to the ice cap and over the Pole towards America. And this key point of contention between Russia and the United States was an undersea mountain range called the Lomonosov

Ridge that ran from Siberia beneath the North Pole. It was said to contain a quarter of the world's remaining oil and gas and it stretched from the Siberian mainland, under the pole, and on to America's Arctic doorstep. The Kremlin had been proclaiming for some time now that it belonged to Russia and the international tribunals that judged the geology of territorial claims such as this one seemed to be bound to agree.

And now it had been established that Russia had built the world's first mobile nuclear power station, the needs of the Western intelligence agencies to know if and when it began to be dragged towards the Pole had become more urgent. In summer, it was said, it could be towed across the sea by tugs to the ice cap, while in winter it was to be dragged by tractors across the ice of the Kara Sea all the way to the Pole. For the geography students, this looming international and ecological crisis was so convincing that Anna's mission – had they known of it – could have had no greater importance. And so there had been no need to tell anyone about her real reasons to be on Russian soil, outside the closed loop of Burt's inner circle.

And yet, despite this supposed purpose of clandestine surveillance, and despite the activities of Burt's expedition on an uninhabited edge of the Polar ice cap, what any curious and possibly unwelcome eyes would have seen, had they been present to study the field expedition headquarters, was a meticulously collected and labelled set of specimens and samples made ready by the team to be returned to the biology, geology and geography depart-ments of the mid-western university that was heavily patronised by Cougar and at which Burt had acquired his temporary, and fake, Chair.

With the help of the university's principal, an arrangement had been made with the universities of Tromso in northern Norway and the university of Kuopio in Finland for eighteen Cougar students to spend the late spring and summer in the northernmost regions of Europe, next to the Russian border.

Sealed jars of different varieties of kelp, fossilised shells, the odd fragment of Ice Age mammoth tusk and bone – all these and more were stacked in an orderly way in the open area of the building, in the unlikely event that anyone came to call. There were also carefully monitored readings of sea temperature, local precipitation and even the movements of schools of fish – for which Burt had provided a 'trawler'. But, like the building, the trawler was a festoon of intelligence-gathering equipment. Monitoring fish was simply a way to observe submarine movements on the Russian side.

The building itself had been a real find, Larry had to admit that. The island had never in its history been inhabited, as far as anyone knew. There was no community structure to which Burt's team would have to become attached or with which to blend in. Out on the edge of the European continent, on the far north-eastern tip of Finland, where hundreds of islands dotted the bleak seas, the existing building was an unexpected bonus. There was no human habitation for nearly a hundred miles in any direction. There were no made roads, or even government listening stations, all of which had been slowly dismantled at the end of the Cold War.

In their long search to construct a listening and watching station in the required area, what Cougar's planners had eventually discovered on this small island was, in effect, a set of rough stone fish-preparation sheds long since abandoned in the early twentieth century. The sheds even had their own small but natural and protected harbour.

The discovery of the sheds was just one of his ubiquitous pieces of luck – or his line to God, as Burt preferred to put it. And the buildings on the island were within a few dozen miles of Russian territory.

Through academic channels, Burt had lobbied long and hard with both the governments of Norway and Finland to take over the place on a temporary, summer camp basis. Large sums of money – for academic research, no doubt – had changed hands. The Norwegian and Finnish side of the deal could only wonder at the lavish expense of converting the old and crumbling stone fish sheds into a geography camp for American students. They wished they, too, could have afforded the shipload of equipment that had come in after dark one night in the middle of April. And they put all this down to the vast sums of money available to American universities, donated by their wealthy and grateful alumni, in return for an eponymous library or sports stadium.

And perhaps also, it has to be said, the curious Norwegians and Finns assuaged their curiosity at the sums of money involved by attributing the great expense of the geography field trip to the well-known American need to bring America with them wherever Americans went.

Even when Americans found themselves within striking distance of the North Pole, it seemed, Americana came along for the ride, as if their country's familiar paraphernalia were some kind of fetish that kept them safe from harm, a womb-like comfort zone.

Now up by the prefabs, Burt asked Larry to gather the 'students' in what he called the auditorium – a bare, hastily erected structure that had been added to the sheds. The great Burt Miller was to address his employees, most of whom had never met him and, therefore, their expectations were at a heightened state. Later this afternoon, a sea plane was to pick him up and take him on to Helsinki, from where he'd make his way to London by private jet, and a conference with Adrian Carew, the MI6 chief, as well as another of the few in the know about Anna's real mission, the CIA's head of London Station.

The team in the auditorium were a mixed bunch, mostly in their twenties or early thirties; they had come up through Cougar's training programmes. For most, it was their first active service mission, as Burt called it, in order to induce a sense of the drama that didn't need inducing. There were no seats in the building and the eighteen members of Cougar's team in the Arctic Circle sat on the floor, legs crossed, and looked up at Burt as if at some visiting Indian guru who had arrived with a message of immortality to impart.

Burt stood at the head of the prefab and seemed to glow with a fur halo. 'Although you don't know all the ins and outs,' he began in his usual chatty style, 'you are all, each and every one of you, a part of an enterprise that is important not just to the prosperity of Cougar, but also to the very defence of your country and the preservation of the ecological purity of the Arctic.' His eyes travelled around the building to each and every one of the rapt audience. 'Not to mention the possibility, or even probability, that this new Russian reactor will at some time blow a fuse and inflict a nuclear catastrophe on the entire planet.'

The only four people in Cougar who knew of Anna's mission were Burt, Larry, Clay and Bob Dupont, Cougar's finance chief whose well-worn joke in the corporation was that he was the only person working at Cougar older than Burt. Even the CIA wasn't fully in on Anna's real mission, though Burt had kept its chief – who, to a large part, was Burt's own anointed appointment to the Agency – in the loop as to Cougar's presence on an uninhabited island thirty-eight miles from Russian waters. The Lomonosov Ridge beneath the Pole that the Russians were claiming, he'd warned the CIA chief, was in danger of becoming the chill venue for an actual cold war.

'In the coming month,' Burt continued, 'twenty-four hours a day, seven days a week, what you do here may avert a confrontation between Russia and America more serious than anything in the Cold War. 'He puffed out his chest and looked around the freezing room at expectant faces. 'It used to be thought that Space was where such a confrontation would take place. No more. It's right here, the Arctic. Luckily, Burt's line to God' – he chuckled – 'has given all of us here the privilege of preventing such an event. What you do here in the coming few weeks may save your world and your children's world. It may even save *the* world. Not just the lives of humanity, but also the lives of the birds on this little island of ours, the lives of the seal colony on the far side of where we sit, the life of the very moss and the molluscs which, in their own way, are the first step on the ladder of all our continued existence.'

Burt the Ecologist meets Burt the Saviour of Humanity. Burt the Spy, whose real interest lay in Professor Vasily Kryuchkov, was nowhere to be seen. 'Work hard and good luck,' he intoned, as if he'd stepped on to the set of one of the melodramatic, end-of-the-world movies which he so despised. 'I'll leave Larry now to give you the day's briefing and objectives.'

There was spontaneous applause throughout the room, even though, Larry thought, by Burt's usual standards, this was an unusually tame address. It lacked his usual fire, despite its apocalyptic scenario.

But if anyone had known what was on Burt's mind at that moment, they would not have been surprised that oratory was not his prime concern.

Later, when they were on their own again and the students had dispersed, Larry saw that Burt was greatly preoccupied.

'Above all else,' Burt said quietly to Larry as they walked back down to the beach and the waiting seaplane, 'above and beyond any other consideration, I don't want Anna to be taken by the Russians. Even if it does mean the end of our hopes of Kryuchkov. Or the end of the damned world, for that matter.'

CHAPTER FIFTEEN

ALEXEI PETROV THOUGHT long and hard about what he was going to do, as he did about most things. Compulsive actions were not a part of his character and the chaotic thoughts that habitually precede difficult decisions he was usually able to keep under control, and then disentangle. But the presence of the three American students on the ferry — as he'd ascertained they were after a day's journey north — was a temptation, nonetheless. He'd overheard them speaking excellent Russian in the restaurant and bar and they were clearly linguists, well-educated people, at any rate. But he was wary of easy temptations.

The contents of the documents which, at all times, he kept about his person were inevitably explosive, or Bachman wouldn't have been killed, in Petrov's belief. He'd decided almost beyond doubt that the German's death and the concealment of the documents must be linked in some way. The disappearance of the woman Valentina Asayev, however, who was now just under twelve hours in front of the faster ferry Petrov was on, was another matter. She might or might not be a piece of the problem. Both possibilities existed and he would decide that when, and if, he caught up with her.

But it was a fact that the American students could, in theory anyway, be approached and given a very limited sight of one or two of the equations, perhaps, that peppered the documents. Neutral, non-Russian eyes. It appeared like a gift from the skies. But before he did so he decided to look at the Russian prose the documents contained, one or two paragraphs of which he remembered were lost in the sea of equations. When he'd looked at the documents for the first time, in his apartment, he'd been so overwhelmed by the incomprehensible nature of them that he realised now he had not bothered to read the Russian writing with any focus.

Petrov walked along the upper deck to a covered area where he kept his rucksack and where he'd bedded down in a sleeping bag for the first night on the river. Apart from those who, like himself, were travelling on the deck, the deck was packed from bow to stern with cars, containers, packages large and small, crates of vegetables and rack after rack of boxes containing mainly alcohol. The latter was the cheapest and easiest way to turn a profit in the north.

He sat in the shadow of one of the ferry's lifeboats, checked he was alone, and withdrew the waterproof sachet that contained the documents from his inside pocket. He took the first sheet out and put the others back. At the top of the first page, what he saw was the first of two paragraphs of prose, written in handwriting, like the equations. The actual paper itself, he now realised, was clearly torn out of a notebook. There was no sign that this was some properly prepared or academic study. It was a scribble. The whole effect was of a man in a hurry to get whatever it was down on paper before someone or something prevented him. Maybe he'd been working in a dark room, Petrov thought, or was being watched and had just minutes to write what he'd written.

At the top of the first page, Petrov read the Russian scrawl, first checking once again that he was alone on this part of the deck.

As has been well known since the 1960s, Petrov read, *muon catalysed fusion involves the sub-atomic particle capturing two hydrogen atoms and fusing them. What has restricted the commercial development of this process, however, has been the uneconomic nature of producing muons with pions.*

Petrov stared at the paragraph without really seeing it. His mind glazed over. He realised that he was none the wiser than before. He had no clue what a 'muon' or a 'pion' were, for one thing, and only a very hazy idea of what 'fusion' meant, or even 'catalysed'.

He withdrew the waterproof packet from his pocket, re-inserted the first page and took out the last page, on which was the only other writing in prose. But when he looked at this paragraph, all it seemed to be doing was explaining, in even more obtuse scientific language, the process described in the equation that immediately preceded it. He replaced the page in the waterproof packet and put it back into his pocket. He sat and stared over the wilderness that was sliding past the ship. An eagle was dipping its wings high up in the sky and, above it, another circled. Mates or potential mates, perhaps.

Then he thought again of the Americans. Could he dare to ask them, perhaps, what 'muon catalysed fusion' meant? It seemed innocent enough, if it had been known since the 1960s. But he smiled at the prospect. It didn't exactly sound like a topic of conversation that could be casually raised between strangers on a boat on its way to the Arctic Circle.

But Petrov decided, nevertheless, to return below decks and see if he could at least become acquainted with the three presumed students. And then he realised that his Evenk background might be just the way to do that. They were tourists on a trip through his people's land, after all. Educated Americans, such as they were, would surely be interested in someone who was from the sparsely populated area into which they were going. They had their own Indians in America, didn't they? Well, maybe he could attach some of that mysticism to himself. On his way below decks, he stopped, returned to where his rucksack lay, and picked up the deer-skin drum his grandfather Gannyka had given him.

In the bar area which was really just an extension of the restaurant on a deck that spanned the width of the ferry, Petrov found the three Americans sitting together at a round metal table, the same as usual when they weren't gazing at the endless green panorama from up on deck. And that was seldom. For a moment, he thought about this. For tourists in Siberia, they seemed to spend a lot of their time below decks. Odd. Most tourists were out on deck the whole time. He looked at them and saw they were drinking bottled juices of different colours and, as usual too, they had their guidebooks and a map with them.

He went to the bar and ordered a beer. When it came, he paid and remained leaning with his back against the bar and looked around the restaurant as if he were trying to find someone he knew.

At first, he felt rather than saw the three Americans. They seemed to shrink into themselves. Their shoulders may have hunched forward infinitesimally, their heads may have bowed, or it may have been that Petrov felt – sensed – their attitude becoming more private when he was present and once he'd started to take in the whole deck, them included.

That was strange, he thought momentarily. Vaguely he'd felt a similar sensation when he'd seen them on one or two occasions previously on the ferry. They seemed to withdraw from him, close in, put up a wall, as though it was something personal between them and him. He was alerted to something about their withdrawn behaviour, but he didn't know to what. Theirs was the attitude of people who didn't wish to catch his eye, and who had something to hide.

He half dismissed the sensation from his mind. Maybe they were nervous about the trip northwards, he thought. Perhaps they realised how out on a limb they were up here and trusted no one they met. There were no other foreigners on the first ferry of the year. Yet it seemed to Petrov that it was only him and not the other Russian passengers who evinced this reaction from them. Finally, he walked across to their table, clutching the beer in his right hand, and stopped beside them. None of them looked up at first, until the woman raised her head.

'Tourists?' he said.

The two men could no longer avoid him. They, too, looked up at Petrov now.

'Yes,' the woman replied.

'From America?' Petrov asked cheerfully.

'That's right.' The woman again. Not unfriendly, but not welcoming either.

'My name is Alexei. Perhaps I can explain something about where we're going?' Petrov said, and then immediately thought that they would suspect he wanted money. 'I'm not a guide, or even a fake guide,' he joked hastily. 'But I saw you and thought, well, I know this country. Northern Siberia. My family is from the Evenk people who live up where we're going. Perhaps you've heard of the Evenk? I'm half Evenk myself and I know the area. I'm visiting my grandfather up in their reindeer-herding lands. He's ill.'

He thought perhaps he'd said too much and he noted again how easily using the story about his grandfather came to him now.

They didn't reply, just stared at him in what seemed like either confusion or consternation.

Petrov pulled up a spare chair. 'May I?' he asked.

'Of course,' the woman replied. 'Why don't you join us? We'd be interested in anything about the country here. It's a visit very few people in America have made.'

Petrov sat down at the table. The woman seemed to be

recovering her equilibrium better than the two men, he thought, though he was still at a loss as to why they were nervous of him in the first place.

Eileen shifted her chair a little so that Petrov would have room at the table.

'My name's Alexei,' Petrov repeated. 'But my Evenk name is Munnukan. It means "hare".'

'Eileen,' the woman said. 'And this is Clay. And Sky.'

'So what brings you here?' Petrov asked. 'It's an out of-the-way place for Russians, even. We don't get many foreigners up here.'

'That's probably because it's so difficult to get a pass,' Eileen replied. 'We had the trip booked before we arrived in Russia, but then they told us in Krasnoyarsk that our passes were invalid. So we had to start over again.'

Petrov laughed. 'That's typical,' he said. 'And you had to pay more, no doubt.'

'That's right.' Still the woman talking, he noted, and she was tense, though less than the others. The other two hadn't spoken, even to introduce themselves with a handshake.

But what Petrov didn't know was that, for the three Americans, it was indeed a moment of extreme tension. As soon as they'd seen Petrov board the boat the day before, Clay had recognised him as the cop who had first turned up at Anna's apartment block and who had called in the MVD. Then, on watch later that night, Clay had seen the same cop return and spend an hour in the apartment, before leaving and going to an Internet café. Now he wasn't wearing his uniform, it made them feel more uncomfortable, as if he were working undercover.

'My father was Russian, but my mother's family is pure Evenk,' Petrov said. 'I can show you the village where they live. Potapovo. The northern one. There's two. Not much of a place, but if you want to get the feel of how the ethnic Siberians live up here, I'll be happy to show you around.'

'We'd be very interested,' Eileen replied, and seemed to glare briefly at the other two, as if they were acting like rude or sulky adolescents and needed to mind their manners. The two men then made a visible effort to engage Petrov.

He explained to them the way of life of the Evenk, their history and the current threats to their existence. 'The huge nickel smelters at Norilsk have poisoned the land for a hundred miles around the city,' he said. 'The trees can't grow there any more. But the pollution has spread far further, invisibly. It damages the moss the reindeer eat. And it's destroying our way of life. Once the white moss the reindeer like to eat has been killed off, it takes thirty years for it regenerate,' Petrov explained. 'I'm afraid this pollution, along with Moscow's attempt to assimilate the native peoples, has damaged the core of the Evenk. You'll see a lot of drunkenness, I'm afraid, unemployment, laziness. They've lost their way, many of them. But my grandfather and mother and her brothers and some of their children still have a herd of deer they pasture every summer. They'll be preparing reindeer-hide tents for the summer months, moving hundreds of miles between now and September in search of the moss. In winter they live mostly in wooden cabins back at the village,' he added. 'Or they travel even further north. The deer can dig for the moss beneath the snow. But now the very north too is under threat. The oil companies are starting to exploit the beds under the Kara Sea. Your companies too. American ones. And then they plan to drill even farther north up in the Arctic itself. Beneath the Pole. None of it is good news for the Evenk and other tribes.'

He laughed awkwardly, as if to make light of foreign companies coming to Russia.

He realised he was caught now between portraying his tribe's relatively primitive existence and a desire to show his family were also modern, or modern enough to live in winter in wooden huts at any rate. It made him feel uncomfortable for a moment.

'These foreign oil companies are already coming to exploit the Kara Sea, in partnership with our Russian state companies,' Petrov went on. 'There will be far more pollution than ever. This is Russia, remember, where anything goes. Our state companies and your huge private companies have the technology to drill under the Kara Sea and right up under the North Pole. Or so they say. But I fear there'll be more devastation of the ecology as a result. Russia isn't too careful about cleaning up its pollution. You'll see when we get further north.'

'The Lomonosov Ridge?' This was the second man, Sky, Petrov noted, who suddenly seemed animated.

Petrov laughed pleasantly, his big round face creased into a benevolence that he felt, for some reason, unnerved the Americans. 'You know about the Lomonosov Ridge?'

he said. 'Of course. It's becoming an international incident. It's a mountain range three miles beneath the Arctic Ocean that runs all the way from Russia, a thousand miles under the ice, beneath the North Pole and all the way to Canada and Greenland. And, of course, the Kremlin is saying it belongs to Russia. Putin had a Russian flag made of titanium planted on the sea floor under the North Pole three years ago.' Petrov laughed at the absurdity of a flag on the sea bed. 'Like you planted your flag on the Moon,' he added.

'Russia is only *claiming* the shelf all the way under the Pole,' Eileen replied.

'That's right,' Petrov agreed. 'And your government, and Norway and Finland and Canada are disputing it in the international courts. But it's the international courts that are saying the Lomonosov Ridge most likely belongs to Russia. A quarter of the world's oil is under there, so they say.'

To Petrov, the stilted nature of the exchange suddenly seemed like a highly diplomatic and absurd attempt to resolve the international dispute on a ferry bound north-wards along the Yenisei.

This wasn't the way he wanted the conversation to go, he felt suddenly. It seemed to put him at odds with them, through the confrontation between their governments.

'Who knows what will happen?' he said, almost apologetically.

'There's more oil and gas there than anywhere in the world, if it can be drilled,' Eileen said. 'A quarter of the world's resources, you say, but there are scientists who believe there's more. America won't accept a flag planted three miles under the sea.'

'Yes,' Petrov agreed. 'So they say. Oil. Always oil. Oil and gas.' He sighed with a genuine sadness. 'When will they find something else?'

There was an awkward silence that Petrov's sorrowful remark didn't seem to dispel. Then it was Clay who spoke.

'Are there still shamans up here?' he said.

For the first time, Petrov saw it was the big man who had spoken. He could have been a member of a Russian special forces unit, Petrov thought, he was so well built, so fit. He looked like a military man to Petrov, or maybe he was just one of those pumped-up, American super-sportsmen.

'Are there? Are there shamans among your people?' Clay persisted.

Petrov paused and frowned.

'They went underground in the Soviet period,' he explained finally. 'But there are still some, yes. Very few real ones now. It's a thing that used to get passed down in families, to women as well as men. But when the Russians forced our people into their schools, they broke the connection. Maybe we can find you a shaman if you're interested.'

He was glad they'd got off a subject that implied conflict. He brought the drum out from under the table. 'This was made by a shaman, my grandfather. It was made with wood from a tree struck by lightning. That's the way we make them, from those trees.'

'I'd be interested to meet a real shaman,' Clay replied.

Petrov wanted to buy them a drink, but he also felt that it would arouse their suspicions, suspicions that he was out to get something from them. He'd seen the way some Russians worked on foreigners and he was eager not to appear to be looking for any gain. And it didn't seem the right moment to bring 'muon catalysed fusion' into the conversation, whatever it was. But he wanted to establish a bridge between him and them, something unthreatening.

He picked up their map, which was half open on the metal table, and began to point out villages along the river and give them a brief description. He also showed them the sites of two former Gulag camps they would pass, and a four hundred-mile rail line built by Stalin's slaves in order to join the Yenisei and Ob rivers, but which had collapsed into the melting earth and was never used. It had cost the lives of more than ten thousand victims.

They seemed interested and began to ask questions. But he still noted a reserve in them and put it down once more to a suspicion on their part that he wanted something in return.

Finally he got to his feet. 'If you're interested in anything, just ask me. I'm on holiday, but my grandfather is dying,' he added, and felt a sensation he hadn't felt for a long time, of real freedom. 'We'll be on the boat for another day or two and I'd be happy to show you things. And I would be honoured to tell you more about my people, if it interests you,' he added.

CHAPTER SIXTEEN

B Y THE LATE afternoon of the third day the old, slow-
moving *Rossiya* had reached Yeniseiysk. During the
course of the fading non-day, grey and heavy with rain
clouds that never quite shed their contents, the ship had
passed several small settlements. There was a torpor on
board that fitted the lowering skies. The mood of the
passengers hung motionless like the weather, mirroring its
weight and presentiment. A calm before the storm.

On the east bank of the Yenisei the *taiga* was thick
with a close weave of trees that stretched for thousands of
miles, an incomprehensible wilderness of forest. The huge
expanse contained one quarter of the world's timber.
Perhaps the endless, grim impenetrability of the forest also
added to the heaviness of the passengers. People talked
about the 'Siberian Madness' that afflicted the Russians
who'd settled – or been forced as prisoners – up here.
And in the mid-afternoon they passed the first of Stalin's
Gulag camps in the region, the first of several they would
pass as the ship headed towards the Arctic Circle.

The great, bleak land of Siberia itself seemed to have
effortlessly absorbed the millions of dead, however. It
seemed to have no memory. But some of those women

on board whom Anna had spoken to in the hold were the daughters of the survivors of the death camps and they did have memories, even if only at second hand. These women were the people who had never been able to escape the place of death, people with neither the money nor the permission to move elsewhere in Russia, outside the *krai* of Krasnoyarsk. Permanent exile was handed down from parent to child like a genetic default.

And it was known by one woman she had spoken to that even the *Rossiya* itself had once been a transport for the Gulag victims. They were packed tight, the woman had told her, locked in its cargo holds like so much freight. Some of them had frozen to death on the way, or starved or been beaten to death before they'd reached the camps.

After her interrogation by the Wolf, when Anna had gone below to the hold where the women were, there was a deep air of suspicion at first. No one – historically – wished to be associated with the accused or those under suspicion.

But finally one old woman who was returning to Igarka as she did every year for the summer work camp – a daughter of a Gulag victim herself, who had been released in 1976 – came up to her and offered her a chunk of bread and some jam from a tin.

'What did the bastards want?' she said gruffly.

'The man who hired us, Ivan . . .'

'That dog!' she spat.

'They say he's disappeared,' Anna said quietly.

'Then good riddance.'

'Some people saw me with him last night.' She looked at the old woman. 'He was trying—'

'I can guess what he was trying. He's a shit, that Ivan,' the woman interrupted. 'He's no good and never was. God help him,' She crossed herself four times in apparent regret at wishing him ill.

It was then they heard the anchor running out in the sheltered bend of the river where the current was slower, as the ship moored off the small port of Yeniseiysk.

Most of the women got to their feet and someone opened the metal door and a slow line of people shuffled up the staircase, like refugees from the light, out into the fading day.

Anna immediately saw the Wolf standing at the bow and looking down and across the water to a line of huts and wooden houses above the bank.

The old woman saw him too, and the OMON badge. She froze. Then she snapped at two men ten yards away from them who were standing on the deck waiting to disembark for the captain's regulation two-hour stop. They both came obediently and waited in front of Anna and the woman.

'These are my sons,' she said, and looked at them superciliously. 'Take care of this girl,' she instructed them. 'She's called Valentina and she attracts much too much attention. Stay with her on the ship and onshore.'

The men nodded sheepishly, like children, even though Anna saw that they must have been in their late forties.

As the four of them descended the metal stairs down

the side of the hull to one of the waiting boats, Anna saw the Wolf watching her from where he still stood up at the bow. The dread that still haunted her was that Ivan's body was somewhere behind them in the river, and that it would slowly catch up with the ship in the current while they were stopped. She wished now that she'd had time to put a weight on it, sink him for good.

As they waited at the foot of the metal ladder to step into the boat, the Wolf was suddenly behind her. He boarded the same launch and they took off for the hundred-yard trip to the beach.

When the boat scraped up on the mud bank next to a small wooden jetty, he took her arm and the old woman and her two sons fell behind at once. The woman's instruction to them was hopeless. Nothing would make any of them go up against a special forces officer from OMON. Their protection was futile against any all-powerful official of the state.

The Wolf guided her along the jetty and they walked up to the stalls and tables that sold the village's few offerings.

'What do you want here?' he said conversationally. 'Something to buy?'

'I just wanted to get off the ship,' she replied.

And it was then that she saw two more OMON officers, with the same wolf embroidered on their sleeves. They were standing in the twilight by some sheds at the top of a slipway.

The Wolf guided her away from them. 'I'm not like that layabout Ivan,' he said as if to reassure her. 'I treat women with respect.'

They walked up into the village.

'You're probably wondering what I'm doing here,' he said. 'And those other two men back there.'

'I don't enquire about such things,' she replied.

'Very wise. But I'll tell you. You might be of some assistance. We're after some dangerous men. Terrorists. We believe they're preparing some kind of sabotage.'

He stopped and looked up ahead towards the end of the village, where the forest closed in around it like a devouring tide of green.

'Saboteurs,' he said, and she saw he was relishing the word, rolling it around his mouth.

Saboteurs. For a moment Anna's mind reeled back to Soviet times, and the ever-present memory of Stalinist Russia. In those days 'saboteur' was a catch-all word for enemies of the state, anyone, in fact, who the state wanted eliminated. It was as if some small crack had opened to let in those dark times.

But all she said was, 'What is there to sabotage up here?'

He looked at her sharply, but then his face relaxed.

'Here? In this village? Nothing. But there are important state projects at the end of the river and this is the way an enemy of the state would approach. Norilsk, for example,' he said slyly, 'is a closed area to anyone without a permit. This river is the only way anyone could approach those areas without being automatically stopped.'

She didn't reply to his inquisitive look, but she felt her heart freeze.

'You seem a smart woman,' he said, conversationally again. 'You can use your eyes and ears.'

'I will. Of course. For the Motherland,' she replied.

There was a small, dilapidated wooden building at the end of the main street which served as a hospital. He led her into the building under a sloping wood porch and they waited in a room and listened to shouting and curses from the back. There was one doctor there and when he saw the wolf on the man's shoulder, he nodded and led them through to the back.

There were a few filthy beds on the floor and the room seemed occupied solely by the mad and the drunk. One man was tied to an iron bed, quietly raving almost in a whisper and wild eyed. There was an ethnic Siberian sitting on the floor at the far end, silently nodding his head from side to side and in a circle. An Evenk tribesman, she thought. The Wolf looked around, as if hoping to identify one of the hopeless in the room as a potential saboteur. He looked disappointed.

'This is what we get,' the doctor said and shrugged. 'But there's no medicine. We ran out of everything except painkillers back in January.'

'This country drinks too much,' the Wolf said.

'Maybe, but if people had something else . . .' the doctor said.

But the Wolf had turned and left, bringing Anna with him by the arm.

Outside in the mud street, night had fallen, briefer than ever as they travelled further and further north.

When Anna and the Wolf boarded the launch to get back on the *Rossiya* the two other special forces officers she had seen by the slipway came with them. One of them looked at her lasciviously, the other didn't acknowledge her presence at all.

'You have other clothes?' the Wolf asked once they were aboard the *Rossiya*.

'Very little. Just jeans and a shirt,' Anna replied. 'So I can wash these.'

'Wear them instead,' the Wolf demanded. 'I want you to join me for supper this evening,' he insisted. 'In an hour.'

'You haven't told me your name,' she replied.

'Dmitry Pavlovich. Call me Dmitry,' he said, and smiled in a way intended to let her know it was not his real name.

When she returned dressed in different clothes, she saw the Wolf had apparently turfed the captain out of his cabin and taken it for himself. As Anna entered, he had a wooden table set for two, a bottle of vodka opened, and a dish of frozen fish and a few vegetables as a centre piece. There were just two plates.

'I know you drink vodka,' he said smiling, and poured them two glasses. 'Sit down.'

He watched her. She was dressed now in more figure-hugging clothes and she felt self-conscious under his gaze.

'What shall we drink to?' he asked.

'To Russia,' she said.

He raised his glass. 'Good. To Russia!' He drained the glass and watched her drain hers. 'Please,' he said then, 'help yourself.'

She forked some of the frozen fish, a Siberian delicacy, on to her plate and he filled the glasses again.

'Tell me about your parents, Valentina,' he said.

'My father was born in Odessa, but came to Russia at the start of the Patriotic War when he was two years old.'

'Jews?' he said, suddenly alert.

'No. Ordinary Russians. Good Communists.'

He seemed to relax.

'His father – my grandfather – was transferred to the factories they were building east of the Urals,' Anna continued. 'My mother was from Bratsk. I don't know how they met, but it was in Bratsk. Both my grandfathers died in the Great Patriotic War. I was brought up in Bratsk.'

'You never left Bratsk?'

'I went to Moscow once,' she replied. 'To visit my grandmother.'

'Where did she live?' he said keenly, and studied her face closely.

'North of the city.' She shrugged. 'I don't remember the street. I was only five.'

'And all these years you've been in Bratsk?'

Anna shrugged again. 'You get used to anywhere.'

'I'm sure you do,' he replied. 'You have a husband?'

'I did once. He was a drunk. I threw him out.'

'Children?'

'No.'

She felt his pencil-thin eyes watching her face. But now she thought it was nothing more dangerous than that he wanted her.

'You don't have to stay down in that stinking hold,' he said easily. 'You can stay here. With me.'

'What will the others think?' she said.

'Does it matter?'

She looked directly back at him and didn't answer his question. But they both knew she would be shunned by the rest of them if she stayed with him.

There was a knock at the door.

'Come!' the Wolf Dmitry ordered.

The two other OMON officers with emblazoned wolves entered. Dmitry stood and looked at Anna. 'I'm doing this for your own good,' he said. Then he looked at the two officers. 'Stand her up.'

They took her by the arms and dragged her from the chair, pinioning her against the wall.

She knew the training the OMON went through – she'd gone through something similar when she'd trained for the Russian foreign intelligence service. One of the final acts before acceptance into the ranks – and one which most applicants failed – was to fight bare-handed against five other men. Pinioned against the wall, even she had no chance.

Dmitry came up to her slowly. He looked at her with black eyes. Then he punched her face, once to the right eye, then the mouth, and then once to the left eye.

She reeled at the blows and the two officers held her head up against the wall for more.

She waited for further blows to rain down on her. She couldn't think, only endure. But through her crushed eyes, she saw Dmitry turn and walk casually back to the table. He sat down and poured himself a glass of vodka. When he'd drunk it, he said, 'That's enough.'

The two officers dropped her and she slumped against the wall.

'You'll have two black eyes and a lot of swelling by the morning,' Dmitry said. 'That way the rest of the people on this damn boat will trust you, won't they,' he sneered. 'That's what you wanted.'

He got up from the table, then, and walked across the room, stopping in front of her. He looked at her slumped head harshly and lifted it by her chin with his fingers so that she was forced to face him in the eye.

'Use your eyes and ears, Valentina. Here, and when we get to Igarka. I want to clear this ship of any suspicion. There'll be no saboteurs coming up north in the *Rossiya* while I'm in charge. And there'll be no one coming through that shitty little timber town who shouldn't be, either.' He slipped his fingers intimately along her chin and then wiped them deliberately on his uniform trousers. 'Now get out,' he said.

CHAPTER SEVENTEEN

ALEXEI PETROV WALKED back from the bridge to the the port-side steps that led below decks. It was lunchtime and he was hungry. Maybe it was all the fresh air of Siberia after the yellow polluted smog of the city that had made him hungry, but whatever the cause it was convenient to be heading for the restaurant for other reasons. The Americans, he'd noted, lunched at the same time every day.

When he reached the mid-deck and had walked to the restaurant, he saw that it was as it usually was at mealtimes. There was just himself there and the three Tajik business-men from Krasnoyarsk who were selling a container full of electrical goods; some Armenian salesmen who seemed to own most of the vodka the ferry was carrying to the north; a Russian technician who worked at the nickel smelters beyond the Arctic Circle; and the three Americans. It was only the rich – or the relatively rich at any rate – and the tourists who could afford to use the restaurant. And he now knew the three Americans were the only foreign tourists on board at this time of year. He'd checked that on the manifest. And so the restaurant was almost empty as it had been since the voyage began.

This time he didn't order a drink at the bar or hang back for other reasons, he went straight to the table where the three of them were sitting and with a cheery 'Hello' took a seat without asking.

'It's time for your first lesson,' he said. 'I must teach you some Evenk before we reach Potapovo.'

As usual, the Americans didn't seem pleased to see him, but the woman Eileen at least made some effort at small talk. Over lunch, which he noted they ate quite sparingly as if they were on a diet or in training for something – or perhaps just afraid of Russian food – Petrov told them some useful Evenk words and phrases and then, just for their amusement, he told them of words the Evenk possessed that could be found in no other language.

There was the Evenk word for 'the noise a bear makes walking through cranberry bushes', for example, and another word for 'the noise a duck makes landing silently on water'. It was Petrov's obvious charm and easygoing nature, as well as the little insights of the Evenk world that he gave them through his native language, that finally seemed to thaw them – even endear them to him. He was hard to resist, asking for nothing, giving everything, and all with a sense of spiritual calm – as Eileen later described it to the two boys – that seemed eventually to allay whatever fear they had of him. Temporarily at least. And Petrov was genuine in his friendly manner and this genuineness shone through. He displayed no artifice, despite holding the question in the back of his head that, if the opportunity arose, he would politely lay on the table what he really wanted to ask.

Over coffee, Petrov slowly reintroduced the awkward subject that had come up in their first conversation; the international incident that was slowly unfolding between Russia on the one side and America, Canada, Norway and Denmark on the other – the ownership of the Lomonosov Ridge, three miles below the ice all the way under the Pole. By this time, Petrov had drunk three beers and, though in a festively inebriated mood, still had his plan for the conversation he hoped would lie ahead clear in his mind.

'It seems to me,' Petrov said, 'that whoever owns this subterranean mountain range won't be able to exploit the oil and gas in it anyway. Not yet. As far as one can tell, there's not the technology to drill beneath the Pole.'

'One day they'll know how to do it,' Sky answered him. 'If they don't already. That's why everyone's laying claim to it now. Technology will follow. It's the same with the growing of illegal crops like marijuana. The big cigarette companies have been buying up land in South America for decades, just waiting for it to be declared legal.'

'Is that so?' Petrov said in genuine surprise. 'And the environment of the Arctic?' he asked gently. 'What about the effects on that up here, in one of the world's most sensitive areas?'

'Ah,' Clay said, with a deep cynicism in his voice, to Petrov's mind. But the American didn't elaborate.

'They always find the excuses they need to bypass environmental questions,' Sky answered him.

'But there's the nuclear reactor the Russians built,'

Petrov protested. 'The first of its kind. It can be dragged across the ice, they say. Surely there'd be an international outcry!'

The three Americans looked back at him uncomprehendingly. But it seemed to him, nevertheless, that they knew exactly what he was talking about.

'It's probably classified information,' Petrov said in a falsely mock-whisper. 'But then everything is in this country.' He paused as if wondering whether to go on. 'The State is building – maybe already has built, I don't know – a nuclear power station up in the restricted area by the Kara Sea, up near a place called Dikson. They plan to float it across the sea in the summer, or drag it with tractors across the ice in winter. Towards the Pole itself. The problem with drilling there is power, as well as the depth, of course. That's the solution from the Russian point of view. The world's first transportable nuclear plant on the ice that can drive the drills through the thickest ice and then three miles down into the sea and the rock below that. A nuclear reactor up near the North Pole. And a Russian one at that,' he said in a voice laden with misgiving.

'The question of ownership still isn't decided,' Eileen said rigidly at last. 'The ridge is still in dispute.'

'But didn't you know that one major international tribunal has granted the whole ridge to Russia?' Petrov replied. 'According to normal questions of judging these things, the ridge is part of Russia – geographically, geologically it's joined to Siberia – even if it does go under the Pole to Canada. The tribunal is only going according to these set rules, they say.'

'But the other countries are still appealing the decision,' Eileen protested.

'And in the meantime, Russia has its reactor ready and waiting,' Petrov replied.

There was a silence at the table.

'I know nothing of these things,' Petrov said, half-apologetically. 'But I've been reading quite a bit about them. Because of the effect all this has on my people. All of it affects the native peoples, mine included. It could be the end of us altogether.'

'A nuclear reactor that can be dragged across the ice sounds like just the sort of end-of-the-world scenario we need,' Sky said.

'As I say,' Petrov replied, again with apology in his voice, 'I know nothing about nuclear science, but it sounds pretty dangerous to me too. Even when they're on dry land, they pose enough danger. Look at Chernobyl. Another Russian-built nuclear disaster,' he said generously. 'Then Japan. And you had one yourselves in America. And that's just three we know about.'

He sipped his coffee, now tired of the beer.

'And there are the best Russian nuclear scientists up there, isn't that right?'

This time it was Eileen who spoke, in a statement, but one that sounded like a question. And Petrov noticed there was the faintest hint of tension in her voice.

'I've no idea,' Petrov said. 'But of course there are nuclear facilities way up in the north. All for research. But that's double double double classified information, I imagine. And I'm just a regular cop.'

His open declaration seemed to intensify the tension he'd noticed in them before and Petrov wondered why again.

'A cop on holiday,' he added, and smiled a serene smile. 'But at least if you run into any trouble, I can add that to any help I might be able to give you.' He sipped his coffee again and leaned back in his chair. 'You all look like intelligent people,' he said. 'Have you been to university in America?'

They nodded.

'Linguists?'

The two boys shifted in their seats.

'You all speak such perfect Russian,' Petrov explained. 'I'm amazed, to be frank.'

'Clay is a Russian literature student. I studied science,' Sky said. 'Eileen works in advertising. But we all learned Russian for this trip.'

'You're a scientist?' Petrov said.

'That's what I studied. But just for three years.'

'One thing I was reading recently about all these nuclear plans mentioned something called muon nuclear fusion. I've no idea what that is. Perhaps you can help?'

This time, the tension around the table was almost tangible. It was as if a wall of non-communication had suddenly gone up between him and the three Americans. But he also detected confusion, amazement even. He saw that they all stared at him, before realising they were giving something away and returning their gazes to the table, only to then attempt some normal behaviour; picking up a spoon in Sky's case, looking around for the bill in Eileen's. Sky got up from the table, said 'Excuse me,' and left.

With his hands squarely on the table in what looked like a preamble to springing over it, Clay replied without more than a brief glance in Petrov's direction.

'Just what is it you want?' he said to Petrov.

It was a deliberately aggressive question. Eileen put a warning hand on his arm, but Clay wasn't to be deflected.

'What are you doing here, Petrov? Following us? What do you want?'

CHAPTER EIGHTEEN

S IBERIA EMERGED FROM the short night in a display of pre-dawn pyrotechnics. Long before the sun appeared to the east, the western sky was a kaleidoscope of swirling colours. There were the normal pinks and reds and oranges, but also blues and greens which were reflected in the high, ice-crystal clouds in the western skies. The whirl of ever-changing tints seemed formed by some invisible Impressionist's brush that painted the skies.

The glow reflected by the clouds from below the eastern horizon was so strong that it transposed the dawn light on to the eastern banks of the Yenisei from the western sky first, dappling the trunks of the spruce and fir trees. Then the sun finally appeared above the horizon and shone directly on the western bank, lighting it for the first time.

By now the landscape was showing signs of the tundra ahead, slowly beginning to leave the *taiga* behind as the *Rossiya* crept closer and closer to the Arctic Circle. But still the vast forests dominated the view as far as the eye could see and way beyond. The town of Igarka lay less than a day's journey ahead.

Anna lay on the bench in the hold. The old woman,

whose name she'd discovered was Evgenia, had placed some kind of herb potion on her face and then some muslin over the top of it. When she'd staggered through the metal door and down the steps the night before, the lights had still been switched on in the hold and everyone saw her condition. Many of the women now came up to her as they woke and asked her what had happened. And why. Why did he do this? Through puffed and cut lips, Anna told them she thought he'd hit her just for the fun of it. To them it seemed a perfectly plausible explanation. At least he didn't break your teeth, one of them said.

'My father was a Gulag victim, as I told you,' Evgenia said slowly. 'When he was sixteen, he was sent to the place that came to be known as Devil Island. On the Ob river. Its real name was Nazinovo. There were six thousand of them and they were left on this island at the end of May – about this time of year. They were given a little flour, that's all, a few clothes and no shelter. It was snowing. On the first morning they buried over four hundred of the prisoners. That happened morning after morning. When the little food ran out, they began to eat each other. That's how my father survived. He ate other men. By the end, there were fewer than two thousand of the original six. They were put there because the Kremlin called them "outdated elements". Not even outdated people. What that strange phrase means to anyone outside the NKVD's self-strangling bureaucracy would be impossible to fathom. To the NKVD, predecessor of the KGB, it meant they were no longer human. But my father lived. There may be no such places in Russia now, but we are all still treated with the same contempt. That officer upstairs, he's no different.'

Such atrocities were committed by people like her father, and her grandfather, Anna thought, yet here she was being looked after by the children of their victims. She had nothing to say in reply, as Evgenia stroked her forehead.

She hadn't slept, except in a few brief doses of pained and shattered dozing. She was exhausted, her face hurt and her eyes had puffed up so that it was difficult to see. She could barely use her mouth to eat. Now, she thought, now at last I've become like one of them. Dmitry the Wolf had given her the perfect disguise.

She went out on the deck before the sun appeared and watched through running eyes the colours in the sky. Then she was joined by Evgenia and a few of the women.

'Many of us have men on board,' Evgenia said. 'Sons, brothers, husbands and other good-for-nothings. They won't like this.'

But Anna heard in the tone of her voice that betrayed her that they were all utterly helpless in the face of a brutal OMON special forces officer. And now there were two more. If they aren't corrupt, they're brutal, she remembered. And if they're not one or the other, it means they're both.

As the day began, the men, too, appeared on deck. The atmosphere was exactly the same as on the previous days, but they, too, noticed what had happened to her and one or two of them, as long as the Wolf and the other two officers weren't present, expressed their sympathy, gave her things to eat, a bottle of beer or a cigarette. From knowing nobody, from being entirely alone in a country whose power wished only to destroy her, she was now surrounded by well-wishers.

It was then that the young man with the wispy beard whom she'd seen staring at her two days before approached her. Again, she thought she recognised his face. He sat down next to her and opened a bottle of beer, offering her the first sip, which she took.

'So you're from Bratsk,' he said.

She handed back the bottle. 'Yes.'

He turned to look her in the face. There was a smile on his lips which she saw was friendly. 'So what were you doing in Kyzyl down near the Mongolian border eight days ago?' he asked.

She sat completely still. So that was where she'd seen his face – and where he had seen her. She remained perfectly calm.

'Picking something up,' she replied without pausing.

'Oh?'

She didn't reply.

'What would anyone be picking up down there?' he persisted.

She turned to him this time and she saw the same smile hovering around his mouth, the same burning eyes. 'From across the border. From China,' she said. 'Just cheap electrical stuff.'

'But in Kyzyl you were pretending to be a woman from one of the villages there,' he gently protested. 'You had all those apples for the market. It was a good disguise.

What were you picking up? TVs? Computers? Or something more interesting?'

She thought for a moment. 'That's my business,' she said finally.

'And where were the things you were picking up illegally from China?' he said, the same smile on his lips.

'My brother took them.'

'So why pretend to be going to market?'

She shrugged. 'This country thrives on pretence,' she answered.

He laughed this time. He had wide open eyes that still flared with a fierce intensity like they had when she'd first seen him on the boat. But as she'd now found, that wasn't the first time she'd seen him. She remembered his voice now too, from the morning in Kyzyl and the bus journey north.

As they'd headed north downriver his sunken cheeks had become raw from the cold which seemed to affect him more than it did the others. But he either affected indifference, or physical pain was of no interest to him, a badge of honour, even. He looked to Anna like someone who'd been in a dark room or in an office or a library all his life.

'Oleg,' he said, and held out his hand. She took it briefly. 'And you are Valentina?'

'That's right.'

He looked at her steadily, neither believing nor, as far as she could tell, disbelieving. 'They really gave you a beating,' he said finally, looking at her puffed face and split lip.

'It was just one of them,' she replied, 'and it was only three blows.'

'That OMON guy? The first one who came aboard? What did the others do, stand you up? Those other bastards?'

'That's right. On all counts.'

'You want to get your own back?'

She looked at him, a thin young man who looked more like an adolescent but with all the strength of ten men in his eyes. She didn't answer him.

She now began to feel deeply uncomfortable in his presence, despite his apparent friendliness. They sat in silence for a minute or two, watching the bank of trees passing endlessly by. Then he looked at her again.

'You know,' he said, drawing slowly on a cigarette and taking infinite care with his words, 'it's only the completeness of your disguise that gives you away. You're too good. It was the same when you were in Kyzyl. Too good. But I and the others know.'

'Know what?'

He smiled more broadly. 'That you aren't who you say you are, that's all.'

She looked at him angrily. 'Are you working for them too?' she snapped. 'Have they asked you to watch me?'

He put his hands up in mock surrender. 'No, no, you misunderstand me, Valentina.' He watched her eyes with the burning coals of his own. 'I trust you,' he said. 'That's what I want you to know. Not just because they beat you up, but because I know I can.' He paused. 'As for us, we're not who we say we are either,' he finished.

She looked directly back at him. But she didn't ask any questions.

He leaned in towards her. 'We're activists,' he said. 'We're going north to commit a great act.'

He pulled back the flap of his grey jacket and she thought for a moment that he was about to do something crude. But then she saw a glint of metal above the waistband of his trousers, a black plastic handle above it. He was showing her he had a gun. It was an old pistol, a Makarov, by the quick look of it which he allowed her. Then he dropped the flap of his jacket again.

'You won't get very far with that,' she said. 'Whatever great act you're planning.'

'Oh, it's not just this and the few other weapons we've brought with us. We have friends. Up in Norilsk. They can get their hands on the explosives they use in the mines there. That's where we're going. And thermite too,' he added.

Thermite was like a highly explosive paint. Once a surface was coated with it, it would take only a small fire to ignite it into a huge explosion. She felt her discomfort in his presence deepen. Saboteurs. That's what the Wolf had said. They were looking for saboteurs.

'They'll find you and they'll kill you,' she said.

He laughed. 'We're going to commit this great act for the world,' he said. And she believed he meant it. 'It will be on the front page of every newspaper in the world, too.'

'What are you? The three musketeers?' She wished to remove herself from his presence, but too much had already been said.

'There are six of us.' He smiled. 'And a few more at the mines in the north.'

He leaned in towards her again. 'The guys that beat you up? They're our enemies too. And our enemies' enemy is our friend. So join us.'

This time it was she who laughed. 'I'm just a saw operator,' she said.

'Like I told you, it's the completeness of your disguise that gives you away. To me, anyway,' he added. He looked at her with an amused, almost playful expression on his face. 'Think about it, Valentina.' He showed her the old pistol again. 'You want to return the favour to that OMON bastard? We'll help you.'

She looked at him, genuinely aghast this time.

'You mean, do I want to kill him?' she said, and laughed again, but laughing hurt her mouth too much. It was a short pleasure. She saw he was smiling too, eagerly this time, the calmness gone.

'You should hide that away,' she said. 'They're looking for you. That's why they're on the ship. If the OMON guys see it, you're in deep shit.'

'They won't,' he said.

'And I wouldn't talk to people you don't know about this,' she told him. 'Including me. You must be crazy.'

But looking in his eyes again, she knew his intent was genuine.

'I know I can trust you,' he said. 'And I've persuaded the others. Join us. I know you're lying about what you were doing in Kyzyl and you're lying about what you're doing here.'

She turned on him savagely. He put up a hand in passive defence.

'No, no . . . Valentina. I'm not interested in telling anyone I saw you there,' he said, and then added, 'And I'm not interested in getting anything from you with the knowledge.' He paused. He seemed to be weighing alternatives. But he was someone who decided things quickly. 'I'd like to kill that bastard too,' he said finally. 'But you can have him first. If you want.'

'You are crazy,' she answered.

She wondered now if this was a set-up. The Wolf had told her to keep him informed of anything that suggested sabotage. 'Use your eyes and ears.' If she told the Wolf about the boy and his friends, it would be safer for her. If she didn't, she might pay for it with her life. It was an obvious choice – to report what the boy had said. Then, if it were a set-up, the Wolf would trust her, or trust her more.

But again, just as at the border, some deep misgiving held her back. And she wondered again if she'd lost her edge, her ruthlessness, the single-minded course of action that had kept her alive so long.

'Maybe a little crazy.' He grinned.

Looking back directly at him again she knew that what he'd told her was the truth and that he was neither joking nor crazy.

CHAPTER NINETEEN

THERE WERE TWO Russian military helicopters on the mud bank by the river. The ship was just outside the village of Kostino, under half a day's journey from Igarka, when she saw them.

From Anna's viewpoint on board the *Rossiya*, the soldiers in the helicopters and sitting around them on the wet mud and snow bank seemed to be mostly *sapari*. In the hierarchy of the Russian conscription system, this meant they were 'fresh meat' – conscripts with less than a year of service – and, for the most part, they were abused, underfed and disgruntled teenagers. Like the boys at the border, she thought. But they would enjoy nothing more than to find people even lower down the pecking order than they were, and the *Rossiya* was full of them.

There were four officers with them that she could see, each of whom evidently had at least two or three years' service, and then a couple of career officers in charge of the whole group. All told, she estimated there were a little over fifty troops waiting on the bank, roughly twenty-six from each helicopter.

Dmitry the Wolf was on the bridge with the two other OMON officers and he was evidently directing the captain to stop. Kostino hadn't been on the list of places they were stopping at. The ship curved in a circle until it faced the current and then dropped its anchor. From speakers fixed up on the bridge came the tinny instructions for everyone to get out on deck on pain of arrest. Crew members were lowering various small craft from davits on the port side, nearer the bank. With a crewman in each, they set off to the shore and Anna heard the shouted orders from the bank for the conscripts to get up.

The Wolf descended the steps from the bridge and the other two OMON officers went to stand at either end of the ship, weapons drawn now. It seemed to her that they were preparing for someone on the ship – or more than one – to make a break into the icy river. If so, anyone attempting such an escape would be shot as soon as they hit the water.

The conscripts crossed the narrow stretch of river from the bank and boarded the ship. They clearly had their orders. Most of them fanned out at once against the guard rails all around the ship, while half a dozen took up vantage points high above the deck, either on the bridge or on a single container in the stern. These troops trained their weapons down on the milling passengers who had slowly emerged from below. When the work crews were all in place, the senior career officer walked up the deck and conferred with the Wolf.

Some of the passengers sat, heads bent, others waited anxiously in twos and threes, smoking nervously. Nobody talked. From the speakers came the new instruction: 'Men in the bow, women in the stern. Be quick about it.'

She saw a dozen conscripts now leave their posts around the ship's guard rails and, with the career officer and one of the 'walruses' – a conscript with two or three years of service – the conscripts were then ordered to go below. It was a search, Anna saw, as she walked head down to the stern of the vessel with the other women, and she wondered if she'd concealed the Thompson well enough. From the bridge the speakers issued further instructions: 'Strip down to your underclothes!'

Slowly, the complement of workers began to take off their clothes. Where Anna stood, plump old and middle-aged women and some younger ones like herself began to strip. It's like the camps, she thought. The officers were acting like the prison guards had. Finally, most of the women stood in bare feet, shivering in the feeble noon sun. There seemed to be no hurry to inspect them. Anna looked up the ship and saw that the men had already stripped, far quicker than the women with her, some of whom still grumbled in rage, seemingly oblivious to the penalty that might be meted out to them for disobedience.

She saw a man in the distance up by the bow light a cigarette and then she looked as it was knocked out of his mouth by the butt of an SPK which connected ruthlessly with the man's jaw.

It soon became clear that they were to be kept waiting and stripped in the cold until the search below was complete. Anna thought about the hiding place where she'd dismantled and hidden the Thompson Contender. But she guessed she was better at hiding something than these inexperienced youths would be at finding it.

233

More conscripts were now descending below decks from the bow, while the others trained semi-automatics on the shivering, degraded passengers. It was a deliberately harsh tactic, designed to debilitate and humiliate. Next to Anna, a woman who was in her late fifties, she guessed, began to cough. It was a harsh bronchial sound that seemed to rattle her insides. They waited like this for nearly an hour.

At first, the conscripts came up from below in twos and threes. There was an officer with them and each conscript was carrying an assortment of weapons. They were put in a pile between the bow and stern. From where she stood, Anna saw that there were three or four AK47s and a collection of handguns, a pile of hunting knives and even a whip. But she couldn't see if the Thompson was among them.

The officer went up to the men's end of the ship first. She saw that a few men, on command, came out to claim their knives. No one claimed any of the guns. Clearly no one had the required licences for a gun. They were hard to obtain and the guns were almost certainly illegal, even if they were only used for hunting. The officer put the claimed knives to one side and then walked the length of the ship.

'Anyone with a weapon, legal or illegal, come and identify it now!'

No one among the women moved.

He turned and walked back, now at last ordering the conscripts, who had all returned from below to the deck, to begin searching the clothes that lay in bundles all around the bow and stern of the boat. The teenagers who came up to the women's end lifted up the women's clothes with bayonets or knives and sometimes searched them when they felt any weight. They were laughing and poking fun at the semi-naked women, letting their eyes feast on the younger ones and making obscene suggestions.

After nearly another hour more, the process was finished. No more weapons were found on anyone's person. It had been a cruel two hours in the freezing cold and some of the women around Anna were showing signs of hypothermia and sickness. Finally the officer came up and ordered them to dress and remain on deck.

Now, Anna knew, the real interrogations would begin. The ownership of the guns was to be established. One by one, the men were brought out, bullied, beaten and casually hit in a process which the conscripts were evidently enjoying. At last they had their moment of power, after suffering the same treatment from their more senior conscripts back at whatever base they came from. Despite the treatment, nobody claimed a single weapon. Anna watched as Oleg and his friends received similar treatment. She saw he took the blows and made it worse for himself by refusing to appear subdued.

But as they sorted through the pile of guns, she saw the Thompson wasn't in it.

Before the sun began its slow fade to the west, a camera was brought and each of the workers for the Igarka mills was made to stand up straight, hat and cap removed, and then photographed. From behind the conscripts milling in front of her, Anna saw that an old-fashioned fingerprinting machine was being set up on a table in the centre of the ship's deck. Then each of the workers was forced to line up and be printed.

When Anna's turn came, she began to calculate the time it would take for their prints to be helicoptered out, then examined in Moscow, before finally, the alarm bells were rung. It was lucky that they were using such a crude method. It might take days, or even a week, depending on the sense of urgency. Not for the first time, she thanked the inefficiency of the system, including its security forces.

The pile of weapons, maybe two dozen in total, lay on the deck and the Wolf summoned the captain and his crew. It was now the turn of the ship's personnel. Anna couldn't hear the words that were exchanged between them. But it was clear that the Wolf was blaming the captain. It was the captain's responsibility that there were illegal weapons on board. No one could have brought assault weapons on to the ship in the small bags people carried. There must have been collusion back in Krasnoyarsk. One or more of the crew were responsible, he seemed to be saying, and the whole serious problem was ultimately being laid at the captain's door.

Anna watched as one of the two other special forces officers handcuffed the captain. An example was to be made. He looked ill, hungover and white. They took him somewhere below.

The Wolf then took three of the crew with him on to the bridge and the ship's engines were started. Some of the conscripts descended the steps to the launches and headed back for the bank and the waiting helicopters. About thirty stayed onboard. Then a metallic announcement came out across the deck from the bridge through the speakers.

'This ship is impounded by the Russian state,' the Wolf intoned. 'Once we reach Igarka, there will be a full investigation. No one will leave the ship until this has been completed on pain of death.'

The anchor rattled up into the hawses and the *Rossiya* left for Igarka.

CHAPTER TWENTY

BEHIND ITS SHELTERING island, the town of Igarka was tucked into a bend in the river. The water was over half a mile wide and the bend in the river had caused a deep channel to be cut where vessels with a big draught could anchor close to the shore. But the *Rossiya* stayed well away from land.

Sawmills and piled logs dominated the shoreline, with the mainly spruce forest pressing in close behind the town. The functional town – no more than a logging operation – stood on the edge of the Arctic Circle and vast rafts of cut timber waited anchored in log pools for the river's mouth finally to be declared open from ice. The industries of sawmilling and small-ship repairs dominated the shore and these and the power houses that fuelled them were the only buildings visible as the *Rossiya* dropped its anchor out in the channel in the slower-moving current of the river's bend, the chain rattling from the ship into the river floor.

From the deck Anna studied the floating wooden wharves that had been rebuilt after the water surge of spring. She judged the distance from the ship to the nearest wharf and knew it was too far, even if a swimmer weren't spotted in the water. Otherwise she saw the lingering grey pall of a town that was little more than a huge rubbish dump. Nothing was collected from here that couldn't be burned and there were piles of non-inflammable waste that lay randomly discarded.

Anna continued to look from the deck as the sun sank behind her. She watched the piles of waiting timber stacked on wooden trestle roads that were built on the shifting muddy slopes of the banks and, higher up the banks, the concrete roads pitted and gouged by the winter ice. She looked carefully across the sparse township but could see no military helicopters or other military presence. There were just the piles of rounded timber and mountains of sawdust, stacks of planking and the spruce forest pressing in behind the small town.

Roadways made of logs led from the town into the forest. Placed on top of the logs were planks, and on top of these were spread moss and sawdust. The streets were built up high, away from the winter frost. The little patches of concrete visible had thin hopes of success in the Arctic temperatures of winter and any pilings that supported them needed to be sunk deeper into the frozen earth than the slaves and underpaid workers who had built Igarka since 1928 were able to achieve. Beneath the raised roadways grew moss and heather appearing for the brief summer growth.

The half-dozen other ships were moored close in at the log wharfs, but it was clear the *Rossiya* was to remain here, too far from the bank for anyone to make an escape. Even if an escapee weren't shot, the water was so cold that muscles would seize before the bank could be reached.

She saw that her options were narrowing sharply to nothing. By anchoring out here, the intention of the OMON officers was clear. Nobody was to be allowed ashore and there were no boats that had come out from the town as they had done at previous stops. Like the others on board, she realised she was now a prisoner on a prison ship.

From the deck she sniffed the breeze coming off the land. The acres of timber wharves, timber roads, timber houses – miles of sawn planks, lakes of floating logs – gave off a sweet scent of pine and the more pungent odour of sawdust. There seemed nothing else. Just the trees, dead or alive. And, behind the town, the Arctic tundra had finally replaced the *taiga* further south.

She turned and looked up at the bridge. She saw the Wolf and two crewmen behind the windows. There seemed to be no further activity now that the anchor had been dropped. She guessed he was waiting for something, most likely the arrival of someone more senior. A decision was to be made that he couldn't take responsibility for. All she knew now was that she had to get off the ship.

She turned back and saw Oleg. His wispy beard and sunken cheeks were raised towards the shore as if he, too, were judging distances, times, the chances of success and failure. She had a sense that he'd been waiting for her near the exit from the hold. She approached him and leaned on the guard rail and he turned and smiled as if at some sort of triumph.

'They didn't get my gun,' he said. 'Too well hidden for those ignorant pigs.'

'Nevertheless, there are thirty *sapari* with thirty automatic rifles trained on us,' she replied.

'So we have to get off the ship, haven't we?' he said, grinning. Then he looked directly into her eyes and she saw the flame of unbowed determination flare briefly. He was suddenly serious. 'There are six of us,' he said. 'With you, that makes seven. A crewman told me they're going to lock us in the holds before long. They're waiting for others to arrive. We'll be here until they've checked up on every one of us back in Moscow. Tomorrow may be too late. We have a few hours.'

'And even if we did get to shore, what then?' she asked.

'Siberia's a big place,' he said.

'They have dogs, helicopters,' she replied. 'We don't even have darkness. It's light here now for almost twenty-four hours a day.'

'And we have the forest,' Oleg stated, as if it were poised to reach across the water and come to their aid.

He watched her silently. 'I know you have to get off the ship,' he said. 'Just like us. But we'll do it better together than apart.'

She considered this. One person might – just – avoid detection in the river if they threw themselves over the side without being seen doing so. But seven wouldn't. She worked alone, anyway, and certainly not with a bunch of star-struck kids inflated with their own sense of immortality and some purpose she'd yet to define.

She looked down and watched the river's current. Even here, in the slower part of the river, it must still be moving at three knots or so. A swimmer would be swept away from the ship at around thirty yards a minute, she estimated, maybe double that using their body to propel themselves with the current. The current curved towards the bank about half a mile away. Half a mile in freezing water. It was unlikely. Even if they weren't spotted from the deck or the shore.

She looked to the left, past Oleg, at the anchor cable, two-inch chain links attached to a drum somewhere in the anchor hold. She studied where it entered the water and imagined where it was lodged somewhere in the mud below. The ship swung away downriver from the cable as the current swept past it.

'All we have to do is get out of this prison before morning,' he said. It was as if sheer will were going to achieve this feat.

And now, as she looked towards the bank, she saw three men, one shouting instructions, the other two flailing in the water at the river's edge with long metal boat hooks. They were gesticulating and trying to reach towards an object floating in the water.

She looked up at the bridge and saw the Wolf had spotted this scene on the bank too. He was watching closely through binoculars, eyes steady, mouth set in a thin line.

On the bank, she saw that the men were launching an aluminium boat. The object was too far out for the boat hooks to reach. They started the outboard and moved slowly, following the object in the current until they drew level. One of hooks snagged on something, one of the men gave a shout, and the other two hauled with both hooks until they had it alongside. Then they reached down. It was heavy. She didn't need binoculars to see what it was. It took all three of the men to lift out the dead body of Ivan from the current and land it inside the boat like a game fish that had given up the fight.

CHAPTER TWENTY-ONE

MIDNIGHT ON THE *Rossiya* and the hallowed quiet of a silent ship at anchor. Only the distant hum of the generator that operated the lights for navigation, as well as the constantly blazing bulbs of the gang walks below deck and the radio communications room, rolled across her consciousness. But the hum of the generator itself had become a part of the silence.

Anna waited until the deadest hour of the night, between midnight and one in the morning in the northernmost climes, before the sun began to tip the rim of the world at 2 a.m. She lay listening to the sounds of sleep in the women's hold, the occasional grunts and sighs, the cries from dreaming sleepers, the turning of bodies in the darkness. She didn't so much rise from her sleeping place as roll to the side, careful not to disturb her neighbour, and then she crawled away, standing only when she found a space that wound between prone bodies and led to the latrines at the far end of the hold in the direction of the bow. She picked her way carefully, stopping when a sleeper turned or emitted a noise, then waiting for deep sleep to claim them again.

She knew the only way out of the hold was from the

direction she was going, the latrines themselves. The soldiers had battened down the hatches of the holds which contained everyone on the manifest, all of the workers. The hired hands on their way to summer work were now truly like slaves in the hold of the ship. The soldiers' orders were clear and had been broadcast throughout the ship on loud speakers; only MVD troops were to be in the open during the brief period of darkness.

When Anna was clear of the bodies, she tiptoed towards the latrines and hoped there was no one else there. There was no door between the 'sleeping' area and where the women relieved themselves. Even in the dark she could follow her nose towards the stench of the uncleaned latrines. The faintest light coming from a bulb outside a porthole showed her where to place her feet.

Once in the confined space with its basic twin shit holes in the floor that led to pipes which twisted their way through the lower depths of the ship to eject the waste a few feet above the plimsoll line, she waited as her eyes became accustomed to the greater darkness. There were no portholes in here, just the twin holes in the floor and a boxed steel ventilator shaft that protruded above her head through the bulkhead to the next section of the ship. And the disused pipe where she'd hidden the gun and ammunition. She emptied the pipe cautiously and found the gun. It was carefully wrapped in plastic. Then she retrieved the ammunition.

She took a tool from her pack which she unslung now from her shoulders and instead hung it loosely over her right shoulder alone, easy to free when the moment came.

There were two small one-inch pipes, shut-off pipes from the ship's water system that came out of the bulkhead below the ventilator and were sealed closed. She would stand on these to get to the ventilator. But it was a big reach for her leg to get to the left-hand one of these short pipes. She had to use one arm to lift her left leg up while balancing herself with her right arm against the side wall above the holes in the floor, so that when she finally had her foot on the water pipe it was almost at the level of her head. How could she get the leverage to haul herself up so that both feet were balanced on the twin pipes? She took some cord from her pack and looped it around the ventilator, hoping the thin metal casing wouldn't come crashing down with her weight. With great effort, hauling with her arms and pressing with her left foot against the water pipe, she slowly, agonisingly, pulled herself up the side of the steel bulkhead, listening to the metal casing of the ventilator groan and waiting for the snap or twist of metal to shatter the silence. But with the greatest effort she finally reached the precarious standing position, five and half feet above the wet, urine-swilled floor, without generating more than a squealed complaint of strained metal.

She steadied herself, her feet on the two inches of pipes that protruded from the bulkhead and her hands clasping the ventilator shaft, which was now just above her head. When she was calm and rested again, she took the tool from her pocket and felt with the hand that held it for the bolts that joined the ventilator casing sections together, and hoped the builders a hundred years before hadn't welded rather than bolted it. With one hand holding the ventilator casing and the other hand holding the tool, she located six bolts, painted over so long ago she guessed that the paint would no longer be an obstacle to their release.

It was a tortuous process, balanced on the balls of her feet on the pipes as she was, one hand holding the ventilator for support, the other slowly guiding the tool over the first bolt until she felt it lock, and then using all the weight of her right arm to turn the bolt. There was no response at all at first. She tried again, but it wouldn't budge. She then jammed the tool over the bolt and hammered it with the ball of her hand until she felt the bolt nudge slightly, and all the time praying the tool wouldn't fall with a clatter into the darkness below and possibly slide into one of the latrines' holes and be lost. But once the first bolt was loose, it was easy to release.

One by one, with great care and enormous pressure on her wrist and arm, her left arm clinging all the time to the ventilator, she loosened each bolt. The last but one of the bolts was the worst. She hammered the tool with the ball of her hand, but it was on top of the casing and the leverage she could get was very little. She was sweating profusely, the muscles of both arms taut and strained to the maximum, her calves equally strained from standing on the balls of her feet, but finally she felt it loosen. And then when that penultimate bolt came free, eventually she was able to remove the last bolt with ease. Each time she placed the bolts into her pocket so that they wouldn't clatter to the steel floor.

She was at the end of her strength, stretched and pulled

and strained to the limit. She simply stood and clung on to the ventilator with both hands now until she felt her muscles ease a little, lifting one foot, then the other, from each of the pipes in order to give her calves a rest. She felt herself panting in the darkness, inhaling the foul stench of the latrines with each gasping breath. She shuddered with the pain and with the effort of keeping herself balanced, but slowly she felt her heart pounding less frantically and her breath coming more easily.

When she felt ready again, she pocketed the tool, and prepared for the last, desperate throw of the dice – the sliding of the metal flange away from the rest of the fixed ventilator's casing. It was the hardest part from the point of view of her wilting strength. She could no longer cling to the ventilator as she had done, or it wouldn't slide away. She searched blindly with her right hand and finally found a handhold, on the far side of the ventilator where it disappeared into the steel bulkhead. It was just a small hook and it dug into her hand, and she clung on to the hook with three fingers – all that would fit from her hand. With her left hand she then began to push and pull the end of the loosened ventilator from side to side, knocking it with the ball of her hand on one side, then on the other, trying to free it from any paint that still clung after the decades.

There was inevitably some noise now, her hand ringing a hollow, dull echo from the empty ventilator, but she couldn't help that. Once she thought she felt it loosen, but then it stuck again. With only one hand she couldn't guide it out straight, but only tap it from one side to the other. She felt it loosen a little, then come away slightly, and then she knew it was free.

Clinging to the hook with her right hand, she now lowered her left hand and found the cord in her pocket, looping it with that hand around the end of the loose casing and tying a firm knot. The loosened casing was directly above her head. Once she was satisfied with the knot, she let the other end of the cord fall over her shoulder behind her and raised her left hand again to nudge and push the casing further and further away from the bulkhead until she could feel the edge of the main casing. She now picked up the loose end of the cord and, gripping it in her left hand, she nudged the casing with the same hand towards and above her until she felt the whole of the end of the casing begin to fall.

Her right hand dug into the hook and she felt the blood flowing freely down her wrist and up her arm. The heavy casing fell towards her head. She leaned away fast, gripping the cord tightly, and wound around her left hand, until it snapped taut with the weight of the casing and jolted her whole body, jarring all the muscles and bones down its whole length. Her left arm was wracked with the pain and stress of holding the fallen casing, but she held on, her right hand's fingers digging deeper into the hook on the bulkhead.

But she felt the casing swinging safely below and behind her now, away from the steel bulkhead and she somehow held its weight. She swiftly and silently lowered it to the floor. Now her left hand was free to hold the gaping hole of the ventilator shaft and give her right hand a rest. She hung there, sucking the blood from the wound in her hand, panting with the effort.

After a few minutes of gasping and shaking, she recovered sufficiently to push her pack into the ventilator hole and shove it well down inside. She then placed both elbows inside the hole and began to haul herself up to the opening. Everything was agony now. The hole of the shaft was large – maybe two and half feet across – but was it large enough to take her body with her elbows supporting her weight? With a final supreme effort, she felt the point of balance in her body mass shift from hanging down the bulkhead wall to resting on the lip of the ventilator, her head twisted sideways in the hole to fit. Once she had her weight right, she kicked her legs and inched into the ventilator shaft.

She must have lain concealed inside the ventilator for fifteen minutes, she thought. It was more than pitch-dark now, but she could do no more than slump, her whole body stretched along the shaft, the pack pushed ahead of her. She might have fainted for a minute or two and thought she had, waking with a start, her heart beating with surprise at the total blindness that almost rose to panic. And then she began the long, slow crawl down the ventilator shaft in the direction of the bow of the ship.

The ventilator dog-legged twice and it was hard to turn in a right angle. She had to turn herself on to her side so that she, too, could make a right angle with her legs twisted from the waist. There was a grille to her left that showed, in the light of another bulb outside a porthole, the men's section. She eased herself past this, fifteen feet above the sleeping male forms on the floor beneath her. Another grille was bathed in light and she inched carefully past it. The room inside was brightly lit and four or five MVD troops sat playing cards or dozing against a wall. She slid by, silently hauling herself on her elbows, her clothes providing a smooth passage on the pristine metal of the inside of the ventilator.

She guessed it was about thirty yards from the start point when she came to another grille dead of her. Whatever was beyond was in pitch-darkness, but it had to be the anchor room.

Anna tapped at the grille with the palm of her left hand, the unwounded hand. The grille was stiff and she removed the tool again from her pocket with great difficulty and tapped with it until she felt the grille begin to come away from the casing. It was simply fitted without bolts. She hooked the fingers of her right hand through the grille to hold it and kept tapping until it was free. Then she turned it and drew it inside the ventilator shaft at an angle and deposited it gently behind her. She inched forwards and looked over the edge into the blackness.

There was no way she could turn in the shaft and drop her legs down first and she saw at once that it was too risky to go down head first without knowing what was below. It was a danger, but she knew she had to use the small pen torch in her jacket pocket. She fumbled until she found it and turned it on first into the palm of her hand to see how badly wounded it was. There was a deep hole at the base of the fingers which had gripped the hook. There was nothing she could do about it now. As

252

she turned the torch on to the floor of what she hoped was the anchor room, she saw a length of coiled rope twelve feet below her. Flicking the torch up a little, she saw the far side of the room, where the ship's bow was, narrowing the space where the anchor chain was locked in position around the drum. She switched off the torch.

There was approximately a twelve-foot drop, of that she was sure. There was no time to delay now. It had taken a long time loosening the casing at the beginning of the ventilation shaft. She dropped her pack down on to the coiled rope and then began to inch her body through the opening. If she landed right she could take the initial shock of the fall with her arms and then go into a roll. There was no other way. It was now all or nothing. She waited in order to calm her mind and prepare herself mentally. Then she edged her body mass further into the black void. When she fell, she felt her shins scrape across the shaft's sharp edge but all her concentration was on the landing.

She hit the coiled rope with outstretched arms, immediately bending the elbows to absorb the shock and almost instantaneously going into a roll. Her head hit the steel floor, but by that time her fall was broken by her arms and shoulders and the roll took her cascading over the coiled rope, turning her over three times before she came to rest against the anchor chain's drum. She was winded, hardly able to breathe. Her wrists had taken more force than she'd intended, but she thought nothing was broken. Only a spreading pain that went from her head down the side of her body on which she had fallen, all the way to her legs and the scraped shins. She realised that she had barely survived the fall intact and lay still again, concentrating on the pain, focusing her mind on to it until it receded slightly in the face of her focused attention. Then she dragged herself upright.

The room was in total darkness still, no light came through from outside and she realised there were no portholes. She could switch on the torch again. In its light she saw the lever that held the chain. It was locked into place in the cogged wheel that arrested the chain at the right length for their anchorage.

She got to her feet and saw the sledgehammer the crew would have used to free the chain. She lifted it and calculated as she had already done before in the women's hold the force of the current, and the distance to the sandbank that jutted out downstream from the ship as the river curved around slightly to the west. The ship was hard on the chain and the current pulled it downstream. It was anchored away from the bank, but not close enough for anyone to jump in safely and swim to shore. She lifted the sledgehammer to shoulder height and brought it down on the lever. It sprung away with a crack and suddenly the room was filled with the deafening noise of the chain slowly beginning to unravel as the drum was freed and the ship was dragged by the current.

Then it began to pick up speed as the current took hold of the ship fully, with nothing to hold it now. She guessed that the river flowed at four or five knots here. She felt the ship slowly drifting with the current as the drum unrolled the chain. How long was the anchor chain?

Would it allow the ship to travel far enough in order to ground it? The chain was unravelling faster now as the current picked up the ship still further, and then its own momentum began to push it away from the anchor embedded in the silt. Thirty seconds, forty, the ship was probably doing a knot of speed now, two knots maybe.

Then she felt a judder as the stern, the deeper part of the vessel, touched the bottom, but the current still forced the vessel on.

Someone above would have noticed what was happening now, even if they didn't know why. She pulled on a military cap, took her pack and waited in the lee of the hatch. Almost immediately she heard shouts, and the hatch to the anchor room was flung open. Two crewmen entered rapidly. She heard shouts outside. Then the bow of the ship struck an immovable object on the river floor; a rock maybe. She heard a grinding, ripping sound echoing up through the hollow steel of the bow. It was too late for the crewmen to arrest the drum. It was running wildly.

Anna silently slipped through the hatch and on to the deck as the ship began to tilt to the side. She heard the crashing of unsecured objects on the deck, the clatter of boots, then shouts and curses as the ship began to heel violently. Men were sliding, dropping their weapons as, keeping to the shadows, Anna made the rail on the side where the ship had heeled and threw herself over it into the fast-flowing water.

As she hit the water, floodlights went on, but they now all pointed down into the river nearest the ship, at the angle to which the ship had tilted, and soon she was away, yards from the shore and she struck out in the darkness until she felt sand beneath her feet. She was freezing, the water ice cold, and she ran up the shallow incline of the shore towards a group of trees. From the eastern horizon, the sky was beginning to lighten.

CHAPTER TWENTY-TWO

THE WOLF DMITRY was fast; faster than anyone on the ship to respond to the imminent disaster that was unfolding. In the commandeered captain's cabin, he felt the movement of the ship through a sleep that was never deeper than the slightest slide from wakefulness. And with a mind that suspected sabotage in anything, his instincts told him almost at once that it was the woman.

He sprung half-dressed from the bunk and automatically picked up a loaded GSh-18 locked breech pistol on a chair beside it.

As the ship grounded it wasn't hard for him to see that the approaching catastrophe was no accident. An anchor as big as the *Rossiya*'s held fast here in the silt at the bottom of the river and so some human agent was responsible. What had happened? That he couldn't guess, and it was anyway unimportant. Only the agent of the disaster was on his mind.

He swiftly put on his boots and jacket. He was out of the cabin as the ship's pace picked up and then suddenly shuddered to a near halt as it struck the river bed. By the time the hull ground itself further into the silt and, then, what felt like rock tore at the metal shell and the whole structure began to heel violently, he was on the tilting deck and had the pistol gripped in his right hand like an extension of himself. The heeling was now more than ten degrees and any unsecured items on the deck were beginning to slide in the darkness, knocking unwary conscripts against the guard rails and over the side. There were shouts and crashes and cries in the darkness. Then the deck was listing at twenty degrees and still the ship kept turning its port side towards the surface of the water.

He shouted up at the bridge deck to a panicked crewman to switch on the floodlights. The man dragged himself up the slope of metal inside the bridge. And Dmitry began to search in the darkness for the person he knew in his angry heart was the cause. It must be the woman. The body of Ivan the evening before had told him that. The man's face was mashed by broken glass. He had never quite believed her story. There'd been something wrong about her from the moment he'd seen her. She was different. The discovery of the foreman's body the night before only now confirmed what he'd sensed when he'd had her standing against the wall and he'd seen how she'd received his blows with what could only be described as a practised resilience. He knew he should have locked her up then, the previous evening, after the body was found, and that made his heart blacker and now his fury slowly ground itself into a sharp, focused point.

But he hadn't locked her in the ship's brig. Instead he'd wavered, his mind on other things, perhaps – on a paranoid idea of saboteurs everywhere that had clouded his judgement and induced him to overlook the single element, the woman, who posed all the danger. Instead of locking her up, he'd merely sent the picture of her that was on the dolt Ivan's phone, which had been found in his cabin after he'd disappeared, to his superiors. Dmitry had looked through the pictures on it the night before – all women, and all women that a drunken fool like Ivan would never have had a chance with. But he'd sent her picture on to Moscow during the night. He knew there was something not right about her. Better to be safe than sorry and Igarka was the first place they'd come to on the river where there'd been any mobile phone reception. He'd missed his chance to neutralise her the night before but he wasn't going to miss it again. His career was on the line, but personal rage was what drove him.

Now as he gripped the rail with his left hand and as the ship heeled further over with every minute, he looked out into the darkness and he knew she was there some-where. Maybe she was still on the ship, or already in the water. He shouted again at the bridge for light.

The problem was that in the darkness and with the river now churned up with conscripts who'd fallen from the deck, he couldn't find the body which he hoped would shortly be a corpse. If he could only calm his furious mind and sort out the dozen or so drifting figures. In an instant he instinctively judged that those who'd fallen accidentally were drifting slowly downstream, flail-ing their arms in the current, shouting half-heard calls for help. Some of them undoubtedly wouldn't know how to swim. But he didn't care for them. What he was looking for in the dark waters wasn't a drifting or drowning figure at the mercy of the current, it was a determined, planned escape, a body that was neither flailing nor shouting for help, but was aiming itself straight to the shore, out of the current.

All he could see as his eyes adjusted to the darkness was some white water where bodies thrashed the surface and he shouted at the bridge again, screaming for his orders to be obeyed. The ship's floodlights suddenly burst their blinding light over the water. The ship was still tilting, it looked as if it wasn't going to stop. It must have grounded on a shelving bank, he thought, next to a trough in the riverbed. And it was falling slowly and inevitably into the cutting. Feverishly he examined the whiteness of the water where humans were disturbing it.

And then he saw it: a straight, aimed kick of white water; it was not heading for the ship, which would have been logical if it had been a conscript, nor drifting help-lessly in the current as others were, but directing itself at the bank, only yards away from it now, the kicking of the water behind the figure forming a line of foam, the direction straight and true.

He raised his pistol but the floodlights on the ship were now pointing close on to the water with the ship's tilt. Their light wasn't spread away from the hull but down into the water at the sides. The dart of white water he'd seen was suddenly lost in the darkness again, where the lights now failed to reach. He was at the edge of the deck. He gripped the rail more tightly with his other hand, his feet sliding on the metal, wet with the night's dew. He remembered where he'd seen the white water and fired four, five shots slightly ahead of where he'd seen it, and then beyond. It was guesswork, but he was highly trained.

The ship tilted violently again and the water began to lap over the sides, flooding into his boots, and he felt the freezing sensation grip his ankles and shins. He only just kept his grip on the rail which was now at an angle of thirty or even forty degrees. The short recoil-operated action of the gun worked perfectly but there was no cry of a wounded person. The shots must have been too low or wide, dipping into the water behind the line of foam as the ship leaned suddenly again, and he tried to steady himself once more. He heard himself shouting vile curses at the woman and saw the helpless conscripts drifting past him, trying to grab the guard rails which trailed in the water. Others were already lost in the darkness behind the vessel.

The barrel of the pistol rotated again, he planted his feet wide, his body flat against the guard rails where the gravity of the angle had thrust him. Now he could get a fair shot and he blasted two more bullets into the darkness ahead of where he'd last seen the line of white water. And then the ship shuddered to halt, almost on its side, and he needed both hands to grip the rail or he would have gone over the side with the others. The bullets, where were the bullets? In his urgent departure from the cabin he must have left them behind. The rotating barrel was empty. Dmitry leaped over the rails which were now half underwater and seized a rifle from a conscript trying to get back up again over the rails, thrusting him back with the rifle butt into the water as he did so. With the rifle over his head he swam on his back in the direction where he knew she'd gone.

Anna felt the last two bullets pound into the mud on the bank to the left of her as she ran on to a harder surface of stones and then tore ahead for the cover of the trees. The trees now showed dark against the lightening of the sky to the east and she made it into a small covey of stunted, twisted trunks and branches and then ran on without pausing until she'd put them between her and the ship. She knew she had almost no time. If she could make it to the shore, then so could others. And now she saw lights coming on in the town in response to the shooting and to the ship's floodlights. The catastrophe would be immediately visible to anyone in the town who saw the ship's lights directed down into the river.

She didn't pause to catch her breath but ran on. She'd noted the low buildings of the town from the evening before, and their arrival at Igarka. Before she and the others had been locked in the holds.

Now she ran towards one low building in particular. It was one of several that served the lumber factories and she saw it was surrounded by piled logs and sawn planks; a sawmill. She was in the lee of the sawmill less than thirty seconds after she'd passed the trees. She felt her feet treading deep wood chippings and saw the sawdust on her boots. There was a door on the north side of the corrugated structure. She tested the handle and found it locked.

She unstrapped the Thompson Contender from her back and tore off the plastic waterproofing and hoped that her improvised efforts to keep it dry had been successful.

She didn't bother with the silencer. From a distance of two feet – dangerously close to be shooting into metal – she fired off a round into the lock and saw it twist and collapse. She jammed her shoulder into the door and it gave way easily.

As Dmitry hit the bed of the river with his feet, he heard the single shot and judged the direction. He hauled himself on to the shore, the rifle still held high. Then he felt the ground harden under his feet and knelt and saw the footprints, the smaller prints of a woman's boots. He stood and ran towards the trees, stopping briefly to find traces of the boots where the ground had become harder and it was difficult to see. He was through the trees, when a light came on outside what looked like a long corrugated iron warehouse. The light illuminated the river frontage of the warehouse, on the western side. He saw two figures, uncertain what to do. He ran towards them, levelling the weapon until he saw they were workers, a foreman perhaps and another man. He shouted instructions. But they wavered. They saw a man in soaking trousers and jacket waving a rifle who could have been, from their point of view, the problem not the solution. Dmitry fired the rifle into the air.

'Get everyone out here!' he screamed. 'I want the town surrounded.' The authoritative violence of his voice was enough to delay them no longer.

Anna heard the voice and recognised it. She also saw the glow of the lights on the eastern side of the building where the light crept around to shed some illumination on the north door where she'd entered. There was little time. She walked steadily into the blackness of the mill feeling along the walls and the worn wooden surfaces of work benches, bumping occasionally into equipment. There would be a cupboard, a metal cupboard most likely, but what she was looking for might also be lying around loose, locked up at night. And there would be more than one, a dozen or so probably. She followed the interior metal wall, came to a cupboard, opened it and scrambled around inside it with her hand. She felt the sharp pain of a saw blade, followed it back to the handle and knew it was a chainsaw. She lifted it out, shook the machine with her hand and found to her relief it was full of fuel.

Then she stopped and looked back towards the door where she'd entered and which she'd closed as best she could behind her with its lock now shattered. A thin sliver of light from outside outlined the door jamb. Too risky. They – he – would find it. But perhaps that would work in her favour. He'd enter through there and she would exit at another door. She walked slowly, the chainsaw in one hand, the Thompson Contender in the other, towards the eastern side of the building, then felt along it until she came to another door. Padlocked on the outside. She put down the chainsaw and felt with her left hand for the slight gap between the door and the jamb, then knelt until she could see the bolt the padlock held in place against the lightening eastern sky. She placed the barrel of the gun into the gap and fired two swift shots and felt the bolt shatter. And then lights went on in the mill and she was out of the door as a rifle bullet sliced into the door frame to her right.

Outside the building there was a pandemonium of men without a leader. She saw a Niva jeep across the mud and sawdust and a man getting into it. She ran for it and opened the door, dragging him out and knocking him cold with the pistol butt. She flung the chainsaw into the passenger seat and, finding the keys in the ignition, started it at the second try and gunned the engine into life. With no lights she aimed straight along the wooden road that was now just visible in the dawn. The jeep crashed against the ill-fitting wooden beams of the road until the wood road ran out at the edge of the town and she was on a dirt track that headed northwards, into the forest. The jeep slewed in the mud, bumped against a thin tree trunk to the side and very nearly turned over. But she was in trees, the thin silver stems of trunks picking out the thinner light of the dawn coming from the east. Two shots rang out but neither hit her or the jeep. She'd reached beyond the small town and she jammed her foot on the throttle.

CHAPTER TWENTY-THREE

WHAT ALEXEI PETROV saw from the foredeck of the *Sibirski* ferry just a few hours later was nothing like the Igarka he'd seen before. A ship, which he soon found to be the *Rossiya*, wallowed on its side, half-submerged. Its funnel was pointing almost at the bank. But it was on the banks themselves and around the town that the scene erupted in his eyes and in his mind. There appeared to be an army camp in the making. It was as if half a regiment had suddenly arrived in this town of just a hundred or so permanent inhabitants.

A launch was coming towards the *Sibirski* as the ferry slunk behind the island that protected Igarka from the main river. Through a megaphone from the launch, a Federal Security Service officer ordered the captain to moor at anchor and not approach the jetty which had been just completed after the spring torrent and which would normally have received the vessel. The captain obeyed at once. The man with the megaphone, Petrov saw, was a colonel in the FSB, or KGB as it had once been known and was still called privately. That's what it was in everything but name. The ferry's anchor began to be prepared and was dropped several hundred yards upstream from the *Rossiya*.

As the ship slewed to a halt, its stern swinging downstream in the direction of the current and the stricken ship, Petrov took in the scene in greater detail. There were thirteen troop-carrying helicopters that he could count. Some were the older Hind versions – gunships to carry troops into forward battle. Others were the newer Mi-24s that were replacing the Hinds. Both were attack helicopters used in the wars in Chechnya or, in the case of the older ones, in Afghanistan in the eighties. Around the helicopters were tented camps, hastily set up in the past few hours, by the look of them. He saw soldiers from the GRU, Russia's biggest foreign intelligence agency, as well as OMON groups and FSB officers and one or two MVD uniforms amongst them. It was a display of Russia's disparate and, frequently warring, security forces. Then, straining his eyes, he thought he saw on the bank nearer to the ferry an FSB general.

Petrov had once visited the set for a film about the battle of Stalingrad. They'd had a front line of World War Two T-34 tanks and, behind them, five thousand modern tanks, their modern design concealed from the film's audience. That was what Igarka looked like, a film set, he thought. It was as if the hundreds of men were preparing for a small war and, as he looked, he heard two more gunships approaching and he watched them land on hastily improvised orange plastic crosses on the edge of the town.

Petrov stood and looked in awe that was swiftly

followed by a deep trepidation. It was a scene from a war on foreign soil, but they were here, deep inside Russia, and entering the heartland of the Evenk people. Like the Wolf Dmitry felt when the ship began to ground, he somehow sensed that the arrival of so much manpower, backed by the most senior security services, must in some way be connected not to an imminent battle but to a single person. And he thought of the woman again and of who on earth she might be. But he had no idea why he thought of her or how all this could be connected to her. The idea seemed to him impossible.

He turned away from the bank, as if to blot out the scene from his mind. Behind him, ten yards or so away on the deck, he saw that the other passengers were gathering for disembarkation at the ferry's final stop. But they, too, were standing amazed, enthralled at the sight of the small army ashore. Then he saw the three Americans. They'd avoided him since the last conversation they'd had. They hadn't appeared in the restaurant since the day before. But as he watched them closely, he saw they were exhibiting a different kind of nervousness than they had in his company. Theirs was a look bordering on extreme anxiety. And to Petrov it seemed that the Americans, too, felt some kind of personal significance in the events onshore. And again, it all seemed to be connected to the woman. But he didn't know why he thought that. Why did the woman keep entering his mind, even when he was watching the Americans?

The passengers waited on deck for nearly an hour before several more launches arrived at the same time at the ferry's side. GRU troops climbed up the steps which the captain had dropped and they were followed by four GRU officers and some uniformed FSB men. It was unusual to see the GRU and FSB apparently working together, Petrov thought. They were the fiercest of rivals in matters of internal security.

An FSB colonel ordered the passengers to form three lines, one for Russian citizens, another for citizens of the former Soviet republics, or 'the near abroad', as the Russians called them, and another line for foreigners. The Americans were the only ones in the foreigners' line. And then Petrov saw yet another launch approaching and he saw that it contained the FSB colonel he'd seen. It was coming to a halt at the foot of the steps. The colonel stepped out of the launch and walked stiffly up the steps on to the deck.

Petrov saw it was the Americans who were dealt with first. There was an intense scrutiny of their papers, questions on the deck first, and then they were taken below with the FSB colonel and two troopers. Then some of the passengers from the 'near abroad' were singled out for interrogation, first on deck like the Americans, then taken individually below decks. When it was the turn of his line, Petrov had his papers ready, the ones which showed he was a *militsiya* lieutenant, as well as the permit from his boss Sadko to travel to his family village and beyond. He was the only police or security individual in the line and he was at once taken below by two FSB men.

They sat him in a chair in the ferry's radio room. The

FSB colonel sat on the far side of a table opposite him, another more junior officer beside him, with two troopers standing behind Petrov, in case, he assumed, he made a break for the door. One of the officers had both sets of his papers on the table, his *militsiya* identification and his special permit for travel.

'Lieutenant Petrov,' the colonel said.

'Yes,' Petrov replied.

'I'm Colonel Fradkov of the FSB.'

Petrov nodded his head in acknowledgement.

'As you see,' Fradkov said, 'we have a serious situation. You might be of help. Where are you travelling?'

'Into the mountains east of Norilsk,' Petrov replied. 'Around the Putorana, where my family take the reindeer in summer.'

'You'll be going there straightway?'

'Yes, colonel.'

'You're from Krasnoyarsk,' the colonel then stated, looking at Petrov's papers. He was a man in his thirties, like Petrov, with dark, close-knit eyebrows and a thin nose. His skin was very clear, no signs of a dissolute life, and he looked fit, with eyes the colour of agate.

'I'm in charge of the quarter around the docks in Krasnoyarsk, yes,' Petrov replied.

The officer then looked at his permit.

'Why are you travelling north?' His voice wasn't pleasant exactly, but it lacked the usual aggression Russian citizens expected. 'Just to visit your family?'

'My grandfather is ill. They say he's dying.'

'A tribal man?' he said.

271

'Yes,' Petrov replied, though it was clear from his own features that he wasn't a Slav.

'Call his commanding officer, this Sadko,' the officer said to his second in command. 'Tell him to text a photograph of Petrov.'

The officer left the room and returned a few minutes later. Meanwhile Petrov and the colonel sat in silence. When the second officer returned, he just nodded.

'He's getting about it right away,' the second officer said.

'And the permit is genuine?'

'Yes, colonel.'

'Good.' He looked up at Petrov. 'There was a body of a dead foreigner found in your quarter three nights ago,' Fradkov said.

'Yes. A German. I was the first to examine it – at least the first person from the security forces,' Petrov said. 'As it was a foreigner, I handed the case immediately to the MVD in Krasnoyarsk.'

The officer looked questioningly at him.

'A major called Robolev,' Petrov said.

'Good,' the colonel said again.

This time the second officer didn't need to be told. He left the room and returned moments later with a nod to his superior. 'It's confirmed,' he said.

'So your papers check out, Lieutenant Petrov,' the colonel said. 'And your story. How are you planning to travel north?'

'I'll wait for one of the small privately owned boats that can make their way through the ice floes. There are plenty every day at this time of year. For a fee,' he added.

The colonel seemed to be considering whether to add anything further. Then he leaned his elbows on the table and looked into Petrov's eyes, his own agate-coloured ones hard and expressionless.

'You may be wondering why there's so much military presence here,' he said.

'Yes,' Petrov answered. 'I was.'

'There is a highly dangerous terrorist also apparently heading north,' he said. 'The eyes and ears of you and your people may be useful.'

'How can I help, colonel?' Petrov asked.

'How can you help?' The officer seemed to be thinking, but he didn't take his eyes away from Petrov's for a second, and Petrov saw he was only pretending to be considering his question. 'The terrorist is a woman,' the colonel replied and his eyes hardened on Petrov's, but Petrov didn't blink or look away. He managed to form a simple expression of curiosity.

'All this,' he said, 'for a woman?' and he indicated with his eyes upwards to the top deck and away to the shore where the army camp was forming.

'She's no ordinary woman and she may not be working alone,' the colonel said. 'But if she is, this is a big place for an individual to lose herself in. That's why you – as a Russian *militsiya* officer – as well as your people can add your special knowledge to the search. Out in the terrain of the Putorana you may be most useful. We will hunt her until we find her.'

'A terrorist?' Petrov said.

The colonel seemed to consider again whether to add further to the description. 'A highly dangerous terrorist,' he insisted finally. 'We believe she – or they – plan to blow up a nuclear reactor outside Dikson. The papers she's travelling under say her name is Valentina Asayev.' He looked back at Petrov's incredulous but steady gaze. 'If she succeeds, your people will be wiped off the face of the earth,' he said.

Petrov's detective mind tried to unravel what he was hearing.

'You mean the new reactor? The one they're planning to drag to the Pole?'

'You know about that,' the colonel stated.

Petrov shrugged. 'Everyone talks about it, that's all.'

The colonel retrieved a mobile phone from his pocket and played with it until he found what he was looking for.

'This is what she looks like,' he said, and for the first time Petrov saw a picture of the woman who called herself Valentina Asayev.

Then the colonel stood.

'You're to report into me personally. Every day.'

'That might be difficult,' Petrov said. 'Communications are non-existent up there outside the towns.'

Colonel Fradkov nodded to his junior, who left the room again and returned with a satellite phone.

'You'll take this and report to me at this number . . .' he took a card from his breast pocket, '. . . every day,' he repeated. 'I'll be expecting it.'

Then the colonel placed his elbows on the table.

'We also believe the dead German's suitcase has been found,' he said. 'It was an expandable leather briefcase. But there's a German maker's mark on it. It wasn't with the body when you found it?'

'No, colonel. I'd wondered about that. Where was it found?' Petrov asked.

'On a dump, not far from where the body was.'

'Did it contain anything?'

'Apart from the man's underclothes and washing equipment and so on, nothing except a bald wig.'

Petrov looked blank.

'Do you know anywhere in Krasnoyarsk where you might buy such a thing?' the colonel asked.

'No,' Petrov replied. 'I doubt such a place exists.'

The colonel looked at him and then went back to his paperwork.

'Every day, understand?' he said, without looking at Petrov.

'Yes, colonel.'

Petrov paused. 'What will you do with the Americans?' he asked, though he didn't know why he should involve himself further.

The colonel looked up from the papers on the table sharply. 'You've met the Americans?'

'Yes,' Petrov replied. 'I spoke to them several times.'

'And?'

'They seemed odd, not the usual tourists you expect on the ferry. They barely looked out at all from the upper deck. They stayed below. It wasn't . . . it wasn't quite natural in my opinion.'

The colonel regarded him for a moment. 'Good. You're observant, Petrov. Just as your boss said you were.'

Petrov was surprised to hear this commendation from Sadko.

'We'll take the Americans to Krasnoyarsk, in answer to your question,' the colonel said, looking back at his paperwork. 'For the time being we'll pretend they're spies.' He looked up. 'Just to frighten them, you understand.' He looked keenly at Petrov again. 'Just so you know, Lieutenant Petrov, if you catch this woman, you will no longer be Lieutenant Petrov, but General Petrov. Understand? You'll have an apartment in Moscow and a dacha in the country. You'll be given a pension that will enable you to live in New York, if that's what you want. The State will be eternally grateful, in other words. Do I make myself clear?'

'Yes,' Petrov replied, but his mind was reeling.

'Remember it,' the colonel said. Then he returned to his papers again.

The second in command now stood and issued an order to the two troopers who stood behind Petrov.

'Take him ashore and make sure he sees the Communications unit and knows how to use the phone,' he said.

As Petrov stood on the deck waiting for the launch to arrive and take him into shore, he saw the three Americans again. They'd been brought back up on deck. He saw the woman, Eileen, look directly at him and then he noticed in her eyes that there was something urgent.

There were a lot of people milling around on the deck and Petrov was able to move closer to her without attracting undue attention. Then he saw her drop something – a small piece of folded paper – on to the deck and she turned away immediately.

Petrov sidled towards where she'd been standing. He watched as the three Americans were handcuffed and taken down the steps to a waiting launch. The security services were exercising their usual hard tactics, he observed.

He watched as they were whisked across the narrow water to a smaller jetty away from the main harbour and then taken to a helicopter which immediately rose into the air and headed south. To Krasnoyarsk, he assumed.

Petrov kneeled and picked up the paper Eileen had dropped and put it into his trouser pocket. And as he did so, he thought about his recent conversation with the colonel. If the woman – whoever she might be – was planning to blow up the reactor in Dikson, why did these security forces who now carpeted the town need the support of his people in the Putorana? The two were hundreds of miles apart. No one going to Dikson would go closer than a hundred miles to the Putorana. The only thing in the Putorana apart from the wilderness of his people were the ICBM silos and the nuclear research facility. Bachman's visit to Norilsk was as close to the Putorana as you could get.

CHAPTER TWENTY-FOUR

I T WAS DARK by the time Anna decided to pull off the forest track. The track was now an indistinct, snow-covered way that she had occasionally lost in the light of a half-moon that filtered thinly through forest branches. Twice she'd had to retrace her route to find the track again. No one had been this way since the snow had last fallen and there were no tyre marks to follow ahead. And along with the increasingly difficult progress she was making, she sensed that, even more than twenty miles north of the town, she was still being followed.

She cut the engine and listened for sounds from where she'd come. There was nothing at first, except the sound of an owl and an answering call from further into the forest. But then she thought she heard a low, constant sound, dense and distant. It would fit the sound of a rasping jeep's engine. She checked the petrol gauge and saw it was nearly on empty. She would have to dump the jeep now anyway and find her next route northwards.

She started the engine and began a slow crawl through the trees to the left of the track that eventually brought her to the river. The trees finally cleared, giving way to snow-covered rock and she came out high up on a cliff face, seventy feet at a guess from the river. Here the moon was free of obstruction and she caught the occasional glint of water and the lighter shades of the remaining ice floes. Some of the floes were travelling north in the current, others were caught on the bank. She looked over the cliff and saw a way she could scramble down to the river. Then she removed the chainsaw from the passenger seat.

She started the engine once more, put the jeep in gear, and jumped clear as it hovered, then scraped and tore at the cliff's overhang, before tumbling to a shingle beach below.

She followed the way back she had taken in the jeep on foot as far as the track. First she stacked branches against where she had turned into the trees and then scattered more along the track ahead of where she'd turned off. It was the only way to obscure, temporarily at least, that the jeep's journey had ended here. She piled heaps of branches for ten or twenty yards or so ahead of her turn-off. It was a delay, but not much of one. Then she listened again. This time she heard the unmistakable sound of a grinding, tortured gear change and she knew the Wolf wasn't going to give her up.

She found a suitable branch for her purposes, away from the track and back towards the cliff edge, and she cut and trimmed it as she wished. Then she dragged it towards the descent to the river she'd spotted from the cliff. With the trimmed branch in one hand and the chainsaw in the other, it took her nearly ten minutes to reach the shingle bank below.

Here in the patchy light of the silver moon she stopped

and listened again. Nothing. There was no sound this time, just the cool flow of the river. She thought that either it was because sound didn't reach over the cliff from the track or because her pursuer had already reached the blocked track and was checking the way ahead. He would soon find there were no wheel tracks continuing northwards beyond the piled branches.

She walked down the rounded shingle bank to where the river curved away a little and saw several floes stacked against each other up against a broken tree. Then she waded out to the floe that was deeper into the river and which still floated. It was caught, pressing itself against the other grounded ones. She yanked the cord of the chainsaw twice before it started. Then she began to cut a hole the size of a human being deep into the centre of the fifteen-foot monster.

Dmitry the Wolf halted at the obstacle of branches and carefully climbed out of the jeep. He noted that he couldn't pursue her much further. It had taken hours to travel the distance to where he was and fuel was low. But maybe she too would be shortly running out of fuel. The branches ahead suggested that the track turned to the right, away from the river, but in the faint light all he could see were the dark silver trunks of trees that way. He walked into the forest slowly, the rifle in an attack position like a hunter. By the time he'd gone twenty yards, stopping every yard or so to listen, he knew that the branches on the track were a deliberate feint.

He came back to the track again and walked along the edge of the forest until the way ahead was clear of branches and he saw that the track continued, but that the wheel marks in the snow that he'd been following did not.

He carefully skirted back to where he'd left the jeep. She might be waiting for him, waiting to get a shot. They were two animals circling each other in the dark and he realised now that she had only a pistol of some kind – the shot he'd heard in the sawmill – while he had a rifle. But shooting at distance in the semi-darkness of the forest was going to be of no advantage to him. They would have to be up close just to see each other. He crouched beside the jeep and contemplated his next move. Then he saw the piles of branches to the left of the track and, walking beyond them, leading towards the river, he saw there were the marks of wheels.

Anna finished carving a hole in the ice floe and switched off the chainsaw. She waded back to the shingle bank and crouched down behind the broken tree. He would find the tracks that led to the cliff – eventually. Maybe he already had. Then he would see the jeep smashed on to the shore below the cliff and, like her, he would see the descent. He would spot her footsteps in the snow that led down to the river. She could run, or she could wait for him, but she didn't need to think long before she decided which choice she would make.

She cranked the chainsaw again, twice, three times before it sprung into life. There was a little fuel still left. Then she tied the throttle to On and wedged the running saw into a crook of the broken tree. She crawled backwards now, away from the tree and the ice floes, up the shingle bank, following the river's curve for twenty yards, before she found a rock. She took up a position behind the rock and unslung the Thompson Contender from her back, checked the barrel had a centrefire rifle cartridge, and slid the safety catch. She chose a big game round, rather than the rimfire bullets she would normally use to disable or kill a human or small animal. But after what he'd done to her on the ship the Wolf was now big game to her. She got up from behind the rock as the chainsaw ran on, cutting empty air, its noise excluding all else in the silence and creating a fatal focus of attention. Then she walked up the shingle bank and ascended the cliff in a different place from where she'd first come down.

Dmitry grabbed at a rock on the way down the cliff to stop himself from sliding and almost lost the rifle. He was exposed, too exposed on the gently sloping descent, and now he knew – even without the sound of a chainsaw – that he was close to her. Her steps on the descent were firmly printed in the snow.

He reached the foot of the cliff and looked up the shingle bank towards the sound. There was her jeep, crashed over on its side. He would check it, but without expecting her to be inside it. It was no accident, he was sure of that. He crouched low and approached the jeep. Through the driver's window now facing the sky, he saw at once that it was empty. He walked back still in a low crouch to the edge of the cliff.

It was dark down here, but not quite dark enough. Against the snow he could be seen and so he followed a route right against the cliff where snow hadn't been able to settle. His first thought as he crept with the rifle ready and the catch off was that this was going to be easy, easier than he'd expected. Unless she was looking right at him, she would see virtually nothing and the noise of the chainsaw meant that she would hear even less. He crept further against the lee of the cliff and picked out a collapsed tree up ahead. It was leaning in towards the river and a few ice floes were jammed up against it. That was where the noise was coming from. She must be behind the tree. Cutting wood for a fire maybe. The bitter cold coming off the river was chilling him to the bone now even with a jacket, as he no longer had the warmth of the jeep.

He came closer – thirty, twenty yards away from the broken tree – and then something began to trouble him and the thought made him instantly duck down against the cliff. There was no cover here but the darkness.

The thought that snapped suddenly into his mind was that the noise of the chainsaw was steady, consistent, without revs, without the higher then lower pitch of whining that it should be making, without the different, lower sound of a blade cutting into wood. And he realised then that it was cutting air and that there was no hand on the throttle.

He looked up and saw a rock between him and the broken tree; cover of sorts. And he began to crawl on his belly tight to the ground, his right knee bending up to give him traction, his left leg long, dragged along by the right leg, and the rifle an inch or so off the stones, held in his left hand up ahead of his body, leaving his right hand free to press the trigger. He felt himself break into a sweat.

He knew he was crawling into a trap and only the darkness, and the rock, could come to his aid. And then the chainsaw stuttered, ran on a little, stuttered again and stopped, leaving the river and the shingle bank and the high moon smothered under a deafening silence.

The blow that struck him like a metal whip across the cheek came from nowhere. He reeled out of the crouch he was in behind the rock, dropping the rifle that clattered on to the stones, and let out a sharp cry of surprise and anger, as much as pain. He fell heavily onto his side, but was on his feet in seconds. It was her, the long barrel of a kind of handgun he'd never seen before levelled at his head, her hands steady, both of them on the gun, her feet apart and, from the moon's dull glow, he thought he saw a smile on her face.

'You would have been a hero,' she said in the deep silence.

He put his hand to his cheek and felt blood.

'You don't know who I am,' she said. 'But they would have made you a general. If you weren't such a fool. If you'd killed me or locked me up. As it is, I'm going to kill you.'

Anna put the long-barrelled handgun down, on to the surface of the rock behind which the Wolf had been hiding. For a split second this perplexed him. But then he launched himself at her. As his body almost flew across the stones at her still figure, she stepped slightly aside, away from the rock, and he felt the agony of her boot in his neck as her right leg kicked high and with immense force into him. In his off-balanced position, he was flung aside by her boot and landed heavily on to the rock, the twin agonies in his neck and now his side making his head swim. He thought he'd broken a rib and he howled in anger and pain as he slid from the rock, but all the time his eyes were on the gun that rested a few inches away.

With as much force as he could muster from his winded and broken body, he catapulted himself towards the gun. Her boot crashed on to the back of his hand and he felt the fingers snap between her boot and the rock, and then a second blow directly in his face that sent him reeling backwards so that he lay flat and splayed on the stones.

'That's for what you did to me,' she said.

The Wolf struggled painfully to his feet. He had beaten five men in hand-to-hand combat to be the man he was and now he was being slowly, measuredly, beaten by this woman. But her first attack had been out of nowhere. She'd weakened him first. He felt a rush of anger, as if she'd played an unfair move in a training exercise, and he saw her smile – more of a snarl – across the six feet that separated them.

He held his good hand up to his cheek where the barrel of the gun had smashed into it, then scraped down it, all the way to his mouth. The blood was still pulsing down on to his arm and chest. His other hand was a mess of broken bones and his left side where he'd been thrown on to the rock sent a searing pain up into his lungs where the breathing was restricted. He knew she could kill him now.

'Lie on your face,' she commanded, and he did so. If

she was to put a bullet in his head then she might come close. That would be his last chance. But she might just shoot him from where she was.

But he heard her boots crunch on the stones towards him.

'Put your hands behind your back,' she ordered him.

He did so painfully and heard her behind and above him. Then he felt a rope twisting around his wrists and he cried out in pain as it caught one of his broken fingers. The knot was tightened. She stood with one foot on his back, near the rib he suspected was broken, in order to get the leverage to pull the knot tight. He nearly fainted with agony. Then, with one boot she turned him over.

'Get up.'

It was a struggle anyway with his hands tied, but with his injuries it was impossible to stand without causing himself the most extreme pain. But finally he was on his knees, rasping breath rushing from his chest in an agonised burst, and then on to one foot and then the other, until he was standing in front of her.

'Turn around. Walk back the way you came.'

The journey back along the shingle bank was hell enough, but the scramble back up the ascent of the cliff blotted out any thought in his mind but the searing pain when he stumbled and had to get up again, feeling the long barrel in his back, and her sure-footed steps behind him. He thought of turning, one last throw of the dice, and trying to kick her off the side of the cliff. All that prevented him from the attempt was a dawning belief that she might not kill him.

They reached the top after a struggle of pain and fear.

'To the jeep,' she ordered. 'No rest.'

He staggered on, through the trees where the moon's light darkened, past the branches she'd laid by the track, until he saw the glint of metal which was the jeep's side.

'Get in.' She held the door open for him and he half fell, half stepped up on to the seat as she shoved him all the way inside. He almost fainted again then, and he vomited with the pain, choking the contents of his stomach on to the passenger seat. He could do nothing now but lie there.

He heard her in the back of the jeep and the terror of his imagination brought an image into his mind of her circling the jeep with a fuel can – that she was going to burn him alive. But then she returned and tied his feet together with some cord she must have dug out of the rear of the jeep.

Then she stood and looked at his half-upturned face for what seemed like an age.

'I sent them your photo,' he rasped. 'To Moscow. To Balashiha. You didn't lose his phone when you killed Ivan.' The thought seemed to give him the brief strength of a final victory over her. 'Whoever you are,' he said, 'you're finished.'

But for Anna, the Wolf's threat was now irrelevant.

'If you don't freeze to death,' she said, 'when they find you, you can explain how you managed to lose Russia's most wanted defector. A former SVR colonel.'

Then she turned and he lay in floods and waves of pain and felt the blood slowly begin to coagulate on his face.

The last thing she did before leaving him was to sling his rifle across her shoulders.

Anna retraced her way to the cliff, down on to the shingle bank, and along to the broken tree. She picked up the branch she had meticulously cut and waded into the freezing waters at the edge of the river until she reached the floe where she'd made the hole. With some difficulty she climbed up on to it, using the branch for support and, once she was inside the hole she had cut with the chainsaw, she pushed against the jammed and grounded floe in front of her. The makeshift pole and paddle forced itself against the floe and, using all her strength, she finally felt the ice floe on which she had taken refuge dislocate itself from the others, turn slightly in the current, and then it was free. With the branch she guided it and her towards the main current of the river to the north.

CHAPTER TWENTY-FIVE

O N THE FOLLOWING morning at just after five o'clock, Alexei Petrov sat with his elbows on his knees in Igarka's harbour office and waited.

Outside the poorly fitting window there was a bitter wind blowing from the north that was following the course of the river. A low grey sky hung over Siberia. From the wooden bench next to the wood burner where he sat, he could see how the wind blasted the young trees sideways on the edge of the town and he felt its chill as it crept under the gaps in the door of the office. A slight snow had fallen overnight. Despite the fact that it was June, the wood burner flamed in the corner of the office, packed with wood, and Petrov was still dressed in a padded jacket.

Early on in the evening before, a member of the GRU Communications unit had shown him the simplicity of the satellite phone and he'd made a test call to the FSB colonel, Fradkov. It had all worked. Now he waited as the Igarka harbour master was out somewhere and, whatever else he was doing, was hopefully checking to see who was going downriver to Dudinka in one of the sixteen-foot alumin-ium boats that were lithe and manoeuvrable enough to avoid the remaining ice floes to the north.

But now, at this particular moment, Petrov was alone and he took the piece of paper that Eileen had dropped on the *Sibirski* the day before from his pocket. It was just a scrap from the inside of a cigarette box and it had been folded roughly in two. He looked at the small writing in Russian, a scrawl merely, and wished he had his wife's magnifying glass that lay in the drawer at home with the rest of her things. Petrov sighed at the thought of his wife's few possessions. Then he squinted one eye half shut and read what the scrawl said. *MNF is nuclear power without danger or waste, from sea water.*

Petrov crunched the paper into the ball of his fist as the door to the outside swung open and the harbour master entered in a gust of wind that blew a twisting billow of snow into the room. He slammed the door behind him. The wind's noise was cut as if with a switch.

'It's like autumn out there, not spring,' he said and stopped by the wood burner to warm his hands. He was silent until that was done – a man who wasted little effort, Petrov noted, and did things in the order that suited him. One of the great unhurried, and Petrov silently approved. When he was done with his hands, he turned.

'There's a man who lives up in Dudinka leaving in half an hour,' he said. 'Pay for half his fuel and he'll take you.'

Dudinka was about a hundred miles north of Igarka. With luck he'd be there in the late afternoon, Petrov thought. If the man had a decent outboard, that was.

'What kind of boat?' he asked.

'Aluminium open boat with a forty-horsepower engine. You know the kind. He's reliable.'

'I'll take it. Thank you.'

The fuel cost relatively little, but it would still knock a hole in the money he'd brought with him. But there was no other way north of Igarka and he'd known that.

The harbour master opened a half-empty bottle of vodka and put his thumb and index finger into two glasses and put all three things on the table. He poured them both a shot. It was just after 5.30 in the morning, Petrov noted, looking at his watch for the first time that day. The harbour master proposed no toast – perhaps he'd exhausted them all long ago – but simply raised his glass to Petrov, who raised his own. They downed the two shots in one go. The harbour master filled his own glass a second time, but Petrov put his hand over his own. The harbour master grunted, lifted his own glass and took it straight down. Petrov tried not to watch him, as if the man might be embarrassed, but he didn't seem to care. Life expectancy for men up here was about forty-six years, Petrov knew.

The man who was to take him north looked about fifteen years old, Petrov thought. When he came into the office, it didn't occur to Petrov that the boy could be his ride to Dudinka. He'd assumed he was the harbour master's son. But down on the jetty outside the office, he watched the man, who told him his name was Roman, and admired the businesslike quality of his arrangements. He took great care with the preparations. The river was dangerous and if you went in up here you might last less than a minute.

Roman took the lid off the outboard and checked inside the cowling and, to Petrov's eyes, it looked well oiled and cared for. The tank was full and there were a dozen more portable military metal cans that held five gallons each. There was little room in the boat for anything else and Petrov jammed his pack into the bow of the metal boat, underneath a tarpaulin. Then he sat slightly forward, where Roman indicated, in order to balance the boat; not too heavy in the stern where the outboard dug into the water, but not too low in the bow either, or the waves that were chopped into high crests by the wind fighting against the current would come over into the boat.

Petrov offered the boatman some bread and cheese he'd bought at the shop the night before, after his lesson with the satellite phone. They sat in the boat that bounced against the wooden posts of the jetty and ate in silence. Roman gave him an apple in return. Then he turned, checked the outboard again, and pulled the cord. The engine immediately came to life and sounded clean and good.

With the wind countervailing the current, it was rough and the journey was going to be slower than Petrov had thought unless it died down. Roman pulled out not quite into the centre of the current, trying to find a happy medium between gaining the maximum from the flow of the river, while avoiding the highest waves in the centre. He hasn't even asked to be paid upfront, Petrov realised, and his liking for the boy grew.

The noise of the engine and the wind was too great for more than the occasional shouted remark and they soon fell into silence, leaving Petrov with his thoughts. And, in particular, the thought of the note he'd read and had flung into the wood burner before he'd left the office. *MNF* – that was Muon Nuclear Fusion; a safe, clean way to providing nuclear power.

To Petrov, it sounded like some Holy Grail – and with about as much chance of existing, let alone of being discovered. But then he thought of Professor Bachman's documents in the inside pocket of his jacket and knew they contained a secret that was, perhaps, some Holy Grail, the unimaginable – at least to him. And he thought that his possession of them must be of some significance. Why him? Why a *militsiya* lieutenant, a tribal Evenk, a childless, wifeless dot on the fringes of an anyway disintegrated society? Except, as Petrov knew deep inside himself, it wasn't he who was disintegrating.

And then, as the waves' spray soaked the outside of his padded jacket and he felt the water running down his face and neck from the oiled cap on his head, his mind turned to the woman. Who was she? And what was *her* significance? The FSB colonel had told him she was a terrorist. Petrov was inclined to think the opposite – not just because that thought came naturally when you encountered anyone from the intelligence services, but because somehow, over the past few days since Bachman's murder, a picture of her was slowly forming in his mind. And this instinctive picture wasn't taking the shape of a terrorist. It was dim, that was true, coming and going in waves of native intelligence, but every time he tried to attach the epithet of 'terrorist' to it, it disappeared altogether. But then there was the small army gathering at Igarka and the 'search and rescue' helicopters that occasionally flew low over the boat and then turned over the forest, scouring it, and this small army was there because of her.

Was she a murderer? Had she killed Bachman? That picture didn't seem to fit either. But he felt a slow realisation that the woman and the documents he carried were inextricably connected, nevertheless.

They'd been riding the river for four hours at just over half revs in the turbulent water, and Petrov was icy cold, a thin film of frozen river water on the sleeves of his jacket. It was then that on the right-hand bank of the river, in the flat, grey light of the day in which nothing stood out against anything else, that he saw something. The river was broad here, half a mile across, and it was hard to see but he knew what he was looking at wasn't a thing of nature.

He pointed at the bank and shouted at Roman, who slowed the throttle slightly while he looked in the direction Petrov was pointing. The struggle against the wind to hold the outboard with its long extension made from a wood pole had kept Roman relatively warm. As the boy looked, he slowly edged the boat at more of an angle towards the shore, careful not to let it turn too far so that the waves chopped by the wind didn't come broadside against the boat. He looked back at Petrov when he was satisfied with the boat's new course. He had a questioning look on his face. He could see nothing strange.

But now Petrov could make out the lines of a jeep, turned on its side on the shingle bank and in the lee of a low cliff. The snow on the cliff was being lifted by the wind in plumes that snaked and spiralled up only to settle in a new location on the rocks above the bank.

Petrov cut the air with his hand, indicating that Roman should go in closer.

The boy was careful, not allowing the boat to turn sideways into the waves, and they came up on the shingle ahead of the jeep, passing it with the angle of their course, and where the water was calmer. And by this time, Roman had seen what Petrov had.

The metal boat crunched on to the shingle and they hauled it with difficulty a foot or so on to the stones, then weighed down the anchor with a boulder higher up the beach. Then they walked back down the shingle until they were standing by the crashed jeep.

Petrov was suddenly Lieutenant Petrov again. It surprised him how much that life had slid away from his consciousness in the past few days. He looked down into the driver's seat, the window facing up towards the sky, and saw both seats were empty. Then he pulled back some canvas in the rear that was snapping in the wind and would soon be shredded by it. There was nothing – or rather nobody – inside. He looked up at the cliff from where it must have fallen. The nose of the jeep clearly had been crushed by the fall. It hadn't been thrown up on to the bank from the river's flood in the past weeks. Then he saw some footsteps in the scuffed, wind-blown snow. They went in both directions, but Petrov began to walk back, in the direction from which they'd come, until he saw that two sets of indistinct footsteps were visible in patches where the new snow had been blown off the frozen snow beneath. He signalled to Roman who was still inspecting the jeep, perhaps looking for things to salvage. Petrov wished he hadn't left his pistol in the pack on the boat.

The two of them ascended the low cliff, Petrov stopping to look at the footsteps from time to time when they appeared; a bigger and a smaller foot, he thought, the smaller one a boy's – or a woman's.

When they reached the top of the cliff, they followed where the occasional appearance of the steps indicated, into the forest, Petrov leading. A hundred yards or so from the cliff top, Petrov stopped. Through the trees he could see another jeep. Slowly this time, as if he were approaching a living crime scene, Petrov advanced under the trees and stepped over a pile of loose branches, until he was standing next to the jeep. Inside it through the closed window, he saw a man, partially tied up as far as he could see. He wore the insignia of the OMON.

Petrov took a hunting knife from his jacket and indicated to Roman to stand away.

Then he opened the door. The man was lying half on his side across the two seats. He had his eyes closed and Petrov couldn't see any suggestion of breathing. Petrov was once more a *militsiya* lieutenant. He didn't know it yet, but it was the last time the learned instincts of police work would be pre-eminent.

He untied the feet which were bound together expertly as far as he could tell. He was able to reach across and grasp the rope which tied the man's hands behind his back. As he did so, Petrov saw the ignition key was switched to On. But the motor had died. He checked the key to see if he was right and he had been. The jeep must have run out of fuel with the engine running. Then he cut the rope around the man's hands – another expert knot, which he used in arrests if he didn't have cuffs with him – and saw a flicker in the man's eyelids. Petrov touched the skin of the man's face and it was icy. The fuel – and the jeep's heat – must have ceased several hours earlier.

He put an arm round the man's neck and slowly pulled him upright, using the shoulders as far as possible, on to the driver's seat. A groan came from blue lips. The face was drained of blood. Hands all but frozen. A body that lingered somewhere between life and death. Petrov began to rub the man's hands, but the man groaned in agony and Petrov saw that one hand was smashed.

From behind him, he felt a tap on the shoulder. Roman had approached and had a metal flask in his hand. Roman unscrewed the cap and gave it to him. Petrov poured some of the liquid around the man's blue lips and watched most of it dribble down his chin, but some stayed in his mouth. Not quite dead yet, he thought, but soon. Roman came through on the passenger side of the jeep and took one of the man's arms between his two and joined Petrov in trying to get some circulation going. Neither of them spoke. But Petrov could see that Roman's face was shadowed by fear; the fear of being found with a dead or dying OMON officer, perhaps.

After half an hour, Petrov felt a faint breath on his

cheek as he leaned across the man. It came and went, not proper breaths. He saw the side of his face was slashed by a sharp object, a blade perhaps, no, the butt of a gun, he guessed. The blood had congealed. And then he felt a whisper, rather than heard it.

Petrov leaned in further, his ear next to the man's mouth. There was a long wait before the strength for even a whisper returned, but Petrov heard the word this time.

'The woman . . .' the man rasped and fell silent again.

Petrov looked at the man's eyes, but they were still closed. The breath very faint, coming at dangerously slow intervals. But he saw the blue lips twitch and a flicker in the eyelids. He put his ear to the man's mouth again.

'SVR colonel . . .' he heard. 'The woman . . .' again. Then the word, almost inaudible, 'Traitor.'

The intervals between breathing became longer and finally stopped altogether. The man was dead.

On the way back to the boat, Roman asked Petrov what the man had said.

'I don't know,' he replied.

Roman stopped by the crashed jeep on the beach. They heard a helicopter somewhere over the forest to the east.

'Let's go,' Petrov said. 'We don't want to be associated with this.'

Roman dragged himself away from the potential booty of the jeep and they pushed the boat out into the river, the engine starting immaculately again.

Chapter Twenty-six

S HE DIDN'T KNOW when it was exactly that she crossed the Arctic Circle, but it was some time between the forest track where she'd left Dmitry and Dudinka, the port of Norilsk, where she was heading. The place where she was now on the river had little more than an hour of darkness in twenty-four and soon there would be nothing but white nights. But instead of the clear blue skies from the day before, there were wide, low clouds that seemed to stretch and curve around the world.

The constant light meant that the helicopters didn't cease their patrols, eyes in the sky looking for her over a terrain of river and forest. She'd watched them fly low down the river, checking small craft, or over the forest trying to find tracks in the remaining snow, or a lone figure walking. She wondered if they'd found Dmitry the Wolf yet. Most likely. She'd left him and the jeep on the only forest track north.

She'd also seen one or two patrol boats stopping any traffic on the river. But an ice floe attracted no attention.

She'd stayed low in the hole she'd dug with the chainsaw and she was dusted with snow and ice from the wind that was coming from the north. It was only the dark pupils of her eyes that were not white.

By four o'clock in the cloudy, lit–up morning, she'd reached a point a few miles south of Dudinka. She could see in the far distance the bare, concrete, four–storey workers' quarters of the city and the high derricks of its big river port that exported the nickel and palladium, the copper and platinum from the Gulag city of Norilsk, an hour's drive to the east. Now was the time to find somewhere to come ashore, before she approached the city. Closer in, there would be roadblocks.

She listened and heard the chop of a helicopter's blades receding somewhere over to the left, the west. Maybe it was going towards the oil and gas fields of Vankor. Perhaps they thought she'd try to make a break for it there. Reach the fields to the west where she could lose herself among construction workers and oil gangs. But if they thought she would make a break, they didn't know her determination now to complete what she had come to do.

After the sound of the helicopter faded, she listened until there'd been a silence broken only by the river's flow and which lasted for several minutes.

She unlashed the pole she'd made back in the forest and which looked, she'd hoped, like a small tree trapped by the ice of the floe. Then she came out of the hole a little way and looked around. A white ice figure in an ice floe.

The banks were still an empty wilderness, now made up of a forest of the small larch trees that were the only ones to grow this far north. But soon there would be the little wooden houses that preceded the outskirts of the city; the fishermen's huts, or the weekend dachas by the river. It was time to head for the shore before she reached them.

She dug the pole behind her back and wedged the end of it against the floe for leverage. Then she dipped its rough-sawn blade into the river and with great effort began to haul herself and the floe against the current of the river. Coming out of it was far harder than it had been to get into the current; twice the pressure of the floe's weight against the paddle in the water nearly forced her from the hole and into the river. But slowly, sluggishly, the large floe began to nudge away from the faster current in the centre of the river and began to inch diagonally towards the larch bank where the current lessened. It became easier the further she was from the main current, but she was becoming more exhausted by the second, the pressure of the pole in her back agonising.

There was hardly any foreshore, just trees. As the floe crossed into shallower water where the current was hardly moving, at last it became easier to manoeuvre the huge block of ice. And then it touched the floor of the river a few yards from the trees. The floe rocked on its own weight and Anna stepped into the icy water and was swiftly on the bank. Freezing now from the snow and ice, soaking wet from wading through the river's edge, she felt her pulse as soon as she was on dry land and found it was dangerously low.

She felt as if she were made of ice; the wind and the proximity of the floe around her body had reduced her temperature to a dangerously low level. She knew she would have to risk making a fire before she could go on. But there was no darkness to hide the smoke and, from the patrols she'd seen from the river, she guessed there was now a full-scale manhunt out for her.

But she walked into the covering of the larch trees anyway, snapped some twigs and dug a small hole in the hard ground with a jagged stone. Then she lit the smaller, dry twigs and nurtured a feeble flame until it took hold and she began to stack on larger bits of any dryer wood that she could find. It would take half an hour, maybe, for her to warm up to a safe temperature and to dry her clothes a little but, unless she did, it wouldn't matter whether they caught up with her or not.

When she was warmer and relatively dry, she doused the fire with snow and swept some stones over the pit and then she scattered branches randomly on the floor of the forest to hide all traces. There'd been no helicopters for half an hour and she'd been lucky with that. But the smoke might have been seen by anyone on the ground. They might be pin-pointing any sign of smoke in the city's environs. But her other problem now was hunger.

She set off through the larch forest, skirting to the south of the city of Dudinka, taking care to stay clear of roads or, if she had to cross, to make sure there was no one in either direction who might spot her. There would be a dacha somewhere in the environs of the city, in the forest itself, and one which was hopefully empty until the weekend or longer. If she kept to the trees and stayed away from roads and tracks, eventually she would find a track that led to a dacha.

It was afternoon by the time she saw it. She was warmer from the hard walking through trackless forest. She had now skirted round the south of Dudinka and was east of the port, heading in the direction of Norilsk nearly seventy miles inland from the river. It was here that she came to a well-used track that was too neat for a logging road. She stayed deep in the forest but followed its course, fifty to a hundred yards away from it in case of traffic, until she saw the house. It was simply made of rough-sawn logs, criss-crossing each other at the corners, with a pitched tin roof over the top.

She went around it in a circle. There might be animals, a guard dog, perhaps, if it were permanently occupied. But she saw no vehicles around it. It was a place not just where she could find food but where she could spend the night, recuperate, sleep, before going on. Finally, sure there was no living presence nearby, she approached a door at the rear of the dacha. There was a small window that looked out into the forest next to the door and she looked through the dirty glass to the interior; an old sofa, a wood burner, a carpet worn to its colourless threads, some books, an icon on the far wall. That was all she could see. She tested the door but it was locked on the inside as she'd expected, and padlocked on the outside.

Next to the door and window was an outside privy and then a shed. The shed too was locked, but easier to break into than the house. She was soon inside. She found a few tools, some seeds ready to plant in the coming month – a task for the coming weekend, perhaps – and some old burlap sacks containing potatoes and other root vegetables. On the shelves around the shed, she felt in the gloom for the trays that would contain the remains of the winter vegetables. There was something for her to eat at least, and there might be more in the dacha, tins most likely. She gathered an armful of the vegetables together from the trays and the sacks. She would eat them later, once she'd broken in.

Then she found a crowbar, lying on the earth floor and, taking care to look in every direction again as she exited from the shed, she made her way to the rear door of the dacha and broke open the padlock easily. It wasn't hard to snap the primitive lock on the inside by levering the crowbar against the door and the jamb.

She realised now that she was trembling, from the cold maybe, but also from some unfamiliar feeling; aloneness, loss, home, Russia. She felt some premonition, but she didn't know what – the end perhaps. She shook herself out of this and entered the dacha.

The house had a musty air – the confinement of winter, the stillness of dust and the lack of living things for long periods of time. It seemed there'd been no one here for a while. That was good. She saw there were just two rooms. The kitchen was part of the living room which had windows at the front and back from where she could get a view of anyone approaching in either direction. The bedroom, through an old thin wood door, just had a single window that looked out to the front. That would be from where the danger would come, if it came.

In the living room, she took the Thompson Contender from its sleeve in the back of her jacket and, unwrapping its waterproofing, laid it on a low wood table. Then she began to take it to pieces, dismantling every part and laying them out carefully. She meticulously oiled each part from a tin she found on a shelf in the kitchen, before putting the gun back together again. She counted out the ammunition she had. She would have liked to have had more of the powerful rifle rounds. Maybe there were some here, in the dacha. It was a place for hunting.

Then she rolled up her sleeves and peeled the vegetables, filled a pot with water and boiled them on a propane stove. She found some tins in a cupboard and filled her pack with them, saving one to eat with the vegetables. Then she ate hungrily, too fast, and felt a pain in the pit of her stomach which went away and then returned. She knew, too, that she was on the edge of exhaustion. She didn't make it to the bed, but lay on the sofa, the loaded gun on the worn and splintered wood floor beside her. Then she slept.

It was not lights that woke her. There was no need for lights in the near twenty-four hour daylight she was in now. But there was a noise and it was that noise which broke through the thin skein of her sleep and brought her out of it into an immediate wakefulness. When she'd been sprung from semi-consciousness – though what the noise was she had as yet no idea – she rolled immediately on to the floor beside the sofa, away from the window, concealed, and had the gun in her hand pointing towards the dacha's front door.

She lay breathing deeply on the wood floor and listened. Then she calmed her nerves, shattered from broken sleep, and her breathing quietened. It was the noise of a vehicle, she was certain of that now. When the engine was switched off, she heard the voices that had also perhaps woken her from the shallow sleep; two men, it sounded like.

She crawled around the sofa and into the bedroom. The voices were coming from directly behind the front door now, out of sight to the left of the window in the bedroom, but they'd been right outside – feet away – when she'd been lying on the floor of the living room. She took the risk of looking up, over the sill of the bedroom window, to the left, and saw an army jeep, with two uniformed conscripts standing a little way from it and looking at the front door. Then they looked in at the window of the living room where she'd been sleeping.

She couldn't hear what they were saying but she could see they didn't know what to do, or were just bored with performing their duties. They'd probably been ordered to scout the area and would certainly not have been told what – or who – they were looking for. Just a woman, that's all, with papers in the name of Valentina Asayev, or most likely no papers at all. No doubt they were just a small cog in the huge operation to track her down that she'd seen from the river. Their role was probably to check all the forest dachas in the sector of this part of the city's outlying areas. Were they ordered to shoot on sight, she wondered? Perhaps, but she doubted it. Her arrest, that was what the SVR wanted. They wanted to put her on parade, the defector, the traitor, not lifeless in a coffin. Then they would kill her.

She lowered her head from the sill. She hoped they would go away, after a cursory, uninformed check on one of several scattered properties in the forest. They would say to their officer that they had looked and found nothing.

She crouched behind the window, waiting for them to leave, and out of sight to anyone who looked in, even from close to the window. And then she heard a key being inserted into the lock of the front door.

Anna rolled under the simple wood-frame bed, all the cover she could find. She heard the door open, a creak of un-oiled hinges, then their boots on the bare wood floor. She didn't see them close the door behind them. From under the bed, she saw only their boots now. They'd walked into the living room, and stopped. Looking around for any sign of a break-in.

'Let's go home,' she heard one of them say. 'There's no one here.'

There was no reply. So they were a local militia, she thought, talking of home in the city.

'Come on,' the same voice complained, 'we're off duty in an hour. It'll take that time to get back to the city.'

'What's so important there?' the second voice spoke.

'It's my girlfriend's birthday.'

'So?'

'We're going to a movie, then having some dinner at her friend's place. Come on, let's go. There's no one here.'

But she saw from beneath the bed that their boots

didn't move. The man who wished to leave was apparently not in charge.

'The smell,' she heard the other one say then. 'I thought they said this place had been empty for a month.'

Then she watched a pair of boots – his, she presumed – walking to the kitchen part of the room. But the kitchen area was out of her sight from beneath the bed. Then she heard the sound of the iron pan she'd used for cooking being picked up.

'Someone's used this. Recently. Look around the back,' the soldier in charge said. 'Someone's been here.'

She heard the sound of a pistol being primed and watched the pair of boots still by the front door turn and leave. He wanted to get this over with and leave.

She knew that if he looked half carefully, he would see where she'd destroyed the lock from the outside, even though on the inside she'd drawn down the wooden bar to lock it.

She heard the cooking pan being put down, carefully, it seemed now, not banged on to the stove. They – or he, in any case – was wary now, thinking of a living presence nearby.

Then she heard a shout. It was coming from the back. She couldn't hear the words, but she knew the second soldier had found the broken lock. She heard the wooden bar being lifted from the inside and the second soldier entering, apparently showing where the lock was broken. Then, she guessed, the next noise was of metal – they'd found the crowbar in the kitchen – a deep, almost hollow sound of thick iron.

'We should radio,' the leading soldier said.

'Ah come on! It's probably just a common break-in. Let's leave the fucking place.'

The lead soldier was silent. Then she heard the sound of footsteps and she saw his boots as they turned towards the front door. 'No. We'll radio. Then we'll wait for instructions.'

At that moment he saw her. And they were the last words either of them spoke. From the doorway to the bedroom, Anna Resnikov fired two bullets from the Contender, each to the head. The lead soldier had just seen her, a fraction of a second before the bullet entered his forehead, maybe simultaneously. His companion was facing sideways and received the second bullet through the temple. They fell down, crumpling in two piles of flesh, like figures with their bones removed.

Anna walked over to them and looked down at the floor. One of them had fallen over the other. They resembled bodies piled up after a scrappy execution.

She stared down at them, the gun butt in both hands, a faint heat coming from the barrel. But then she realised the heat was coming from her, not the gun. She saw two kids. They were just like the guards at the border. Carelessly trained youths, out of their depth. Conscripts who didn't even want to be in uniform. They were in their late teens and at the mercy of the brutal Russian army system – and now they were dead by her hand. Yes, it was an execution, but not a scrappy one.

She looked at the second soldier, the one who'd wanted to leave and who'd gone around to the back. He would miss his girlfriend's birthday, she thought, a movie then dinner afterwards at her friend's house. And then Anna felt the unfamiliar wave of remorse rising that she'd felt for the first time at the border. The disgust, or fear of the nullity of other people's deaths, was coming over her again.

But this time she shook it off at once, shut off her mind to thought altogether. She knelt and took their guns. Then she began to strip the uniform from the second man's body. There was less blood on this one. When she was dressed in the uniform, she went to the shed, picked up more vegetables and two animal traps. Back in the dacha, she found a hunting rifle and ammunition. She didn't check whether the ammunition fitted the Contender, she just took everything there was, filling her pack and her clothes, stuffing pockets until they overflowed. When she left the dacha, she was dressed in the dead boy's uniform.

She rammed the jeep through the forest, bouncing it against the hard permafrost and the broken branches. It was as if she were seeking to destroy her thoughts by destroying the jeep. But all the time her mind was on the task in hand, to head east, away from the river, towards Norilsk – and then on, further east, to the Putorana mountains.

It was roughly seventy miles from here to Norilsk, she guessed, and she knew if there were roadblocks around Dudinka on the river, there would be an impregnable ring around Norilsk. They must know she was heading beyond there, to the secret military and nuclear base, and to reach where she was going she would have to get through the city. There was no other road, even in the forest and on the bare tundra. She joined the metalled road that headed towards Norilsk a few miles to the east of Dudinka and checked carefully that she wouldn't be running straight into a roadblock. There was normal traffic here. Nearer to Norilsk, that's where they would form their stranglehold.

She drove fast for around twenty-five miles through an icy rain that made the road dangerously slippery. Then the trees began to fall away to leave just withered stumps. Closer to Norilsk, all the time now, nature was dying. It was here that the pollution of the world's largest city beyond the Arctic Circle began to tell. For the remaining miles to Norilsk all the trees would be dead. The sulphur dioxide and the other chemicals from the city's smoke stacks had killed the land itself. She'd seen the stacks of Norilsk once before, many years ago from the air when she was on active duty. They made Norilsk look like a city on fire.

Her body leaned forward, into the steering wheel, as she saw the wasteland unfold along the road's edges. They said this wilderness produced over one per cent of the world's sulphur dioxide pollution. And it did so in order to make from its palladium and platinum the catalytic convertors in the West so that western cars ran more cleanly.

As she got to within thirty miles of the city, a smog descended over the land and the acid rain began to fall. The permafrost land was no longer any good for growing living things, but she knew the soil was now harvested for the quantity of heavy metals it contained.

She saw it from a mile away, along a straight stretch of road. It was a poor place for a roadblock. If they'd thought about it harder, had longer to think and set it up, perhaps, they'd have put it just around a corner where was no opportunity to see it in time and flee. But it was undoubtedly a roadblock; there'd be spiked chains across the road and some other kind of barrier. But it was the gathering of jeeps and the helicopter that caught her eye first. She slowed to take in the number of jeeps, the probable number of men, the helicopter. It was a heavily manned obstacle and she knew she wouldn't get through it.

CHAPTER TWENTY-SEVEN

ALEXEI PETROV STEPPED off the aluminium boat on a sleet-driven beach of mud and shingle. They were two miles south of Dudinka. The boat had just passed the village of Sitkova and the place where it was now beached contained a few simple wooden houses like some Arcadian vision from Tolstoy. The wind had died and lazy grey smoke came from metal flues that protruded from the rough, bark roofs of one or two of the dwellings.

Petrov stood on the beach, lifted his head to the sky and filled his large chest with the pure air. What a feeling it was to be back, to be here where his life had begun, and from where his spirit had never quite been severed. He felt it growing all the time. The feeling of space, the space in the blood of a nomad, after the confines of the city and the ferry, was at first almost disorienting. Home? he thought. Here in the north, in the wilderness, home was everywhere. To the north and east there were thousands and thousands of square miles of empty tundra, and there were thousands more of forest, the Siberian *taiga*, to the south and west. Norilsk and the nuclear facilities in the Putorana mountains, with their ICBM base, were the only, though not inconsiderable, blot on the pristine, untouched landscape of the far north. But the city's foul, polluting chimneys increasingly leached their baleful influence over the wilderness, and the city was still nearly a hundred miles away. He would avoid it, Petrov decided, skirt to the south and follow where he knew the reindeer were being driven.

It was here that he'd chosen to leave Roman and to seek out his tribal family. Roman had changed his own plans. He had now decided to go much further upriver, far beyond Dudinka and towards the estuary that led to the Kara Sea. He was going fishing, he told Petrov, if the authorities were letting people like him pass through.

Petrov turned. His big, round face broke into a smile of gratitude at the boatman. He handed over money for his half of the fuel and warmly shook Roman's hand. It was funny how you could meet someone for the briefest time, travel with them for a few hours in conditions that made it impossible to talk, and still feel you had made the deepest connection, a friend for life. Then he walked up towards the few wooden houses that were set back, safely up on the bank and away from the cataclysmic spring torrent of the river. Already back on the river, with a wave of his hand Roman was gone.

Petrov stood longer in the silence and stillness, feeling his way into the natural world. With the wind gone, he felt as if he was the last person left on earth. Then he came out of his quietness and walked past the first few houses, shuttered and locked, until he came to a house at the back of the village, furthest away from the river. There was a man sitting on a porch, whittling a larch stick, and there were wood carvings of animals he'd made which were dotted around and hanging at odd angles on the log walls. A bottle of vodka was open on the boards beside him. The man was his mother's cousin.

Petrov exchanged a greeting – the man wasn't drunk yet, he saw. But the cousin hardly spoke and merely pointed in an easterly direction.

'How long ago?' Petrov asked.

'They left four weeks ago, maybe a little more,' the man answered. 'In time for the reindeer to calve up by the Putorana.'

Petrov eyed the snowmobile next to the man's house. 'Can you take me there?' he said.

The man looked at him steadily, then drank slowly from the vodka bottle. 'Some of the way,' he said eventually. 'But look, the snow's going, in some places it's nearly gone. We'll see how far we get.'

'Okay. How much?'

The man finally stopped whittling the stick but he made no answer.

'How many of them went this year?' Petrov enquired.

'Twenty-five . . . thirty. And they took a thousand reindeer.'

Petrov recalled that in his childhood there would be eighty or a hundred herders, men, women and children, plus all their dogs and several thousand reindeer on the trek to the east and the summer feeding grounds. Now, too often, his people went to the cities, confused by the Russian schooling they'd been forced into, tempted by the pittance in wages the cities offered. And he supposed that he was one of them, one of the lost. Unlike him, however, most of his people ended up drunks, in jail, or dead before their prime.

'Pay for the fuel and a hundred roubles on top,' the man said.

'That's steep.'

'It's up to you.'

'Okay. We can go now?'

'Anytime. But, like I say, the snow is going fast. We'll only make it part of the way.'

Petrov decided to take his chances.

The snowmobile was old and the fuel was evidently mixed with something else, Petrov guessed. Its engine stuttered and choked and barely came to life. It sounded sick. But they set off, slowly at first as if the engine was getting used to some new medicine, and then they wound their way to the end of the village, Petrov clinging to the rear of the vehicle with both his hands behind him. Once they were clear of the scattering of dwellings, the driver kept to the shade of the trees where the snow was deeper and melted last. It was slow and precarious finding the good snow, but it was a lot quicker than Petrov could walk and he knew he would have to walk a long way when they ran out of snow, a day and a night perhaps, before he made it to the edge of the plateau they called Putorana; 'the land of lakes and steep shores' in the Evenki language.

The herders, his mother, a brother and some cousins, would also have taken a southern sweep, away from the pollution of Norilsk. There was nothing for the reindeer left to eat near the city. They must already have crossed the land on their reindeer-pulled sleds, when the snow was deeper than it was now, and when they could also cross the countless rivers and ponds and lakes on the thicker ice. With the summer almost here, the permafrost was already beginning to soften on the surface and the whole area, through six time zones, would begin to turn to bog, except up by the plateau. It was when full summer arrived – soon enough now – that the giant Siberian mosquitoes would start to plague every living creature. The plateau protected the animals and men from them too. Its elevation kept the insects away, preferring lower, wetter ground.

The snowmobile bounced and crashed its way through the larch forest for dozens of miles, until finally Petrov guessed they must be south of Norilsk. Maybe the city was a hundred miles away to the north of them, maybe less, he couldn't tell any more. He was numb from the ceaseless movement and painful thudding of the snow-mobile and it was only by looking at his watch and guessing their speed that he could hazard a guess. He'd hardly seen anything in the crashing and swerving of the vehicle, and he'd heard nothing above the engine. The blur of the violent motion had shut down his senses. They'd stopped four times to refuel from tanks strapped to the back.

The forest then began to thin and open out into treeless tundra, where the moss and lichens grew that fed the reindeer. Out in the open, the diminished snow was left only in great patches where it had drifted, around which the melt had begun to reveal the white lichen and moss the reindeer liked and which they had to dig through the snow to find in winter.

But they kept on, somehow, still heading east, in twists and turns to follow the available snow, skating sometimes across watery patches that thrashed the engine into an ear-piercing roar of protest. Finally, after several more hours, his mother's cousin pulled over and cut the engine. The way ahead now made it impossible for the snowmobile to continue.

Petrov dismounted and picked up his pack. He gave the man a hundred roubles, and then added twenty in gratitude. It wasn't much, but it would keep him in vodka for a week or two. The snowmobile started again and the man turned and headed back towards the river village without a look or a word.

In the blessed silence, Petrov stood still and pondered the way ahead. A day and night of walking, he guessed, before he would catch up with the herders. The sun was growing hotter, out here summer was arriving more slowly but at least it was arriving.

Looking down in a shrinking patch of snow, he saw the recent tracks of a wolf, a sacred animal to the Evenk. They would use its hide for warmth, but never ate the meat. They would eat a bear and use its hide. But the wolf was not to be eaten, only buried in the four corners, bone by bone, to the north, south, east and west. Above him, high in the sky, a white eagle circled slowly in ceaseless vigil. Petrov made sure his gun was loaded. A wolf and an eagle; the eagle could sometimes kill even a wolf, and both could put an end to him.

He began to walk in an easterly direction across the frozen and sometimes boggy ground and after several miles came across the spoor of reindeer and the occasional, broken lines of sled tracks in the little remaining snow. There were different types of reindeer that pulled the Evenk's wooden sleds to the ones they kept for meat or hides or breeding.

As he walked in the timeless landscape, his mind turned again to the woman. He knew where she was heading now. She was also going to the Putorana; the place of infinite wilderness, all but inaccessible to anyone except the natives and the wild creatures. But also the place where the nuclear missiles were buried in silos hollowed out deep in the mountains and where the nuclear research and development facilities were hidden from view. The ICBM silos were a secret place – almost like a sacred site in a perverse way – but a secret that his tribe knew well, even though they chose to ignore it.

It took him slightly less than a day and a night to reach the meadow where he knew he'd find them. It was just as he'd thought. Before he saw the tribes' *chooms* – hide tipis – ahead of him on a slight rise of meadow that led up to the plateau, he heard the barking of dogs and came across the reindeer herd feeding. There were young calves with their mothers, and the young men of the tribe were picketed at outposts long before he reached the meadow. They were there to guard against a wolf or bear attack.

And up ahead, rising from the tundra, were the

extraordinary twists and turns of canyons and tumbling rivers, falling from two thousand feet. A magic place that almost nobody knew of.

On the journey, he hadn't slept, just walked and stopped occasionally to fish for the easily caught Siberian char, which he ate raw. It was as if he were slowly, steadily becoming a different person from the *militsiya* lieutenant with an apartment in the city and a car and regular hours for sleeping and eating.

Twice he'd stopped to call the FSB colonel from the satellite phone and now, before his arrival prompted a celebration and he was caught up with his mother and the rest of his family, he stopped again and called. The colonel answered immediately.

'Where are you?'

Petrov told him and then listened to a long, almost contemplative silence.

'She's been near Dudinka,' the colonel said finally. 'She shot two men – soldiers – at a dacha outside the city in the forest. Then she stole their jeep.'

Petrov was silent.

'We assume she's going to the research facilities in Putorana now,' the colonel said. 'Not to the north where the reactor is. She's in the sector where you are.'

The sector? Petrov thought. It was hard to imagine how this empty land could be anyone's sector.

'To Putorana?' Petrov said, but he'd known somehow that this was where she was going.

'Your people are there?' the colonel said without answering his question.

'It's where they take the reindeer herds in summer,' Petrov answered. 'They're here.'

'Never mind their fucking reindeer!' the colonel snapped. And now Petrov felt a dislike for him he hadn't felt up to now. 'I want all their eyes and ears looking and listening. She'll be out there. Somewhere. On foot. If she makes it past the checkpoints.'

Petrov was about to protest that the herds were his people's livelihood, but he didn't. There was no point.

'Yes, colonel,' he replied.

And then he stayed where he was, the dead satellite phone in his hand, and began to think. The incongruity of the phone out here in the wilderness, the contrast of his own existence in the wide emptiness with his existence in the city, and finally the woman. The woman. Why were they so afraid of her? An SVR colonel, the dying man in the jeep had said. A traitor. But a traitor to what? How could this woman possibly justify the scale of their operations? For some reason he couldn't understand, he began to feel an affinity for the woman that transcended everything he'd been told. Somehow, whatever she was doing seemed to be right.

Before he entered the camp, he felt through the padded jacket for the crunching of plastic, the waterproof package which contained the strange, incomprehensible documents that he'd found on Professor Bachman's body. Reassured, he walked on and saw his mother emerge from the *choom* nearest to him. She embraced him, as if he'd been expected all along, and they went into the reindeer-hide tipi.

There was a wood stove in the centre, and a pot boiling reindeer meat. Some berries were piled in a pyramid on a low table and round the edges of the *choom* were the reindeer-hide bedrolls of ten or more people. His mother, he noticed, was wearing a dress of reindeer hide. He picked up a handful of berries – he was hungry. Then he began to remember the words in his own, Evenki, language that he had told the Americans but had allowed to fall into disuse in his long years in the city. 'The noise a bear makes walking through cranberry bushes.' 'The noise a duck makes landing silently on water.'

CHAPTER TWENTY-EIGHT

ANNA PULLED THE jeep off the road and stopped. She was now just under half a mile from the checkpoint. Other vehicles continued past her towards the roadblock ahead and she waited, looking in the mirror until the road was empty of traffic.

She could see the checkpoint with her naked eye, but there were binoculars hanging from a hook on the passenger side of the jeep and now she took them and trained them on it. First she carefully watched the troops milling around the area. She saw their attention was exclusively focused on the line of vehicles and their drivers waiting to go through. There were jittery conscripts mixed with regulars and special forces.

Beyond them she saw glimpses of a metal barrier that was lowered across the road and which rose occasionally to allow a vehicle through. And beyond the barrier, a large spiked chain had been dragged across the tarmac in case anyone broke through the barrier. That too was hauled back each time a vehicle went through the barrier. It was the second line of defence.

There was a line of trucks and cars and jeeps waiting to get through in the direction of Norilsk. The drivers' papers were being meticulously noted, the vehicles searched exhaustively inside and out. Even the undersides of the trucks were being examined with mirrors. She saw that it took twelve soldiers an average of twenty minutes for a vehicle to be thoroughly checked and to pass through the two barriers. The area on and around the road was crowded with thirty or forty well-armed soldiers, with a small group of special forces troops who kept their automatic rifles trained on each driver.

She lowered the binoculars and considered the options, and found none that had a chance of succeeding. Then she raised them again and trained them on to the guard house next to the road. It was a hastily constructed edifice put together in pre-built sections, in military fashion, and there were more soldiers she could see through a transparent plastic window. They seemed to be keeping a more distant look-out than the soldiers on the road, eyeing the whole queue of vehicles for any unusual movement. The roof of the guardhouse bristled with temporary communications equipment and there was a machine-gun emplacement next to it, surrounded by sandbags. Next to and behind the guardhouse she saw several trailers drawn up in a haphazard formation; for accommodation, perhaps, and no doubt here'd be a kitchen and a bathhouse of sorts. Between the guardhouse and the trailers, around the perimeter of the guardhouse, numerous army vehicles were parked facing in a semi-circle towards the road and there was a troop carrier on the far, Norilsk, side which had a mounted machine gun on the turret.

The whole area was a teeming melee of military personnel and equipment that would ensure no one without papers could get through and no one could break through without being instantly eliminated.

She swivelled the binoculars again, to the right of the guardhouse.

About thirty yards behind it on some flat ground there was the helicopter. A Kamov Ka-60 Kasatka, by the look of it. It was a relatively new design, built to replace an older model that had been in service since the Afghan war. It was a machine built for adaptability. It could be used simply as a means of transportation, or for reconnaissance work and was sometimes even employed in an attacking role. Two crew and up to sixteen men, she recalled. She trained the binoculars around the fuselage and found the two crewmen, a pilot and a navigator or gunner. They were standing beside the fuselage and smoking cigarettes.

Anna put the binoculars down on the seat next to her and sat in the cab of the jeep, the engine still running after nearly fifteen minutes. It was still thirty miles to Norilsk and then, beyond the city, another fifty or more to the beginning of the Putorana plateau.

She finally withdrew the Thompson Contender from her coat and armed it. Then she screwed on the silencer. She made sure the two guns she'd taken from the dead conscripts were armed also. All three guns she placed beside the binoculars on the seat beside her. Then she revved the jeep's engine and pulled out, back on to the road in the direction of the checkpoint. If they didn't yet know about the dead conscripts and the theft of the jeep, it would give her an extra few seconds. And she knew she could rely on the obsessive secrecy of the people in charge of the operation. The intelligence people were naturally miserly with information, even pointless information, and that was their weakness. And so she trusted that only the special forces troops doing the checking at the roadblock, looking at the drivers, examining the vehicles, would know they were looking for a woman.

As she pulled on to the road, she checked the cloud cover. It was thick and grey and very low now, discharging the sheets of acid rain over the wet landscape.

She drove at regulation speed and it was, perhaps, the longest half a mile she could remember. But her thoughts were focused, accurate, and she resisted the temptation to put on speed, to get what was about to happen over with. In fact, her mind was as close to being empty as it was possible to be. There was just action; a gear change, a foot pressing gently on the accelerator, her hands, now without gloves, guiding the loose steering wheel, her eyes watching the approaching roadblock for any movement outside the normality of a heavily armed checkpoint that she'd observed through the binoculars.

There was the line of vehicles getting nearer, just ahead of her now, exhaust fumes twisting upwards. The rain lashed on to the tarmac. And then she saw where the military vehicles that were stationed at the checkpoint had pulled off the road two hundred yards before the guard-house. They had created a rutted track in the snow and melting earth. The track was off to the right of the road,

on the side where the guardhouse and the small encampment were, and by turning off on it – just one more
military jeep – she could also turn away from joining the
line of vehicles trying to make it through to Norilsk.

She was two hundred yards from the guardhouse when
she gently swung the wheel of the army jeep to the right
and followed the tracks, very slowly now, no fast movement to alert anyone watching. She saw a few faces turn,
recognise the military nature of the jeep, and one or two
stayed watching it. But she went on, down a small earth
embankment at the side of the road, swinging the wheel
gently again to the right, until she'd left the guardhouse
well ahead and to the left of her. With every few yards,
she was coming closer to the area of ground that had been
churned up by other vehicles, and the small military camp
behind the road. Here she posed no immediate threat to
the activities around the barrier and the guardhouse where
all the attention was focused.

She approached the trailers scattered across the area a
hundred yards or so to the rear of the guardhouse, pointing the jeep away from the direction of Norilsk, away
from suspicion. Unless they knew about the dead men
and the jeep. But still she wasn't challenged, the jeep
bumping casually over the churned–up ground. Unhurried. All the troops who knew what they were doing
there, and why, were up by the barrier, or around the
guardhouse, or manning the machine gun on the top of
the troop carrier. That was what she hoped.

She finally swung the jeep over beside the second of
the trailers and cut the engine. No shout, no command,

no order to identify herself. She put the three guns into her jacket, keeping them below the jeep's window as she did so. One or two men watched from a hundred yards or more away by the guardhouse and the road, but she was on the far side of the jeep from them as she stepped out on to the ground and walked with slow deliberation in a direction still further away from the guardhouse, until she was behind the second trailer. She was more than a hundred yards from the barrier and the guardhouse now, concealed behind the trailer, and her vehicle was halted and quiet. She was in military uniform, and evidently not someone trying to challenge the barrier or the troops.

Behind the second trailer, there was another, third, trailer, perpendicular to it. It smelled of urine and there was a pit hastily dug beneath it. She ducked around behind this trailer, putting the three trailers now between her and the mass of troops up ahead and behind her on the road. Ahead of her as she walked away was the helicopter, thirty yards from where she was now, its two crewmen smoking, chatting. She put her hand in her pocket and withdrew an order paper she'd found on the lead conscript at the dacha. This she waved ahead of her, not too high, but just enough to attract the attention of the pilot, as she now saw the man on the right to be.

He stood up from his leaning position against the side of the helicopter, a cigarette still in his hand, but which he swiftly stubbed out on the earth. There was a quizzical expression on his face. She was within twenty yards from the two of them now, when her other hand without the order paper dipped into the inside of the jacket and withdrew the Contender, its eighteen-inch barrel augmented by the five-inch silencer. It was an unmistakable intent. There was no going back. She was committed.

But as the two crewmen first stared in amazement, then looked outraged and finally began to scramble for weapons of their own – all this taking place in a second or two – she fired twice, two dull thuds of a silenced weapon, bullets into flesh. They both dropped.

She continued her measured stride without a pause.

As she climbed over the bodies and into the fuselage of the helicopter, she heard the first shout, but altered nothing in the swift, smooth flow of her movements. Over the first seat, into the pilot cockpit, as she pressed the Start button, turning only briefly to the left to shoot dead, through the open door, a lone running man in uniform. Her brain now wired into the next action, and the next and the next, almost wired into the helicopter itself, as the rotors began their slow turn. It took ten to fifteen seconds to get the engines going fully, with no time to allow them to warm up, the centrifugal clutch engaging the rotors at the tail and above. She heard nothing now beyond the roar of the engines as she pushed down the feed and gave it the full blast of aviation fuel, and now the blades were whirring level and then at a steeper angle for a sudden, violent take-off, when the first shot was fired in her direction, but she didn't duck or alter anything as the machine rose first from its nose then fell down to the ground again – too quick – then rose from its nose again and this time stayed up as the tail, too, rose from the ground, and she seemed to hover before the helicopter began its roaring motion upwards at ten metres a second, in a hail of fire now. She dipped the joystick to the right to swoop the machine low and give the shooters less of a target, no longer broadside on now, and she was suddenly in the first wisps of a low-scudding cloud that flew past the machine and then began to envelop it. The rattle of bullets, the smashing of metal against metal.

Her first fully conscious thought was the blindness of the clouds, the zero visibility, and she suddenly realised where she was, up above and to the south of the encampment. She was airborne. And she looked down inside the cockpit and saw a constellation of bullet holes that studded the fuselage like stars, the crew door smashing loose against the sides until, in a hideous moment before she tried to reach it, it broke away from its hinges and flew spinning backwards and away, missing the tail rotor by inches.

She steadied the machine. Lost in a greyness. Nothing she could see at all. Then she headed south at first, flying at 170 miles per hour at just over 500 feet, still seeing nothing beyond the screen, until she estimated that she was about thirty miles south of the checkpoint and the road to Norilsk. Then she swung the helicopter to the left, to the east, so that she would pass well to the south of the city. There was still nothing in view, the grey wedges of thick cloud parting with the thrust of the machine's nose and shrouding everything. Even the nose of the helicopter was barely visible. Then it would appear again, where the cloud ahead was exploded by the motion, and disappear.

She would keep inside the cloud cover for as long as possible. The tundra was dead flat until beyond Norilsk, where it began to rise towards the Putorana. She would leave it until the last minute before she rose above the cloud bank for the approach into the plateau. There were no power lines in the way in this north–south direction; they all led from the city to the east, along the road to Dudinka. She had a map of the whole area in her head as if it were on a screen in front of her.

It took another twenty minutes before she was sure she had passed Norilsk to the north and she kept her elevation and speed the same, counting seconds now, not minutes, checking the speed, the altimeter, her hand steady on the joystick, her ears filled only with the roaring of engines and the beat of rotors.

She dared wait no longer and began to lever the machine up – 550, 600, 670 feet – but the cloud still shrouded everything. Further, up to 800 feet, and there was still nothing ahead but the grey shroud of invisibility. Still forcing her way through at 170 mph into the dead space where, somewhere up ahead, she knew there'd be an escarpment or a sheer cliff to meet her without warning, the final embrace of twisted metal, the end. She levered up again, saw a lighter grey in the cloud, the surface perhaps, and up again twenty, thirty feet until she saw a break, then more clouds and another break and she was free for the first time in forty minutes to see half a mile ahead the flat tabletops of the Putorana, glittering in sunshine, as if the cloud dared not proceed to the mountains.

She was heading straight at a high top, way above her, 2500 feet perhaps, and she violently sheered the helicopter to the right, passing rock 100 feet to her left and up into a thin canyon where a tumbling sodium river shone brightly from below. Cascades of water, white and green, pouring itself on to the flat tundra below. She chased the canyon eastwards, rising up with it until she broke over a tabletop thirty feet below, the engines screaming with the effort, and a huge vista opened up of broad blue lakes, ringed with black rocks and bright green vegetation, of winding narrow gorges branching away from them like fjords, and crashing waterfalls everywhere that dug deep into the mountains.

She had minutes, maybe less, to get down before her hunters appeared. They would come from the north of where she was, from the nuclear facilities and the ICBM site.

She spotted a narrow defile that led from a huge blue lake that reflected the colour of the sky and she dropped a little way into it, looking for a flat spot to land. Out on a small ridge that jutted from the mountain was a small green parchment of grass, a meadow inaccessible to anything but the bighorn mountain sheep, perhaps, but she would have to risk it. She took the machine down, steadying its rocking as best she could, until she saw the walls of the mountain that sealed the tiny meadow were feet away from the rotors overhead. But then she felt the skids touch and bounce, and just then an enormous blow of the overhead rotors against rock shattered the rear of the machine as they snapped and fragmented, shooting backwards into the tail, and she jumped from the helicopter as it began to settle and a roar of flame exploded upwards from the tanks. She rolled and rolled until she found herself clinging to a rock ledge over the lip of the meadow as the burning fuel ballooned outwards and up and she felt a gigantic heat even though she was protected from the direct explosion.

Anna clung to the rock above her, her feet tight on the ledge, her ears burning from the sound of the fuel explosion. The remains of the helicopter tilted on to its side, somehow remaining perched on the tiny meadow, and she saw the thick, black cloud of burning fuel rising up into the sky like an invitation.

She looked around and beneath her, to a sheer drop that fell away into a gorge a hundred feet below. No ropes for climbing, no path down. She hauled herself over the lip on to the meadow and past the blackened, burning beast, following the lip, looking down for any route away from the meadow. Here, if they saw her, she was a target in a shooting gallery, and she didn't want to climb up from the meadow on to the tabletop. That would only expose her more. She saw a cut in the rock where she could wedge her legs on each side to prevent her fall and she climbed down into it and began the precarious descent hoping the cutting wouldn't fizzle out and leave her hanging in limbo with no way out, down or up.

She levered herself down the first ten feet. Maybe they would think she'd died in the crash, though they wouldn't trust it. But as long as she could disappear from view, there was that chance. They would have seen the smoke

335

by now, diverted their hunt to the canyon, and they would drop men down on ropes. They would see the carnage of the helicopter, examine inch by inch the terrain and the near impossibility of escape from it. If they didn't find her, they would hope, though only hope, that she was dead. But they wouldn't lower their search. She had gained the plateau; before her, a thousand-mile stretch of wilderness devoid of roads or habitation — just the secret base and the nuclear research station where Professor Kryuchkov was their prisoner.

CHAPTER TWENTY-NINE

THROUGHOUT THAT LONG, white Arctic night, Petrov sat with his dying grandfather. Gannyka lay on wooden sled runners with packed grass bound into sheaves over them and then a reindeer hide over them to keep him away from the dew. His eyes were suddenly bright, Petrov noticed, and had lost the cloudiness of before, earlier in the bright night, but he still insisted he was dying.

'This is my death bed,' he told Petrov. 'It is my time.'

At one point he looked up at Petrov who was sitting on a wooden stool beside him and asked, 'Who will carry on the tradition? Who will perform the magic now?' But Petrov had no reply. Shamans were grown by their elders early on, he knew that, or they simply appeared, either from birth or later in adolescence. Those who become shamans were the most sickly or those affected by severe nervous disorders – the 'Arctic Madness', as Slav academics called it, but it wasn't that. After all, there were shamans all over the world. And the native tribes in Siberia felt no nervousness living in the Arctic. But the sickness that was common to a shaman's initiation was part of the ritualistic necessity of becoming a shaman. The sickness took them to places ordinary mortals never went. And if they survived whatever ailed them, they became stronger than anyone in the tribe and then they could heal the sick themselves. Gannyka, Petrov remembered, had started his secret life as a shaman in the 1940s when he had cured two children with smallpox and some syphilitics who'd escaped from the Gulag camps.

The long day of night was completely silent. Somewhere, wolves would be tracking a moose, or trying to get inside the reindeer corrals, and the bears and foxes would be hunting, but Petrov heard nothing. At some time between two and three in the morning, Gannyka began to talk in a low voice, almost as if he were speaking in a trance of words. Petrov recalled that the Evenki had around four thousand words in their language, but the shamans of the tribe spoke in a secret language with more than ten thousand words. The shaman speaks the language of all nature, as his grandfather had told him when he was a boy.

'My story began when I was sick with smallpox as a boy,' Gannyka said. 'I was unconscious for many days, so near death that my family almost buried me. In my sickness and raving I was carried to a great sea. It was there that the smallpox spoke to me. "The Lords of the Water will make you a shaman," the sickness told me. Then the husband of the Lady of the Water, who is Lord of the Underworld, gave me a sable and a black rat who guided me to the underworld. There, those who had died from smallpox, syphilis, plague and other deadly diseases to humans, first tore out my heart and then they tore the flesh from my bones and they put all my bones in a boiling pot of water. They boiled them for three years. Later, they took out my bones and counted them to make sure they were all there and then a smith in the underworld welded them together again with metal plates and put new flesh on me. He gave me new eyes so that I could see differently and he forged a new head for me so that I could understand what is inside it. Then he made me my shaman's costume, which is hidden near here in the cave where you will bury me. It is this smith who forges the shamans. I was born then as a shaman. After that, the other sicknesses of humanity that live in the underworld taught me how they tortured mankind. The sicknesses of the head, as well as of the body. The Lord of Madness taught me how he, too, tortured humankind. They all taught me these things so that I would be able to cure men.'

He seemed to come out of the trance and looked at Petrov, perhaps to see if he was listening. From beneath the wooden sled runners Gannyka took his own drum. 'It is made from a tree struck by lightning,' he said. 'Like the one I gave you. Rub vodka on the skin.'

Petrov took a small vodka bottle from his pocket and filled the palm of his hand. Then he rubbed the deerskin top of the drum with the vodka.

'You have your drum that I gave you?' Gannyka asked him.

Petrov took the small tambour drum that he'd kept in his apartment all these years from beside him and showed it to Gannyka. The old man studied it and then looked at Petrov with a piercing stare.

'This is all finished,' Gannyka said. 'With me. There is no one else.' He fell back on his shoulders. 'The black rat and the white sable then escorted me from the underworld,' he continued. 'They took me to the Tree of the Lord of the Earth who, as you know, is the eagle, and he taught me about the nine herbs and their healing qualities. After that, my escorts then took me to a cave in the mountain where there were two naked women, their skins growing reindeer fur. One of these women was pregnant and would give birth to two reindeer, the animals that give us food and help us in everything we do. The cave has two openings, one to the east and one to the west. Through each gate, the young woman sent a reindeer to serve the people of the forest.' He looked up at Petrov again. 'I have had three wives, all orphans, as it should be. But the Great Mother of the Animals is my true wife.'

Petrov placed his hand on the old man's forehead. It was burning.

'I have many souls,' Gannyka said. 'Many, many animal souls.'

Then Gannyka sank back as if for the last time. Petrov saw a great peace descend over his forehead and into his eyes. It was like a bright sun cloud. The burning on his forehead eased.

But the old man opened his eyes again and fixed them on Petrov with all the harshness he'd ever possessed. 'You, Munnukan,' he said. 'You have a great secret. But you don't know that you possess it. You are like the shaman before he becomes a shaman. The old ways are gone, my ways, but you possess the secret of the new ways.'

Gannyka turned his eyes away to the sky towards the east. Without looking at Petrov again, he said, 'After my death, you will see a wolf. Then you will find and finally believe in the secret you possess.'

The wolf, Petrov thought. *Irgichi* in the Evenki language Gannyka had spoken. They were his last words on earth. *Irgichi* was also the word for 'son', Petrov remembered. A sacred creature, the wolf, whom it was a sin to kill. Like a son.

The funeral took place in the early morning at around six o'clock. Though it was daylight, it was still night in terms of the dead man who was being guided by his spirit to the underworld and who was joining the spirits of his ancestors, the other shamans.

The whole camp was dressed in ceremonial clothes of deerskin and eagle feathers, small metal charms hanging from their clothes in imitation of their shaman. Some of the metal was just bottle tops, or small bits of ironmongery they carried with them on their nomadic journey. As if in a dream, Petrov found that he too was dressed in the deerskin leggings he'd brought, and moccasins and a deerskin jacket he'd been given for the ceremony. He carried the drum Gannyka had given him in his hand, while the old man's drum was placed on his body which was now carried on the bed which had become a bier. It was carried by four men who were not of the shaman's family.

They walked in a slow, winding procession up through

the meadow towards the rising mountain and the cave. Some of the people carried flaming torches, others beat ordinary drums in a monotonous rhythm that sent the senses to sleep. The walking and the drumming were in themselves trance-like. Occasionally, one or other of the participants broke into an Evenki funeral song, and the others stamped their feet to the rhythm as they walked. Petrov discovered he could remember little of the songs, but soon he was able to join, from some distant childhood memory, in one or two of the choruses.

The procession stretched for a hundred yards, with the old man on the bier at the front and Petrov – at his mother's and Gannyka's insistence in their conversation during the night – behind it. By now they were on a slow, wild sheep path that climbed in switchbacks up the side of the mountain and the men carrying the bier had trouble keeping to it. Everyone else walked in single file. Back and forth across the mountain they walked for an hour until they were at the entrance to the cave.

There they stopped, the bier was laid down, and the people gathered around while prayers were said and some chants were sent to the sky and to the earth below. A tree had been planted at the entrance of the cave, with its roots facing to the sky. There was an east and a west entrance, Petrov noted, just as the old man had told him there had been in his long dream nearly eighty years before.

Finally, at some undetermined signal, the bier was lifted and carried into the cave. It was a huge cavern stretching back some fifty yards into the mountain. The rock was wet with ice and water from the streams and lakes on the plateau above and Petrov saw various charms and small flags, bowls of incense and wood carvings. He saw the carving of a man's hand, huge, with its palm open. It had been made in the previous week at Gannyka's instruction. It was the symbol of his parting.

Finally, the bier was hoisted by ropes on to a high ledge where animals couldn't reach it. More prayers were said and Petrov saw his mother disappear into the back of the cave, the only place of total darkness on this Siberian summer morning. When she returned, she was carrying a coat. It was of faded red material and had a great number of metal discs attached to it, with feathers on the arms for flight and a wolf's skin around its collar. She walked up to Petrov and gave it to him.

'He kept it here since 1941,' she said. 'When the persecutions were at their height. He came up to this cave to conduct his ceremonies alone, his ecstasies, and to commune with his spirits. He told me to give it to you.'

Petrov looked at it, first in amazement, then embarrassment. Finally, he saw that the others were all looking at him. He took the coat from his mother and they stood in silence while herbs were burned around the rock at the foot of the ledge where the body was laid.

'You must leave last,' his mother said.

Petrov stood in the semi-darkness as the others filed outside.

'Wait until we reach the foot of the cliff,' she said.

Petrov stood still. His mind was empty and he seemed to see with eyes other than his own.

Down in the valley, coming on to the meadow where

the reindeer were, the procession went. Petrov stood at the front of the cave now, in the sunlight, the coat over his arm, like a businessman, he thought, on the way to a meeting, and who was prepared for rain.

When he saw they had all reached the meadow below, he came out of the cave, pausing once to look back at his grandfather. He couldn't see that far back into the dark cave, high up on the ledge where the old man lay. It was a look that required no eyes.

From the top of the sheep path, he looked to the left, towards the eastern gate. There, around a hundred yards away from where he stood, he saw a wolf. It was standing stock still, though unthreatening, not in a crouch or making to run and attack. For an uncomfortable moment, Petrov felt that the wolf was just there to see him and to be seen by him.

Then he felt a dull boom that shook the air. He turned to the right, the west, and, after a few moments, he saw a black cloud of smoke rising straight up into the skies in oily billows. Petrov stared in astonishment, the wolf for a moment forgotten. The plume of black smoke was some way off, coming from burning fuel, by the look of it, aviation fuel, Petrov guessed. It was coming from one of the countless canyons that lay deeper inside the plateau.

CHAPTER THIRTY

ANNA STOOD UP on the escarpment, thirty feet above the military road that led to the Putorana nuclear research station. Beyond the road, the land stretched away on a flat plateau as far as the distant mountain where the ICBM silos were located, where the research facilities were also buried in the earth, and where Professor Vasily Kryuchkov was being kept prisoner.

She'd rolled two large boulders down the slope on to the road, at a juncture in its twisting path through the higher ground she now stood on; an arc in the road where the boulders would be concealed from traffic coming in either direction, until they were almost on them. Using heavy branches, she'd also managed to manoeuvre several smaller boulders in a line on the escarpment that would take only a small amount of leverage with the branches to tip them down the hill and on to the road. Whichever way a jeep or a military vehicle or two came, she was ready to attack. Only if a troop carrier or several jeeps came along the road would she hold back. The odds against her were high enough as it was. But if she could take a vehicle and then head for the nuclear base, then she would be ever closer to the man she needed.

It had been a long and dangerous scramble down the sheer cliff face from where the helicopter had crashed. She'd slipped twice and fallen heavily on to a ledge on one occasion, her death only prevented by a last-minute grab with her left hand on to a rock that jutted outwards. But she had cut the left hand to the bone and there was a deep gash in her left thigh. She had stemmed the blood eventually, swamped the wounds with bandages from her pack, and then reached the foot of the cliff. She'd lost a lot of blood and she knew she was weak.

It was only when she'd reached the foot of the cliff that she'd heard the sound of the first helicopter, arriving to investigate the smoke and finding the crash. It hovered high above her, above the rock wall she'd scaled down and high, too, above the small meadow where she'd landed. Down in the canyon now, hundreds of feet below it, she'd been able to stay out of sight, dodging around overhangs and protruding rock walls until she was at least a mile away. When she looked back, she saw three other helicopters arrive and then ropes coiling downwards towards the stricken helicopter. But by that time, before the men began to descend down the ropes, she was around a dog-leg in the canyon and on her way north. Northwards, that was where the road to the research station lay. It crossed just on the other side of this stretch of plateau which she'd walked beneath as the canyon turned north.

She waited now on the escarpment, two, then three hours. She ate from two of the remaining tins in her pack that she'd stolen from the dacha and drank from a stream.

She felt some strength returning, but it was feeble compared to her usual strength. After some time between four and a half and five hours she finally heard the sound of an engine. And then she saw in the far distance on the lower-lying ground before the road began to wind up towards where she stood, three vehicles. Three. Too many, that was her initial reaction. She could maybe take out two, but three . . .

But with her strength ebbing again and the pain of her wounds throbbing and tearing at the nerve endings, she decided it had to be now.

She watched carefully through the binoculars, keeping them away from any flash from the sunlight. There were the three vehicles; two jeeps and, in the middle, another vehicle, a low, covered truck. The jeeps seemed to be the truck's escort. They were coming from the direction of the research station.

In the first jeep were just two men, a driver and passenger, and in the second the same. In the truck between the jeeps, she saw a driver only. But were there more men hidden by the truck's cover, a platoon even? Yet the slow cortege was odd, she thought. If it had been a bureaucrat's limousine rather than a truck between the two jeeps, it would have looked more natural. There was something in the truck that needed an escort of sorts, but not a heavy escort. Whatever the truck contained couldn't be so important, then; and anyway, as many troops as possible were now either diverted in the search for her, or would be guarding the fences of the research station. She decided there were no troops under the truck's canopy, and she would have to deal only with the five men she could see.

She lowered the binoculars and walked to the left along the escarpment to the first of the line of smaller boulders she'd prepared. Below her, on the road which arced into the mountain, the two huge boulders she'd managed to heave down the slope stood immovable, preventing a vehicle from passing easily. They would have to stop and then carefully go around the edges of the boulders, avoiding the chasm that opened out on the far side.

She watched as the three vehicles disappeared behind a jutting ridge below the higher ground where she was. The next time she'd see them would be when they appeared around the corner and into the arc of the road, and they saw the boulders.

She sat down and armed the Thompson, stringing a band of ammunition around her jacket; a single firing gun, but one with great accuracy. Then she made doubly sure the two pistols she'd taken from the dead conscripts were also armed, and she thrust these into two diagonal pockets in the jacket. They had maybe three miles to cover before they reached the arc in the road. She tested the first branch under the boulder and felt how little leverage it would take, then she tested the others. She would go from one to the other. Another line of prepared boulders lay over to her left, but they were useless now. They were in case a vehicle approached from the other direction, the other side of the boulders in the road.

She finally caught the distant sound of a rasping jeep

engine and then the truck's gears clanking down as the vehicles climbed up the plateau. Two minutes, three perhaps, before they appeared. She looked up in the sky and saw an eagle circling high above. Then she saw two hawks lower down, wary of the eagle above them. But maybe they had already sensed the approach of carrion.

The first jeep came into view and at once the two men inside saw the boulders on the road. The truck and the second jeep hadn't appeared, both slowed down by the truck's weaker engine, she guessed. The first jeep pulled up twenty yards or so from the first boulder in the road. The driver stepped out, looked up at the escarpment and, seeing nothing, slowly walked up to the boulder and checked the width of the road to the side of it, before it dropped into the chasm. Then he walked to the second of the boulders. Satisfied, he turned, looked up again, and Anna shot him through the heart at thirty feet.

It was then she heard the truck's roaring, grinding sound as it appeared around the bend. The second jeep was behind it. Once they'd gained the flat ground on the slope from beyond, where she could see, they were travelling at greater speed in order to catch up with the first jeep; twenty or twenty-five miles an hour. She didn't look at the passenger in the first jeep who was now out of it, walking towards where the driver had fallen, but she shot at a hundred and fifty yards, through the screen of the second jeep and hit somewhere near the driver's neck. The jeep slewed, even at its relatively slow pace, and she knew she had a hit. And then, to her great good fortune, the whole jeep continued its slewing motion across the road and over the edge into the chasm, taking the dead or wounded driver and his live passenger with him.

Anna saw the face of the truck driver now; confused, unaware of a shot above the noise of the truck's engine, but still seeing – in the truck's mirror – the jeep behind him swerving erratically, swinging from side to side as though it were being shaken, and finally tilting over the edge into the chasm. Then he looked ahead and saw the first jeep stopped. The truck driver was unaware too, perhaps, of the boulders in front of it. When he saw the halted jeep in front of him, the truck driver slammed on the brakes and it skidded to a halt, huffing and growling from the hood, brakes strained to the maximum. He was just fifty feet away from Anna and she shot him through the chest too. Three bullets, time for loading between each, no need for the conscripts' pistols to back up her firepower.

But when she looked back at the first jeep, its passenger was out of the seat and had disappeared. He'd seen the driver shot as soon as it had happened and there'd been seconds, but valuable seconds, to get out and conceal himself. Anna scanned from the dead body of the first driver, past the empty jeep, to the slumped driver of the truck behind and the flailing tracks of the jeep that had disappeared over the edge. Nothing. A sudden silence. One on one. That must be how it was now. Otherwise, if the truck contained men, they'd have been out of the back by now, deployed along the road, concealing themselves as best they could. But there was no one else; just the first jeep's passenger.

From behind the rock where she lay flat on her stomach, she armed the Thompson again, this time with a high-powered rifle round, and took one of the loaded pistols from her pocket. The scree slope that led thirty feet to the road below her contained no cover. But there was only one place the man could have hidden, could still be hiding – behind the first jeep. He was waiting too, also armed and ready now, and aware perhaps that he was the only one left. There was only one thing she could do to draw him out and that was to come out herself.

Finally ready, she stood up from behind the rock. The pain in her thigh coursed up through her body, the conscript's pistol in her bandaged left hand dug into the wound. But her right hand was free for the Thompson; thirty feet with a rifle round was devastating. She had one advantage – her height on the slope above him. He had another – cover. But he would have to show himself to shoot and, while she was supremely deadly, fearless, he was undoubtedly terrified. He'd seen the entire cortege wiped out, but for himself. He had no idea who, or how many, there were up on the slope above the road. But she knew he wouldn't dare to try to surrender, no matter how much he might like to. Surrender was clearly not the game with two dead men on the road and another two at the bottom of the chasm.

She began to half walk, half limp down the slope, the two guns ready, and she aimed at the jeep. She saw now that the driver had opened his window, the window nearer her, as he'd first looked out at the boulders, and then descended from the jeep to his death. The air was

351

still. There was nothing living except her, the man, and the eagle and two hawks which still circled lazily above. But the opened window seemed like an invitation.

She descended ten feet, then fifteen. She was halfway to the road, limping painfully on the steep rocky slope. Fifteen feet; she would risk it. She had the height and he hadn't shown himself. With the Thompson aimed at full arm's stretch, she shot the rifle round through the opened window, and downwards, through the inside of the flimsy passenger door of the jeep on the far side. The explosion shattered the silence, but she heard nothing after it, just the ringing in her ears. She crouched, swiftly rearmed the Thompson with another rifle round, without ever taking her eyes off the jeep. She descended a few more steps, fired again, the same trajectory, through the open window and the door on the far side. This time, she rearmed as she continued down the slope to the road, rolled on to her stomach and looked beneath the jeep.

What she saw were two military boots, their toecaps facing upwards, then legs in fatigues and an arm splayed to the side in death. She didn't know which of the shots had killed him, but it didn't matter. She stood and walked around to the far side of the jeep and saw his face had been blown to indistinguishable meat.

Anna stood up, pocketed the conscript's pistol and walked over to the first man she had shot. Then she turned and walked back the way the cortege had come until she reached the truck, its driver slumped over the steering wheel. She went to the back of the truck and opened the flap, untying cords that held it to the tailgate.

She flung back the flap, fastening it open, the Thompson drawn and ready. In the dark of its interior, she saw nothing at first. It seemed entirely empty. But then she saw a box, made of heavy wood, by the look of it. She climbed over the tailgate, her leg an agonising presence, using her right hand only to claw her way over and leaving the Thompson momentarily inactive. She stood inside in the half-darkness and breathed away the pain from her body, until she felt her head begin to cease its spinning. She threw open the other flap of canvas to let in more light.

Then she walked over to the box.

Before she was five feet away, she saw that the box was a coffin. The cortege was escorting a dead person; another death.

She looked around the inside of the truck until she found a tool box and, deep inside it, a tyre wrench. She put down the Thompson and picked up the wrench. Then she returned to the coffin. She dug the sharp edge of the wrench into the crack where the lid was nailed to the base and began, with one hand, the slow, hard process of heaving up the lid. Each nail came away, one by one. The lid was half free by the time she was able to yank it free completely with a splintering crash of wood and torn nails.

There was a winding sheet of sorts and she pulled this away, using the wrench as if to touch it with her hands might contaminate them.

Under the sheet was a face she recognised at once; the craggy, deeply lined face of the 68-year-old Professor

Vasily Kryuchkov. She stared, first in horror, then in shock, and finally with a sickening, dead feeling that her life – all the lives – had been wasted. She turned her head and retched on to the bed of the truck. When she'd choked up everything she'd eaten from her guts, she looked back at Kryuchkov's face again, lifting the veil for the last time. Too clever to die, but finally too dangerous to live.

She dropped the wrench on the truck bed, picked up the Thompson, and walked to the back of the truck. As she stepped painfully over the tailgate on to the ground, she heard a crack, then felt a stinging sensation in her side. She half turned, half fell. She saw the truck driver lying, crawling on his belly, a pistol in his hand, raised again for the kill. She aimed the Thompson without thinking and fired, blowing his skull in two through the bridge of his nose.

Then Anna fell, slammed down on to the road, and remembered nothing.

CHAPTER THIRTY-ONE

PETROV FOUND THE body of Anna some two hours later. From the entrance to the cave, he hadn't returned to the funeral feast that was being given for his grandfather. The billowing black smoke, of aviation fuel, so he thought, changed everything. And maybe the wolf too, which had lurked stationary for half an hour, until finally it disappeared over a ridge in a steady, loping run.

He'd turned towards where the smoke was coming from, and began to walk, first up over a ridge and into a canyon, then up another ridge and down again into another canyon. The shaman's coat was still draped over his arm.

But he was too wary to approach up close to the site of whatever it was that had crashed. All he knew was that it was the woman, somewhere the woman was near. The woman was behind everything he thought and did now.

From down below the small plateau where the burning of the helicopter had died down, he saw three or four more helicopters hovering high above and then he saw the occasional movement of men on the plateau as they explored the accident. He caught sight of them only when they came close enough to the lip of the plateau to catch a glimpse of an arm or a leg, the side of a body in military fatigues. But he kept himself well hidden, under overhangs in the rock, and walked swiftly away from the scene of devastation until he could no longer hear the sound of helicopters and the world was silent again.

It was later that he saw the footprint. More than an hour of walking had passed when he saw it in the deep cleft in the canyon, just after it had dog-legged to the north. He knelt and examined it and saw at once that it was most likely a woman's boot. For several miles after that he followed her tracks, losing them occasionally as she climbed over rocks, then finding them again after much searching. But he knew it was her. He walked for ten miles or more, until the tracks started to lead upwards, out of the canyon, towards a ridge beyond which, he knew, was the road that led to the missile silos and the research station thirty miles to the north. When he reached the top of the ridge, he looked down and saw on the road a still life – a jeep, a truck, three bodies lying at intervals in the road. A still death.

He went to the body of the woman immediately. He saw the gash that had opened in her thigh, her bandaged hand, a long-barrelled handgun he'd never seen before, fallen by her side, a Russian military pistol thrown aside by her fall. And then he noticed bleeding from above her waist. The blood had slowed to a stop some time before. He pulled back her jacket and saw the bullet wound where it had entered just above her hip, through just flesh, and exited an inch or two behind. A surface wound, but one that had been enough, along with her other injuries, to bring her down and leave her down.

He knelt on the road and put his ear to her mouth. He felt nothing, not a breath. But he kept his ear there and placed a finger on the pulse of her right hand. He could feel the faintest movement, a jagged, muted struggle for life. And then he felt the thin, interrupted breath from her mouth. It seemed to last a minute between each breath, but it must have been less.

He looked up at the jeep and thought he should lift her into it, drive her to the nearest hospital in Norilsk. But at once he knew he couldn't take the woman there. Whoever she was, Valentina Asayev, a former SVR colonel, a traitor, a defector, a terrorist, or . . . none or few of these.

He slung the shaman's coat over her inert body and picked her up. Then he walked back up the slope, and over the ridge until he was out of sight of the road, then down again, scrambling, crawling, sliding into the darker depths where there would be water. Several times he put her body down, to rest certainly, but also to try to cover his tracks up from the road. It was most important they didn't find his tracks up – or hers down. When he was thirty feet or so above the road, he saw the smaller boulders she'd arranged and evidently hadn't used. He set them rolling down the slope and then tried to cover where she'd set them.

He walked over rock wherever he could, and finally found a sloping rock ridge that would take him to the foot of the canyon on the far side of the road from where

357

he'd first come. There would be water there.

He bathed her wounds in a stream and dribbled some water into her mouth. She was pale, bloodless, but one time he felt her lips move a little as he wetted them.

Time no longer existed here, not any more, not amongst his own people, or in the land of endless light.

He walked on ten, fifteen miles along the broken canyon until he was at the foot of the slope that led up to the cave and the meadow where the camp and his people were. He never knew how he'd done it, no matter how strong a man he was. It was a superhuman effort, he thought dimly, something that he could never have done in the ordinary way of things.

For nearly two days, Anna lay on a palliasse of bound grasses with a deer hide laid over them before she was able to speak. She was in Petrov's and his mother's *choom* and it was Petrov's mother alone who treated her wounds. Many herbs were used. Petrov noticed nine herbs in all and he remembered his grandfather's story the night that he died, about the teaching of the nine herbs. Maybe, he thought, Gannyka had passed on the shaman's language to his mother. But she never replied when he asked her.

In the meantime, Petrov made his daily calls to Colonel Fradkov. He learned of the crashed helicopter that he'd seen and Fradkov informed him of the ambush on the military road. Petrov intimated surprise and shock. He was then ordered to stop all his people's usual activities and to command them to spread out along the roof of the plateau.

'We have other developments,' Fradkov told him on the second day. 'Four terrorists have been arrested in Norilsk. They, too, were on board the *Rossiya*. They had explosives and a highly dangerous explosive material with them. From our interrogations, we understand they were heading to the far north towards Dikson. Apparently they intended to blow up Russia's new and unique Arctic reactor. After further questioning, they will be executed, of course. But from our interrogations, we know there are at least two others still free.' Fradkov paused. 'Those we've captured are being questioned twenty-four hours a day. There will be little left of them before they're shot.'

And Petrov knew the dark meaning of his words.

Petrov asked him if they were connected to the woman.

'Everything is connected,' Fradkov replied angrily. 'Find the woman. Remember what I told you. The rewards will be astronomical for you. Failure, however, may have other implications,' he added threateningly.

They will blame everyone but themselves, Petrov thought.

In and out of consciousness, Anna thought of one thing only; the death mask of Professor Vasily Kryuchkov. And with it, the failure of her mission, the waste of life, the loss of what she knew was a great — if not the greatest — opportunity for mankind. Sometimes in these moments she struggled for life, at others she felt the peace of near death and almost welcomed its embrace. But the attentions of Petrov and his mother, as well as her own deep desire for life, somehow always prevailed. She knew she would recover, though she understood in her rational mind that there was little point in doing so. Her mission had replaced her life.

On the evening of the second day, she was well enough to speak and Petrov's mother left him with her. He drew up the small wooden stool he'd sat on as his grandfather died and sat next to the grass palliasse where she now sat, painfully, but upright, leaning against the backing of wooden sled runners. Petrov's mother had made her a cup of tea – more of the herbs she seemed to know so well – and he offered her a drink of vodka from the bottle. She drank a little, then two mouthfuls, and she was alert again.

Petrov sat and watched her for a long time without speaking. And she, too, studied his face intently for the first time.

What she saw was his brown skin at first and, even without the surroundings of a reindeer hide tent where she lay, he was clearly from one of the tribes of the north. She noted a dilated face with a frontal retraction at all three levels – intellectual, emotional and instinctive. The man's forehead was well differentiated, his eyes set back, protected. It told her he had a clever, deductive mind. On his forehead she saw a round-ish mark of curved lines, rather than the normal straightness. She believed then that she was looking, not just at a man who was clever at the twists and turns of life, but at someone who had some great spiritual quality. His high, full cheekbones, straight and protected nostrils, were a sign that he lived his life through passion, yet a passion that was guided and controlled by honesty and discretion. His jawline, she noted, was immensely strong. Whoever sat before her possessed a vital force and the capacity to carry on to a designated goal with great determination. As her eyes travelled across his gentle but strong face, her training told her that here was a man it was possible to trust.

Finally, he spoke first.

'Did you kill Professor Bachman?' he asked her gently.

It was such a strange and unexpected question, she was lost for words.

'In Krasnoyarsk,' he prompted her eventually, and again with a great, gentle inquisitiveness.

'I know of no one called Bachman,' she said finally. 'And I killed no one, not in Krasnoyarsk in any case.'

The straightforwardness of her admission caused his mind to be at rest. After all, he'd seen the road littered with bodies and the OMON officer in the jeep in the forest and heard from Fradkov about the killings of the conscripts at the dacha and at the checkpoint on the road to Norilsk. Who knew, there might be others.

'Why are you here?' he asked.

'Did you find me on the road and bring me here?' she said, without answering his question.

Petrov nodded.

'How far was it?'

'Twenty miles or so through the canyons. I had to take a roundabout route. There's a great deal of military activity in the area. They're looking for you,' Petrov added. 'As I'm sure you're aware.'

Anna was amazed that a man could carry an inert body

so far through such difficult country. That he'd bothered to do so at all and not turn her in to the authorities lifted her confidence in him further. She felt her trust in him becoming embedded. She decided she would slowly open the doors of her knowledge and trust.

For his part, Petrov had no intention of hurrying her, and so he withdrew from the direct question he'd asked. He would lead up to it.

'I saw the wreck of the *Rossiya*,' he said. 'Was that you? How did you do it?'

She told him about the freeing of the anchor chain, and the grounding of the ship. 'I was lucky,' she added. 'It grounded on a ridge next to a trench in the riverbed. That's why it turned completely on its side.'

Petrov considered this for a moment.

'And all the time you were heading north?' he asked her. 'You never had any intention of remaining in Igarka?'

Yes, she thought, to trust him was the only way. 'I was trying to reach the Putorana nuclear research station,' she replied. 'That's what I'm doing here.'

He sat and watched her in silence. If she was going to tell him, then she would.

His silence was one of intense calm, she thought. And she knew that, if she wanted their contact to mean anything at all, any communication would have to come from her.

'There is ... there was a man there, in Putorana. A great scientist in the nuclear field. We believe he'd made a discovery of truly life-changing proportions. His name was Vasily Kryuchkov. Another professor. I found him in the back of the truck on the road. But what I found was his dead body.' She looked intensely at him. 'I believe the State has killed him, in order for the world to remain ignorant of what he found.'

Petrov decided not to ask her what 'We' meant. 'We believe . . .' Who believed, he wondered, who did the woman work for? But he was not going to pursue it. It didn't seem to matter much anyway. And so he sat in silence once more. Let her come to him, if she would.

'Who is Professor Bachman?' Anna asked suddenly.

Petrov let out a small sigh. His mind reeled back to the morning at the apartment block on Sverdlovsk Street, the discovery of Bachman's dead body, and his own extreme diligence – peculiar, he now thought – by which he'd discovered the papers in Bachman's shoe, papers that he still carried in a shirt pocket beneath the deerskin coat.

'My name is Alexei Petrov,' he began at last. 'Lieutenant Alexei Petrov of the *militsiya*. But my mother's family is here, all around us. It was up here where I was born, and up here where my spirit lies. My Evenki name is *Munnukan*. It means "hare". But for many years I followed my Russian father's demands to be Russian and to join the *militsiya* like him. It was me who first examined the body of Professor Bachman on the morning of the third of June. It was found in a trash alley at the side of an apartment block on Sverdlovsk Street.'

He saw her eyes widen, her body stiffen, but he didn't pause. 'It was lying face up next to the same apartment block where you had rented a room in the name of Valentina Asayev from a woman called Zhenya. That last information I alone found out. The MVD investigators there were not told your name, nor of your presence there. They must have found out in other ways about you.'

Anna thought of the photograph the foreman Ivan had taken of her on his mobile phone.

'I was photographed on the *Rossiya,*' she said. 'It must have been passed on.'

'Then your face is obviously well known in Moscow,' he stated, without demanding affirmation from her. But, from her eyes, he knew he was right.

'I searched the body of Bachman,' Petrov continued. 'Even though when, almost immediately, I'd found that he was a foreigner, I knew the case should be handed at once to the MVD. I found he had a return ticket from Norilsk that day. I also saw that his clothes had been slit. Someone had been searching for something he was carrying, no doubt illegally or, at any rate, something that the authorities would not wish him or any other foreigner to possess.' He paused. He didn't know – not yet – whether he should reveal what he'd found in the sole of Bachman's shoe. 'I checked up on this Bachman,' he continued. 'He is, or was, a very eminent nuclear scientist from Germany who has written many papers, is very respected throughout the world, and had been researching a highly secret nuclear project for many years – as far back as the sixties, I believe. It seemed clear to me then, as it does now, that he was murdered for whatever it was he was carrying. And that must have been something that he'd brought from Norilsk that afternoon.' He paused again. He didn't want to tire her. 'Norilsk is a hundred miles to the west of us from here, from this meadow, and only a little more than that from the Putorana nuclear research facility.'

He paused, watching her face all the time. He saw that a whole wild flock of thoughts were crossing her mind; calculations, assumptions, and just guesswork perhaps. But she was making connections without pause and he saw this from what was in her eyes and what was written in the changing lines on her forehead.

'So,' he continued. 'An internationally renowned German nuclear scientist is found dead in an alley in Krasnoyarsk on the third of June, the same day you left on the *Rossiya*. With something evidently valuable concealed on his person. For that, surely, was why he was murdered. And then, eight days later, an internationally renowned Russian nuclear scientist is found in a coffin in a truck on the deserted road over there,' he pointed vaguely north-wards, 'leading away from the nuclear research facility which you were trying to reach.' He leaned forward on the stool, but it was a movement without threat. 'You were trying to reach Kryuchkov too, just like Bachman was and, perhaps, did . . . yes? And you believe this Kryuchkov was murdered by us, by the Russian State. And again, he was murdered in order to conceal something. The connection, it seems to me, is obvious. Bachman met Kryuchkov – or maybe some go-between of Kryuchkov's – in Norilsk on the second of June. Something was exchanged between the two of them, or between the go-between and Bachman – and it was for this that Bachman was murdered. And now Kryuchkov is dead also, and his secret is presumably intended to die with him.'

Anna pulled herself up on the palliasse until she was more upright against the sled runners. It was painful, but she wanted to find out how painful, how difficult it was for her to move.

'What you are looking for,' Petrov continued, 'has, I believe, something to do with what was exchanged between Kryuchkov and Bachman. You wanted to find Kryuchkov at the research facility, in order to find what you are looking for, yes? And you knew nothing of Bachman and what apparently took place between them on the second of June.'

Anna looked back into the dark, intense eyes of the man who sat beside her, a *militsiya* lieutenant who hadn't put her under arrest, but had saved her life.

'And so that is why you're here,' Petrov concluded. 'Just like Bachman. Kryuchkov.' Petrov paused. He didn't know what he possessed in the pocket of his coat. 'Had Kryuchkov discovered something so terrible, so dangerous, that first Bachman, and then Kryuchkov himself, were murdered?'

Anna sat and watched the man's gentle but determined face in front of her. She knew she had little – no, no options – now but to open herself to him.

'My name is Anna Resnikov,' Anna said quietly. 'I was an SVR colonel, my father and grandfather were both senior officers in the KGB and its predecessor, the NKVD, before that. My father was head of station in Damascus. I defected from Russia five years ago.'

Petrov just nodded. Then he sat deep in thought, looking down at his hands clasped on his knees in front of him. He still felt that there was no dilemma, but he had no idea why he felt that.

Then he withdrew the satellite phone from a leather bag beside the stool.

'I was given this by a Colonel Fradkov of the FSB, in Igarka three, four days ago. My orders are to call him every day. My other orders are also to find you. I have seen how much they want you. To destroy you too.' He wasn't sure how to go on, so he persisted with facts for a moment. 'This Fradkov has said that if I find you, I will be made a general. I will be given a pension, an apartment in Moscow, a dacha, enough money to live in the West, if that's what I want.'

'As far as anyone can trust the FSB, I believe that's true,' Anna replied at once. 'They will give you all those things. Medals too, anything you want. You will be a great hero.'

Once more, Petrov was impressed by her straightforwardness.

'But even if I were interested in those things,' Petrov said, 'that would not be a reason to hand you over to them. There would have to be other reasons.'

'I've killed eleven Russians in the past eight days,' Anna said. 'That should be reason enough for a *militsiya* lieutenant.'

'Instead of those things they've promised me,' Petrov continued, ignoring the provocation of her response, 'I've actually decided to downgrade my position. I no longer wish to work for the *militsiya*, let alone become a Hero of Russia. I intend to remain here, with my people, at least for as long as they allow us to live our old way of life.'

They sat in silence then, but it was a complete, comfortable silence, one of two old friends who had no need to talk. Finally, Petrov looked up from his clasped hands.

'There were others on board the *Rossiya*,' he said. 'Like you, they also escaped when the ship collapsed. Four of them have been arrested, according to this Fradkov. Up in the area of Dikson, where our new mobile reactor is waiting to be taken to the Pole. Were you with them, part of them?'

Anna thought of Oleg, with his fanatical eyes and his determination to commit 'a great act'.

'I met them onboard, or their leader, anyway,' she replied. 'He wanted me to join them, but he didn't tell me what for. He told me they had access to explosives and a highly dangerous explosive substance called thermite.'

'And you had no connection with them other than talking with their leader?' Petrov asked.

'None.'

'Good,' Petrov replied. He was relieved about her reply and, more importantly, he completely believed its honesty. 'They were arrested, apparently, these boys, before they were able to blow up this reactor. A highly stupid thing to do. To save the world? Is that what they were trying to do? But in doing so, risking the exact damage they purported to be fighting against. Nuclear fall-out – and up in the Arctic of all places.'

'They were fanatics, certainly,' she said. 'The act, for them, was more important than the fall-out – in both senses of that word.'

So, Petrov thought, the way was now clear for him to go on. She was not connected to the stupidity and violent danger of the boys who'd been arrested. It was time to pursue his course to its core.

'Tell me, Anna,' he said quietly, 'what is muon catalysed fusion?'

He saw her whole body tense then, despite the pain of muscular contraction. Her eyes were suddenly wild. Or was it amazement, or confusion? She seemed ready to leap from the palliasse, to reach out at him. In violence? No, he thought not. It seemed to be some kind of desperation.

'Is it what Professor Kryuchkov was working on? What Bachman was working on?' he said. 'What you want?'

'It's what Kryuchkov had been working on for many years, and no doubt Bachman too,' she replied tensely.

'Then you know what it is,' he said.

'And you too,' she replied.

'I know nothing. That's why I'm asking you.'

Anna was silent, her mind reeling. What did the *militsiya* lieutenant, the Evenki tribesman, know in order to ask such a question?

'I'd like to stand up,' she said.

'Of course. If you feel up to it.'

Petrov stood and began to put his arms around her back to help her. But she put her hand on his right arm and looked at him.

'I can do it on my own,' she said.

He watched as she struggled with the pain, until she'd heaved her legs over the side of the low palliasse.

The poultices his mother had put on her wounds were good, she thought, whatever they were. Her hand barely hurt. The gash in her thigh was worse than her hand, but she saw it was well wadded with bandages under which a few sprigs of some herbs were protruding. Only where the bullet on the road, fired by the dying truck driver, had ripped her right side was the pain still very great.

She rested on the edge of the palliasse for a moment and he made no move to help her. Then she pushed her way through the pain to stand on her feet. She stood, panting slightly from the pain, but she was steady.

'Let's have some vodka,' she said.

He got up from the stool and picked two cups from an upturned box and, clutching them and a vodka bottle in one hand, placed them all on a low table in the centre of the *choom*. Then he threw some wood into a wood burner and lit it. There was an icy wind coming under the flap of the *choom*, from the north. He thought from the smell of the wind that there would be snow tonight – and then he wondered how he had developed the sense to know that.

When the fire was blazing, he filled the two cups, gave one to her and raised his own. They both sipped from the cups until he put his down while she held hers, perhaps unable to bend easily to the low table. He then sat cross-legged on the floor. Anna continued to stand, as if to test herself and her strength.

'In the late 1940s,' Anna began, 'our Professor Sakharov predicted that there was a possibility, theoretically in any case, of producing muon catalysed fusion at some time in the future. A muon is an unstable subatomic particle. It's like an electron, but two hundred times bigger, or more. If a muon were to replace one electron in a hydrogen molecule, they would therefore be drawn at least two hundred times closer together. When they're this close, the possibility of creating nuclear fusion is greatly enhanced.'

Petrov looked and concentrated and began to feel that the mystery – the 'secret he didn't know he possessed', as Gannyka had told him the night he died – was closer to being revealed.

'Fission and fusion are therefore two very different things. The word "fission" means "split apart". In the case of normal nuclear reactors – or bombs – uranium atoms are split apart producing gigantic amounts of energy; millions of times more energy than any other type of fuel. But they also produce gigantic and unstable amounts of nuclear waste and, in the case of a damaged reactor, for example, or a bomb, they produce a huge amount of fatal radiation. Radiation from the bombs at Hiroshima and Nagasaki more than sixty-five years ago is still killing people. The disaster at Chernobyl will still be killing people in decades time. Perhaps in Japan too, from its recent reactor disaster.'

Now she sat down on the thin rug inside the *choom*, and faced Petrov directly. She was keen, he saw, to make him understand the point she was heading towards. She couldn't cross her legs, with the gash in her thigh still not properly healed, but she kept them straight out and leaned against the stool Petrov had been sitting on.

'Fusion,' she continued, 'is different. It fuses muons on to the electron in a hydrogen molecule. It can be done at room temperature, or even less, while thermonuclear fission requires extremely high temperatures.'

She sipped from the tin cup of vodka and this time placed it on the floor beside her.

'However, it is difficult to produce muons in large enough quantities to make much of a difference. Another problem is that the muons decay away before they pro-duce more than a few hundred nuclear fusion reactions. Muon nuclear fusion works in a laboratory, in other words, but not in a practical, commercial situation in order to produce the energy we actually need and use. And so, in 1957, an American scientist concluded that muon nuclear fusion would therefore be impractical as an energy source.'

Each of them felt the wind outside the *choom* pick up again from the north and some iced flakes scudded under the flaps at the entrance. When the gust had died down, Anna continued.

'If a way could be found to bring it out of the laboratory and into the world, four things would result. First, it would be much cheaper than normal nuclear fission reactors. Second, it would produce almost no radioactive waste, perhaps none at all if it were properly efficient. Third, it would produce almost no greenhouse gases. Fourth, it would eliminate the need for fossil fuels altogether, including coal, oil and gas.'

Petrov thought about this extraordinary possibility for a moment. But then his mind returned to what the American professor had said in 1957.

'And there's been no progress?' Petrov asked, 'since the 1950s?'

'None of any significant kind. There needs to be a cheap way to produce muons and that has never been found. Muons can only produce as much energy as it takes to produce that energy. The only things that can produce muons almost indefinitely – and therefore produce inexhaustible energy – are something called pions. But no method has been discovered to do this.'

'And you're going to tell me, I hope, what a pion is.'

'A pion is also a subatomic particle – any one of three, in fact. There is effectively an endless supply of them. All the seas in the world produce an almost infinite number of pions. But how to make these pions produce muons – that is what scientists have been working on for more than sixty years. It is called an "almost success". In other words, it's useless.'

Anna sipped from the vodka cup again and looked back at Petrov once more.

'If muon nuclear fusion could be realised by channelling ordinary seawater to produce an endless supply of muons, then a city such as Norilsk could be run from a building no bigger than a small house. All its factories, all its transportation systems, all the domestic use of a city of a hundred and seventy-five thousand people. There would be no danger of radioactive escape or of nuclear waste. All it would need is a pipe, carrying seawater, to the city. Or simply an energy line from a fusion centre based by the sea. Every car on the planet could be run on electricity provided by muon catalysed fusion. Safely, cleanly, without waste. Every village, town and city on the planet.'

Petrov stood. He realised he'd drunk half a cup of vodka. But he poured himself another and saw that Anna's hand was stretched up towards him, with its cup also empty. Then he sat down again opposite her.

'And this is what you believe Professor Kryuchkov had discovered? How to make muons from pions – from the sea! From seawater! From almost nothing!' he said.

'Yes.'

Petrov was bemused. He couldn't understand what he was hearing, and yet he could. But there was one other thing at the back of his mind that now worked its way to the front. It was something that utterly and completely baffled him.

'But if this discovery of Kryuchkov's is so momentous,' he said, 'so world-changing, so beneficial to the planet, why does the Kremlin wish to conceal it? Why have they killed him? Why do they want to deny his discovery to themselves, let alone to the world?'

CHAPTER THIRTY-TWO

BURT MILLER STOOD on the shingle beach on Cougar's rented island and looked towards the east – the Barents Sea and, beyond that, the Kara Sea, and then the mouth of the Yenisei river, three days' journey from where he stood. The tenth of June had come and gone and Anna Resnikov had not made the first rendezvous.

Larry stood beside him, also looking into the blue expanse. The sun was low, but bright, the sea calm and empty of vessels. But the chill was intense. It was just after two o'clock in the morning.

'The State Department has heard from our ambassador in Moscow,' Burt murmured, barely audibly. 'Pressure has been applied and it's been partially successful.'

'What's the news?' Larry asked his boss.

'The Russians have released Eileen and Sky. That's their concession so far. But they're holding Clay in Krasnoyarsk.'

'Why?'

Burt didn't reply immediately. He just scuffed some stones beneath his feet and kicked one into the gently lapping waves. They were right on the shore, the water almost reaching their feet.

Burt turned and began to walk up the beach, away from the stone buildings and the prefab huts Cougar had erected, as if there were anyone who could hear them anywhere. Larry followed.

Finally, as he continued to walk slowly along the shingle, Burt spoke, but still in tones so low that Larry had to lean in slightly.

'They're charging him with murder,' Burt said.

Larry was struck dumb.

He felt a deep anger coming from Burt, rather than hearing it in his voice. It seemed to steam invisibly out of him.

'But that's crazy,' Larry exploded at last. His mind was working fast, thinking of the possibilities, the implications. 'Have they found some link between him and Cougar? Is this their way of extracting something from us?'

'I'm afraid not,' Burt replied.

'Then what?' Larry demanded, exasperated now by Burt's low and halting delivery of information.

Burt stopped again and turned towards the sea. 'He's being charged with the murder of a German professor. A nuclear scientist. The man's name is Bachman. According to our German friends he's been missing for twelve days or more. Now the Russians say they've had his body all along. They've also found a briefcase of his, they say. Contains the usual things a man takes on a short trip.' Burt stopped talking again and Larry restrained his impatience this time. 'But along with the underwear and the shaving things and the change of shirt, they found a bald wig in the case,' Burt said finally. 'The Russians say the wig contains DNA that matches Clay's.'

Larry was ready to explode.

'Where's the evidence?' he almost shouted now.

'Oh, the Russians are being surprisingly co-operative,' Burt answered quietly. 'They've invited FBI investigators to Krasnoyarsk.'

'But it's obviously a fix!' Larry said. 'They've just planted the DNA. They must know something about what Clay was doing in Siberia. They've let the other two go and kept him. So. They must be asking for something. They must be trying to screw us.'

'I'm afraid not,' Burt said again, towards the sea. 'They're not asking us, or the CIA or the State Department, or any of us, for anything at all. They're charging him with murder and they intend to pursue it. They want nothing, no bribe, to make them drop the charges, as they usually would. They see it as some kind of publicity coup, perhaps. A way to show the world they can solve a murder committed by a foreigner, even if they somehow fail to solve the murders they commit against their own journalists and MPs and anyone else in Russia who dissents from the Kremlin's line.'

'But it's an obvious set-up, for Christ's sake!' Larry said, demanding the answer he wanted now, screwing his right foot into the shingle in anger. 'You know that! They know he's connected to us and they're going to frame him. "Stop sending your spies on to our soil", that's their message, that's what it's about.'

Burt turned towards him, for the first time since the conversation had begun. 'Of course, we've been making our own inquiries,' he said softly. 'That was also my opinion, naturally. A frame-up. This Bachman had been to Norilsk. He'd intended to meet Kryuchkov, but we hear he apparently failed. Kryuchkov no longer meets anyone. We believe he met another man in a hotel in Norilsk, however. Perhaps something passed between them, we don't know. But Bachman was a marked man after that.'

'But not marked by Clay! Jesus, Burt, stop talking this crap! It's obvious the Russians are sending a warning shot across our bow. They know Clay isn't who he says he is, that's all. Maybe they even know he works for us, or believe he's CIA. Who knows? But that's what they're doing. Straightforward extortion.'

Burt briefly put a hand on Larry's shoulder. He knew Clay was close to the man standing next to him on the beach. He saw his distress. It was Larry who had recruited Clay initially and then Cougar had hired him after all the normal checks on the man had yielded favourable results. So it wasn't Larry's fault, Burt was thinking, but, nevertheless, Larry would blame himself. Burt knew that.

He removed his hand from Larry's shoulder.

'I repeat, they're not trying to extort anything from us,' he said. 'And as I say, we've been making our own inquiries,' he continued. 'And not just in Russia. We've been working on this back in the States twenty-four hours a day.' He paused. He didn't want to go on. But finally he sighed and began to complete the story. 'It seems Clay has a bank account in a small private bank in Mexico City. Under the name Santorio Mondragon, would you believe. There's five million dollars in the account.'

Larry looked at him aghast.

'The provenance of the money has been harder to discover. But we have, finally, discovered it. In double-quick time too. A company called Friar Tuck Invest-ments . . .' Burt gazed up into the sky. 'Where do they get these names?' he wondered aloud. 'Santorio Mondragon . . . Friar Tuck . . . It baffles.' Then his face turned down towards the shingle and, from the side of his face, Larry saw that he was frowning. 'The company doesn't exist, of course,' Burt continued. 'Or, at least, it exists solely for the purpose of depositing money to Santorio Mondragon. To Clay,' he added delicately. 'It is in reality a snake's nest of entities, a poisonous soup of different ingredients, a consortium, in other words, of different companies, all of which are competitors in the normal way of things, but who, on this occasion, share the same interest.'

Burt violently kicked a pebble into the sea. Larry was too stunned to speak or even think.

'Apparently, representatives of this consortium knew about Bachman's visit to Kryuchkov and, even though he failed to meet the Russian professor, they must have had reason to believe that he'd taken something with him back to Krasnoyarsk, something the people in the con-sortium wanted very badly indeed. Evidently, this was communicated to Clay. A little taster of five million dollars was paid into the account in Mexico City. No doubt the eventual reward, if Clay found what they were looking for, would have been ten, a hundred times greater. What this consortium want is the same thing that we want – Kryuchkov's magic formula,' Burt said dryly. 'If it exists. And I now believe it does. In any case, assuming Clay did kill Bachman, did he find anything on the German? Kryuchkov's equations? If he did, the Russians have now relieved him of them. But they'll never let him go. Maybe he's hidden a copy of them – if indeed he did find anything on Bachman. Maybe he's even smart enough to keep the equations in his head. Who knows?' Burt paused. 'I'm sorry, Larry,' he said, turning towards the taller man. 'But it seems that Clay did murder Bachman. And if he found anything, no one's going to get a sight of it in the West or anywhere else. Clay's lost, buried for good, he'll probably catch typhoid, or "commit suicide", or get shivved by a fellow prisoner in a Russian cell in Moscow or Krasnoyarsk, or far out of the way in one of their prisons in the middle of Siberia. Once the Russians have presented us and the FBI with irrefutable evidence, he'll be tried *in camera* for the murder and convicted. Correctly, I'm afraid. That will be almost a first for Russia; a correct conviction. Then he'll simply be disappeared. Too dangerous to remain alive – if he did get sight of what Kryuchkov has found. If he didn't, the Russians won't care. They won't take the risk. They'll kill him. In one of their well-appointed dungeons. If he's lucky, they may not even bother to torture him first.'

Burt now stuck his gloved hands in his pocket. Larry hadn't asked him the question he expected him to ask. Not yet. But Larry's mind was for the moment twisted into a fist of conflicting lines of thought that were tighter than a golf ball.

'Bachman,' Larry said. He felt a fury grip him. 'The Bachman you courted so assiduously before this operation began.' He looked like he might lunge at Burt. 'Was Bachman working for us? For Cougar?'

Burt turned towards him and looked him directly in the eyes. 'Larry, you should know better than anyone that Cougar doesn't employ amateurs.' Then Burt gave a hollow laugh of incredulity. 'You think I'd employ Bachman? Really, Larry. But someone did, or may have done.'

Larry stood silently and the silence stretched into more than a minute as he tried to believe Burt.

'So Anna is our only chance,' he said finally.

'Just as she always was,' Burt added.

'If she's still alive,' Larry wondered.

'If she's still alive or not, we've had another piece of news,' Burt said. 'Last night, out of Moscow. A formal press announcement, as it happens. To all the wire services. Professor Vasily Kryuchkov is dead. A heart attack, the Kremlin is saying. The Kremlin is hailing him as a Hero of Russia, a nuclear scientist greater than Sakharov, greater than anyone, they're saying. He's to be given a state funeral. And this time – now he's dead – all his international colleagues will be invited to meet him at last. At his funeral.'

'They've murdered him,' Larry whispered.

'I would say so, yes,' Burt replied. 'The lid is being slowly screwed shut.'

He turned to Larry.

'When's the next rendezvous?' he said.

'In five days,' Larry replied faintly. 'I'll be on the ship. It should be arriving not far from us here in the next twenty-four hours. That's when I'll board.'

'Good. For God's sake, get her out, Larry.'

And then at last Larry's mind began to form itself itself into some kind of order. The second question Burt had been waiting for rose slowly through its dark depths and finally broke the surface.

'Who is the consortium?' Larry asked him. 'Who the hell is Friar Tuck Investments?'

Burt looked up at the taller man again.

'It's obvious, isn't it, Larry. It's the people who stand to lose most from Kryuchkov's discovery – to lose everything, in fact. Our own people, our own oil companies in the West. Our all-powerful energy companies. The richest corporations in the world.' Burt paused. 'They'll be wiped out completely.'

He brooded towards the sea.

'Who knows?' he continued slowly. 'Maybe our own government is involved in the cover-up? To support our all-important energy companies. In return for their support, of course, for our government. Maybe,' he said, and there was now a look of slight alarm on his face, 'maybe I don't know everything there is to know about our own men of power.'

There was a silence between the two men. Only the lapping of the water, as it rolled on to the shingle, disturbed the total peace of the pristine island.

'Can you imagine the kind of sum they offered poor Clay to avoid that fate,' Burt said.

CHAPTER THIRTY-THREE

A NNA STILL SAT on the earth floor. The fire had gone down and Petrov got to his feet and put more wood in the burner. It flared warmth into the *choom* and they both felt it in their bones. It reinvigorated her. She was beginning to feel strong again.

'What date is it?' she asked.

Petrov realised he had no idea. His links with his previously normal life seemed to have been severed almost completely. He looked in blank surprise for a moment, then got to his feet again and rummaged in his pack by the grass bed on the far side of the tent from Anna. He finally found his watch.

'The twelfth of June,' he read.

Four days, she thought, four days until the next possible pick-up. And she knew that each delay was bringing greater danger to the men who came into the small gulf off the Kara Sea in the 24-hour daylight. But it was the nearest pick-up point to Finland and the most remote from people, the best. Three hundred miles to the north of where she sat, a hundred miles east of Dikson, Siberia's northernmost town. Around a thousand miles from the North Pole.

But even then, even if she made it, she would be returning with only failure.

Petrov waited. She hadn't answered his question from earlier. And so he tried again, uncharacteristically forceful now in his demand for an answer from her. 'Why?' he asked again. 'Why is the Kremlin destroying all the evidence of this discovery? Even down to the presumed murder of Kryuchkov?'

Anna stretched out and then curled her unwounded leg into her thigh. She felt the good muscles respond as if they were eager to get going, to be on the move again. To go north.

'The Russian economy,' she began, 'is hopelessly dependent on oil and gas. The Government is interested in no other investment in the country. And now there's the oil and gas they wish to exploit under the Pole – with this new mobile nuclear reactor they've built up at Dikson to power the drilling. Oil and gas make up at least thirty per cent of Russia's GDP. They are two thirds of all Russian exports. They account for around half of the Federal State budget. A one dollar decrease in the price of oil on the world markets means a one per cent reduction in Russia's GDP. And, of course, a similar increase results in the opposite.' She stretched out her leg again, so that both were straight out and flat to the floor of the *choom*. 'Without oil and gas, Russia would be a truly Third World country. It would disintegrate as a world power. It couldn't afford its Space projects or its nuclear technology. It couldn't survive in its present form. Its people would become poorer than they are even now. It couldn't afford its vast security and intelligence services that keep the lid on popular discontent. Russia would have to change at last. Start to become a modern economy. But that's not what Russia's leaders really want, no matter what they say. Most important to the Kremlin and its spy cronies, without oil and gas the thieves who strip the State energy companies for their own personal advantage will no longer be able to do so.' She clasped her hands in front of her and leaned her neck back, stretching her torn body as best she could. 'In the West,' she continued, 'in certain Western intelligence agencies, in any case, they believe Vladimir Putin is now unofficially the richest man in the world. The graft and percentages that come to him and others from the State's companies are vast.' She paused and looked Petrov in the eye for the first time during this exchange. 'That's why they don't want Kryuchkov's discovery to reach the world. The spy elite in the Kremlin will become irrelevant. No more the *siloviki* – the men with power – but the men without power. And so they're prepared to inflict ever further damage on Russia and the rest of the world with their pollution and their drilling and extraction and their highly dangerous and volatile nuclear reactor up at Dikson, ready to be dragged to the Pole. And the world, including your people, the Evenki, will pay the ultimate price for their greed.'

'And Kryuchkov's discovery?' Petrov asked.

'. . . would have made the world a far, far better place for everyone except the few who go on growing richer,' she answered him.

Petrov sat deep in thought. But he knew what he was

going to do now. It had been building in him for two days.

He'd always known he was going to do it, he supposed, somewhere in the recesses of his heart. He knew the woman he'd been searching for and who now sat in front of him was somehow pre-ordained. They had been brought together for the purpose. And so finally he spoke.

'I found something on the body of Professor Bachman,' he began slowly. 'It was overlooked by the killer, it was concealed too well.' He put his hand into the inside of his jacket under the deerskin coat and withdrew the package he'd been carrying for ten days now. And he thought again of Gannyka, who'd told him that he possessed a secret that he didn't know he possessed. He handed it to her.

Anna unwrapped the waterproofing and then found an old leather wallet, from inside which she extracted three pages of a small notebook. She stared at the first page, first with incomprehension, then amazement, and finally with a near shattering of all rational thought. What she saw was Professor Kryuchkov's handwriting, studied and memorised by her at Burt's Cougar Ranch in New Mexico. It was unmistakably his writing.

She quickly scanned the first page, then the second, and then the final one, and saw the jungle of equations, the two paragraphs of prose – everything that Petrov had seen but which had sent his mind into a dull waking sleep.

'Where was it concealed?' she asked him, not daring yet to approach the possibility that it was what she'd been sent to find.

'In his shoe,' Petrov replied. 'I noticed the stitching was different on the left shoe to that on the right. More crude. Russian stitching. I cut the sole away and found it inside. Then I took it. I'd never done such a thing before in all my career in the *militsiya*. I don't why I took it. But after I'd taken it, I handed the murder case over to the MVD as I had to do.'

'So Bachman met Kryuchkov?' Anna said.

'I don't know. Somehow I doubt it, though. But he met someone who knew Kryuchkov. That's my best guess. Someone who had access to him.' Petrov got up and sat next to Anna. 'Look,' he said, 'it's been written extremely hastily, perhaps in a dark room, I thought. Or perhaps he was being watched constantly. But somehow he got it out.'

Petrov looked at the papers in her hand. 'But what does it mean?' he asked.

Anna scanned the pages again. She couldn't fully understand them, though she'd studied everything there was to know about muon catalysed fusion. But she knew the formula in front of her was what she'd been looking for – the commercial development of a new, safe and clean nuclear technology, sprung at last from its previous laboratory-only status. A holy grail that had been pursued for more than seventy years and finally been written off.

They both sat in silence, but another question was forming itself in Petrov's mind, and one that had been there all along, since he'd found the woman lying on the road.

'I believe I can trust you,' he said, 'but what about the

people you work for? Whoever they are. The "We" you talk about. Might it not also be in their interest to suppress it, just as the Kremlin has tried to do?'

Anna didn't reply immediately.

She thought of Burt Miller, the great, grandiose and bullish multi-billionaire who'd built Cougar from nothing into the world's largest private intelligence agency; the man who had been a star CIA agent in his youth, who'd been stationed unofficially throughout Central Asia and in the south of Russia itself more than thirty years before. She thought of the nature of Burt Miller, the man she'd known well for nearly three years now, and had worked for tirelessly against her own country. Larger-than-life was not a big enough description of Miller. He was his own man, but a man of power too, like the *siloviki* in the Kremlin, a man who could subtly appoint the head of the CIA from within the ranks of Cougar, in a system of revolving doors between the private and the public intelligence communities that he'd exploited to his own massive advantage; a man who had the ear of the president of the United States and knew what was discussed in each daily briefing between the President and the CIA chief. Miller was one of the elite that ruled America behind the scenes; a man with a seat at the highly secretive Bilderberg Committee, with the Kissingers and the Rockefellers and the Perles. Miller was a businessman, and his business was intelligence. He walked the same corridors with the other men of power, including the men who controlled America's and Europe's and Asia's energy needs. With the formula she held in her hand now given over to Miller, would Miller the businessman stick with his own? Would he quietly file it away – and in return take a stake in the companies that it would destroy – in return for more billions, and shares and stakes in the world's biggest companies?

But Miller, most essentially – beyond business, beyond his authority among the world's men of power, beyond anything – was a supreme individualist. A man for whom money itself meant little. At the core of Burt Miller was a lust for personal glory, for a place in posterity, in history itself, which more money and acclamation from politicians and the great couldn't outweigh. While they would soon be forgotten, Miller would want his place in history to be remembered for ever – alongside that of Vasily Kryuchkov; the men who changed the world, saved the world, even. That was something, Anna was sure, that he wouldn't be able to resist, no matter what the cataclysmic effect Kryuchkov's formula had on his business peers. Anna smiled slightly. She was imagining Miller, at some huge and extravagant press conference – with all the drama and the melodrama that he loved – announcing to the world that he, Burt Miller, had come to save it. It would be his moment of greatest glory.

Yet, as she looked at the fine-boned face of Petrov sitting beside her and saw his quiet concern, she realised she could not explain this to him, let alone convince him.

She took a notebook of her own from the pocket of her jacket and gave him a pen.

'Copy it out,' she said. 'Carefully. Check it three, four times, to make sure you've got it right. Then when it's done, waterproof it well, seal it in a metal box and bury it somewhere in the Putorana.'

Petrov knew he would bury it in the cave with his grandfather.

'That's your insurance,' she said. 'But I believe you'll read it soon in the world's newspapers, hear it on every radio and see it on every television. I'll find a way to contact you from the West. So you'll know.'

The journey from the reindeer meadows to the small river took them half a day. Some of Petrov's people carried her on a stretcher, even though she insisted she could walk now.

They'd built her a boat, more of a raft, something they used themselves to hide on when they went on expeditions to shoot duck and geese. It was strongly made of crossed branches, bound with rope, beneath. But the top was a medley of brush and smaller branches and grasses set and bound with grass at odd, natural angles. From above it looked just like the normal flotsam of the river's vegetation.

'From the air,' Petrov told her, 'from a helicopter, for example, it will look the same as one of the countless bundles of foliage that the snowmelt washes down these rivers at this time of year. You'll be concealed underneath the top layer.'

Hidden beneath the tangle of brown and green, on the actual raft structure itself, a small rudder fashioned from a branch, protruded into the water. Lying concealed on her front, she could operate it with her feet, without ever being seen.

'It's about twenty miles along this river before you reach a tributary that goes off to the left,' Petrov said. 'Follow that for another hundred miles or so and you'll reach a larger river that will take you to the gulf you're looking for on the Kara Sea.'

He then gave her his *militsiya* pistol and ammunition.

'I won't be needing this any more,' he said.

A look of concern crossed his face.

'I should come with you, Anna. It would be safer.'

'No,' she replied. 'You have something far more important here . . . if I don't make it.'

Petrov nodded.

'We have an Evenki saying,' he said. ' "The deer and the wolf do not follow the same path".' He paused. Then he smiled at her. 'I think I'm the deer.'

Finally, he gave her bags of food and then a bag made of grass. She looked inside it and saw a sea of red, with circular metal discs sewn into it, and feathers she thought were an eagle's sewn on to the coat's sleeves.

'It was my grandfather's coat,' he told her. 'He was a great shaman. It will keep you safe.'

And this seemed to Petrov now a perfectly natural statement.

CHAPTER THIRTY-FOUR

THE RUSTED HULL of the freighter *Rosa Mundi*, out of Hamburg, picking up timber from the port of Dikson, followed the path cut through the ice floes of the Kara Strait by the Russian nuclear ice-breaker a quarter of a mile ahead.

Larry stood at the stern, the bridge of the vessel between him and the Russian ship. The ice-breaker was certainly necessary, but he knew that on board would also be officials whose job it was to make sure nobody got on or off the freighter. They were well inside Russian waters.

On the left of the freighter now was the island of Novaya Zemlya, that curved like a dented and damaged gibbous moon towards the North Pole. Ahead was the Kara Sea and the Gulf of Yenisei. They'd reached the point.

He turned and shouted an order.

A boat was winched from the opened hold below. It was attached to the stern davits and Larry, with four other men, one a medic, the other three former special forces officers like himself, climbed up a ladder and into the boat. This was the crucial moment.

As the *Rosa Mundi* passed the first promontory of the

long, curving island, the boat was lowered from the davits over the stern of the freighter, out of sight of the Russian ice-breaker. If the captain did his job right, and turned slightly south, presenting more of the freighter's port side to the ice-breaker ahead of it, Larry and the others would be shielded from sight by the freighter until they could reach the cover of a rocky point on the south-westernmost part of the island.

The boat was fitted with a jet engine beneath the hull, and old twin outboards at the stern, for travelling near inhabited areas, or in case they encountered other Russian vessels, or spotter planes or search helicopters.

All five men onboard the aluminium boat, disguised as a small fishing vessel, were Russian speakers, all carried false papers that named them as five of the two thousand or so inhabitants of Novaya Zemlya, and the boat was fitted with nets, net-haulers for fishing, and the usual winches and grabbers a small fishing vessel of its kind would be equipped with. All five men were dressed in the regular gear of Arctic Russian fishermen. There was even a refrigerated hold that contained fish they'd supposedly caught. But in the false floor of the boat was an array of weapons and ammunition that could fight a small war.

It was the third attempt to pick her up and Larry had been on both of the previous ones. But Burt was determined that the northernmost pick-up point would be the one she came to. And Larry would keep returning until either he found her or he was blown out of the water by a Russian naval patrol boat.

They reached the rocky promontory of the island and

saw that, every inch of the way from the freighter, they'd been shielded from the Russian vessel by the brief and tiny change of course the *Rosa Mundi* had made. And they now began to track their way north, as the other two bigger vessels turned south. They were making their way up the western coastline of Novaya Zemlya and towards the thin Matochkin Strait that cut the island in two. This was the slowest part of the journey, under the power of the twin outboards. But once they were through the Matochkin Strait, and to the east of Novaya Zemlya, out of sight of the island, they would enable the jet engines that would carry them through the relatively calm seas at seventy knots and weave them through the floes and growlers that were coming up from the Yenisei, or down from the Pole.

And as they made their passage half a mile off its western coast, Larry pondered the island for the third time; in 1961, the most powerful nuclear weapon ever detonated – the *Tsar Bomba* – had been exploded here and caused an earthquake that reached nearly 7 on the Richter Scale. But over the years, from the 1950s onwards, nuclear weapons had been detonated on the island with a force equivalent to 265 megatons of TNT. By comparison, all the explosives used in World War Two, including the American atomic bombs, were equivalent to just two megatons of TNT. The island and its subterranean caverns had been bombed to pieces.

They reached the narrow Matochkin Strait without incident and turned to the right, making their steady way through the centre of the island until they reached its eastern shore that looked towards mainland Siberia. Then, for mile after mile, they kept their speed regular on the power of the outboards alone, the boat's fishing nets ready to be off-loaded from side davits if they needed to look busy. But once they were out of sight of Novaya Zemlya and there were no other vessels as far as the horizon, and nothing in the air to see them, the jet engine came on. They would reach the rock and ice coastline they were looking for, to the east of the Gulf of Yenisei on Siberia's northernmost coast, in less than four hours.

The monotony of the aluminium boat's slamming against the light waves became a thing that was part of the men. But all the time, the horizon was scanned with high-powered binoculars in case of the presence of another vessel or plane. They encountered nothing, except the bergs and floes, some as tall as tower blocks, others that lurked dangerously close to the waterline. And finally, they saw where the coast of northern Siberia curved to the east, reaching out five thousand miles, eventually as far as Alaska. They were fifty miles north of the port of Dikson where the freighter and its escort were headed.

From here they hugged the coast, once more on the boat's outboards even though the coastline was unin-habited. But it was too much of a risk to use the jets in sight of land. For another four hours, they dodged from bay to bay, curved from promontory to promontory, following the jagged flow of the coast and, in doing so, shielding themselves from whatever danger might lie ahead around the next corner. They were giving themselves time and the chance to see anything untoward before they were upon it.

Finally, Larry told the steersman to take the boat on to a small spit of ice-covered shingle. It was the bay before the pick-up point and he wanted to reconnoitre before exposing them to whatever lay beyond, stay behind the cover of more iced rock. He wanted to land, and look, crawl up the gentle ice and rock slope and carefully spy over the ridge at the top and survey the place where he hoped she'd be.

And, at that moment, one of the others, an eagle-eyed twenty year old with a marksman's accuracy, saw something. He immediately waved his arm frantically downwards at the steersman, while still staring straight ahead, never taking his eyes away from what he'd seen.

The boat slowed to a near halt, the outboards quietening to a low rumble. The twenty year old gave Larry binoculars and Larry saw at once what he'd seen with his naked eye, through the glasses.

There was a chain, at an angle, coming up from the water. It was the chain of a boat at anchor, the boat to which it was attached out of sight beyond the rock wall ahead. If the wind hadn't been blowing lightly from the north, the boat would not have been pushed inland towards the shore and they would have been seen by the people on it at the same time as they saw it.

The boat beached gently on the ice spit. Clouds were gathering in a grey mass above them and it looked like it would snow.

Larry took an automatic from the bottom of the boat.

Then he began the slow walk across the spit and finally the crawl and the climb up the rock towards the ridge. He carried the SCAR-L MK16 assault weapon with a twenty-round magazine across his shoulder. After a tortuous climb over ice and rock he at last reached the peak of the ridge.

The first thing he saw over the top of the ridge, keeping his head flat to the rock and ice, was a Russian naval patrol vessel at anchor. It swung gently on the anchor chain in the light sea swell. A Stenka class maritime border patrol boat, by the look of it. Nearly a hundred foot long and armed with short- and middle-range guns.

Then his eyes swivelled to the right, to the ice beach which was the pick-up point. There was a fire burning, he saw, two small boats beached, their anchors dug into the ice and stone. Around the fire were ten men, the crew, he assumed.

Larry tried to remember how many crew a Stenka normally carried and he cursed himself for not being certain. The men were cooking something over the fire, fish presumably. Vodka bottles lay on their side or were dug into the snow and ice. It was a party then. An impromptu landing. They were preparing for nothing but eating and drinking. They'd sneaked into the mouth of the small gulf for an hour or so, for as long as no one would notice their absence. Presumably, Larry realised, they would have a radio man, at least, still on board, just in case of sudden orders.

But what he then saw on the ice beach was the strangest sight he'd ever seen in his life. There was another figure there. It was walking slowly towards the group of men, its back to Larry, maybe two hundred yards from the men now. But they hadn't seen it yet. The figure Larry stared at in utter bewilderment wore a long red coat.

Larry reached for the binoculars. Through the powerful lenses he now saw that hanging from the coat – the back of it that he could see, in any case – were a couple of dozen circular metal discs. They waved with the figure's movement, from side to side, right to left with the figure's loping walk. From the neck of the figure he saw a fur collar and from the sleeves there protruded large feathers like a bird's wings. On the figure's head, above the fur collar, was a hide and fur cap, pulled low against the cold. The figure walked with a slow, fatalistic and halting step towards the group of men.

Larry fitted the magazine. It was a four-hundred-yard shot. He now wished he'd brought a second magazine with him.

Then he picked up the glasses again and watched the figure a second time. The coat reached down below the calves of the walking figure, the metal discs swaying in the rhythm of its walk. It was around a hundred fifty yards from the men now. Larry looked at the boots of the figure through the glasses. Small, he thought. A native inhabitant of Siberia.

When the figure was a hundred yards from the men, one of them suddenly noticed it, and they all looked up or around from the fire. Larry could see their expressions; surprise, bemusement, a little laughter – he couldn't tell whether it was nervous laughter or not. One or two of the men stood. Larry saw holstered pistols. He scanned the area of the fire, but saw no automatic weapons. They were all watching the figure now; a strange apparition in red with its sparkling discs of metal. The coat must be heavy, Larry thought.

One of the men shouted at the figure, but Larry couldn't tell whether it replied or not. It just kept walking, the same, half-steady stride, and he noticed now that it had a slight limp.

Around twenty-five yards now. The men were shouting, some angrily, some laughing, whether from the sight of the strange figure in the middle of this empty place, or from the vodka they'd drunk. It was hard to tell. But by the expression on one of the men's faces, it seemed to Larry that he was telling the figure to stop. But it kept on walking.

The man who'd shouted fingered the leather holster at his side, unclipping the cover. He put his hand on to the butt.

And then Larry heard the dull bang of a pistol and he saw the man instantly fall. And then there was another dull bang. The second man standing also fell. And now all the men, eight left now, Larry noted, began to stand, shouting and looking for their weapons. And the figure walked on, as if it were prepared to walk right into the centre of the fire.

And it was then that Larry realised the figure in the red coat with the strange metal discs was Anna.

Anna shot the first man through the heart. It was an easy shot. Then, immediately, she shot the second and then the third of the men standing. She could feel the wound in the side of her body, and in her leg where the gash was healing, and it was painful. She couldn't walk quite straight, she knew that. But her right hand – her good hand – and its trigger finger were still working well. But she had five shots left with Petrov's *militsiya* pistol and there were seven men. With her left, wounded hand, she drew a long knife.

She knew this was her only chance. If her rescuers saw the patrol boat, as they surely would, they wouldn't come in. That would be another three days on the beach, if she survived this. But even if she survived this, she knew she wouldn't survive another three days on this ice beach. Her strength was waning. She would have to kill the men, then sink their boat, so her rescuers wouldn't see it. That was her only chance. And so she walked straight, or as straight as she could, into what would soon become a hail of gunfire.

She felt the great weight of the coat on her shoulders. There were thirty or forty metal discs that swung from it, front and back, and some were six inches in diameter. Petrov had told her that they represented the metal joints the smith of the underworld used, to weld the bones of the new-born shaman together after they'd been boiled for three years. Petrov's grandfather, she thought dimly, as if he were there beside her. She knew she was now in a sort of semi-ecstatic state herself, though she was still just conscious enough to know it. She felt that she could do anything, fly, travel to the underworld, see the women with the reindeer fur skin, stand beneath the Tree of Life, with its great eagle perched on top, see the Source of all Existence and The Lord of the Water.

A bullet struck her, but it had come from the side and it glanced off a metal disc. If it had come straight on, it would have pierced the thin metal and her, but still it knocked her back, back on to the wounded leg, but she felt no pain now. She was in the midst of them, firing round after round, until the bullet got her, somewhere it got her, but she had no notion of where. She dropped the gun, empty of rounds, and tried to transfer the knife to her right hand. But she had no strength left. Something was draining very fast from her and she knew it was blood. She fell. Well then, this must be the end.

As soon as he'd heard the first shot fired by the figure he knew was Anna, Larry had shouldered the SCAR and taken aim, first at a seated man whose hand was already on his pistol and his finger closing on the trigger. He aimed a little high at the distance, but the man slumped over. And now Anna was between him and the rest of the men. There was no clear shot. He saw four men down on the ground and he fired twice more, around the red figure, and then a burst of five. More of the men – two, three maybe, he couldn't tell, tumbled to the ground, or slid sideways from their seated positions, or crumpled as they tried to stand. There was no time to view anything except through the gunsight. And then he saw the figure in red go down too. She didn't move, didn't try to get up. But the view was clear now, with her fallen.

He fired burst after burst, until the magazine was empty.

He heard the engine of his boat in his left ear and saw

through the corner of his eye that it was racing around the promontory, heading for the beach, until a burst of fire erupted from the patrol boat. And then it switched direction towards the patrol boat and he saw the grey curve of a grenade, launched from the shoulder of the twenty year old in the bow. It burst on to the deck, accurate to the millimetre, from a boat that was smashing into the water at forty knots.

Larry ran down the other side of the ridge, unarmed now, and ran and ran along the ice beach for four hundred yards until he stood over the scene of carnage that now spread out from the glowing wood where the fish that nobody would eat still cooked. He ran to the figure in red and turned it over and saw Anna's face. There was blood on her mouth. He flung the coat back and saw more blood on her stomach.

He stood and shouted, screamed at the boat out in the bay, for assistance, and saw it turn, sure now there was nobody left on board the patrol boat. It beached yards away and Larry screamed again, this time for the medic, who ran up the ice slope of the beach and knelt beside the red-coated figure, felt her pulse, looked at Larry.

'I don't know,' he said.

'Is she alive?' Larry shouted at him.

'Yes, she's alive. But only just.'

'Fix her, for Christ's sake, fix her, goddammit, fix her.'

The medic ran back down the beach to fetch a heavy titanium case. He struggled back up across the stones until he knelt beside Anna. He opened the case and took out a defibrillator. He tore the clothes away from her upper body and attached the wires to her chest. Then he pressed the red button. Larry watched as her back arched and she seemed to leap up from the stones, only to settle back lifelessly. The medic pressed the button again and her body arched once more in a terrible spasm that lifted her and dropped her again.

Larry turned and ran to the edge of the water. He shouted at the others in the boat to sink the patrol boat. It must not be seen by prying spotter planes or helicopters. They had a ten-hour journey ahead at seventy knots, back to Finland, and he wanted nothing suspicious that would lead to the evidence of the massacre on the beach.

He ran back up the icy stones to Anna, at some point hearing a dull thud of explosives out to sea.

The medic was kneeling beside Anna, pressing the red button – her body grotesquely reacting to the charge – pumping her heart, attaching a drip, stemming the flow of blood that ran from the wound in her stomach with thick anti-sceptic wadding, injecting her, putting his mouth to hers and all the time keeping on pressing down on her heart with great thumps and breathing deeply into her mouth with his.

Larry was crying, he realised.

'Save her. Just save her,' he said, but quietly, desperately, despairingly now.

And then, through the tears that he felt coursing down his cheeks, he saw something shine from a deerskin jacket she'd been wearing beneath the red coat.

He knelt and slipped his hand inside the jacket and withdrew a plastic package – the shiny glint he'd seen. He saw the plastic was waterproofing. And as he gripped it in his trembling hands, his grief almost overwhelming him, he knew that, somehow, she had done it. He knew that what he was holding in his hands was the end of the old world and the beginning of the new.

Larry put his fingers around her wrist. Nothing. The medic pressed the button again. Larry held on, desperate for a response. He felt a flutter underneath his fingers, a faint, broken pulse. It grew stronger, more regular, and he tightened his fingers on the inside of her wrist in terrified hope. Now her pulse began to beat, then a break, then a return to a steady motion under his fingers. And, at last, Larry knew that she would be part of this new world and would not depart with the old. He wept.

ACKNOWLEDGEMENTS

I would like to thank certain people who wish to remain nameless in the city of Norilsk, Russia, the second largest city in the world north of the Arctic Circle. They are the sons and daughters of the slaves who built this dreadful place, where life expectancy is forty-six years. Their generous hospitality and help to me during my visit in the brief period when the Kremlin allowed foreigners to visit the city in the 1990s was invaluable. I would also like to thank those in Russia who are prepared to break ranks with the corrupt regime currently in power there. They are brave people whose wish for democracy, the rule of law and a political system not dominated by the spy elite often invites vilification, gaol and even death. I would like to thank Stephen Horvath, Hungarian-born engineer, inventor and nuclear scientist for his inspiration and genius. My thanks too to AR for his skills in the dark arts. And, as always, my thanks are due to my editor Martin Fletcher and my agent Piers Blofeld.